CATAPULT

TALES OF A WITCH'S FAMILIAR
BOOK THREE

ALBA LOCKWOOD

Dad, Aunt Loretta and Aunt Sharon, this is the last page you read. This book is not for you. I want to be able to look you all in the eyes.
I'll tell you what happens without the spice.

Everyone else...Carry on.

CONTENTS

CHAPTER 1

CLAWDIA

"*I*s anyone having déjà vu?" Charlie asked as he threw the car into the next gear and had us speeding away from the collapsed warehouse and, more importantly, the dragon escaping from the rubble.

The dragon was all I could allow myself to call it. Acknowledging who the dragon was—who he was to me— threatened to break my already fragile mind.

"What is déjà vu?" Zaide croaked, indulging Charlie's dramatic tendencies.

"When you feel like you've done this before," he replied quickly, his eyes shooting to the rearview mirror, then darting back to the front window in time to throw the wheel and dodge a pothole. Pain sparked up my arms as I slammed against the door. Charlie continued, "Except ... no, we definitely have done the racing away from the dragon before. Only I didn't know I was related to it, then."

"I wasn't there for that," I said, trying to distract myself with the conversation and strapping myself in. I couldn't see what I was doing in the dark, and it took a few panicked jabs before I managed to get the seat belt into the clip.

"Oh, you were there. You were just unconscious because your power had just brought the fucking thing back to life."

I flinched at the blame in his words. Even if I didn't consciously raise the dragon, it was my fault that they'd come rescue me from his clutches. I'd portaled myself there without a plan.

The dragon, Fafnir, who was the mythical Norse beast a hero named Sigurd killed.

Fafnir, who was accidentally raised from the dead by scared witches and shifted to his human form to begin living as Mr. Jenkins.

Mr. Jenkins, who I was forced to marry in my past life. And who Charlie, apparently, was a descendant of.

I swallowed a lump of bile as the fear I'd pushed back while I dealt with the reality of him being alive, being a dragon, being a creature that consumes magic and wanted to kill me and my soul bonds, caused my body to shake.

A horrific thought crossed my mind. *Am I still married to him?*

As though the world had suddenly slowed down, I stared at Zaide, my soul pair, who'd searched the realms to find me. He was battered and bruised, his golden skin turned bronze with his injuries as he rested his head against the seat, eyes closed. His purple scars glowed dimly in darkness as though they didn't have the power to glow as brightly as they did before.

I turned my gaze to Charlie, the first man I'd ever desired and who'd ever offered me affection. His brows were pulled down into a thoughtful frown as he skillfully drove us away from danger. Ash covered him, making his dirty blond hair look darker and messier. He was shirtless, his skin littered with cuts and soot.

I loved them both so much I couldn't bear seeing them hurt. I wanted them safe more than I wanted my next breath.

CHAPTER 1

But dread filled me at the thought of explaining what had happened once we were home. If we got home.

Are they going to feel different about me when they find out Fafnir is my husband?

A deafening roar drew me back to the moment, and I peeked over my shoulder through the back window of the car to see flashes of green wings under the streetlights and yellow, furious eyes.

"He's following us," I whispered.

I knew Mr. Darren Jenkins to be a proud man. He wouldn't have allowed anyone to make a fool of him. He wouldn't stop until we were dead or worse. Especially since he saw me. Watched me change from cat to human, felt the power in my soul bonds and believed I looked like his previous wife.

I was a puzzle to him. One he would find and decipher no matter the cost. And when I no longer held interest for him, he'd destroy me, like he would have in our past life. Only I didn't give him the time nor the opportunity to, and I prayed it would be the same this time.

I rubbed my sweaty palms on the t-shirt Charlie gave me and tried to control my breathing.

Light and heat suddenly flooded the darkened road behind us, and sweat prickled my brow from the intensity of it. Another loud roar followed, sending my pulse racing.

"Charlie," I whimpered as I turned to see the beast getting closer. Each beat of his wings seemed to get stronger, sending him surging toward us. The orange underbelly scales glinted as he darted above the streetlights. He would have been pretty if he wasn't completely evil and trying to kill us. "He's healing as he flies. He's getting closer."

"I see him."

"Can't this car go any faster?" I asked, glancing at the

speedometer. The needle ticked in the middle, but I had no idea what that meant.

"I didn't think I'd be racing fucking dragons when we picked up this rental, so you'll have to forgive me for the horsepower," Charlie snapped.

Zaide reached back and patted my hand. He peered at me through hooded, swollen eyes. "Try not to worry, Little Cat. We will be fine."

Another thunderous roar, so close I could feel the vibrations in my bones, seemed to negate his statement, and I bit my lip.

"How?" I whispered.

We were trapped in a tin box, moving at the fastest we could go with a very angry dragon attempting to panfry us alive. It was hard to see the positives.

"I have faith," Zaide said simply, his deep voice a calming balm for my racing heart.

I sent a quick prayer to whoever was listening. *Please, please let us escape.*

Taking a deep breath, I leaned into the distraction he offered me. I caressed his face and rubbed at the drying blood by his temple with my thumb. "Are you all right? You're really hurt … Is this from our escape?"

He shook his head and nuzzled into my hand, placing a soft kiss on my palm. "I was with the task force on our way to you when our car was pushed off the road."

I gasped. "What? Why? Who would do that?"

"I can't begin to imagine." He coughed and sighed. "I didn't see who they were. But none of the task force leaders nor Alcor were conscious when Charlie found me at the side of the road."

The cut on his head trickled a drop of blood again, and I swiped it away gently. I knew the head was a delicate area, but he was still bleeding, and it worried me.

"Let me heal you," I demanded. He needed to be at his best in case our escape went pear-shaped, and more importantly, I hated to see him in pain and suffering.

He shook his head and offered me a small, tight, smile. "You are drained, Little Cat. Do not lie. I can feel it. We all need time to heal from tonight once Charlie gets us home."

An intrusive thought said, *If Charlie gets us home.*

"Jesus fucking Christ!" Charlie shouted, bursting our bubble.

I whipped my head to see a car hurtling toward us. The headlights were so bright and dazzling I didn't notice the car had strayed into our lane as it turned around the corner.

Charlie turned and braked, gritting his teeth and cursing under his breath. The seat belt jarred so I didn't get flung across the passenger seats, but my head followed the movement and whipped to the side. I gasped as an ache began pulsating painfully where my neck had snapped.

"We might find out who pushed the task team leaders off the road quicker than we wanted to," Charlie added breathlessly as he straightened the car and glanced at the giant vehicle in the rearview mirror.

His eyes widened.

"What is it?" Ignoring the ache in my neck, I turned to see the car skidding to a halt in front of the dragon.

Fafnir roared, and flames burst from his mouth, lighting up the sky, but he didn't aim directly at the newcomers. He hovered in front of them, almost as though he was curious.

Why isn't he trying to hurt them? What does he know that we don't?

All four of the tinted windows rolled down. Guns appeared, quickly followed by the arms and heads of those aiming their weapons at Fafnir.

"They seem to be attempting to kill the dragon," Zaide replied.

5

"He just survived a building falling on him." I sighed heavily, not getting my hopes up that these people might beat him.

Charlie chose to ignore my comment and cheered, "Nice meeting you, Granddaddy! See you in Hell." He put his foot down on the accelerator, and we sped away.

Despite starting to feel sick, facing backward in the car, I couldn't take my eyes off the scene in front of me. Sparks flared from the guns, and shots rang out. I flinched instinctively, trying to follow the trajectory of the bullets with my eyes as Fafnir roared.

I couldn't tell if they'd hit him or if he was just voicing his annoyance at these strangers attacking him, but he flapped his wings, making a gust of wind that knocked some weapons from their hands. He inhaled.

I turned around before I could witness people being barbecued. I'd seen enough horrible things for one day. But as we raced away, I saw no blast of light surround us, felt no heat, heard no screams.

We were too far away now to look back, but my anxiety doubled not knowing what just happened. *Why didn't he hurt them? What else might he have done to them instead?*

"Do you think they are another supernatural task force?" Zaide asked.

Charlie scoffed. "A task force that uses guns? Pretty sure the supernatural community has better weapons."

"But he can eat magic. Maybe they are trying to keep their distance," I added.

Charlie shrugged. "Maybe. But this just reeks of government intervention."

"You think?" I did find it curious that he could light up the sky with flames along a motorway and not be reported or found by the government or army.

"You don't think? The dragon's been on national news.

Probably international too. I don't know how high the supernatural council is in the human political food chain or if even there's communication there, but I'm sure every government has intelligence branches to deal with weird stuff like this."

I huffed a tired laugh. "I think you watch too much television, Charlie."

"Look around, Clawdicat. This is everything paranormal sit-coms are made of. All we need is a wolf shifter and a sparkly vampire, and we are ready for Hollywood."

We drove in silence for a little while, letting the lights flash by while we sat with our thoughts.

"Do you think they killed him?" I asked finally. It was the only explanation I had for why there'd been no retaliation from Fafnir.

"No," Charlie admitted with a sigh. "But they've helped us get away from him for now."

Zaide had just tipped his head back to go to sleep when I noticed bright lights glinting in the rearview mirror. And they seemed to be approaching fast. Really fast.

"Who the fuck is this now?" Charlie exclaimed, and Zaide's eyes flashed open.

I could only sigh and asked, "Is our luck really so bad that we'd be chased by the same people who just attacked Fafnir?"

"I think it is, Little Cat," Zaide replied grimly.

"Come on, you little shit box. We're so close now. Get us home." Charlie tightened his grip around the wheel and leaned forward as he jeered the car.

The car behind us crossed into the empty opposite lane, and I could see it more clearly without the headlights blinding me. It was indeed the same large, black vehicle with tinted windows that had attacked the dragon.

Only now it seemed they'd turned turrets to face us.

Charlie glared. "Remind me to get something faster next time I rent something."

7

The windows facing our side rolled down, and they aimed their weapons at us. I gasped, and fear struck me like lightning. I couldn't move. I just stared at the half-covered faces of the men—and they must have been men from the size of their hands and thick, muscled arms—who were now trying to kill us.

Charlie swerved away just as a shot rang out. I ducked and closed my eyes tightly, trying to keep low and steady as the car weaved and dodged. Two more shots sounded, but nothing seemed to be hitting the car.

"Jason, you big, beautiful thug bastard. Who would have thought your random lesson on dodging bullets in a car chase would actually come in handy? I hope you're eating chili-heatwave doritos wherever you are." He kissed his fingers and raised them to the sky.

"Charlie, please keep your hands on the wheel," I squeaked as he suddenly turned the wheel again, but with one hand.

"Who is Jason?" Zaide asked, slightly slurred. Which only alarmed me more. I leaned forward, took his hand, and squeezed.

"Zaide, are you okay?" He blinked and seemed to become more aware at my touch. I quickly, discreetly, pushed power toward him, hoping it would help him stay more alert and heal faster.

"Little Cat, I am fine." He narrowed his eyes, which must have been hard to do considering they were already so swollen, and said, "I know what you are doing."

"Anyone got a banana?" Charlie asked cheerfully as the passengers of the other car paused their shooting when they were forced to move back into the lane behind us to prevent colliding with oncoming traffic.

I shook my head, ignoring his question. "If I didn't know any better, I'd say you were enjoying this."

"Mario has trained me well."

"I didn't realize the human realm was so plagued with such chases that one needs to be trained," Zaide frowned. "This is a common occurrence?"

"I'll introduce you to gaming—" Charlie began but stopped as the other car moved out suddenly. They accelerated until they were driving alongside us and their weapons were drawn yet again. "Fuck," he cursed and looked around. "Okay, hold on."

We turned sharply off the main road and onto a small, forested track as the other car zoomed past, not able to turn in time to follow us. Bullets rained, popping loudly against the trees. It was a show of their frustration, and thankfully, nothing hit us. We were too far away.

When I heard the screech of tires stopping, spinning and the rev of an engine heading toward us, my heartbeat ticked up another notch.

I bounced in my seat as we rolled over dirt hills and dips. But the small track was getting smaller, tighter, more enclosed by trees, and soon, I saw the end of the road. We could go no further.

But they are right behind us.

Charlie answered my growing fear before I had a chance to ask. "We are going to run. Get ready."

We stopped, but Charlie didn't turn off the car. He left the lights on and the keys in the ignition while I threw my seat belt off and flung myself out. The sting of pain as my bare feet hit the ground, and the cold air around my almost naked body, were ignored.

Charlie whispered, "Follow me," and took off running.

I followed him, trying not to wince, trying to be strong and quiet as I scrambled over dirt, leaves, branches, and tree roots. With only the headlights offering some illumination of the forest, I stumbled often, until Zaide scooped me into his arms.

"What are you doing?" I hissed.

"You have nothing protecting your feet. I can't stand to watch you hurt anymore," he whispered and held me closer to his chest as he continued to run after Charlie.

I caught his wince as I accidentally brushed my hand over his shoulder. "I'm hurting you. Put me down."

"You are not leaving my arms, Little Cat. Stay still," he growled in a way that made me immediately still. A blush covered my cheeks at the sudden zing of arousal he'd caused just from his voice.

I opened my mouth to suggest that I change form so I could run faster—and without shoes—but the loud squeal of a car grinding to a stop made my breath catch. The bright headlights flashed through the trees, and moments later, doors slammed shut.

Charlie, responding to my rising panic, told me through our bond, *"We aren't far from town. I think we can make it before they catch us. We can hide until tomorrow, and hopefully they will be gone."*

I relayed the message to Zaide in a whisper, and we continued to run in silence for the next few minutes.

A voice shouted into the dark brush. "We know you're there, freaks. We'll find you. And when we do, you're dead." Then guns blasted loudly in the quiet woods, frightening sleeping birds from the trees.

Zaide dropped to his knees and curled over me. I flinched as bullets whistled past, my heart in my mouth as I prayed that nothing hit Zaide or Charlie, who I couldn't see. Footsteps hurried toward us, and suddenly, I was hauled back into Zaide's arms, and we were running again.

Charlie swerved and began heading toward the men following us.

"Charlie," I mentally hissed at him. *"What are you doing?"*

"This way. Quick," was all he said in reply.

Zaide raced behind him, unquestioning, trusting Charlie would know what to do and how to get us to safety. But he was flagging. I could feel his arms shaking, hear his loud panting and rapid heartbeat. Sweat formed on his brow.

"Please put me down, my love. I'm hurting you," I whispered, my lips grazing the shell of his ear. He shuddered but shook his head, holding me tighter as he ran down an embankment that, at one point, must have been a river, because to our right was an old stone bridge.

Underneath the bridge, where an archway should have been, allowing a long-dried-up river to continue through, was now rubble, thick undergrowth, bushes, tall weeds and grasses.

Charlie stood right at the bottom of the embankment, waiting for us and holding out his arms as though ushering us in front of him. He swept a hand over the tall grass under the arch, and something flickered. An illusion shimmered, coming apart like it was a drawing on a curtain. Beyond it was the darkness of the secret space underneath the arch.

I gaped, but Zaide didn't wait for me to process. He walked straight into the black, Charlie quickly following and letting the magic grass curtain sway close behind us all.

Have we broken the magic, or are we behind the magic grass curtain and invisible? I couldn't see the barrier, and in the distance, lights from torches roamed the woods. They hadn't given up. They were still looking for us.

"I think we're safe here for a moment," Charlie whispered. "I can feel the magic is still in place."

I let out a sigh of relief, and Zaide released me. He placed me deliberately so I stood on his feet like a little girl that dances with her father and didn't allow me to escape the circle of his arms.

"How did you know this was here?" I asked with chattering teeth. It was dark, and the damp, cold stones were like ice to my sparsely covered body.

Zaide tugged me closer to his chest and rubbed my arms to warm me.

"I love you." He didn't respond, but I could feel the swell of affection and love that surged to meet me, despite his unbearable fatigue.

"Same way I can find things," Charlie replied. I could barely see him in the darkness, and he felt far away. "Quiet," he suddenly whispered as he stepped in front of me, caging me between him and Zaide. His lips grazed my forehead, and his cold hands wrapped around my back.

From beyond the curtain, footsteps crunched across the forest floor, and heavy breathing—someone else's, not our own—echoed in the silence until two men stood only inches away from our hiding place.

One was short with a round belly, while the other was tall and lean. They both wore black sportswear, their masks covering all but their mouths, and a jacket with a distinctive symbol. A red arrow.

Their weapons clunked against them as they paused to look around, and I swallowed thickly. Up close, the guns were even more frightening. Large, long assault rifles. The kind I'd seen spoken about in mass shootings.

"Shit. I thought for sure they'd gone this way," the tall one growled and lowered his weapon. What surprised me most was his accent. He wasn't European. He was American.

The short one smiled and shrugged nonchalantly. "Your tracking has never led us wrong before, Brian." His easygoing manner suddenly disappeared, and an evil snarl twisted his lips. "But I bet they used magic to get away. These freaks are always getting away like that."

His accent was harder to place, but it was clear he wasn't European either. He sounded South African.

Have they really traveled this far to hunt us down?

"I'm just pissed we gave up the chance to bag the dragon over these unknowns, and now we've lost them," the short one continued.

"I'm telling you, Stan, the group in that car were more powerful than the dragon. Our radar went nuts for them. We'd have gotten more with them than the dragon." Brian kneeled to look closely at the ground.

Gotten more what?

Brian touched the grass, shifting through it, looking for something. "We'll find them again. We always get our prize."

"Yeah." Stan kicked at the dirt and pouted as he mumbled, "The dragon looks cooler, though."

"Got to wonder why the dragon was following them." Brian crawled closer to the archway, following a track I couldn't see, and slowly stood up to stare at the curtain that hid us. I gripped Charlie's hand tighter and held my breath.

Stan's scoff drew Brian's attention, and I slowly let out my breath as he said, "Why do I have to wonder about that? It's a beast, and they are freaks. Maybe they've abused it like a circus animal. They're evil."

Brian chuckled. "You know, that actually makes sense. You're not as dumb as you look, Stan."

"I'm going to take that as a compliment instead of kicking your ass and making you look bad in front of others."

"Like you can make me look bad. I've got thirty-seven confirmed kills."

I gasped and covered my mouth. *Thirty-seven confirmed kills. Thirty-seven supernatural people he'd killed just because they were supernatural?*

"Did you hear that?" Brian's face snapped toward us, and

even though the curtain protected us, I felt his eyes staring straight at me.

"What?"

I swallowed a whimper.

They waited. Listening. Brian took five slow steps toward us but stopped an inch from the curtain. "Nothing. I thought I heard something, but it could have been the wind." He glanced around again. "Anyway, let's head back. I got a glance at them, and we can probably use the car to find out more about them."

Oh my God. They are going to try and find us again.

We waited, frozen, trying to control our breathing and panic until they'd been gone for at least ten minutes. Then we pulled back the curtain and headed toward town again. Zaide took my hand, and we began jogging slowly. I watched my feet as we hurried, concentrating on every step and not how far from safety we might still be.

The fact that he didn't pick me up again was not lost on me. It told me he was close to his limit. We needed to get him home. Now.

Charlie raced ahead, his bare back glistening with sweat in the dim moonlight. The movement of his shoulder blades was mesmerizing, and a shot of lust blasted through me.

It's not the time for that. I told myself and reluctantly dragged my eyes away from his back. *Who knew that was such an arousing sight? I can't be held responsible for my reaction.*

"Almost there now," Charlie gasped.

I almost cried at the sight of the streetlights, shops, and other buildings. Exhaustion was setting in quick and fast, and every step felt like I was trying to walk underwater.

"Stay here," Charlie said. "I'm just going to pull money from the cashpoint. Don't move until I'm back."

I opened my mouth to protest, my anxiety rocketing at the thought of us separating, but he was already gone.

Zaide and I huddled in the corner of the alleyway, his arms wrapped around me keeping the chill from seeping into my bones. I tugged the shirt over my legs and ran my hands up and down Zaide's arms.

"Thank you for coming for me," I whispered.

"Don't leave me again, Little Cat. When I woke up to see you missing ... I can't describe my fear. I can't lose you again."

I shook my head fiercely. "You won't. I'm sorry, I won't do it again, it's just ... I needed to see him. Face him."

"I don't understand. Why would you need to face—"

Zaide's words were swallowed by the humming of powerful magic, and a blue light flashed in the darkness. Swirling in the center of the wall opposite us, the blue light expanded.

A portal.

I flinched away into Zaide's chest, and his grip on me tightened.

Oh, Lord. Won't this day ever end?

CHAPTER 2

CHARLIE

I snatched hundreds of krona out of the cash machine, keeping one eye looking for supernatural hunters and the other watching the sky for signs of my evil grandad.

How has it only been a day and so much bad shit has happened?

Shoving the money into my wallet, I dashed back to my familiar and her soul pair. When I saw a glowing blue light and heard the whooshing that came with a portal opening, I panicked.

As I ran into the alleyway, Zaide stepped fearlessly in front of Clawdia, his arm stretched back to keep her away, even though it looked like a strong wind could knock him down.

When I'm grown up, I want to be as badass as Zaide.

"Stay back, Charlie," he warned, not taking his eyes off the giant blue swirl in the wall.

Exhaling slowly, I steeled myself to deal with the next disaster.

"Ahhh, friends. We thought it would be a good time for a stroll around the town," Savida's cheery voice sounded. Relief hit me like a gunshot, and I sagged against the wall, sighing.

A large, black body, leathery wings, and flame-red hair came through the portal, closely followed by Daithi.

"Savida. Daithi. Thank Christ," I breathed.

Even though we'd left things on bad terms after they confessed to being manipulative bastards with Zaide, I could've kissed them for turning up in the nick of time. They'd just made my job of getting us all out of here so much easier.

Savida frowned when he caught sight of us all. "You're all dirty. Have you been rolling in the mud together?"

"No—" Clawdia began.

"Say no more. I remember the passion of new love. Although, I don't remember the dirt," he eyed Daithi contemplatively.

I barked a laugh as Daithi shook his head. I said, "Nice to see you saving us for a change. Let's get the fuck out of here. We need to get my laptop and stuff before we leave."

"Leave? The apartment?" Savida's expression turned from confusion to despair. "Charlie, you can't still mean for us to … Zaide has forgiven us. We are helping."

I didn't know that. Zaide looked at me, his swollen face shrouded in the darkness, and nodded.

While I really wanted to know what they'd said to get back into Zaide's good books, I didn't have time to ask questions.

I shook my head. "No, I don't mean you and Daithi. I mean all of us."

"Ah. Good." His wings sagged as he sighed, but he tilted his head in confusion. "But why?"

"We are being tracked by some people who kill supernaturals," Clawdia replied quietly. She gripped Zaide's hand tightly as he swayed.

"I knew this realm was cursed," Daithi muttered.

"Where is Alcor?" Savida asked, his wings fluttering anxiously as he looked around.

"He's … in safe hands. I hope," I replied, thinking of the strangers who told me to leave him with them and rescue Clawdia with Zaide.

But my vague response only made the demon more concerned. "Shall we go and retrieve him?"

I hesitated, glancing at Zaide, who looked worse by the second, then shook my head. "Let's get back first. I want to get us set up somewhere safe, and then we can go get him."

"Of course. Let us go," Daithi said, turning his back to us as another portal burst to life on the wall.

"Thank you for coming for us," Zaide whispered to Savida, then slapped him on the back.

Savida shook his head. "Wasn't my idea. Daithi saw you all running, and so here we are."

Daithi stepped into the portal, and as I took a step to follow him, Savida shoved me out of the way and charged into the blue swirl, shouting, "Last one through the portal is a Lagworm!"

WE STUMBLED INTO THE APARTMENT, littering the floor with ash and dirt. As much as I wanted to go to sleep for a thousand years, there wasn't time to relax. The portal closed behind us with a blinding flash and snapped me into action.

I fell onto the sofa and plugged my phone in to charge on the side table. Turning back to my ragtag group, I started giving instructions.

"Go shower. Both of you," I told Zaide, who could barely keep his eyes open, and Clawdia, who was shivering.

"Are we not leaving soon?" Savida asked, his wings fluttering anxiously.

"I'm going to call the council. Update them and then get us somewhere to go. The quicker we move, the safer we'll be."

"Shower, then pack." Clawdia nodded and tugged Zaide toward the bathroom.

"Charlie, before you call the council ..." Daithi started, perching awkwardly on the other sofa and staring at me.

I waved my hand, already knowing what he was about to say. "If Zaide has forgiven you and you are helping instead of hiding, then you don't need to say anything else."

He raised a green brow. "It's that easy?"

"There are bigger issues, so yeah, for the moment, it's that easy." I rubbed my head, nursing the epic headache brewing in my brain.

Savida took the seat next to me. "We do want to apologize. We didn't rescue you in the cave despite everything you did to help save me. That wasn't fair, or kind."

"Apology accepted," I said.

Daithi's lip turned down a fraction. "I do not believe you are telling the truth."

I huffed out a breath of frustration and stood up. "I understand you want to clear the air. You want to apologize. I get it. But I don't have the headspace for it. And honestly, Clawdia needs an apology from you more than I do. After all, you were going to use her to get Zaide's titan powers back. You hated her, blamed her, turned her into a human and a cat against her will. Then let her rot with your friend in a cave." I shook myself. "I'm getting angry again just thinking about it, and I don't want to be angry. Point is, you were an arsehole, and you need to fix it."

"I will." Daithi stared steadily at me despite my pointed finger in his face, and a gleam of sweat covering his skin.

Is he sick?

"Thank you for your forgiveness, Charlie," Savida added.

His quiet remark let all the air out of me. "Don't mention it. Now go pack. And Daithi, maybe have a lie-down. You look like shit."

Daithi's eyes suddenly rolled into the back of his head, and he collapsed on the sofa.

"It definitely wasn't me this time," I announced quickly as Savida rushed to his soul mate's side.

"It's all right, Charlie. He has just fallen into a vision." Savida frowned and stroked Daithi's brow, smoothing out the wrinkles. "I should have thought. After a vision and creating two portals, he is worn out, which is usually when he is attacked with visions. He will be exhausted when he wakes up." He lifted Daithi into his arms and carried him to their room.

Seeing Daithi cuddled and unconscious in Savida's arms was a bit of a head fuck. Daithi never seemed vulnerable or small, but he looked that way with a giant demon carrying him.

When their door closed, I unplugged my phone and made the call.

"Hello?" Joseph Northrop's voice was clear and calm.

"Hi, Joe, it's Charlie. I don't know if your team leaders have updated you—"

"Charlie, yes." He sounded relieved to hear from me. "They said you and Zaide left the crash site to retrieve Clawdia and our agent, Rose."

At least it actually was other team leaders that I left Alcor and the others with, rather than hunters looking for an easy kill.

"We did. But I'm sorry, your agent died. We couldn't save her." I'd barely had time to think about the woman we'd had

20

to leave there. I didn't know if Fafnir had killed her or if the collapsed building did. Either way, it was bad news.

Joe sighed. "And the dragon?"

"Is Fafnir. From the legend. He can shapeshift. If we were still unsure, I can confirm he and the protector were raised before." I rubbed my forehead again as my phone beeped a warning for low battery.

"This plot is getting tiresome. What happened to Fafnir?"

"He managed to escape the rubble of a factory he destroyed from the inside out and fly after us. We were then attacked by hunters."

"You are safe now?"

I stared out of the window overlooking the car park. "We are at the apartment, but we aren't safe. They will soon be able to track us down again. We had to abandon the car. I'm looking for a new place to—"

Joseph stopped me. "No need. I think you should come to us. We are moving base and taking the protector with us. The hunters are making aggressive moves, so it's time for all our people to go to ground."

"Go to ground where?" I frowned.

I don't have time to get Savida a passport.

"It's not safe to give that information over the phone, Charlie. Surely you understand that. But it's protected, and we are stronger in numbers."

"I don't need ID?" I asked.

"We will arrange everything you need."

It was a non-answer, but it reassured me. "All right. Saves me a job, I suppose. Can you pick us up?"

"I'll have a team sent your way within the hour."

Before he could cut the call I asked, "Alcor and the others, are they okay?"

"They had similar trouble with hunters on the way back. But they are in safe hands now and getting medical treatment at our private facility. You'll see them when you get here," he informed me and abruptly hung up.

I couldn't be mad. He was saving our bacon.

I plugged my phone back in and headed for a shower, desperate to take off my destroyed jeans. Zaide was leaving the bathroom as I turned down the corridor. His skin looked better, clean and healing, but his eyes were half closed as he stumbled down the corridor with his towel around his waist, his long hair trailing behind him like a soggy rope.

"You can nap for an hour, but then you need to be alive," I called, and he acknowledged me with a floppy wave of his hand.

He looked like shit, but he could sleep in the car. We needed to get somewhere safe before we could all truly rest.

Stepping into the bathroom was like entering a sauna, which felt fucking amazing after spending half the evening without a t-shirt. The steam fogged up the mirror, and as I stripped out of my jeans and boxers, I relished in the warmth.

Throwing my clothes on top of the heap of destroyed fabric in the corner, I peeked around the curtain to see a naked Clawdia with her eyes closed and her head back, letting the water wash over her. Her skin was clean of the soot, but bruises and cuts littered her body. Her arms were tight around her waist.

Like I'd watch a lady hug herself when I could do it for her.

I flung open the curtain and climbed inside.

"Charlie!" Clawdia gasped and made a strange twitch like she was going to cover herself but realized there'd be no point.

"Clawdicat. Fancy seeing you here."

A slow smile crept onto her face. "This is my shower."

"You shared it with Zaide. Probably looked at his wounds

and conditioned his hair. Are you saying I'm not worthy of such consideration? That your witch isn't as important as your soul pair?" I raised my eyebrow, teasing.

Her face fell, and she stared solemnly. "Never."

I pulled her into my arms, and she gasped as our bodies collided in a wet slap. "Good. Because I'm feeling really needy right now." I nuzzled into her neck, and water washed over my head and down my back.

She didn't care that I was getting her dirty again. She squeezed me tight and stroked my hair. "You don't need to feel needy. I love you just as much as I love him."

No one had ever been so open with their love for me. I could count on one hand the number of times I'd heard it from other people. Yet Clawdia handed me her heart on a silver platter and didn't ask for anything in return.

And that shit needed to stop now.

I wouldn't have been so worried about her dying if I didn't love her. I wouldn't be needy and jealous of the time she spends with her soul pair if I didn't love her. I wouldn't be in the shower, hard as a rock and dying to kiss her, if I didn't love her. It was clear to anyone who had eyes and a functioning brain cell that I loved her.

The brain cell must have been hibernating all this time, only getting up to see what had been going on, before cluing me in on my own feelings. And, well ... I had eyes.

They were tracking the drops of water down her gorgeous face and plump lips before staring into her violet eyes. "Fuck past-Charlie for thinking you can't love in the life-and-death moments. He doesn't know shit." I pressed the lightest kiss to her lips and whispered, "I love you too, Clawdicat."

She blinded me with a bright smile before reaching up onto her tiptoes, wrapping her arms around my neck, and pulling me back to her lips.

I restrained a moan when she captured my lip between her teeth, and my hands clenched around her perfect arse. Our kiss turned feral. My cock ached.

"Fuck. Clawdia," I panted between hot kisses. "You don't know what you do to me."

"What do I do?" she asked quietly, almost shyly.

"You can't feel me?" I asked. "You can't feel my cock hard as stone pressed into your stomach? You can't feel how much I want you?"

Her pupils swallowed the violet of her eyes as they dilated with desire. *My girl likes dirty talk.*

"This is what you do to me, Clawdia." I took her hand and moved it between us, wrapping her fingers around my length, and sucked in a sharp breath. She licked her lips as she stared down and gave me an experimental stroke.

Don't come. Don't come, I chanted.

I covered her hand, stopping her torturous motions and kissed the corner of her jaw, below her ear. "This isn't about me. It's about you," I whispered.

She licked her lips. "I want it to be about both of us."

I sucked in a breath as she gently squeezed my cock and lightly scored her nails down my shoulder. "You want to make me come, Clawdia?"

"Y-yes," she replied shakily.

"Ladies first."

I kissed down her jaw, my hands roaming her soft curves until I cupped her gorgeous tits. The perfect perky handful with rosy tips. *Mine.* She whimpered, and her chest heaved, her nipples begging for attention. I bent down and sucked one into my mouth while I lightly pinched and tugged the other.

"Oh, Charlie," she gasped.

And damn if that wasn't the biggest turn on. Her calling my name with that posh accent, delirious with pleasure, made me feel like I was doing something naughty with a Julie-Andrews-style teacher or librarian.

Or a sexy nurse.

I dragged out the torment, sucking, licking, and biting her nipple until she was shuddering and crying, "Charlie, Charlie, Charlie," like a prayer. It was addictive.

Her fingers wrapped tightly in my hair, but the sting of pain only turned me on more.

Do I like my hair pulled? Have I unlocked a new kink?

I swapped from one side to the other to continue the delicious torture. Equal opportunity for nipples. #feminism.

While one hand pinched the nipple I'd just been sucking on, the other stroked her thigh, urging her to separate her legs and give me access to her pussy. She did so unconsciously. She tilted her head back into the shower spray, mouth open, eyes closed, and hands holding on to me like she'd die without me. *Fucking perfect.*

I dipped a finger into her wet heat and grazed over her clit with my thumb. She cried out, and her pussy spasmed.

I grinned as she looked down at me, dazed and shocked. "I must have had you really worked up for you to come that quick, Clawdicat."

"You're evil," she panted. I righted myself but kept my finger inside her, not wanting to leave heaven just yet. She buried her head in my chest and asked, "Your turn?"

I curled my finger, rubbing inside her as my palm rubbed her clit. I shook my head. "I think I'm going to stay here."

Her whimpers were a drug, and I couldn't stop if I wanted to.

She grasped my weeping cock and said, "Let me make you come, Charlie."

Her grip was perfect, and the demand in her words was like a shot of lust straight to my cock. It was almost too much. I'd never been so hard, so turned on. *Don't come. Don't come.*

I groaned. "God, Clawdia. I want to fuck you so bad."

"Why don't you?" she asked as she stroked me, dragging the precum from my tip down the shaft to lube her fingers.

I hissed. There wasn't enough blood in my brain to make coherent sentences. "First time ... not shower."

She seemed to understand what I meant, because she said, "Charlie, our first time is ours. It can be wherever we want it to be."

The fact that she was able to use reason and logic instead of being a stuttering mess like I was pissed me off. *Nope. That's not allowed.*

"Good point." I lifted her up, my arms under her thighs, and put her back against the wall.

She yelped, and I quietened her with my lips on hers. After a frenzied kiss that had her panting and squirming in my arms, I asked, "Can you be nice and quiet while I fuck this tight pussy? Savida and Daithi might hear if you're loud."

She whimpered and nodded. I looked down between us to enjoy the sight of my dick nestled between her folds and nudging her clit. Thrusting between her folds, feeling how her pussy pulsed and clenched, reaching for me, even as I denied her, thrilled me.

"Charlie, stop teasing." Clawdia pulled my head back up by my hair.

Yep, definitely a new kink. Who knew?

"Stop teasing? You want more?" I pressed soft, teasing kisses to her neck and jaw as I thrust against her folds.

"You know I do," she growled.

I grinned. "Say the words."

She hesitated and licked her lips. "Fuck me ... please."

Don't come. Don't come.

I notched my cock at her entrance and slowly slid inside. "Christ," I bit out. "Clawdia. God."

Warm. Wet. Perfect.

Mine.

The mental walls I put up between us came tumbling down, and I felt her again. Not her pain, thankfully. But the pleasure I was causing. It amplified my own so much I knew I wasn't going to last long.

But neither was she.

"You're so tight. So perfect," I groaned, biting at her ear lobe as her muscles squeezed me.

She panted, "Charlie, I can feel you."

Fuck yes, you can. She had that dazed and awed expression on her face again, which bolstered my ego some more.

Her mewls turned to loud moans with every thrust. If I couldn't tell from her sounds that she was seconds from coming, then the resounding pleasure and lust that I felt from her, and her pulsating pussy would have.

"Remember what I said about being quiet," I reminded as I started bounding into her, the slaps echoing loudly in the bathroom.

I didn't mean it. I wanted to hear everything. But with me, she was the disobedient type.

She shook her head and chanted, "Can't. Too good. Too good. Please. Please."

Her breath choked, her pussy fluttered, and then I was locked inside her as she clamped down. Hard. Her orgasm immediately threw me into my own. I came like a fucking hose. Like I wanted to drown her pussy in cum. Like she needed it to live.

My eyes rolled back in my head as the rush of endorphins hit. "Jesus."

We didn't move. We were both shaking and panting and quiet as we recovered from earth-shattering orgasms. My dick, spent and limp, slumped out of her still quaking pussy, and she shuddered.

Her eyes met mine, and she licked her lips before whispering, "I love you."

I pressed a gentle kiss to her lips. "You are everything, Clawdicat."

She smiled brightly, and I gently lowered her back down to stand in the tub. I picked up the washcloth, crouched, and gently rubbed it between her thighs. "Let's finish cleaning up and get ready to leave." She blushed but didn't stop me, even though I could tell she wanted to. I pressed a kiss to her stomach before standing. "I need a proper wash. Wait for me?"

She nodded and opened the curtain and hopped out, wrapping a towel around herself and picking up a brush. "They never talk about cold tiles when they talk about shower sex," she said.

"Who is they?" I asked as I grabbed at the shampoo and began scrubbing my hair.

"Netflix films with shower sex scenes."

"What? Like *50 Shades of Gray*? Or that kidnapping one?" I rinsed my hair and quickly rubbed soap all over. "I don't think you should be basing your knowledge of shower sex on films."

"Consider me re-educated."

I frowned and opened the shower curtain. "I don't like the way you just said that. Does that mean it was better or worse than what you thought?"

She laughed, the mischievous twinkle in her eye. She was winding me up like she used to as a cat.

"I don't even know why I'm letting you get to me. I felt you come so hard we both saw stars. I know it was good," I mumbled and wrapped a towel around my waist.

She was staring at me, her violet eyes turned darker with desire. "See something you like?" I asked with a smug smile.

"I always thought you were a beautiful man, but somehow, you seem … more … now. I don't know why."

"Orgasms will do that to you. Roses smell sweeter too," I teased, and her answering laugh lit up her face.

I could have lost her today. Lost out on this.

I wanted to ask what happened, why she'd left, but mostly, I wanted to know that the old, frightened version of Clawdia wasn't going to return.

I leaned down so our faces were inches apart, and she looked up at me, surprised. "Are you okay?"

She frowned. "Of course I am."

"You were alone with that dragon. With Fafnir."

Comprehension flickered across her face before it went suspiciously blank. "That's true. I was."

"Clawdia. Are. You. Okay?"

She hesitated. "I'm processing. It wasn't the worst experience I've ever had with him."

My brows drew together. "What does that mean? You've met him before?"

Her head bowed and her whispered words made my blood run cold. "He wasn't Fafnir when I knew him. He was Mr. Jenkins. My husband."

CHAPTER 3

ZAIDE

*O*ne moment, my head touched the pillow and my eyes closed; then the next, they jerked open when the bedroom door slammed against the wall.

"Did you know about this?" Charlie asked.

My soul pair squeaked as she was tossed onto the bed beside me.

"Really, Charlie," Clawdia grumbled as I groggily opened my eyes to watch her right her towel. "You can't just throw women around like that."

"I can when I've just found out that she's my great-great-grandad's wife." He ran his hands through his hair and paced. "What a mind fuck."

My body ached as I sat up. While I knew the pain was from a different source, the memories of fighting in a ring or being beaten by my master were close to the surface of my mind and made my mood worse.

But my little cat was already looking so miserable, and I didn't want to further upset her. I hid the pain and fear behind a blank expression and calmly asked, "What is going on?"

"Fafnir is Mr. Jenkins." She bowed her head. "My husband."

"Your husband? The man who beat you? Hurt you? He is alive?" I asked incredulously.

"And a dragon," Charlie added. I glared at him. "I'm just saying, because you have a scary look on your face. Like you want to go and find Fafnir so you can punch him straight in the snout again."

He is not wrong.

The only consolation I had when Clawdia told us the story of her past was that the family and husband that had hurt her so tremendously were long dead. Now to find out he was not only alive but was the dragon we'd raised …

The Fates are laughing at us.

Clawdia placed a hand on my arm. "Are you all right?"

"I'm …" I hesitated, not wanting to burden her with my anger when she was clearly suffering the greatest shock of all of us.

"You don't need to worry about the husband part," Charlie told me. "She died, he died, and the vows only say till death do they part, so they aren't married anymore. Marriage isn't magical either. And she didn't want to marry him in the first place."

I nodded, knowing this. It wasn't what bothered me but perhaps it had bothered Charlie.

"Do you think so, Charlie? My marriage is void because we died?" Her voice wavered.

"You aren't married to that fucking bastard, Clawdia," Charlie growled, tilting her head with a finger under her chin so he stared intently into her eyes.

"I agree. You died," I began. Charlie freed her from his hold, and she turned her attention to me, big violet eyes glistening with tears. I took her hand and kissed it. "He has never touched this body. Your voice might have said vows,

31

but the words did not come from this mouth. You were reborn anew."

She laughed once, a look of shock on her face, and then hiccupped a sob as tears slipped from her eyes and her lip quivered.

Charlie joined us on the bed and wrapped her into his arms. "It's okay, Clawdicat. He'll never touch you again."

"Never," I promised as I kissed her brow.

Charlie and I shared a look as we comforted our beloved. Without saying a word to each other, I knew we were united in our thoughts. We'd do anything to protect her from him. *Anything.*

As she quietened, I asked, "Will you explain what happened when you disappeared from the dreamscape?"

Clawdia wiped away tears and nodded. She told us she'd met Nisha, an akari seer, who told her Fafnir was Mr. Jenkins and that she had to leave us behind to find him.

"It was horrible. Seeing him again … It bought back so many memories. And when he killed that witch …" She swallowed. "It could have been me."

"Jesus Christ, Clawdicat. I'm so sorry." Charlie tucked a curl of hair behind her ear and stared with sympathetic eyes.

Her whimper distressed me, and I squeezed her again while my hand that rested on her stomach rubbed in reassuring circles. "Why didn't you wait for me to come with you? You shouldn't have had to face him on your own."

"Nisha said I couldn't. I was really scared, but I needed to do it … I needed to face him," she explained.

"And who is she? Why are we listening to her?" Charlie asked with his usual skepticism.

Clawdia shrugged. "I don't really know. But she is on our side."

"I don't think you should trust random women who

kidnap you from dreams and tell you about your future unsolicited."

"She wanted to help us so we could help her. I believe her. Trust me."

He sighed heavily and ran a hand over his face. "Help her how? We've got a long enough to-do list without adding her issues too."

"I'm not sure. She made it sound like doing this was also going to help her."

I asked after a slight pause, "Does Fafnir know who you are?"

She hesitated, and I held my breath. "He recognized me but doesn't think it's me. I hope he doesn't find out, but Mary could tell him. I don't know how that could affect us."

"I'm sure we will soon find out," Charlie replied ominously.

"I can't think about that now. Charlie, what did you mean about Fafnir being your grandad?" She paused for a moment before she gasped. "You met your birth mother! What did she say? Was it everything you thought it would be?"

Charlie barked a laugh. "Not quite what I'd dreamed of."

Charlie went on to tell us about meeting his mother. Clawdia practically growled with anger as he explained how his birth mother, Elizabeth, attacked him, tried to kill him, and made him swear a vow to get any witch training at all. He laughed at her, "Calm down, killer. It's fine."

"It's not fine. She tried to hurt you, kill you, and after you were so—" She huffed. "It's horrible. I hate her."

"We left it in an okay place. Maybe we'll grow closer as she trains me."

He continued, explaining that he discovered Mary is his cousin, and Fafnir, the dragon, was his great-great-grandfather.

We sat in shocked silence until I said, "You aren't having much luck with discovering family members, Charlie."

"You're telling me." He rolled his eyes.

Clawdia frowned. "But I left some over."

"What?" Charlie gave me a questioning look. I shrugged in response.

"The vial. I didn't drink it all. I left some for the next wife. But that poor woman had his children. Children that killed her by taking her magic." Clawdia closed her eyes, her shoulders heavy with a burden that shouldn't be hers.

I nuzzled into her neck. "It was a horrible fate, but one that couldn't be avoided. Without such an incident, Charlie wouldn't be with us."

"I make a beautiful silver lining." He winked, and Clawdia reluctantly chuckled.

I envied his ease at making her laugh.

She smiled. "You do."

Charlie rolled to lie on the bed. "Speaking of silver linings and me being amazing, do you want to tell us what happened before I rescued you from the side of the road?" he asked me.

I told Charlie about meeting my brother, Thos, in a dream before I got lost in the dreamscape. Just remembering his chipped tooth and the hope in his eyes made me feel lighter.

That changed as I admitted my shame at attacking Baelen when he found me, because I was lost in the memories of my akari slave owner. Clawdia held my hand and offered me a sympathetic smile.

Charlie's eyes pulled together as I explained that Clawdia, Baelen, and I are soul mates.

"Soul mates like Savida and Daithi?" Charlie asked quietly.

Clawdia was quick to react to the vulnerability in his question and assured him, "You don't need to worry. I'm just as connected to you as I am to Zaide and Baelen. And it's nice I get someone to myself."

He picked up her hand resting on his chest and pressed a gentle kiss to it.

"That explains why you were so into him." Charlie chuckled, remembering how distraught we all were when Clawdia kissed Baelen after our first time. "But I didn't know you were into guys."

I shrugged. "I wasn't into anyone until I met my soul pair and now my soul mate. Bodies are just the shell. It's what's inside that is most important." My lips brushed her neck as I spoke, and she shivered.

"You're a soppy golden giant," Charlie laughed softly.

I opened my mouth to continue the tale but snapped it shut. Baelen and I had been attacked in the dreamscape, but I was pulled out of it before I knew who was there. I don't know what happened to Baelen.

I won't tell her. It will only worry her, I decided and closed my eyes briefly to send a prayer. *My gods, if you are listening, please protect your son from harm.*

Baelen was strong, but he'd created weapons as though he was preparing for war. He was scared. I anticipated the moment when we'd be together again in our dreams and I could see him safe and well.

Charlie brought my attention back to them when he asked, "And you made up with Daithi and Savida when you woke up?"

I nodded. "Savida threatened to leave Daithi if they didn't make things right with me."

Clawdia gasped. "That would destroy them both."

"I haven't seen him so determined … nor miserable. I don't want to be the cause of their misery."

"Well, Daithi is still on my shit list," Charlie scoffed as he played with Clawdia's fingers.

"They both came with me and Alcor to help the witches heal the protector," I argued. "Savida learned his true name. It was incredible …"

I grinned as I remembered the pure joy on Savida's face when he learned his true name and used his gift for the first time.

Clawdia echoed my smile. "I'm glad Savida got a part of his heritage back."

"And you all healed the protector?" Charlie asked. "He's back to normal?"

I coughed, and closed my eyes before saying, "I doubt healing someone would return them to a former age, so perhaps he is not back to normal. But he should survive to tell us what he knows. He was still unconscious when I left with Alcor and the task team."

Charlie finished, "And then someone, probably hunters, ran you off the road."

I nodded. "And then someone ran us off the road."

"And Alcor, is he all right?" Clawdia asked.

Charlie replied, "The council has him, and we can see him when we leave with them."

"We are leaving with the council?" I asked. My eyes popped back open and, I lifted my head to look over Claudia's body to look at Charlie.

"Going into hiding with them." He nodded and offered me a sympathetic smile.

He could probably tell from my face how much I was loath to move right now.

Clawdia frowned, her hand pausing for a moment as she stroked Charlie's chest. "Why are they hiding? People need their help. Fafnir could be flying around terrorizing innocent people, and now with the hunters …"

Charlie replied softly, "Everyone needs to regroup and

think up solutions before they start to do anything. We need to make sure the protector is safe and talk to him."

"You think he will be able to help?" Clawdia asked.

Charlie shrugged. "Sigurd and Fafnir are mortal enemies. If anyone has a clue on how to defeat the dragon, it's him."

"A mortal enemy, a decedent, an ex-wife." She sighed, leaning her head back on my shoulder. "I don't like how connected we are to all of this."

"It makes sense," I said.

Charlie raised an inquisitive brow and asked, "What makes sense?"

"We are supposed to be connected to this problem. The gods and Fates want us to save the titans. But they are going to test us first, make us strong enough to fight our pasts and remake ourselves as saviors."

There was a pause before he scoffed. "You've been watching too much television."

"I haven't been watching any television." I gave him a droll look and played with a strand of Clawdia's drying hair.

"So, this dramatic statement was serious?"

Clawdia ignored Charlie's comments, huffed out a breath, set her jaw, and declared, "If Fafnir is our test, then I'm going to win. I won't let him take my life from me again. I won't run."

I gave Charlie a look as Clawdia helpfully demonstrated my point, which he responded to by rolling his eyes.

He remarked, "That said, we are running right now."

"Only for a little while," Clawdia allowed.

"We are going now?" I asked. The thought of more travel, stress, and fear filled me with dread.

Charlie said, "We're waiting for our ride."

I sighed and let myself fall back into the pillow, my mind close to bursting with all the new information.

Clawdia rolled over to stroke my brow. "I'll pack for you, Zaide."

"Thank you, Little Cat. I don't think I can move yet." But I did feel a lot better than before.

I eyed Clawdia suspiciously as she got off the bed, dressed herself, then began throwing our clothes into a suitcase. She must be getting good at healing for me not to have noticed her doing it while in my arms.

She seemed in reasonably good spirits, but I knew she must be tired.

I was tired. I was tired thinking of how much there was yet to do.

Is it too much to ask to find your soul pair and soul mate and have time together without being in perilous situations and mortal danger?

"How long do you imagine this will last?" The question was out of my mouth before I had a chance to stop it.

"What?" Clawdia stopped folding a t-shirt to frown at me. I felt Charlie's piercing gaze too.

I didn't want to worry them with my dark thoughts or my sober feelings so, swallowing, I chose my words, my tone, very carefully but gave them my honest truth.

"We will have to wait for Fafnir to be defeated and the protector to die once more before the portals are reopened. He is young again now. That is … a long time until I can rescue my siblings. A long time until Baelen can join us."

Clawdia moved to the bed, dropping the shirt and brushing a hand over my hair. "I miss him too. I hope for everyone's sake this is dealt with quickly, but if it isn't, if it takes us years to stop Fafnir, if the protector looks to live another seven decades, we will find a way to search for your siblings and reunite with Baelen."

I hated seeing the concern on her face, although I relished in her soft voice and gentle touch. *Stupid titan, you*

38

shouldn't cause her more worry. You should be strong, I berated myself.

With a stiff smile, I said, "You are correct, Little Cat. I apologize. I should concentrate on the present and not allow myself to get overwhelmed by the vastness of the future. It will all work out. That, I am sure of. I have you and Charlie and Baelen. We are a team, and we will be victorious."

Clawdia frowned and opened her mouth but was interrupted by Charlie.

"That's the spirit." Charlie slapped my thigh as he sat up. "You should start a podcast, you know. It could be called *Titan Vibes.*"

"I do not know what a podcast is, Charlie, but I will take your comment as a compliment."

An undeserved one.

A knock interrupted us, and Savida peered around the door. He looked … scared. "Forgive me for intruding, but Daithi has woken from his vision. I think it's important you know about it."

I scrambled out of bed, as did Charlie. Clawdia was already following Savida into the corridor and toward their bedroom.

We crowded into the room, standing around the bed as though Daithi would not see the morning. His eyes flickered open and locked on mine.

Dread sat heavily in my stomach.

The vision is about me.

A sheen of tears gathered in his eyes.

It's bad. He's never seen anything bad in my future before. Certainly not enough to make him cry.

"Do I die?" I asked quietly.

Clawdia's head snapped toward me as she gasped. "No. Surely not."

Daithi shook his head.

"What did you see, Daithi?" Charlie asked.

"You are imprisoned," he croaked.

"Alone." It wasn't a question. I wouldn't allow Clawdia nor Charlie to end up captured, especially now that I knew it was fated.

"Why alone? Why aren't we with you?" Clawdia asked, panic rising in her voice. She took my hand, gripping it firmly as though holding me now would stop me from being taken from her in the future.

Daithi sat up in the bed, and Savida fluttered worriedly around him. "I'm not certain, Clawdia. I only saw him."

"Don't get upset." Charlie tucked her into his arms and stroked her head.

"I'm injured?" I asked.

Daithi's jaw tensed. "You're ... unable to escape."

Very injured, then.

I suppressed a shiver of fear and told myself, *Don't let this fate make you afraid. You have suffered before and been saved. Keep faith.*

"What does the place look like?" Charlie asked.

"It was dark. I cannot see what precautions they have taken to hold him, but there are humans in front of you, taunting you. They hold the keys to your cage."

"Humans? How can you tell?"

"They call him a freak."

Clawdia, Charlie, and I exchanged a grim look.

Hunters?

CHAPTER 4

CHARLIE

"*O*kay, this isn't the end of the world. Forewarned is forearmed," I state cheerfully.

Although the vision worried me, it was clear I wasn't nearly as worried as maybe I should be.

Alone. Imprisoned. And injured. It wasn't the best fate, but it also wasn't the worst. Daithi didn't know how long he'd be there, but he hadn't seen him dead.

Zaide might have freaked out in the cave cage, but he didn't know he'd be affected that way. Now he did, and now he'd prepare himself. I could see it in the set of his jaw. He wasn't going to fall to pieces.

He used to be a titan slave, for fuck's sake. He's lived through worse than teasing from a bunch of humans.

If Zaide was hiding his fear, Clawdia was demonstrating enough for both of them. She shook in my arms, her breathing uneven against my bare chest, and gripped Zaide's hand like a lifeline.

Daithi glared. "I'm sure you said that before, Charlie, when it was Savida's suffering I saw."

"And look how that turned out. Savida is right here." I

waved my arms at Savida, who gave me a small smile but continued to plump Daithi's pillows and offer him water.

"You aren't usually so positive," Clawdia noted and looked up at me with narrowed eyes.

"Well, someone needs to be. We don't know when this will happen, or why, or who, but we can plan to make sure we can get him back."

Clawdia swallows. "There's nothing we can do to stop it?"

"My visions always come to pass," Daithi answered simply.

Clawdia choked on a sob and left my arms to hug Zaide. He was still frozen, so he didn't move to embrace her.

"But you saw the place. You know where he'll be?" I asked.

Daithi said, "Yes."

"So, you can portal there?"

"As I said, I can't see what protections his captors might have in place—"

"That isn't what I asked."

I knew what he was doing. *He doesn't want to promise to go and get him if it puts Savida at risk.* But I wasn't going to let him get away with that. Zaide needed hope to get him through.

Daithi closed his eyes. "I can portal there now that I have seen it. But I can't guarantee he'll be there when we do. I don't know when this will happen."

"We'll take that risk."

"Will we be able to go and get him?" Clawdia asked desperately, looking at me for reassurance as she rubbed Zaide's back. Zaide's statue impression crumbled under her touch, and he finally hugged her back.

Savida spoke. "No one is suggesting we leave Zaide to suffer his fate for long. As soon as we are able, we will rescue him as you rescued me."

"Don't fear for me, Little Cat. I'll be fine," Zaide mumbled into her hair.

"See, it's going to work out. He'll get caught, and we'll go and get him as soon as we can."

No one seemed to be cheered by my statement. *Tough crowd.*

In the living room, my phone vibrated against the table it had been charging on. I dashed over to it to see the notification. A text that read: *outside.*

I rushed back into the bedroom. "That's our ride. Come on team. Shake off the vision blues. Time to rest, recoup, plan, and do a training montage."

* * *

WE GATHERED our things and headed out to the car park. As the door shut behind us, Savida called out a thank you to the apartment for safe housing while we were there and said goodbye. *Weird demon.*

I recognized the man standing by a car waiting for us. "Laurence, good to see you again. Thanks for coming to get us." I shook his hand.

He gave me a wide smile. "You're welcome. I couldn't leave you all to be eaten. Fafnir with your magic would cause us a lot more trouble than you could cause with us."

"Ah, you've been drastically undersold on how much trouble we are." I laughed as I walked around to the passenger side, opened the door, and jumped inside.

"Glad you found them," Laurence said as he hopped into the driver's seat and looked in the rearview mirror at Daithi and Savida. He turned to me. "They portaled away as soon as Daithi woke from his vision saying they had to go and get you."

Laurence went to put the car in gear and turn the key, but

I stopped him. "Before we go, I just need to hack the building records and security to stop the hunters from finding who we are."

He raised a brow. "You can do that?"

"I'm a hacker. Give me a computer, and I can do a lot."

I flipped open my laptop and, using the Wi-Fi, managed to get into the records pretty quickly. With a few taps, I changed my name and address and added a different credit card number. Then I went in search of the CCTV. The recording was live, so I had to find the storage for the files before I sent a virus and made the files corrupted and unviewable. Then I crashed the live CCTV.

"Okay, we are good to go. They won't see us leaving," I said about twenty minutes later.

I glanced up at the mirror to see Daithi and Zaide fast asleep in their seats in the back of the car and Clawdia and Savida whispering in the middle seats. Laurence didn't wait around, starting the car and zooming off into the night.

"Where are we going anyway?" I asked.

"We're heading to a remote island about thirty minutes away," he told me as he messed with the buttons for the heat since it was a relatively cold summer night. "A few families of witches have lived there in secret for centuries, but they have offered it as a safe haven to other supernaturals trying to escape the chaos of both the dragon and the hunters."

"A secret island?"

"Only a secret from humans. Most supernaturals can see and visit it, but it's invisible to humans."

"How have they kept humans from knowing about it?"

"Magic." He gave me a look that said, "duh." "There are protection spells around it, built up over the centuries they've been there, so it's very secure."

"We are longing for somewhere secure," Savida added and

then gasped as a thought occurred to him. "Perhaps with an excellent shopping facility for a handsome demon to scour."

Clawdia giggled. "I don't think a secret island is going to have many shops."

Savida's face fell. "This is not the correct secure place for me."

"But it's going to keep you safe, so it's your place for now," I told him.

"I've been before." Laurence said, "It's pretty rustic, but it's the perfect place for the protector to wake up in. Much calmer than a city. Can't have him dying of shock and letting people portal here again."

"He's going to be on the island too? Can we talk to him?" Clawdia asked.

"We're just waiting for him to wake up."

I asked, "Do you know where Fafnir is?"

"He flew toward Stockholm, and we lost him among the buildings. We aren't sure what his human form looks like, so we have some agents following multiple suspects."

"I can describe him for you," Clawdia offered, but the pink in her cheeks faded.

"You've seen him?"

She nodded gravely. "So have Charlie and Zaide."

"Clawdia has more … intimate knowledge of his appearance," I admitted.

And boy, did that piss me off. I'd been so focused on getting Clawdia out of there that I hadn't taken the time to really look at and remember his face. I hated that she knew him, had married him, was hurt by him, and on top of that, he was my ancestor. *Fucking winged bastard. I'll kill him.*

"If you can identify the suspect, it would help us immensely."

"I'm happy to help." She gave him a shy smile, and I glared.

"No more smiles," I told her through our bond. *"You'll make him fall for you, and your dance card is full."*

Her eyes flashed to mine, amusement dancing in them. *"You're so silly. No more boyfriends, I promise."*

I didn't know why I was getting so possessive, but it was clear to me that after our life-altering shower, any walls I had standing between us had crumbled away. She was mine.

"What are the plans to defeat him?" I asked, trying to get my mind back to the burning issue. Emphasis on burning.

Laurence shrugged. "I'm afraid the council hasn't shared those plans with me, if they have them. Many agents are hoping that once the protector awakens, he will be able to inform us of his enemy's weaknesses and the best way to defeat him."

"Defeat," I noted. "Not put back to sleep for the witches to raise again?"

Laurence nodded. "Elimination is best for the future of the realms."

Twenty minutes later, we were on a small boat in the pitch-black water, huddled and shivering as the cold wind whipped around us. It wasn't a long crossing. Only ten minutes or so, and God only knows how Laurence could see anything, but just as I was sure I'd lose my dick to frostbite, we slowed and pulled up to a dimly lit wooden pier.

"Thank Christ." I sighed, roughly warming my arms after getting up onto the dock.

I helped Laurence pull everyone up, one by one, holding them for a second as they got their legs under them and then pushing them down the platform and out of the way.

"I can feel the magic in the land," Daithi muttered, his skin like silver under the moonlight.

"It really is protected?" Clawdia asked. "You can feel it?"

He nodded and put a hand on her shoulder. "We should be safe."

It was weird to see him being nice to her after everything he'd said and done to her before, but I appreciated that he was taking mine and Zaide's comments about his attitude toward her to heart and trying.

As I pulled my golden giant friend out of the boat, he almost toppled straight over the deck and into the water on the other side. Savida spread his wings, managing to catch him.

Zaide patted his chest. "Thank you, my friend," he slurred as he spoke, and his knees shook.

Poor Zaide. What a day for him.

"How far is the cabin?" Clawdia asked as she tucked herself under Zaide's arm as though she'd be able to hold him up.

"I'm fine, Little Cat," Zaide tried to assure her, but he still sounded like a drunk sailor.

"You are tilting to the side," she retorted as they walked down the pier, toward the lights of the little houses.

Laurence guided us down a few dark streets until we stood in front of two small cabins. The light from inside the cabins didn't illuminate outside enough for me to really see what the cabins looked like, but I was so tired I didn't care. I just wanted a bed and to rest in the knowledge a dragon wasn't about to eat me.

"One for you." He handed me a key. "One for you." He handed Daithi another. "There's nothing in the cupboards, so you'll need to come to the main house, which is at the top of that hill"—he pointed—"for breakfast. But I expect you'll need your rest after the last few days."

* * *

TUCKED into bed next to Clawdia and with Zaide's dulcet snores echoing on her other side, I closed my eyes, so tired, but I wouldn't be getting a restful sleep. To keep my sworn promise to my birth mother, I needed to dreamwalk to her every night for her to train me. I did as I was taught and followed a connection to her through a fog until I appeared in her living room.

"Charlie," she said, quickly standing up from her sofa. "What happened? Your familiar is safe?"

Elizabeth frowned, stepped toward me and reached out a hand, but stopped short. I collapsed into the armchair and filled her in on everything that had happened since leaving the dream last night.

When I finished, she looked a tad green around the gills and began pacing, rubbing her arms and chewing her lips. "Hunters." She shook her head. "The situation is getting more dire by the second."

"You're telling me. This shit is unrelenting. But hopefully, this protected island will give us time to plan the next move instead of just being smacked in the face by universe balls."

She sighed and ducked her head but not before I saw the slight smile turning the corner of her lips. "Now that you're being chased by hunters, I'm going to teach you more defensive magic. Something that will protect you—invisibility spells, luck potions, barrier spells …"

Books appeared in the middle of the table as she listed protective spells.

I frowned. "I thought I couldn't do potions."

She paused and gave me a wary look. "Why did you think that?"

"Because the way magic was explained to me was that some families do spells, some families do potions, and others track."

If fucking Simon was telling me lies, I'll make his life hell when I find him. Slimy bastard.

She rubbed her forehead. "I'd forgotten you are still so

new to magic and there are so many who don't fully know our history." Sitting on the sofa opposite me, she sighed and said, "Let us start at the beginning. The emergence of witches in the human realm.

"Our realm has been linked to other realms since its conception, and therefore, other beings have always been in and out of our realm, doing what beings do. Reproducing. As generations have passed, the magic in their blood from their ancestors has faded to humans who have extraordinary smell and singing voices. People who can see the future, get feelings about things or push their desires into being.

"Witches are humans who were stricter with their bloodlines. They knew their power came from their ancestors, whatever mix of otherworlder they were, and chose, strategically, to continue and strengthen those lines to retain power.

"Families do have certain specialties; however, there has been so much interbreeding across witch families over thousands of years that there isn't a witch alive who can't do the basics of magic."

A little china dish and cup appeared on the coffee table in front of her, brimming with some kind of fruit tea. She picked it up and sipped.

I waited for her to put her tea down before I asked, "And casting spells. How did that come about? Otherworlders don't have books of spells."

"Spells are just voiced intentions. It's easier to teach if it's spoken because it focuses the brain on the meaning and the intention. Witches have built spells and magic that works for them over thousands of years, enough to separate our magic from the otherworlder's now."

I wanted to ask about my tracking ability, where it came from but I had a feeling it was a longer conversation. Instead, I asked, "How do you know this?"

"Every witch should know their history," she replied simply.

I rolled my eyes. "And yet the leader of the witches has just risen an old man from the ground to protect her from otherworlder slave traders without knowing he'd been risen before or that in raising him, she'd be raising a magic-eating dragon too."

She paused and pursed her lips. "I'll admit it's embarrassing, but I think their lack of knowledge has more to do with Fafnir and his followers than the witches being ignorant."

I raised my eyebrow and leaned forward. My tiredness and irritability faded as I felt the tingle of my magic. *We are on to something here. Finding something.*

"While I don't trust Debs as far as I can throw her, she said Mary gave her a document about raising Sigurd and told her to hide him from the council. Knowing who Mary is now, it makes sense. She wanted to raise Fafnir and got it done by feeding Debs a line about bringing back Sigurd for protection but then hid Sigurd from the council so he'd die before they could help him. Question is, was it Mary's idea to raise him or something Fafnir planned?"

I eyed my birth mother, who sat stiffly. "If Fafnir left a plan for his descendants to enact in order for him to rise again, surely you would have known about it."

CHAPTER 5

CHARLIE

*S*he knew. She must have known he'd been planning to come back.

Elizabeth swallowed nervously, her hands clenched around her tea cup. "As I told you, the family has been completely divided for some time."

"Because one side wanted to free Fafnir and the other didn't?" I crossed my arms and glared. "You said it was about power, politics."

"They go hand in hand." She stopped me when I opened my mouth. "Please, Charlie, I will explain. Just let me start at the beginning.

"You'll remember I told you that the sons of Fafnir killed their mother and her sisters by taking their magic. The daughters, however, were horrified. They'd suffered their father's abuse and had no love for the males in their family. After the deaths of their mother and aunts, they decided to kill their brothers before they could take any more lives."

I interrupted. "How many children did he have?"

"Four. Two boys. Two girls."

"So, the girls killed the boys, and the girls had children."

She nodded. "Killed them in their sleep. Fafnir disappeared. The girls taught their daughters their history and powers but cautioned them against Fafnir. As the terror of Fafnir was forgotten through generations, more descendants became curious about their dragon ancestor and began to learn of him through diaries the family had collected.

"Our family has been hidden for a long time to protect ourselves from those who would seek to use us. It is why Fafnir sought out my great-grandmother; he, unlike others, found her. But around the same time that the family began looking at the diaries, they also questioned why we had to hide. Why did we have to do a duty that gives us no glory."

I frowned. "A duty with no glory? What duty?"

She paused to stare at me, debating something in her mind. The cup chinked against the plate as she put it down, nodded to herself, and stood up. "It is easier to show you."

The room changed in a flash, turning dark and cold, and I dropped to the floor as the sofa vanished.

"A little warning would have been nice," I muttered as I stood from the muddy, gravelly ground, wiping myself down. Elizabeth started walking, and I quickly followed, our footsteps echoing off the stone walls surrounding us. "Where are we?"

It looked like a cave, but it was a lot nicer than the one I'd spent a week trapped in. This one had lit candles in little holders down the tunnel that widened the further we walked.

"Under my home," she replied simply as we approached a curtain of hanging vines.

There's something there. Something hidden.

Just like when I found the magic hiding spot as we escaped the hunters, I could feel magic fizzing under my skin, urging me forward, telling me to find what I couldn't yet see. It was an interesting, if not freaky, feeling.

Elizabeth turned to me, her hand resting on the edge of the curtain. "I guard a natural portal here."

"A natural portal? What's that?" I asked.

"The best kept secret in all the realms." She pulled back the curtain for a dramatic reveal, and blue light poured out. A huge portal took up the entire cave, swirling and humming like the other portals I'd seen created, but this called to me.

Power unlike anything I'd ever felt seemed to bounce around the cave walls, and the fizzing under my skin intensified. I took a step back, suddenly wary of my reaction to it.

Elizabeth began lecturing, and I had to concentrate around the blood rushing loudly in my head. "This portal, and the others like it around the globe, are how the realms are linked together. They keep magic flowing between lands and make sure there is balance across the realms. After the fall of the titans, the Fates took the knowledge of the natural portals from all creatures except a few."

"Why?" I choked out.

"Unrest in the human realm leads to imbalance in other realms. The human realm is the only realm with natural portals to all the other interlinked dimensions. It was a lot like a train station for otherworlders who crossed into this realm, aiming to go to another since their own realm doesn't have a direct portal," she explained.

"A titan civil war caused chaos in the human realm which had a huge impact on the interlinked dimensions and the portals themselves. The Fates felt the Guardians of the Titans had failed in their mission to bring peace around the realms, and so the guardians were made gods, which is a terrible eternal sentence; the titans were punished, their souls cleaved in half; and the natural portals were forgotten to stop otherworlders traveling so easily."

"A titan civil war in the human realm?" I ran a hand through my hair as I tried to take in all the information.

"A ten-year war where the Olympians fought the titans for reign over the human realm."

I raised a brow. "No shit." Another thought hit me. "So, you've been shaking the hands of the otherworlders coming through who are looking to steal humans?"

She gave me an exasperated look. "No, of course not. These portals are forgotten. Nothing comes through."

"Why are you guarding it if nothing comes through?" I crossed my arms, not understanding and getting more frustrated by the second.

Why does every conversation with this woman leave me feeling like I've been given a riddle rather than answers?

She let the vine curtain fall across the portal, the bright blue glow hidden again, until we stood in the dim light of the candles.

"We have always been guardians of the portals. We are the only people in this realm to know where they are, which portal leads where, and can see the connections each portal has to the human realm. The magic has embedded itself in our blood over centuries. We have a kinship, a connection to them."

"You know where that one goes?" I pointed to the vine vale, and she nodded with a smile, a knowing glint in her eyes. "Where?" I asked, my curiosity getting away with me.

"I can't tell you."

Bloody typical. I rolled my eyes.

The dreamscape changed again, and I wobbled on my feet as I suddenly found myself back in the living room we started in.

I glared at my birth mother as she smirked at me and said, "You're going to need to get used to controlling the dreamscape."

"I'll add it to the to-do list," I muttered as I sat on the sofa again. With my head in my hands, and my mind processing, I said, "So, Fafnir came looking for your great-grandmother because he wanted access to the natural portal." I looked up at Elizabeth, who had another teacup in hand. "But how did he find her?"

Elizabeth frowned. "She felt a powerful disturbance and left her portal to seek it out. The disturbance was probably the rise of Sigurd and Fafnir, but unfortunately, she fell victim to Fafnir."

"She didn't tell him about the portals," I stated. If he knew where they were, he'd have already gone in search of more powerful prey.

She shook her head. "She couldn't. Everyone is sworn to secrecy."

"You haven't sworn me."

"You don't know anything beyond that they exist, and Fafnir already knows that. But you don't know where they are. Where this one is. If I ever tell you, you will be sworn too."

I gritted my teeth and huffed my frustration. *She only trusts me so far. She still thinks I'll turn to the dark side.*

"How did Fafnir know the natural portals exist if the knowledge was wiped?"

She paused, took a sip of tea, and stared into the cup before shaking her head. "I'm not sure."

"But you knew he planned to come back for some reason," I prompted, still looking for the answer to my previous answer. She'd talked around the subject so much, but it was obvious. *They knew something.*

She sighed and put her tea down. "You're so determined to see the worst in me."

"You literally tried to dust me last night," I reminded her as I leaned back on the sofa and crossed my arms.

"That was an accident."

I scoffed and asked a new question since I was getting

nowhere with the other one. "Are Fafnir's plans in the diaries?"

"Not the ones I have."

I clenched my fists and stood. "Stop fucking around and answer me straight!" I yelled.

"I can't help but want you to see me in a positive light," she said quietly, her head bowed.

But I was past being patient.

"That ship sailed a long time ago. All I need from you now is training and knowledge." She nodded sadly, and I felt a twinge of guilt. "What did your family, the Fafnir fans, tell you before they split away from the rest of you?"

She stood up, retrieved the photo album she'd shown me last night, and opened it up to the same photo of Elizabeth holding a fifty balloon, surrounded by other women. This time, instead of my eyes tracking straight to Mary, I looked intently at the other faces.

"They told us they'd found diaries written by Fafnir and knew what he planned. Knowing how much power he had, they felt they were wasting their time watching portals when they could be out showing the world what the witches of extremely powerful lines could do. Then they left and took all his notes and diaries with them. They abandoned their posts as the guards of portals and never contacted us again."

"Which ones are they?" I asked, looking down at the photo.

"My aunt, Doris." She pointed at an old gray lady who had her arms around a similar looking older lady. "My cousin, June, and her daughter, Maeve." She tapped two ginger ladies. "My sister, Amalie, and my nieces, Mary, who you know, and Alice."

Her fingers hovered over the blond woman with her arms around a brunette girl and Mary, who had her arms around them both as she stood on a plastic white chair behind them.

"They abandoned their portals? Who guards them now?" I asked.

"We had to split up. My daughters used to be here with me, but now they guard the portals left by my cousin and sister."

"I have sisters," I breathed. The "World's Best Mum" mug on the cabinet had given me a clue, but it still felt like a shock to know I had sisters. Younger sisters.

She pointed at the two blond girls sitting on the grass in front of her. "Yes. Gemma and Kayleigh. They are now twenty-five and twenty-three."

I felt a pang of sadness at the thought I hadn't got to be the annoying protective older brother I would have loved to be. *But maybe when it's all over, I can meet them and have some kind of relationship with them.*

"That's crazy." I wanted to ask more about them, but it wasn't the time.

Getting back on track, I asked, "So, they didn't explicitly say they were going to bring him back, and you didn't know he could be brought back?" She hesitated. "What?"

"We have an old document the witches who raised Sigurd and Fafnir in 1915 had seen. It stated they would need to return to the very same resting place in order to rise again. It cautioned against raising Sigurd because in doing so, Fafnir would also rise. They ignored that, of course."

"So, you did know he could rise again."

"We knew it was a possibility, but we didn't know where he went when he disappeared after his sons were killed. We didn't know if he knew he needed to go back to Sweden to rise again. We certainly didn't think our family would help bring him back."

"You didn't hear anything about the plans to raise Sigurd and think to tell anyone that they might be raising a dragon too?"

"No, I knew nothing of it."

"Because you've isolated yourself from society." I sat back. "I agree with them to a certain extent."

"Agree with what?" Elizabeth asked as she closed the album and eyed me suspiciously.

"You shouldn't be hiding away guarding a portal no one uses. You should be out in the witching world. You could be helping to stop him, especially because your family is involved."

She rolled her eyes. "You've known about this all of a few minutes and think you have all the answers."

"You're right. I don't know fucking anything. You've got all the knowledge that could be helpful in defeating him. You know the history. This wouldn't have happened if you were the head of the witches. Even if you didn't want to lead, you could have advised from afar and under another name."

"Bad things happen when we leave our portals unguarded. Look at what happened to my great-grandmother."

I scoffed. "Sounds a lot like cowardice to me."

Her eyes narrowed, and her voice dropped to a threatening whisper. "You don't get to speak to me like that."

"Why not? You gave me up rather than fight with your family. You tried to kill me before hearing me out, so afraid of me even though I didn't fight or threaten you. You're a coward," I hissed, really driving the dagger in deep.

"You don't know him. The dangers."

I barked a laugh. "Don't know him? I fucking walked up to him and offered him Zaide as a snack to distract him from Clawdia. I've seen him. His ex-wife is my familiar. I know what he did to her, how afraid she is of him, but she still went to face him and attacked him to save another witch. She's far braver than you."

"She's made herself a target for him now. He'll hunt her as

he hunts the portals. And if he finds her, all will be lost." She looked genuinely fearful.

I gentled my voice. "Maybe. We are scared about that too, but she's going to help the council take him down. She wants to help. We are all helping. We know nothing is going to get better without us. We are too wrapped up in the mess to bury our heads in the sand. You are involved, whether you like it or not, and you should be helping."

"I'm telling you everything—" she started.

"Nothing I haven't dragged out of you. You have diaries and spells and all kinds of things in your arsenal that you can't teach me in a few days."

"If he were ever to find—"

I interrupted. "I don't disagree. But I don't think you need to hide yourselves as well as the portal. The portal hasn't been doing anything. You could have lived your life with the witches, finding out what's going on, helping younger witches, anything, but you've just said a big fuck you to everyone and hid under a rock."

"You don't have to make a point with such vulgar language." She sneered, but in the silence that followed, her face fell, and she sighed. "But you're right. We have hidden away."

"I get it. We are hiding right now. But that's only until we have a plan on how to deal with this. We aren't telling the world to fuck themselves. We're putting our oxygen masks on before we help others. You've had yours on for ages now, and the rest of us are turning blue. It's time to help."

"How do you suggest I do that?" she asked quietly.

"Call the council. Tell them everything you know about Fafnir. Give them the names and pictures of your family on his side so they can track them. It might help them find him more easily. Offer help in any other way you can think of. It's not hard."

She stared at me silently. Long enough to make me feel uncomfortable and twitchy.

Finally, she said, "You have not had the life I wanted for you, but you have become a good man, Charlie."

Her words were so surprising I stepped back like she punched me, and warmth bubbled inside me at the pride she had in her eyes. I had to look away as I muttered, "Thanks."

She nodded briskly and put the photo album back on the shelf. "I will call a family meeting and tell them everything I have learned from you. We will see what they have to say. If they agree to help, we will help."

Not a yes, but not a no.

Is that a win?

CHAPTER 6

BAELEN

*Z*aide disappeared, leaving me alone in the dreamscape with the shadows who continued to haunt me.

I was no longer in control of the dreamscape, and it changed from the familiar sight of the healing tent in Akar to a desolate place. Ash fell from a gray sky, scattering on the blackened earth, which had deep scars and craters across the barren landscape. I'd never seen a realm so colorless and dark.

Where am I?

Figures formed in the dimness, two males and a female. The smokey gloom of the environment and the darkness of their skin hid any distinctive facial features. Their thin and flaky clothing, which hugged them like a second skin, allowed for no concealed weapons.

But even if they were armed to the teeth, I expected the shadows had gifts I didn't know.

With my fangs protruding and my mouth pulled back in a snarl, I crouched, ready to attack the moment they moved.

My instincts homed in on the figures, looking for ways to kill most efficiently.

Of course, I found none, since the figures were incorporeal, which only served to make my akari nature more furious. *Invade my dreams. Take my soul mates. Threaten me again. Die. Die. Die.*

In the back of my mind, I was glad Clawdia and Zaide were not there to see me like that. *I do not want them to see the monster that lurks beneath.*

But the events of the past few days were testing my restraint and I could no longer pretend civility.

A male voice barked a laugh. "Put your fangs away, youngling. You cannot puncture a shadow. Especially not with those tiny things."

Anger turned my vision red. I growled, "Remove yourself from my dreamscape, or I will remove you myself."

Although, without being able to see their blood threads or attack their corporeal bodies, I was not entirely sure how to follow through with that threat.

"Your dreamscape? Are you familiar with the desolate landscape of Ombra?" I felt the mocking smile in his tone.

"Ombra?" I asked but didn't move from my stance. *What is Ombra?*

"How interesting. Your fathers and mother have let you grow ignorant of their crimes against my people." I remained silent. "Ombra, the realm of shadows. A realm dying because of you."

The realm is dying? The isolation from the other realms has turned it to ash?

"I wasn't alive at the time of the fall," I replied, my body tensing. *Was I right? Was this all for revenge? Because I could be reached when the gods couldn't?*

"No, but it was your fathers who caused it. Who were too late. Who saved their mate instead of the realms. Who destroyed our natural portal." His voice grew louder with each sentence, the anger palpable.

I asked in a growl. "You want to hurt me to hurt them? You attacked me for revenge?"

He scoffed, and the black figures remained still. "We've made no move to attack you, youngling."

I bared my teeth at the lie. "So the other shadows who attacked my dreamscape and tried to kill me were just a coincidence, then?"

"Not a coincidence. Our seers saw you. Some of my people decided to take matters into their own hands. While I understand their reasons, I can assure you they were punished for their disobedience."

Shadow rebels attacked me? They were punished for disobedience? Who are these people?

Although more questions arose from the shadow's statement, I relaxed slightly as a piece of the puzzle was revealed. "A seer. That's how you have been able to take over my dreamscape."

"Correct." The air around us shifted, and the figures wavered. The male's voice sounded again. "We are not here to harm you, youngling. If we make ourselves visible, do we have your word not to attack us?"

Confused, I righted myself, my fangs retracting. "Why would you take the risk? Why would you trust my word?"

"Risk is essential to change."

I paused. They could have attacked me already, but they hadn't. Control over the dreamscape was theirs, so I couldn't change the landscape to escape the same way I did last time.

I'm powerless against them. I should hear them out instead of trying to fight. Especially if it regards a seer's vision.

"I swear not to take any action to harm you unless you move to harm me first."

"Your conditions are accepted." I heard the grin in his

voice, and the hair rose on the back of my neck as I wondered if I'd made the right choice.

The middle figure stepped forward, and as though he'd just moved into the light, his form solidified, and I could see him clearly. Pale gray eyes stood out against his black skin, and thin braids of gray hair fell to the nape of his neck. He only wore a thin, flowing skirt, which didn't conceal much beneath and bared his muscular chest. He wasn't much bigger than me but held himself like a male of importance.

At his sides, the male and female also stepped forward, revealing themselves. They had the same black skin and gray eyes, but the male had long black hair in thick dreadlocks and darker gray eyes. The female's hair was in tight curls that circled her head like a halo, and her ash-colored gown covered her body like a veil.

They were all beautiful, but there was madness in their eyes. *They are deadly.*

"What do you want?" I asked finally.

"You cannot guess?" the other male asked as he threw out a hand toward the barren landscape.

"I stopped enjoying guessing games as a child."

"We only wish to talk to you. Let me introduce myself. I am Kaatu, king of Ombra. This is my guard, Zillah, and my sister, Sayah." The male in the middle and the voice who'd been speaking to me, gestured to the male and female and his sides.

I nodded my greeting to them. "I won't introduce myself, as it seems you are already familiar with me."

Kaatu raised his brow and smiled. "You aren't curious about what our seer told us?"

"I'm sure you're going to tell me anyway," I drawled and shifted on my feet.

Get to the point so I can get back to my soul mates.

"You are our hope, Baelen of Blood."

I stilled. It was the same thing my mother had told me all those years ago when she set me on the path to become the savior of the titans.

"Hope for what?" I asked.

The female, Sayah, spoke, "Our lands are dying because we have been disconnected from the realms. Our magic is fading. The strength of the shadow people has dwindled until only a few bloodlines can control, move in, and be the shadows."

She waved her hand, and the landscape changed rapidly, showing me images of her home, each one ash and barren, no crops, no water. People starved in their shacks, and their leaders were powerless to help.

I swallowed thickly. The realms were full of suffering, but seeing it so closely was never easy.

"I'm sorry to hear the isolation from the interlinked dimensions has had such a terrible impact on your people," I told them genuinely.

Kaatu nodded. "It happened slowly. We managed at first. But we are on the brink of death. We need help, and our seer saw you."

"What can I do?" I asked. If they needed a savior, I would be that for them. *Perhaps it will show my fathers I am also the right savior for the titans.*

"Bring our portal back," Sayah urged. "Heal it. Allow our realm to connect with the human one once again. You are mated to the soul pair of healing, and you can return our portal to how it was before the fall. Heal our lands."

I paused. There were multiple issues with their request.

"The human realm has been without your portal for many years now. We will need to assess the dangers of reconnecting it before I agree to anything."

"We are a victim in a titan civil war, and now our lands suffer because of it. Our portal was not supposed to be destroyed. It will be as it was and always should have been," Kaatu argued.

I shook my head. "My soul mate and her witch are of the human realm. It's in their interest that I look out for things that could worsen the situation there."

Sayah began whispering in a language I didn't understand. Kaatu didn't take his eyes off me but listened intently. The secrets made me wary, but I stood firm, determined not to show my apprehension.

Finally, Kaatu said, "My sister makes a good point."

"And what was that?"

He gave a sheepish grin. "Now that we are so close to saving our realm and our people, it would kill me to wait any longer."

The guard and princess disappeared suddenly, and Kaatu strode forward, his form flashing back to shadow. My heart stuttered, and I backed away, only to be tripped by the dreamscape changing. Kaatu disappeared, but I saw a blackened spot on the ash ground rushing toward me. I scrambled away, but the ash turned sticky and held me still.

My vision turned red again as panic rushed through my veins like a drug. My fangs dropped, but they were no use against my foe. I'd never been more helpless.

The shadow blot reached my head, and as soon as it touched the skin of my cheek, pain burst across my face like an ink spill. It spread to my mouth, nose, and eyes and seemed to deepen, penetrating my mind.

I gasped and clawed at my throat as I woke up in my bed in Akar. I felt wild, hissing and growling as pain laced through me, my instincts screaming at me to defend myself, but my enemy was … inside me?

A dark chuckle echoed in my mind. Kaatu. I screamed, the violation of it all too much to bear.

The door to my chamber slammed open, and Darshaw

charged in. "Baelen, what in Darkness … What is wrong with you?" He gasped as he took me in. "Your skin."

I glanced down at my hands to see my skin mottled with black patches, then looked back up to my uncle as pain whipped through me and I collapsed to the floor. Only I didn't touch it. My body seemed to fall through it.

Then next thing I knew, I opened my eyes to see the ash ground, which I recognized as Ombra.

What just happened? I winced as I sat up to look around.

"Ah, you're awake." Kaatu's voice drew my attention to the corner of a cave. He sat on a bundle of collapsed rocks.

"What did you do to me?" I croaked around, my still drawn fangs.

"Being the king of shadows means I can live in any shadows." He smiled sinisterly. "The shadows of a mind, of a heart. I can also travel through shadows which is how I've brought you here."

My mind whirled, and my blood boiled. I growled, "You took over my body and made us travel in shadows, across realms?"

"I thought an akari-titan half-breed would be made of sterner stuff, but I've been waiting over a day for you to wake."

A day? I've lost a day? Zaide and Clawdia …

With energy I didn't know I had, I jumped up and rushed him. Gripping his neck, I lifted him up against the stone walls and lowered my voice to a dangerous whisper. "You are desperately trying to save your people, and I understand that more than anyone, but if you ever do that again, I will make sure you fail. Your people will die if you push me too far."

He chuckled and disappeared. "How are you going to achieve that, youngling? You are outmatched. You cannot even portal away, you are so drained." His voice echoed in the cave, and I turned to search for him.

More laughter echoed around the cave, and I hissed my fury at the memory of what he did to me. I felt … violated. Controlled. Powerless.

Worse, the shadow king was right. I couldn't fight him or make good on my threats.

My energy sapped, I fell to the crumbled rocks. I took deep breaths and tried to calm myself to think clearly.

As I opened my eyes and scanned for a clue to the shadow king's location, my hand hovered over the collapsed stones. There was something strange about them. They felt like my mirror. Like a magical item with its own essence. It felt ancient.

"Where are we?" I asked Kaatu, knowing he was still here in the shadows, even if I couldn't see him.

"We are at the rubble of my natural portal in Ombra." His voice gave no clue to where he hid.

These rocks used to be a natural portal? No wonder I can feel power.

I shook my head. "I told you. I won't do anything until I know the effect on the human realm."

"The effect can only be guessed at. Theorized. We will only know the answer when we do it," he argued.

"But in theorizing, we can plan to limit the damages of any possibility. It could kill humans, unbalance the realms, even destroy another portal. We can't be hasty."

"You seem to think you have a choice," Kaatu snarled as he reappeared in front of me.

I held firm. "The human realm is currently dealing with a dragon that consumes magic beings. We believe it could be seeking a way to escape the human realm and prey on more powerful beings. Opening a portal could allow it just that possibility."

He paused, but only for a moment. "I don't care. I've waited long enough. Heal our portal now or die."

"If you kill me, you won't get what you want."

"You have soul mates I could use just as easily as you."

"You cannot get to them. You cannot portal to the human realm."

Kaatu pulled me by the collar of my shirt so I was inches away from his face and whispered, "Don't underestimate a shadow with nothing to lose."

His words chilled me.

He's already displayed a power I didn't know shadows possessed and transported me from Akar to Ombra. I don't know what he's capable of. I can't let my soul mates suffer for me ... or be without me.

Swallowing my pride, I said, "I will try, but as you've already observed, I cannot create my own portal to get out of here, so healing a millennia-old natural portal may not be successful."

He gave me a cruel smile, and I restrained a shudder as I turned to the stones. I closed my eyes and concentrated on my bonds with my soul mates, but the bonds were thin and fragile ... unconfirmed.

Still, I pulled on the power within them and opened my eyes to see healing threads. The stone threads were red, frayed and broken strings poking out of the rubble, but I could see them, and that was a start.

As soon as I attempted to manipulate them, my power faltered, and my bonds with my soul mates strained.

I can't do it. I can't use their power like my own because we haven't consummated our bond. The realization was a relief. *He will have to wait.*

"Why isn't it working? It should be working." Kaatu demanded.

"I am too drained," I told him simply.

He stared at me, and I refused to drop my gaze. "You are hiding something from me."

69

"I am—"

He must have seen something in me because he vanished, and before I could think to run, a black smudge appeared on the rock next to my hand. Pain erupted where he touched as he disappeared under my skin. I growled and struggled but couldn't do anything as he hid in the shadows of my mind and searched for information.

"You haven't consummated the bond," he whispered before chuckling darkly. *"I know just what to do to fix that."*

CHAPTER 7

CLAWDIA

*T*here was a bear in the room. A loud, sleeping bear who's snoring woke me up.

Opening bleary eyes, I found myself wrapped in Zaide's arms, his face nuzzled into my hair and his large inhales and exhales pushed a strand of hair back and forth across my forehead. It was rather hypnotic to watch.

It was another thing the movies didn't tell you about being in a relationship. Men slept loudly.

As if to prove my point, Charlie rolled to face me, a strange, strained expression on his face, and let out a rip-roaring fart. I thanked God he'd faced the other way, because had he done that on me, I would have kicked him out of bed.

I wiggled out from between them, too disturbed to stay in bed any longer, and to get Charlie back, I gently picked up Zaide's arm and placed it on Charlie's side. Zaide, like the cuddle monster he is, snuggled closer to Charlie until they were inches away.

Giggling, I picked up some clothes from the bag and tiptoed out of the room.

The cabin was lovely, considering there hadn't been

people living here for a few years. It was small but with an open plan kitchen and living space and a dining table pressed against the wall, which made it feel bigger. But with only one bedroom, it didn't need to be big.

I dressed in the bathroom, washed my face, and brushed my teeth. My hair had dried strangely, so I pulled it back into a ponytail as I pushed my feet into sandals and then headed to the door.

I was greeted by the view of lush green woodland and little wooden cabins like ours grouped together at the bottom of a hill. In the distance, on top of the hill, a big house sat proudly, blocking the early morning light.

I headed toward the house, hoping they had some breakfast I could bring back to my men.

My men.

A giddy smile lit me up from the inside, and I could have skipped through a meadow, I was so happy.

I was so distracted I didn't hear anyone approaching.

"Hallå, can I help you?" a female voice with a thick Swedish accent asked. I spun around to see a slender blond lady in her early twenties closing the door of a cabin further up the hill. Her smile was wide and welcoming as she walked down the steps toward me.

"I was looking for somewhere I can get breakfast. Am I going the right way?"

"Ah, of course. *Ja,* straight up the hill to the large house. I'll walk with you if you like."

"I'd be happy for the company." I smiled, and we started walking up the hill.

"You arrived last night?" she asked.

"That's right."

"Ah, so you are ..."

"Clawdia."

She frowned, but the expression was gone before I could ask. A warm smile replaced it. "I'm Karin."

I replayed the question in my head. *Was she asking what kind of supernatural I am? Is that something supernaturals are happy to announce to a stranger?*

I shook off the odd feeling as I plucked a leaf from a tree and asked, "How long have you been here?"

"All my life."

"Oh, I didn't realize." My eyes widened, and I guiltily dropped the leaf. "Your home is lovely. Thank you for letting us stay."

"You don't have to thank me. I didn't make the decision, but it is exciting. Even if there is a magic-eating dragon flying around, I've never seen so many people here. It's like a festival. Or what I imagine a festival to be like. I've never actually gone to one."

Her blue eyes sparkled as she spoke, punctuating her words with exuberant hand motions. I chuckled at her excitement.

"Laurence said you're all family here," I said.

Her shoulders slumped, and her excited tone dulled. "*Ja*, although our family is small these days, hence why so many cabins are empty. There's only my grandparents, my parents, my aunts and uncles, and my four cousins."

"You must all be very close."

"Probably too close." She scowled. "That's why I moved out of the main house and into the cabin. I needed to get away from them."

I was a little breathless as we reached the top of the hill. "Do you think you'll ever move off the island one day?"

"Centuries of witches have poured magic into the wards that protect us here. It would be a waste to leave it all behind." She gave me a wry smile. "Although some days, I'd kill to be closer to the shops."

I chuckled. "I can imagine it's quite the expedition."

She shrugged and pointed toward the garden in front of the large house, which held a large greenhouse and many rows of plants. "We're very self-sufficient." She chuckled. "I learned to cut my own hair through videos."

"Wow. It's amazing what you can learn from the internet." I ran a hand through my hair, twiddling with the ends. "I can't wait to do all the things to my hair that I didn't get to do in my time. Cuts, dyes, straightening … although hair straighteners do seem rather dangerous."

"You've never straightened your hair?" Her blue eyes were wide with horror.

I shook my head. "But I watched my witch do her hair a lot, and she always burned her fingers on the straighteners, so I'm a little hesitant to do it without help."

At the mention of Winnie, a morose sensation washed over me, and tears pricked at my eyes. I missed her so much.

"Your witch? You're the familiar?" The strange tone in her voice made me look up from the winding stone path we were walking to the front of the main house. Her eyes were large, and there was something in them that made me uneasy.

"I am," I replied simply since she'd already guessed correctly.

She surged toward me, grasping my hands. "Then you must come by my cabin this evening. We're planning a little party in the main house so everyone can decompress and get to know each other. You'll need something to wear, and I can help you do your hair and makeup. It'll be so much fun. Tell me you'll come."

I backed away, surprised by the sudden touch and eagerness, and stuttered, "I … I … yes, I'd love that. Thank you," despite being a little taken aback.

Her grin spread from ear to ear. "It's my pleasure. I can't wait to get to know you better."

"Ah, Clawdia, there you are." I turned around, thankful for the interruption, and found Laurence. "We were just going to see if you and your men were ready for breakfast."

"It's only me. Zaide's still bruised all over from the car crash, and Charlie's hardly slept for weeks now. They need their rest."

I could feel Karin's intense gaze on me but tried to ignore her and stepped closer to Laurence.

"Come on in. Let's get you something to eat." His eyes moved over the top of my head to look at Karin. "Thanks for walking her up here, Karin. I think I heard your parents are looking for you to discuss the get together tonight."

"I'll go find them," she said. "See you this evening, Clawdia."

"Goodbye," I called faintly as she marched around the side of the house.

I gave Laurence a smile, and he gestured for me to walk ahead through the front door of the house.

Stepping through into the entryway, I was immediately reminded of Christmas by the gorgeous wooden floors, the red tartan wallpaper, and the smell of pine.

"This way," Laurence said as he walked through an archway and into a huge dining room with a table of food sat up at the back of the room. I recognized Joseph Northrop, the faei representative for the supernatural council, and Marianne Liscovy, the vampire representative, sitting at the dining table, talking quietly amongst themselves.

"Help yourself to whatever you like," Laurence said as he picked up an apple and bit into it.

I picked up a plate and started filling it with the hot food. My stomach rumbled, reminding me that I hadn't eaten yesterday. As I stacked an extra hash brown on my plate, I asked, "How are Alcor and the others?"

"Healing," he replied.

I assessed his face and saw the fear that he tried to hide. "Now that Zaide and I are here, we can heal them."

His lips tightened, and he nodded. "I'd appreciate that. But first, let's have you identify Fafnir for us. Then we'll fill your arms with food for Charlie and Zaide, and this afternoon, we can see the team and Alcor."

"And the protector? Has he woken up?" I asked as I pressed the button for hot water.

Laurence shook his head. "He's in the treatment center with the others. He seems fine. We are just waiting for him to wake."

Joseph stood as we approached and pulled out a chair for me next to Marianne. "Clawdia, I'm glad to see you safe."

"Thank you for helping us get out of there." I sat down with my plate and tea and immediately began chopping into a sausage.

"I hear you are going to help identify Fafnir," Marianne said with a smile.

I nodded and swallowed. "Anything I can do to help."

"I hate to interrupt your breakfast, but I'm sure you understand that the sooner we identify him, the faster we can track his movements," Joseph said.

"Of course." I withheld a sigh as I put my cutlery down. My stomach roared even louder since it'd had a taste of food.

"These are the men we are currently tracking that we believe to be Fafnir." He flicked through pictures on his phone, and I frowned, leaning closer to see them.

He offered me his phone, and I wiped my hands on my leg before I took it and flicked through the pictures as he had. Dread filled my stomach. "These are all of them?" I asked after flicking back and forth for a minute.

"Yes."

I looked up as my heart rate increased and asked desperately, "You aren't following any others?"

Joseph pursed his lips. "No."

Marianne could see what I wanted to say on my face because she stated, "They aren't him."

I shook my head and closed my eyes. "He could be anywhere by now."

Anywhere. Doing anything. Killing anyone. I shuddered.

Laurence placed a hand on my arm. "You've saved resources by identifying who he isn't. Now our teams can get back to searching."

It wasn't much comfort, and I grimaced. "I'm sorry. If you have someone who can draw, I can describe him. Like the police do," I offered.

Joseph shook his head. "We don't have anyone here who can do that at the moment."

I tapped my nails on the table as I thought. "Maybe I can ask Daithi if he can give us an image from my mind? I'm not entirely sure how his magic works, but I know he made an image once."

Although Daithi's help was never guaranteed, I had to ask. While it was nice to be safe, I knew we'd never feel truly safe again until Fafnir was stopped and the hunters left us alone. And I'd do what I could to make that happen.

He won't make me give up again. I have something to live for now.

Joseph said, "Give us a basic description. Our team will continue to search and come up with possible suspects. You can let us know which ones are wrong until we can get an artist or your friend can produce an image. Does that seem fair?"

"Yes. Anything that will help." And I did just that. I described Fafnir in as much detail as I could remember. They asked questions that helped prompt things I hadn't thought of, and after a few minutes, Joseph, Marianne, and Laurence left me to finish my breakfast.

"Here we are, my love." Savida's cheery voice echoed through the house, and soon, his big body and flapping wings pushed through the doorway of the dining room. "Look, Daithi, a feast. And Clawdia. I see you have chosen the English morning meal. I approve."

He and Daithi rambled over, gathered a plate of food and a drink, and joined me just as I was putting the last perfectly proportioned bite of bacon, beans, and eggs into my mouth.

"Did you sleep well?" I asked around my cup of tea.

"The bed was lumpy," Daithi grumbled as he picked at his fruit.

Savida playfully whispered to me, "I think he was sleeping on my wing."

I suppressed a laugh. "I should be getting back with some food for Charlie and Zaide."

"Yes, you must keep the harem fed. That is rule one."

He said it so solemnly I couldn't help laughing as I pushed my chair back and moved to stand.

But Daithi stopped me. "Clawdia, please sit for a moment. There is something I wish to discuss." The merriment I felt fled at his words, and I slowly sank back into my chair as dread filled me. "You do not have to look so concerned. It's not about a vision of your future."

I let out a sigh of relief. The fact that Zaide's fate still loomed over us was bad enough. I couldn't take any more bad visions.

"What is it, then?" I asked.

"I owe you an apology."

I frowned. "Whatever for?"

He bowed his head, his green hair covering his face. "My behavior when Savida wasn't with us. For my assumptions about soul pairs, which were not fair to you. For not coming to help you even though you helped me in saving Savida."

I sighed and glanced at Savida. His eyes were downcast as

he experienced all the misery his soul mate felt. Daithi continued, "I have offered my apologies to Zaide and Charlie already, and since you are here alone, I thought it a good opportunity to do so."

"Daithi, we are not friends," I began, and his eyes snapped up to meet mine, shock clear in his expression. "I understood your behavior when Savida was taken, and while I didn't like it at the time, you don't need to apologize for it. Whatever assumptions you had about soul pairs before you found me matter not. And I didn't have any expectations of you to save us from the cave because, as I said, we are not friends.

I took a breath. "But we are family now. Zaide loves you, and I love him. We are going to be forging new paths and a new life together, and I want you to be a part of it because he will want you to be a part of it. So, I accept your apology but would like us to work on being friends so our family is united. A safe place for us all."

Savida had tears in his eyes. "Clawdia—"

Daithi nodded regally, not showing emotion. "Thank you, Clawdia. I would like us to become friends too."

"I have just the way for you to make a start at our friendship." I smiled widely and explained that I needed to get an image of Fafnir from my brain to the Council teams searching for him in his human form.

He tapped his chin as he thought. "Allow me to ponder this for a little while, and I will see if there is anything I can do to help."

I smiled, feeling lighter knowing someone would be helping me on my quest and stood up. "Thank you. I'll see you both later."

I collected takeaway containers of sausages, bacon, beans, eggs, and hash browns as well as two cups of tea before wandering back down the hill to the cabin.

Tiptoeing back into the bedroom, I silently chuckled

when I saw that Charlie had migrated to the middle of the bed and now lay curled up with Zaide's arm wrapped around him. Before they could wake up, I set down the food and tea on the side table, picked up Charlie's phone, and took a couple of pictures of them both.

"Charlie. Zaide. It's time to get up," I called gently, stroking Zaide's brow.

"Five more minutes," Charlie mumbled and nuzzled into the pillow.

"I bought breakfast," I sang.

That got Zaide's attention. His head snapped up, and his nostrils flared as he caught a waft of sausage and toast. "Ummm, yes please."

His hair was messy, white clumps escaping the braid, and there was an indent on his face where he'd been lying on his hand, but he was adorable, and I told him so.

"I'm not cute. I'm fierce. Like a beast." He bared his teeth.

"Beast of burden, maybe," Charlie mumbled and opened bleary eyes.

He blinked a bit more before he realized that the golden hand resting over his hip and the fingers he mindlessly played with weren't mine. His eyes widened, and he quickly shuffled toward me, reaching out like I was going to protect him.

I laughed. "He doesn't bite."

"It's not his teeth that were pressed against me." Charlie shuddered.

I patted his back as he hugged my waist and hid his face in my stomach. "It's okay. You're safe now. The monster can't get you."

"It's too early to be so dramatic." Zaide sighed, rolling onto his back and stretching.

I bit my lip as I admired the delicious muscles rippling

across his chest and the tenting of the sheets around his hard cock.

Is it normal to go from being untouched to craving intimacy all the time? I shuddered with excitement, just thinking about having another experience like the one Charlie and I had in the shower. Who knew opening the bond in such a way could be so powerful.

I wonder if Zaide and I can do the same.

"It's never too early to be dramatic," Charlie replied, unaware of my hungry thoughts. "Did you say you had food?" he asked.

As they sat up, I handed them plates, then crawled between them as they tucked in. Between ravenous bites of his breakfast, Charlie told us about the dream he had with his mother.

"Do you think she will help?" I asked when he finished explaining.

"I don't know for sure. It seems like it's a family decision, but she seemed earnest." Charlie shrugged and slurped the last of his tea.

"I didn't meet with Baelen in my dreams last night. Did you?" I asked Zaide as he put his plate on the side table.

He shook his head but didn't look me in the eye, and I frowned at his odd behavior. Charlie interrupted, saying, "Does it matter if he did? Do you always need to be a threesome? Maybe Zaide wants to have some time alone with Baelen like you did at the start?"

I was taken aback by the suggestion and spluttered, "No … that's … it's not that. I just want to make sure he's okay since I didn't see him." I took Zaide's hand in mine and gave it a squeeze. "I don't need us to all be together if you want time alone, but I'd like to know if you saw him."

Charlie scoffed. "You want the dirty details, you mean."

"Charlie!" I exclaimed. "I do not!"

"I'll require a new book to teach me about sex with a male, Charlie." Zaide said with a teasing lilt to his voice. "I do not want to disappoint my soul pair with having no dirty details nor my soul mate with poor skills."

Charlie burst out laughing. "I got you, man. I'll get you something with some threesomes with a girl in there too. For research, of course."

"Zaide, you got a book about sex from Charlie?" I hadn't heard anything about that. *Is that why he was so good with me even though it was both of our first times?* "Why didn't I get a book?" I demanded hotly. I wanted to research and be good at sex for them too.

There was a brief silence before howls of laughter echoed around the room. Charlie clutched his stomach, and tears ran down his cheeks, dripping from his nose to the pillow, while Zaide huffed chuckles into my hair.

I didn't intend to be funny and was genuine with my question, but a smile overtook my face as their joy filled me through our bonds. Their laughs vibrated the bed. I loved how it all felt, being together and laughing, safe in bed.

"You are very amusing, Little Cat," Zaide said when he could finally catch his breath. He pressed a long kiss to my forehead before throwing the covers off and padding barefoot to the door.

But his kiss made me long for more, and I sounded whiny when I asked, "Where are you going?"

"To the toilet. I won't be long." He smirked, crinkling the scar across his eye, which only made me more attracted to him and pouty.

As the door shut, I sighed, and Charlie chuckled next to me. "Needy."

"I don't know what's gotten into me," I confessed in a whisper, rolling onto my side to look at him. "But it's like a dam has broken and suddenly it's all I can think about. I didn't know anything could feel that good. I want to feel it again and again and again."

A slow smirk began crossing his face. "We've turned you into a monster."

"Is that a bad thing?"

"Not when you've got three guys to give whatever you want."

"Whatever I want?"

"Name it."

I hesitated but decided to be brave. "I'd really like to come. For you to make me come. Please."

"Since you asked so politely …" He smirked and rolled out from under the sheets.

Kneeling in front of me, he lifted my chin to meet his lips in a passionate kiss. I groaned and shifted, my hands roaming his naked chest, relishing in the contrast between his hard muscles, his soft skin, and his coarse hair.

He gripped the bottom of my top and tugged up, my hands automatically rising so my t-shirt could be pulled over my head and tossed into the corner of the room. My nipples hardened as cold air greeted them and Charlie's hands cupped them firmly.

When our lips met again it was like an inferno had been lit inside me. I was ravenous. My nails trailed over his hair and down his back until I gripped his bum. I pressed myself closer to him, as close as I could get, so I could feel his erection pressed against my pussy and stomach.

"Trousers off," Charlie demanded, ripping himself away from me to push me back on the bed and pull off my bottoms, pants included.

He took a moment to stare at me, and it was easy not to be self-conscious when I could see the heat in his eyes. Then he covered me with his body as he kissed, nibbled, licked, and sucked his way down my neck to my chest, paying extra attention to my nipples before venturing further down.

He petted me, gently feeling for my wetness, smearing it all over my nether lips and said, "Is his what you wanted, Clawdia? You want me to finger this sweet pussy? Or do you want my mouth?"

Lord, his dirty mouth. It made my insides clench down and my eyes roll back in my head. I couldn't think, let alone form sentences.

"I need you to tell me," he said as he barely touched me. *Tease.*

"Both," I whimpered. "Please. Both. Anything. Charlie."

"I love when you say my name like that," he confessed as he pressed two fingers inside me.

My eyes crossed as he thrust them and built me up until I thought I might splinter, crack, and shatter. My breath caught in my throat, and from the corner of my eye I saw the door open.

CHAPTER 8

CHARLIE

"*C*harlie, please don't stop. Please don't stop."

I pressed my fingers into her tight, wet pussy, curling them against the ridged patch inside her. She moaned, her legs shook, and I knew she wouldn't last long. Her thoughts were screaming "yes, yes, yes" in rapid succession, and I could feel her orgasm brewing under her skin like a thunderstorm, the lightning of it zapping my spine.

I buried my head between her thighs, biting gently at the soft flesh before pressing a kiss to her soaking wet center. "Savida and Daithi aren't here this time. I want to hear you scream."

I groaned at the taste of her—musky yet sweet. She squealed and flinched away as I flattened my tongue and made thick, long, soothing strokes around her clit.

When she started squirming, her chest heaving, I curled my fingers and sucked on her clit. Hard. She went off like a bomb.

She screamed with tears streaming into her hair and her back bowed. I gripped her thighs and pulled her underneath me, surrounding her before stroking her hair and pressing kisses to her neck, chin, and lips. She shivered from the aftershocks of her orgasm.

I had to hold and squeeze my dick to stop myself from following her into oblivion. Her pleasure flooded our bond. *If that's how women feel when they orgasm, why are guys the ones who are sex-crazed?*

Fuck me.

"God, Charlie." She gasped as she opened her eyes and looked at me. They were clouded and dazed from pleasure, and there was no better feeling in the world than knowing I did that to her.

I made her scream as she came.

She might have been Zaide's first, but by orgasm count, I was winning. My smugness was clear in my grin as I stared into her violet eyes. I wasn't hiding it. Even without the grin on my face, she could feel it in our bond.

"I would like to know how you did that." Zaide's gravelly voice shocked us both, and our heads turned simultaneously to look at him standing with his back against the door.

Clawdia squeaked and tried to cover herself while I froze like a deer in headlights.

It was one thing for someone to say they were okay with their love fucking someone else. It was quite another for them to walk in on the action.

But his words echoed around my head until they eventually registered.

"You want to know what?" I asked incredulously, moving to sit back on my heels, my dick saluting us all. A soldier awaiting instructions.

Mission aborted, soldier. Report to base.

"How did you make her scream like that?" Zaide replied with a smile growing on his face as he stepped toward the bed.

86

"Oh, dear God," Clawdia muttered and covered her face with her hands.

I stared at Zaide in disbelief. "You want me to tutor you?"

"Perhaps we can discuss it another time. My soul pair looks as though she wants to melt into the covers," he said holding back a laugh.

I shook my head and blinked. "You aren't upset?"

"Charlie, I told you—"

"I know what you said, but that's—"

"You just made a joke about threesomes," he pointed out.

"Threesomes. Not foursomes." I ran a hand through my hair. "Threesome being you, Clawdia, and Baelen."

"So, you aren't going to tell me?" He crossed his arms and sighed.

Clawdia's voice drew our attention back to her. "Gentlemen, I am naked, and you are talking about me screaming in pleasure and threesomes and—and—" Her glare fell away as she looked at the ceiling before huffing and spitting out, "And it's all really embarrassing, so just stop it before this blush becomes permanent." She sat up and gathered quilts to wrap around her.

Zaide and I exchanged a glance before bursting into laughter.

Clawdia pouted, but I saw the small smile at the corner of her lips.

As I wiped tears from my eyes, I said, "I'm sorry, Clawdi-cat. We aren't laughing at you."

"You're laughing with me?" She raised a haughty brow and set me off laughing again.

A pillow came slapping in my face, but it only knocked me back on the bed and made me laugh harder. Clawdia's fierce but entertained face appeared for a moment before she tugged the pillow back and smacked me with it in rapid succession.

I held my stomach as I howled, infuriating her further. "Stop laughing, you … you … you dick!" she shouted as she continued to beat me.

"Oh, a bad word, " I gasped between chuckles. Having had enough of being smacked, I grabbed her wrists and sat up, pushing her onto her back and covering her.

Her eyes darkened, and she bit her lip, and just like that, I was hard again. And dizzy from the blood rushing so suddenly back to my dick.

"I will be getting a demonstration, then?"

We looked back over to smirking Zaide, before looking back at each other.

"I love him, and I love you. I'm embarrassed but not uncomfortable for you both to be here with me. It's up to you."

I replied verbally, "I'm not sure I'm about threesomes."

"It's because you are insecure around my—what did you call it? Ah, that's right. Monster cock."

I rolled my eyes. "No. I just think it's going to be awkward is all."

"It certainly is when you're talking about it while lying above me," Clawdia muttered before wrapping her legs around me and rolling me onto my back.

I was a little impressed with how easily she moved me but couldn't think to tell her as her pussy lay over my length and she ground against me. Moaning, I shifted my hips automatically to slide between her warm, slick folds.

"That's cheating, Clawdicat."

Her hands fell to the sides of my head, and her hair fell around us like a curtain, a beaming grin on her face. "I'm sorry, Charlie." She faked a pout and ran a finger down my chest. "But I remember you said that if I wanted to make something up to you, I could give you a blow job."

I swallowed thickly, surprised at her brazenness but really fucking turned on. "I did say that."

"If I want to treat you for making me scream, will a blow job suffice?"

"I think that's a reasonable reward." There was a quiver in my voice that I wasn't ashamed of.

She smiled and pressed a sweet kiss to my lips, then to my neck, my shoulder, my pec. As she crawled down my body, her hair tickling my arms and making me shudder, I looked over at Zaide to see he was staring at us. He didn't look upset. His underwear tented around his erection told me he was enjoying the sight. And surprisingly, I wasn't turned off knowing he was here.

And I definitely wasn't distracted. As Clawdia kissed underneath my belly button, inches away from where I wanted—needed—her lips, my cock jumped, and she flashed me a cheeky grin. I groaned as she ignored my dick and kissed down to my balls.

She cupped them and gently squeezed before licking the sensitive skin around the base of my dick. I yelped.

"What? Did I do it wrong?"

"Jesus. Fuck. No."

"If I'm—"

I interrupted, "You aren't. Clawdia, if you don't put my dick in your mouth soon, I'm going to come without the blow job."

I heard Zaide chuckle but ignored him as she gripped my dick and slowly wrapped her lips around the head. I'm pretty sure I whimpered but don't want to admit to that.

"Yes," I hissed. "Just like that, Clawdicat. Take as much as you can. Pump me into your mouth."

She seemed to appreciate the instruction, because she took to blowing me like a duck to water. It probably helped that she could feel my reactions just like I could feel her orgasm.

"Twist. Ah, fuck. Yes. Just like that. Good girl."

She shuddered and swallowed at "good girl," and I slapped the bed, gripping the sheets as pleasure rushed too close to the surface. Her throat closed around my dick.

My girl has a kink praise.

Her pussy was so wet, liquid dripped from her nether lips onto my leg. I glanced over at Zaide again to see that he was staring at that leaking pussy, practically salivating.

"Zaide, you want that lesson?" I ground out.

His eyes shot to mine, and he nodded. I released my grip on the sheets to stroke my hand through Clawdia's hair and pull her lips from my dick with a pop. "Get your arse in the air, baby. Zaide is going to eat you while you blow me."

Her eyes, already blown wide with lust, seemed to get darker, bigger, and she licked her lips and nodded. I pulled myself back so I was sitting against the headboard and could properly see what Zaide was doing. Clawdia followed me, kneeling between my spread legs and leaning down so her arse was up and pointing at Zaide.

She swallowed me again, and I bit my lip, restraining the moan at how good it was to have her mouth around me. I wrapped my hand through her hair so I could clearly see her sucking on me like she wanted my soul.

She could have it.

Zaide's weight on the mattress drew my attention to him. He was staring at us but waiting.

"Touch her. Stroke her back, her arse. Touch her pussy, and see how wet she is," I instructed.

I felt the excitement from her zip through me, and my eyes rolled back in my head.

"She is wet," Zaide murmured, and I opened my eyes to see he'd dipped a big golden finger into her depths. She whimpered and pushed back, fucking herself on him, and his other hand spanned across her butt check, kneading at the soft flesh.

"Add another finger and turn your hand down so your thumb can rub her clit." I did as I said, and suddenly, Clawdia jumped and choked on my cock, her teeth brushing a little too hard.

I choked as the clenching of her throat, the saliva and precum pouring from her mouth, and the tinge of pain from her teeth overwhelmed me and sent me over the edge.

I came hard.

I came like I was a teen coming for the first time.

I think I blacked out.

Clawdia didn't even get a warning, but she swallowed what she could. I lifted her head from my dick and cum fell from her raw, reddened lips. Her eyes were dazed, and she moaned and buried her head in the quilt between my legs.

I looked up to see Zaide plunging his fingers deep into her pussy. "Can you feel ridges when you curl your fingers like this?" I demonstrated.

He frowned until his eyebrow twitched. "Yes."

"Concentrate on that spot and stop moving your thumb. Just keep it pressed in at the side of her clit and still."

Her legs shook, and her pussy started to sound so wet and juicy that I salivated. She whimpered and moaned and twitched and squirmed.

"Roll her over," I said.

Clawdia rolled onto her back, and I moved her up so her head lay on my chest. Her breath was rapid, and her chest heaved, drawing my attention to her gorgeous tits. I brushed my hands down her neck, over her nipples, to her hips, watching the trail of goosebumps prickle over her skin in wake of my touch.

Gripping her thighs, I pulled her legs apart so they sat bent over my own and trapped her feet underneath my legs. She gasped as she was exposed, and whimpered as I completely ignored her needy pussy. Instead, I pulled her arms up over our heads, and pressed her hands to the head-board. Her head tilted back so she could look at me, shock and heat blazing in her eyes.

"If you move your hands from the headboard, Zaide is going to stop. He's learning, so you can't interfere." She nodded and licked her lips eagerly. "Good girl." I looked up at Zaide and said, "Zaide, get your face and fingers in her pussy and make our girl scream."

Our girl.

He dipped his head between her legs, and after one long swipe of his tongue from her center to her clit, she shook. Her legs tightened and tried to close around his head, but he held her open. Her arms twitched, and I whispered, "Don't move those hands, Clawdicat."

I pressed a kiss to her head and moved my hands over her stomach and up to caress her tits, palming them gently before pinching at the tight nipples. She whimpered, and her back bowed. I looked down to see Zaide's tongue flicking rapidly over her clit and swollen folds while his fingers plunged and curled inside her.

"You like that, Clawdicat? You like having us both tease you like this?" I asked.

She moaned as I pinched her nipples again, and a chorus of "please, please, please" came sobbing out of her.

"Suck on her clit, Zaide," I said.

The moment his mouth wrapped around her tiny nub and sucked, her head flew back, and her eyes seemed to roll in the back of her head. Her mouth opened to let out a scream of pleasure.

The sound, the sight, the feel of her orgasm echoing through our bond had my dick weeping at her back. With her body twitching from the afterglow, I petted her. "Good girl. You came so hard for him, and he loved the taste of your pussy. Your pleasure. Good girl."

Zaide slid his fingers out gently and sat up with a lopsided smile as he eyed his pleasure-dazed soul pair. His dick, however, didn't look happy. Rather than gold, it was now bronzed and jumping for attention.

Clawdia eyed the monster too. "That looks painful."

"It is. But I'm thankful for the pain. It means I found you." *Smooth fucker.*

But Clawdia seemed to appreciate the flowery words, because she sat up to press a kiss to his lips and whispered, "I love you so much."

"And I love you, Little Cat." He angled her head and deepened the kiss.

I had to admit they looked good together. So different and yet so similar. Although the size difference was a bit of a concern. *The train looks too big for the tunnel.*

She gasped into his mouth as his hands cupped her tits and his fingers played with her nipples. Her nails raked over his chest, and she wrapped a hand around his cock.

They were in their own little world. *But they brought me into this threesome, and I'll be damned if they cut me out at the end.*

"Don't tease him, Clawdicat." I got up on my knees to whisper into her ear, "Squeeze him. Get a bit rough with it. He can take it." She shuddered but did as instructed. "Good girl."

While they were busy, my one hand pressed against her belly, pushing her pelvis out, and the other stroked down her arse to her leaking pussy. I could feel the pleasure growing in her again as my fingers petted her. My thumb pressed against her arsehole, and she clenched down, her body jumping with surprise.

"Do you like someone playing with your arse, Clawdicat? You think you could take a cock here?"

She gasped and broke away from Zaide's kisses to rest her

forehead on his shoulder. Zaide watched me with keen interest.

I used her wetness to lube up her arse but didn't press in more than my thumbnail while my fingers continued to play with her clit. When she squirmed, I retreated. When she whimpered, I stilled.

It wasn't long until she broke. "You're such a tease, Charlie! Someone fuck me right now!" She cried out.

I gave Zaide a smirk and moved to the side while Clawdia lay down and dragged Zaide down on top of her.

He raised an eyebrow. "Are you sure?"

"I want you. I always want you. I need you so much," she babbled as his cock dragged through her folds. "Please."

He spared me a glance and sat back on his heels so I could see the moment he pushed into her.

Fuck, that's hot. I didn't know I had a thing for watching, but seeing her pussy stretch around the golden monster was something else. Like live porn with my favorite stars. She groaned, her violet eyes glassy as he thrust into her, her tits bouncing.

"Oh my god, Clawdia. I had my doubts, but look at that. You're taking him so well," I told her.

Everyone deserves compliments for a job well done.

She turned to look at me. I'd been fisting my dick and enjoying the view, but she reached out and took hold of my cock for me. Tightly. I hissed as she moved her hand even as she was mercilessly fucked by her soul pair.

I wondered at his restraint, because no near-virgin could feel what she felt and not come in a heartbeat. *He's making me look bad.*

"Can you feel her too?" I asked.

His eyes moved from where her hand gripped me to my eyes. "Feel what?"

"How she's feeling? Like when we could feel her pain. Can you feel her pleasure?"

His brows raised, and his thrusts faltered for a moment. "If I open my mind to that, this will end very quickly."

Clawdia's legs quaked. "Please, Zaide. I want to feel you come inside me."

He shuddered at her words and bit his lip.

I felt the moment he opened the bond and let her emotions flood him, because suddenly, everything was tripled. I felt his emotions through her. It was like I was fucking her with my monster cock and getting wanked off and getting fucked all at the same time, and it was … a lot.

We erupted together, and I came like I'd never come before. I thought the last time was good, but this converted me. *I'm going to need to start a religion based on the stars I've just seen. Maybe get a sex addict sponsor because threesomes are going to be addictive.*

Screams, grunts and cries were probably heard for miles on the tiny island, and we collapsed in a sweaty, dehydrated lump.

"I think you both killed me," Clawdia finally managed to say breathlessly. She faced me and pressed a soft kiss to my lips, then turned to Zaide to do the same.

She had my come on her chest, her hair was wild, and most of her body was pink, but she'd never looked more beautiful.

When I finally had breath in my lungs, I asked an important question. "So, has the student become the master, or am I still the best orgasm giver ever?"

Clawdia pouted as she glared at me. "Don't make me hit you with the pillow again."

"I just need to know. It's good for us to review our skills and learn and grow."

Zaide chuckled and gave me a big grin. "I thank you for the lesson, master. Research is much better when done through touch." He tickled Clawdia, and she giggled and fought him off.

I smiled, about to join in the torture, but noticed a strange buzzing that seemed to be getting closer and louder by the second. I sat up and asked, "Do you guys hear that?"

Zaide nodded, and Clawdia covered her ears and asked, "What is it?"

"It sounds like a portal, but not," Zaide said and got out of bed.

A strange light appeared from the crack in the door—not portal blue, but like a dusty ash blue. We froze. "What is that?" Clawdia whispered, creeping behind Zaide.

"One way to find out," I said, wishing I wasn't naked but not having the time to dress. I threw the door open only to stop short at the sight of the strangest-looking portal I'd ever seen. I didn't know a lot about portals, but this looked like a portal you'd buy on Wish for a few quid and free lube.

Rather than a swirl of blue and a strong hum, this one was blackened and huffing out ash. It buzzed and rattled like an old car going over fifty on a motorway.

"Gods alive. What is that?" Zaide gasped behind me.

Okay. Clearly not just another kind of portal I hadn't seen yet.

It seemed to cough, and from the lump of ash gathering in the center, a figure emerged. A male figure. But he tumbled out of the portal like a sack of potatoes and hit the floor with a heavy thump.

I was pushed out of the way as Clawdia dashed toward the collapsed stranger.

"Clawdia," Zaide growled, trying to stop her with an outstretched hand that she dodged.

"Clawdia, you don't know if he's dangerous!" I warned, following her.

She wasn't cautious at all as she reached for the man, the weird portal disappearing behind her, and she managed to turn the man over. She gasped, and we all got a look at his face.

"Baelen."

CHAPTER 9

CLAWDIA

"*B*aelen. Oh my Lord." My hands shook as I pressed my fingers to his neck, checking for his pulse. Relief flooded me when I felt the steady beat, and I combed his hair out of his face. "What happened to you?"

Zaide's bare knees smacked into the wooden floor at Baelen's side, and he stroked our soul mate's cheek. "What is this?"

Black patches covered Baelen's body, bruise-like spots that moved like ink under his skin when pressed. I blinked and allowed my thread power to become visible, but as I concentrated on Baelen, his threads were only orange. I pushed power into him, but the black spots did not move. Nor did he.

Charlie hovered above us. "Maybe some kind of symptom from the weird portal?"

"Or from a shadow," Zaide whispered.

"You know what this is?" I asked.

"No." He licked his lips but met my gaze. "But when I left

him in the dreamscape, he thought we were under attack by shadows again."

My chest grew tight. I saw what the shadows did to him last time they attacked in the dreamscape. They'd almost killed him. If I hadn't given him blood ... he would have died.

But I didn't even know he was in trouble. I expected to see him in the dreamscape again last night so we could talk about everything happening. But he wasn't there. He was suffering. Alone.

He could have died, and I wouldn't have ever known.

"And you only just thought to mention that now?" I hissed at Zaide.

He flinched but hardened his jaw. "There was nothing either of us could do to help him if he was attacked."

"It's clear something terrible has happened to him." I ground my teeth and took a breath, trying not to shout. "You should have told me."

There was a firm knock at the door, and before we had a chance to stop the visitor, it swung open, and Laurence came in.

"There was a weird pulse from the wards. Are you—" He stopped, mouth agape, when he saw us all. "What's going on? And why are you all naked?"

Charlie summarized as Zaide moved to block Laurence's view of my body. "This is their soul mate. He just collapsed out of the weirdest portal ever, and now we are all panicking. You might want to check the protector."

Laurence paused for a moment, staring at Baelen's fangs poking out from his mouth. "He's a vampire?"

"Half akari," Zaide corrected.

"Let's get him to the treatment center and check the protector too," Laurence ordered, and we sprang into action, Zaide lifting Baelen with ease and striding toward the door. Laurence coughed. "You're naked."

I looked down at myself. My skin was still rosy from the pleasure and dewy with sweat and cum dried on the inside of my thighs. But I couldn't bring myself to care. There were more important things than my nudity.

I dashed into the bedroom as Zaide handed Baelen to Laurence and quickly dressed. I didn't wait for Charlie and Zaide to finish dressing before rushing out of the cabin to follow Laurence to the treatment center.

As it turned out, the treatment center was an insult to the name. I'd seen better medical facilities in my past life in the 1920s. It was a slightly larger cabin than the one we'd been given, with three bedrooms, a bathroom, and an open-plan kitchen and living space.

The only reason I could see for it to be called a treatment center was the first aid kit on the kitchen cabinet as well as a few open cupboards showing syringes, needles, and other medical instruments.

An older gentleman stood up from the table as we entered. He took one look at Baelen and said, "I assume this is the reason for the wards fluctuating?"

"He has somehow managed to come through a portal and the wards here."

"Place him in the spare bed."

"He's akari," I warned.

The gentleman nodded and followed us into the tiny box room. "I have blood should he need it."

Charlie and Zaide stormed into the cabin just as Laurence lowered Baelen to the bed.

"The protector is fine?" Laurence asked.

"As fine as he was an hour ago. He hasn't been affected by this … being … portaling to our island."

I tapped my foot impatiently in the doorway. Charlie and Zaide crowded around me as I watched the doctor examine Baelen.

077

CHAPTER 9

His threads are green. He isn't physically hurt, so checking him physically isn't going to tell you anything. You should have machines to check his head where I can't see, I angrily thought at the man's bowed, bald head as he listened to the thumping of Baelen's heart with a stethoscope.

Charlie must have felt me vibrating with rage, because he pulled me away. "Let's leave the man to check him over."

I shrugged him off. "I'm not leaving him."

"Don't get pissy with me."

I glared at him. "Did you know he'd been attacked by shadows?"

His mouth fell open. "No, of course I didn't."

"You are always backing Zaide up."

Charlie crossed his arms and sneered. "So you'd rather us be at each other's throats. Is that it? Does this make you happy?"

"Let's calm ourselves," Zaide whispered and tried to move us out of the doorway.

"Zaide was trying to rescue your stubborn arse because you'd portaled yourself into the hands of an evil, magic-stealing bastard, was hit by a car on the way, and has been recovering since. When was he supposed to tell you he thought your soul mate may or may not be in danger? Danger you couldn't save him from?" He leaned close to my face and hissed, "You're not a stupid woman, Clawdia, so don't act like it now."

Tears filled my eyes, and my lip wobbled. Charlie's fierce expression crumbled as I let out a sob. "I'm so sorry."

"Oh, for—" Charlie pulled me into his arms and patted my back. "It's fine. Enough with the waterworks."

I pulled out of his arms and threw myself at Zaide. "I didn't mean to be so angry. I don't know—"

He sighed and tightened his arms around me. "Tensions are high right now, and our emotions are turbulent. But I

101

will never do anything to cause you intentional pain, Claw-dia. I didn't tell you my suspicions because you wouldn't be able to do anything and the worry would drive you mad."

I nodded, nuzzling into his chest. "I know."

Zaide kissed my forehead and said, "Wipe your tears, Little Cat. All is well. Let us heal our friends while we are here."

"These are the healers you said would help the team?" the doctor asked, the disdain clear in his voice.

All of us turned in his direction to glare at him as he walked out of Baelen's room.

"They helped save the protector," Laurence told the man calmly as he closed the door to Baelen's room behind him.

"That remains to be seen," the doctor mumbled as he adjusted the thick glasses on his nose.

"Besides being powerful healers, Clawdia was a nurse in her past life. They'll be able to help."

"Laurence is becoming one of my favorite people. He's a good man," I told Charlie.

"It's the long red hair and beard that really does it for me," Charlie replied.

"And yet cries at the sight of an injured man." The man sneered.

Charlie huffed. "Look, doc, they are fucking titans and can heal almost anything, hence the tears at Baelen because it's clear there's something else the matter with him."

The doctor straightened his shirt and addressed Laurence when he said, "I'll be taking my lunch."

We were silent as he picked up a few items from the table and left the cabin, the door banging loudly behind him.

Laurence sighed and stroked his beard. "Don't mind him. Apparently, he's a grump anyway, but it's worse since the island has been occupied. He doesn't like actually needing to treat people."

"You don't need to apologize for him, Laurence. I've met many doctors with a superiority complex," I replied. *But I won't be leaving Baelen with him.*

Laurence opened a door into a large room with three beds, and we followed him inside. I recognized Alcor but only knew from the story that the other occupants were Arabella and Isaac.

They were all cut up and bruised, as you'd expect from someone in an accident. But the tops of Alcor's wings looked scratched and punctured. While they'd all been cleaned of any dried blood, it was clear the doctor was relying on their supernatural healing to save them instead of medical intervention.

Stupid, arrogant little man.

"How are they?" Charlie asked.

Laurence replied, "Your familiar might be more qualified to say than I."

I focused on the patients, and their threads became clear. "Isaac seems to be healing fine and is improving by the second. But Alcor and Arabella have orange and red threads."

"I will be outside if you need anything," Laurence said quietly and closed the door behind him.

Zaide immediately moved to Alcor's side and lowered his hands to touch him.

"And are you going to heal Arabella too?" Charlie asked.

"Why wouldn't I?" I replied.

Charlie crossed his arms and glared at the unconscious purple-haired woman. "She took Alcor's fire, and he's been buried alive for years."

Zaide, with his eyes still closed and power pushing into Alcor's threads, said, "It's not for us to decide what her punishment should be. We don't know her reasons. It's for Alcor to decide."

"You're a better person than I am, Clawdicat," Charlie

mumbled as he leaned against the back wall. I put my hand on Arabella's arm.

Zaide's eyes opened, and Alcor's threads were green and healthy again. The wounds in his wings had completely vanished.

"I have a feeling not all is as it seems with these two," Zaide added, "She looked shocked to see him. Not guilty."

That's an interesting detail. And from Charlie's raised brow, I could tell he thought the same.

A groan from Alcor and a toss of his flame-blue hair had us immediately crowding around him.

"Alcor? Are you well?" Zaide asked.

His eyes opened, and he flinched away, confused and afraid.

I lowered my voice and gestured for us all to move back. "It's all right. It's only us. You had an accident."

"Accident?" Alcor's voice was rough and unused.

"Yes." I passed him a cup of water from the side table, and he struggled with his sheets as he sat up to take it. "But you're safe. We've healed you."

After finishing his water, he stared at us, assessing. *Something isn't right.*

Alcor confirmed my suspicions when he asked, "Who are you?"

I blinked and leaned back. "You don't remember us?"

I checked his threads and could only see green. *Is something going wrong with our healing? First Baelen and now Alcor?*

"No. Who are you?" His voice lowered. It wasn't a question anymore. It was a demand.

I licked my lips. "I'm Clawdia, and this is Zaide and Charlie. We're your friends."

He shook his head. "I don't remember you. Why don't I remember?"

"You were in a car accident."

"A car? I've never been in a car." He was becoming more panicked, and he looked around wildly. "Where's Arabella?"

I moved out of the way so he could see her next to him. "She's right here."

"What's wrong with her? Why isn't she moving?" He nudged me out of the way as he moved from his bed to kneel at the side of hers, his wings twitching anxiously. "Arabella?"

"Alcor, she's fine," I calmly told him but knotted my shaking hands. "We are just about to heal her. She should be awake in no time."

Should I try to heal her even though I haven't seemed to heal Baelen or Alcor?

"What are you waiting for? Heal her. She's in pain. Can't you see?" Alcor pleaded as he reached out to grab my arm.

I shook off my concerns and tried to channel the fierce nurse I used to be. While Arabella was unwell, the priority was Alcor and his memory. *A confused patient will do more damage to themselves and those around them than the unconscious one.*

"We'll help her, Alcor." I promised, squeezing his hand. "We just want to make sure you're well first. Can you tell me the last thing you remember?"

"What does that matter while Arabella is hurt?"

"The sooner you cooperate, the sooner I can move on to helping her."

He rubbed his head and frowned. "We—we were making dinner. Arabella and I. I can't remember what it was called, but it had strings and a tomato sauce with balls of meat."

"Spag bol," Charlie said, and I snapped my head around to glare at him as Alcor continued to rub his head.

"Does your head hurt?"

"Only when I try to remember more." His frown deepened, and he shook his head. "I'm sorry, I can't—"

"That's okay." I patted his arm. "Alcor, I understand that

cooking with Arabella is the last thing you remember, but in reality, that happened long ago. Your body has been through something traumatic and needs rest. Please try to relax, and I'm sure your memories will be back in no time."

He looked up at me, searching for something in my eyes, before nodding. "Please. Please help her," he said. "She's whimpering."

I looked up at Charlie and Zaide, who were staring at me. I wanted to talk to them. I needed advice. Speaking out loud would upset Alcor and ruin the calm facade I was presenting. Leaving the room would make him more stressed. But using our bond to speak would mean I could only speak to one of them.

Unless I could make them hear me and each other ...

I concentrated on our bonds and imagined wrapping and tying the gold and shining lines between my soul pair and my familiar. Testing my theory, I thought, *"What do I do? I don't want to cause her any brain issues like Alcor."*

Zaide responded first. *"Heal her. I do not believe our healing is impacting the mind, only that we cannot reach it."*

Charlie's eyebrows reached his hairline as heard Zaide's voice. But after a few blinks, he replied too, *"You said her threads were looking bad, so she's better off healing in body even if she loses her memory."*

"But that will not happen," Zaide added.

I took a deep breath and began slowly pushing power into Arabella's threads, turning them green within a matter of seconds. Suddenly tired, I took a seat on the edge of her bed as she moaned.

"Arabella?" Alcor whispered, his face scrunched with such concern and hope that it hurt my heart.

He's going to be devastated when he remembers she betrayed him.

Her eyelids fluttered, and she mumbled, "Isaac?"

Alcor reared back. "Who is Isaac?"

"That's him over there." Charlie pointed at the bed in the far corner of the room, where Isaac slept facing the wall.

Alcor glared at the bed. "He was also in the accident?"

"Yes."

"Isaac?" Arabella asked again more clearly and opened her eyes to focus on me. "Who are you?"

"I'm Clawdia," I replied.

Please, let her remember.

She sat up looking around, the confusion in her eyes cleared. "You are the soul pair we were going to save." I nodded. "What happened?"

"You had an accident."

She nodded, "But after. Did you see Rose? Is she okay?"

I swallowed and looked down. "I'm so sorry. She died."

Alcor couldn't keep quiet any longer and crawled onto her bed. "Arabella, my darkling. I was so worried. Are you truly healed?"

"Alcor!" She jumped back, giving me a wide-eyed look, and Alcor frowned. "I'm—I'm fine."

"What's wrong, Darkling?" he asked and gently cupped her face. "Are you hurting?"

"He's forgotten what happened," I whispered.

Her mouth fell open, and she blinked a few times. Then it snapped shut, and she caressed the hand holding his face. "I'm glad to see you're okay."

"What is going on?" Charlie asked.

"I'm not sure."

Zaide crossed his arms, his expression unchanged, but his voice in our minds was smug. *"I told you there was more than meets the eye."*

"Yes, you're such a powerful and all-knowing golden giant." Charlie's eyelids twitched and I knew he wanted to roll his eyes.

"Is there a way to undo whatever you have done, Little Cat? I do not want Charlie's chatterings in my mind."

"Shut up. You love it, really." Charlie hid a smug smile behind his hand.

"Arabella?" Isaac drew our attention back to what was happening in the room. He threw his covers off, revealing his naked, very muscled chest and moved to join Alcor on Arabella's bed. His eyes narrowed on their hands pressed against her cheek. "What's going on?"

"We should leave," Charlie said, taking my hand and pulling me up.

Arabella opened her mouth, panic in her eyes, but I interrupted, "I'll be back to check on you all later. Rest up."

We exchanged wide-eyed glances as we shut the door behind us. A slow smile crept up on my face, and I covered my mouth as a giggle threatened to escape.

"Is it bad that we left them?" I asked.

Charlie shook his head and threw his arm over my shoulders. "We have enough on our plate. We don't need whatever clusterfuck drama that is. I'm starving. Shall we go and see what food we can get?"

I cast a look at the closed door where Baelen slept. "I don't want to leave Baelen here with that incompetent doctor."

It annoyed me just thinking about the doctor's terrible attitude.

Zaide shook his head. "There's nothing more you can do for him right now, Little Cat. Let's let him rest."

"When he wakes up, we won't be there. He'll be scared."

"There's not much that can frighten akari, and as soon as he's awake, we can rush to his side. I promise."

Please, let him wake up.

CHAPTER 10

CLAWDIA

A knock on the cabin door interrupted our nap a few hours later.

"I'll get it," Zaide muttered and rolled off the bed with a groan. Without his heat at my back, a cold draught chilled me, and I shivered, unable to fall back to sleep.

"What's going on?" Charlie groaned.

"I think they are trying to drag us to the party," I said, my lips grazing against his t-shirt as I smothered my face into his chest.

"A party?"

"You knew about it?" Zaide asked as he re-entered the room.

"Clawdia knew." He stretched, and I sighed, knowing our nap was definitely over.

"A lady I met this morning invited me to get ready with her," I explained, sitting up.

"Look at you, making new friends."

Zaide studied me with his penetrating purple eyes. "You don't want to go?"

"She just—" I hesitated. Karin didn't really do anything to

make me uncomfortable, so I couldn't explain why my gut was so cautious around her. I shook my head and grimaced. "Never mind. I'm sure it's nothing."

"When does it start?" Charlie asked, rubbing his hands together like he was actually looking forward to socializing.

What happened to the grumpy man who would spend his Christmas with the cat from next door?

* * *

FIFTEEN MINUTES LATER, I found myself at the door outside Karin's cabin with Zaide and Charlie standing in the street behind, waving me inside like a parent sending a child to school. I glared at them, but they both smiled and continued walking up the hill to the main house.

Karin flung the door open wide and cheered, "Clawdia! I was just about to send a search party!"

She'd let her hair down since this morning and curled it so it fell in lovely blond waves around her shoulders. Her floral summer dress and matching red sandals were also very cute.

I suddenly felt very underdressed and unprepared.

"Oh, I'm sorry. We fell asleep," I mumbled as she pulled me inside.

The cabin was exactly like ours, except it had a far more homely feel. There were plates on the dish rack, rugs on the floor, pictures on the walls, and a large bookshelf taking up the majority of the open plan space.

"Don't worry about it. I'm sure you need your rest after all the healing you've done today."

I frowned and immediately tensed. *How does she know about that?*

"My father is the doctor." She rolled her eyes and laughed.

110

"He's grateful you've halved the number of his patients in only a few hours."

I instantly felt bad for judging her. *See? She's not doing anything untoward. She's trying to help you. Stop being so paranoid.*

"I'm glad to have helped," I mumbled as I scanned the titles of the books on her shelf. They were all magic-based.

She must be a very dedicated witch.

Karin waved her arm toward the sitting area, and I noticed two ladies I hadn't seen there before. "These are my cousins, Natasha and Naomi."

Twins. They were beautiful girls with brown, curly hair and blue eyes very similar to Karin's. Their smiles were warm as they stood up from the sofa to greet me, revealing their matching outfits. Pink halter tops and denim skirts.

"It's lovely to meet you both."

"I'm Natasha. I wear a pink bracelet." She pointed to her wrist and drew my attention to the braided fabric tied there.

The other twin, Naomi, also waved her wrist and introduced herself. "And I'm Naomi, and I wear the blue bracelet."

Karin explained with a laugh, "They have to wear something to differentiate themselves, or after a few drinks, even their own mother confuses them."

"We won't swap them either. Promise," Natasha said with a devilish grin. I returned it, warming up to the twins more now I'd seen their mischievous side.

Naomi picked up a bag and handed it to me. "We gathered some things from our wardrobe that you might like."

"Oh, wow. Thank you." I opened the bag and peered inside to see a stack of clothes. "I can't tell you how much I appreciate this. I haven't had a chance to go shopping since I became human. I've been wearing Winnie's clothes."

And her clothes didn't exactly fit. If I thought too hard about the number of people, I'd unintentionally flashed in the past few weeks due to a lack of undergarments and over-sized clothes, I'd never recover my dignity.

"Who's Winnie?" Natasha asked as she sat back down and picked up a glass of wine.

I paused before saying, "She was my witch."

"Was?"

"She … she was killed." I swallowed and tried to repress the tears forming in my eyes. It was so easy to forget she was gone when we were busy trying to survive, but when I had time to think, I missed her.

"We're sorry for your loss." Naomi gave me a sympathetic smile, but it didn't help me stop the grief. I looked up and tried to blink back tears.

Karin's cheerful voice sounded strange in the somber atmosphere. "It's absolutely fascinating that you turned human. And you managed to get a new witch? How exactly did that happen?"

I squirmed at the intense look in her eyes but couldn't fault her for asking questions. As far as I knew, I was the only familiar to turn human. And the only one to be transferred to a new witch.

"It's a long story." I gave her a small smile and hugged the bag of clothes tighter.

"Why don't we get you ready, and you can tell us your story as we go, if you're comfortable of course?" Naomi suggested.

"Now that I've had a look at you, I think we have the perfect outfit for tonight." Natasha held out her hands, and I passed her the bag back. She flicked through a few things before pulling out and unraveling a long, thin, grass-green dress. "Here. This is it."

"Oh, I'm not sure. It looks tight, and I don't have a bra."

"No bra needed."

"But my n-nipples …"

"Will be free. As the goddess intended."

"Trust us. We know."

I found myself ushered into the bathroom, holding the dress. When the door closed behind me, I sighed and succumbed to their desires, taking off my baggy clothes and pulling the dress on over my head.

I cast a glance in the mirror, and while the color suited me more than some of Winnie's clothes, my nipples were indeed free, poking through the fabric, which clung to my body like a second skin.

You look like a lady of the night. My mother's cruel voice echoed in my head, and I flinched.

No. No. I look modern. And ... and pretty. So go away. You're dead, and your opinions don't matter.

I exited the bathroom to cheers from the girls. Natasha called, "I knew it! It looks great on you."

"Very pretty, Clawdia." Naomi nodded her approval, curls bouncing around her face.

"Come sit here, Clawdia. Let us do your hair and makeup while you have a drink and tell us your story." Karin guided me to the chair at the table, which now had a glass of white wine on it as well as a multitude of makeup items.

Is all this necessary for me?

Natasha started combing my hair the moment I sat down. "Would you let me cut your hair, Clawdia? Maybe darken it and add some highlights? It would look so lovely, and I don't get to play hairdresser very often."

"Darken? I'm not sure."

"You don't have to, but I think it would look great."

I paused. "Do we have time to do that?"

"Of course. We have a potion here for hair color. It's easy."

A potion? Why did Winnie always do it with boxes she bought from the store, then?

113

Naomi rifled through bags and pulled out a jar. "Here it is."

I stared at the jar but decided to be brave. "Why not? I didn't get to do anything exciting with my hair when I was human."

The twins squealed and did a little dance that made me laugh. Natasha gathered all my hair in one hand and took the jar Naomi passed her. "You won't regret this, Clawdia. I promise."

Karin picked up the glass on the table and handed it to me. "Here, try this wine. It's my favorite. I think you'll love it."

"Thank you." I took a sip, rolling the sweet flavor around in my mouth before swallowing.

I was shocked at how much I enjoyed the beverage. After my father's predilection for alcohol, I stayed far away from it. But I didn't want my past weighing me down. Not my mother's scathing opinions, nor my father's drinking or Mr. Jenkins's abuse.

Just as Zaide said, this body has never been touched by any of them, and I won't poison it with the fears my mind produces. I want to be stronger than that.

"This might be a bit cold," Naomi warned, and my head tingled as she poured the jar on my hair.

"So, how does a familiar become human?" Karin asked, her chin resting on her fist, her elbow firmly planted on the table as stared at me from the opposite side.

With my hair being played with and my recent commitment to being stronger, I didn't allow the odd sense I had about Karin to stop me from opening up to these women.

I missed the companionship of women. I missed Winnie. While she'd never be replaced, I wanted a relationship like the one we used to have. Friendship. Sisterhood.

With another swig of my wine, my tongue and mind

fizzing happily, I told them my story. They all laughed when I told them how Charlie's scream made me realize I could be both human and a cat. And gasped as I told them Mr. Jenkins was Fafnir. And giggled as I told them about Charlie and Zaide and Baelen.

"Three men," Naomi sighed and closed her eyes as if to imagine it.

Natasha chuckled as she put the scissors down on the table. "Naomi, 'I moan' is escaping."

"What?" I asked.

"Naomi spelled backward is 'I moan,' so we like to say 'I moan' is her other self. The naughty side," Natasha explained.

Naomi smiled over the rim of her glass. "And Natasha backward is 'ah satan' so her bad side is the devil himself."

I laughed as the steam of the straighteners warmed my scalp. "That's so fun."

"Not as much fun as you are having with three men. I want details." Naomi winked and nudged me as a blush colored my cheeks.

Karin rolled her eyes. "I'm sure an old-fashioned lady like Clawdia isn't going to want to talk about the details of her intimate life."

I frowned at the term "old fashioned" but agreed. I didn't want to talk about sex. Even if it was incredible and life-altering and perfect.

I don't want to make them jealous. Or for them to look at my men knowingly. They are mine.

The possessiveness in my thoughts surprised me. But I'd never had anything I really wanted to keep before, so it made sense that I was protective.

"Anyway, it's time to do your makeup," Karin said and began searching through the piles of things.

"I don't think I want a lot," I told her.

"No. You certainly don't need it." She gave me an impish grin. "But it's so fun to play with."

I smiled. "I used to watch Winnie put on her makeup all the time. She'd do such bright colors on her eyelids. It was like art. I used to ask so many questions about what she was doing, but she never got impatient with me."

"You miss her." Naomi gave me a sympathetic smile.

"I didn't get to mourn her. I woke up in a cave, and she was gone and I was with Charlie and … the dragon … and Baelen." I cleared my throat and took another big drink of the wine.

"You've been through a lot. But you're safe here. You can grieve." Natasha patted my arm as she turned off the straighteners and sat next to me.

"I wish she weren't dead. She didn't deserve that," I whispered as tears filled my eyes yet again.

Darn emotions. I didn't have this issue as a cat.

"No one deserves a betrayal like that," Naomi agreed somberly.

Karin leaned forward in her chair, her lips pursed as she patted my face with a sponge. "You said Mary cut her throat with a knife."

Naomi gasped and glared at her cousin. "Karin! That's so insensitive."

I frowned at the sudden shift in conversation but nodded. "She did."

"But why did she do that when she could have killed you to kill Winnie? Or killed Winnie before you all arrived?" Karin asked. She picked up a small brush and patted a brown color with it before stroking it over my eyelids.

"When I was in the warehouse, I saw her give the knife to Fafnir as a gift. She said it was cursed with the blood of the betrayed and wanted to use it on the protector," I replied. "Have you ever heard of such a thing?"

I opened my eyes to see her purse her lips and nod. "I've heard of such a thing, but I've never seen it, nor do I know how to counteract its effects." She picked up a tube and pulled out a brush from the lid. Mascara.

"Look up," she instructed, and I did as I was told. She continued as she combed my lashes with the brush. "I could do some research. We have lots of craft books here. If your new witch, Charlie, needs to know anything, he's also welcome to join me in the library."

"That's really kind of you to offer. I'm sure he'll take you up on that. He's keen to learn more about his powers to better protect us all."

She nodded and picked up a smaller tube, revealing a pink lipstick. After painting it on my pouted lips, she snapped the lipstick shut and said, "There look at you. A brand-new woman."

Naomi took my hand and pulled me into the bedroom in front of a full-length mirror. I gasped.

I could barely recognize myself. My hair wasn't gold; it was darker but with blond highlights, making my skin seem brighter. It was straight and silky smooth to the touch. My eyes looked defined, wider. My lips looked plumber.

I look ... beautiful.

My lips quivered, and my eyes filled with tears.

"Why are you sad? What's wrong?" Naomi gasped.

I swallowed. "I spent a lot of time watching films where the girls would have sleepovers or help each other dress and talk about boys, but I didn't have that in my old life. It wasn't the done thing. But I never imagined I'd meet such lovely supportive ladies who would do all this for me."

"Oh, goddess." Natasha put her hand on her heart and closed her eyes.

Karin slapped the hand I moved to rub my eye. "You're ruining all my hard work. No more crying."

It shocked me enough that I laughed. "I'm sorry. I'm not sure what's wrong with me."

Naomi nodded knowingly. "You let the barrier down after grieving your witch, and now you're all tender and squishy."

"That must be it," I replied.

"Cry as much as you like." Natasha gripped my arm and pulled me into a hug. "I'll join you. I'm in the emotional part of my cycle. I have an excuse."

I chuckled. "Thankfully, familiars don't have cycles."

"And you are definitely still a familiar?" Karin asked quickly.

"Of course I still am a familiar. Just not your average one."

I followed Naomi back to the table, where she topped up all our glasses with the remainder of the bottle. I smiled and picked up my glass to take a sip. It seemed to taste better the more I drank and made me feel warm and loose. *I can definitely see the allure.*

"You've met other familiars?" Karin asked.

I nodded as I sat back down. "I have met another familiar. His name was Cedric. He was a raven."

"And he liked being an animal as you did?"

"Oh no, he hated it. I don't know about now. His witch was really old, so they could have passed on already, but he wanted to fly. She wouldn't let him. He called himself an adrenaline junky and died in a skydiving accident. He wasn't pleased to wake up as a familiar."

"That's so sad," Natasha commented as she put all the makeup away.

"Is that often the case?" Karin continued.

I shrugged. "I imagine it depends on the person. People can die before their time in all manner of ways. If they were looking forward to their death, they might feel differently to someone who regretted their ending."

"Someone ..." Karin repeated as though it were an alien word.

The odd feeling I had returned, and I looked at her intently. "Yes. Someone. Familiars might look like animals, but we have human souls. We talk and feel and think just as we used to."

"Let me get you some shoes, and then we can be on our way." Natasha patted my shoulder and went into the bedroom.

"Yes, let's go already. I'm hungry." Naomi stated as she reached for a bag.

Many of Winnie's witch friends came to call when Winnie summoned me. I was used to demonstrating my power, my bond, and my kind. Karin's curiosity was understandable, expected even, but for some reason, it made me uncomfortable.

I decided to be brave and ask, "Karin, why are you so curious about familiars?"

"She's always been like that," Naomi replied, yawning and stretching.

"Curious since the day she was born," Natasha added as she returned holding a pair of white sandals. "Here, try these."

I slid my feet into the sandals, and although they were slightly too big, they had a buckle I could tighten around the ankle.

"That's why she knows so much about magic," Naomi finished. "She's a witch know-it-all."

I lifted my head to look curiously at Karin. She smiled and said, "I've never met one. Or met anyone with one. I just find it fascinating."

It was answer enough for me. I nodded my understanding and stood up, suddenly excited to go to my first party. With my makeover and the wine sloshing around in my stomach, I was filled with confidence.

Natasha offered me an arm to take and gave me a devilish grin. "Now, let's get you to your men. I can't wait to see the look on their faces when they see you."

Neither can I.

CHAPTER 11

ZAIDE

"*A*h, you must be our new guests. Please, come in." A blond female ushered us into the main house. "We are so glad to have you join us."

"Glad to be here! I'm Charlie, and this is Zaide." Charlie matched her enthusiastic greeting and looked around as we walked through the halls. "Let me guess. You're Karin's sister."

On second glance, she did have a resemblance to the woman we'd seen at the cabin we left Clawdia at, but this female looked older.

"You tease me." She waved a hand as a blush rose to her cheeks.

"You're not?" He pretended to be shocked.

I gave him a sidelong glance. *What is he doing?*

"Oh, I'm sure you know I'm her mother." She spared me a look and, with a twinkle in her blue eyes, said, "He's a naughty one, isn't he."

"Charlie, stop flirting with the older lady. It's disturbing." I told him, trying not to show my discomfort on my face.

His laughter echoed through my mind. *"It's harmless. Charming the person that feeds you is never a bad idea."*

The lady continued speaking, unaware of our mental conversation, "I'm Ingrid, and this island has been in my family for centuries. Would you like a tour of the house?"

"We'd love it. Especially if you have any secret passageways or rooms hidden behind a bookcase," Charlie said as we followed her through the dining area and kitchen. "I'm thinking about getting one of those installed in my house to hide all my new witch gear."

"No secret rooms since our island is already so well hidden, but we do have a large library. My daughter is quite the researcher."

"What does she research?" I asked.

She stopped at the top of the stairs to turn and look at me. "Magic. Everything to do with magic. I'm sure you and your friends will be the talk of everyone here tonight since you're all so powerful and from other realms. I know my daughter will be eager to ask you lots of questions."

Charlie and I exchanged glances when she turned back to guide us through the upstairs halls. Neither of us wanted to answer the same questions all night. We just wanted a night to forget our troubles. I wanted to create memories I could hold on to when I am taken from them.

I gritted my teeth. *Don't think of it. Enjoy the moment.*

Ingrid pushed the door open to a large room filled with bookshelves. "Laurence mentioned you have only recently become aware of your heritage. And gained a familiar so fast. You must be very powerful." She addressed Charlie but also seemed to glance at me before spreading her arms open, a wide grin on her face. "Of course, you'll be welcome to spend your time here, learning about magic. My daughter will be happy to help. Very happy."

Charlie rubbed the back of his neck, his charm fading as

her strange behavior made him uncomfortable. "Er, thanks. I might take you up on that."

She clapped her hands and fluttered back into the corridor calling, "I'll let you rejoin your friends. Please, help yourself to food and drink."

Charlie sighed as we made our way back down the stairs. "Was that weird, or was that just me?" he mumbled.

"I told you not to flirt with her."

The entryway was getting busier by the minute, and we squeezed past people through to the garden. A recognizable winged body made us head toward a small table in the furthest corner from the square center where two strangers bravely danced.

Savida cheered when he saw us coming. "Ah, friends! Please, join us for a tiny cake." He raised his food and motioned toward the three empty chairs.

My heart warmed at the sight. They'd been waiting for us all. Wanted us to be together amongst these strangers.

"A cupcake," Charlie corrected as he sat down.

"But it is not in a cup." Savida frowned. "Why would it be called cupcake?"

"I don't make the rules." Charlie shrugged and ungarbed the cupcake of its paper.

"Who does?" Savida asked.

I stopped listening to Charlie and Savida's conversation as I looked at my faei friend. "You don't look well, Daithi. What is wrong?"

His green eyes and hair were dull; his skin was sallow and had a sheen over sweat covering the usual glow. When I looked at his threads, I could see strands of orange tied tightly around him. I rested my hand on his where it gripped the arm of the chair and slowly healed him.

He blinked and quietly said, "Thank you."

"You're welcome. Now tell me, what's wrong?" I asked,

although I didn't want the answer. Not because I didn't care, but because I thought it was to do with his visions about me.

He spoke quietly. "More visions are assaulting me."

I nodded calmly but my stomach clenched. "Of me?"

"I cannot say."

"Why not?" I frowned.

His eyes met mine, and I could see a deep fear in them. "Because for the first time, I've had multiple visions of the same event but all with different outcomes. I'm unsure what speaking of the vision would do. What path it would create."

"You've let these visions control you for too long, my friend." I sighed and patted his hand before pouring us both a drink from the bottle on the table. "Clawdia recently met an akari with the gift of sight and said she saw multiple versions too but knew what actions affected each thread. She seemed to be able to check as she pleased without falling unconscious."

"I am not her."

"No. But perhaps seeking out visions in a safe place would mean they no longer assault you," I told him but knew he would either heed the advice or not.

There would be no convincing him if he didn't wish to hear. He was a stubborn faei, and despite always suffering with his visions, he'd never sought help or mentorship for them. I wouldn't waste my breath unless he really wanted my help.

I handed him a drink and took a sip of my own, my eyes now watching the crowd, waiting for my little cat to appear. She is who I wanted to spend this night with.

He paused for a moment before saying, "You've changed."

"I have." I was no longer afraid of losing his good opinion. I no longer looked up to him. I saw his faults.

He took a sip of his drink and sighed. "How do you believe I can control them?"

I hesitated, shocked he'd asked and then worried. *The visions must be truly terrible for him to ask for help.* I shuddered at the thought. *Perhaps it is better if I don't know about them.*

"Meditation," I began. "Allowing the visions to come to you when your mind is relaxed. Changing your mindset from hatred to gratitude. Learn to ask questions and receive answers."

He snorted. "So simple."

"The mind is not so easily tamed, but it can be done. Every creature in the realms is able to control the gifts they are given as long as they are willing to learn how."

"You know my reasons—"

"I know, but it is long past time you forgave yourself and healed."

His lips tightened, and he sighed. "Clawdia asked me to help her create an illusion of Fafnir to show the council. Apparently, they are tracking the wrong men." I was unaware of that but allowed him to continue. "I've thought about it, and if you are able to control the dreamscape, she need only pull me into a dream and show me an image. I can then use that to show the council. "

I shifted in my seat, frowning. "The dreamscape is no place to guess around in. If anything went wrong, we could lose you."

"You wish for us to wait until Baelen is awake?"

"No. But it may be safer. Or try to induce a vision of Fafnir, which you can present to the council." Both ideas had merit, but both could be dangerous in different ways.

But we need the council chasing the right man. We need to know where he is so when the protector awakens and tells us more about our foe, we can plan our attack and finally defeat this evil.

My mind was fit to bursting with the amount we had to do. Destroying Fafnir was just step one, and yet that step was huge.

Savida, turning his attention back to us, interrupted with his cheerful manner. "Such talk of visions and safety are left until morning. We are at a party. It's been so long since we were able to drink and be merry."

I smirked, suddenly cast back into the memory. "It was at the full moon party in Mestaclocan, wasn't it?"

"It was." He looked at Daithi mischievously. "I had to fly us home because you were climbing the trees, were you not, my love?"

"We do not speak of it." Daithi glared, but his lip twitched.

"Daithi." Charlie gasped dramatically. "I didn't know you had it in you."

"Are we anticipating a similar incident tonight?" I asked.

"Fingers crossed," Charlie said, a mischievous glint in his eye.

"Don't mind me," a voice from behind said. I turned and recognized Samuel, the shifter representative on the council. He pulled back the empty chair, the chair intended for Clawdia and said, "I heard y'all mention Mestaclocan and couldn't help but listen in."

"It's your ancestral home." Savida nodded. "Your curiosity is valid."

"I'd love to hear more about it," he said with his drawling voice and leaned in, the green bottle in his hand forgotten.

Savida got into his storyteller persona, his black eyes alight with excitement. He shifted in his seat with a flutter of his wings and began in a low voice. "It's as rich and diverse as this realm, but as you know, the people house beasts within them, which make tempers fraught. It can be dangerous in some places. But in others … I've never seen more gentle or understanding people. It's from them that Zaide learned to meditate."

Samuel spared me a glance before saying, "We teach our

children to meditate. It's how many learn to communicate with their animal."

I gave Daithi a look before turning back to Samuel. "The practice lives on with you. I'm sure those in Mestaclocan would be glad to know you honor their ways."

A female listening nearby came into the conversation and sat on the armrest of Samuel's chair. "What would you say is the most interesting place you've been to in the realms?"

Savida jumped to take the question. "In Daithi's homeland, Álfheimr, there is a small island called Santrix, and it's full of people who have hair that changes color with their mood. You might not think this is unusual, but they never leave their island. They have a group of women who can heal but only at the cost of their own life, and they are treated like goddesses. And anyone who approaches the island is shot at with arrows. We once took a ferry to see if we could see them, but after I received an arrow through the wing, we decided they weren't ready for visitors."

The table, and everyone listening in on the conversation surrounding the table, laughed. Savida preened, completely in his element.

"Savida only believes it to be interesting because no one has ever been there. Everything we know is a myth," Daithi added.

"All myths come from truths," Savida argued.

"The women die if they heal someone?" someone else asked.

"Only if it was a life-threatening wound."

Charlie turned to me. "I'm starving. Shall we get some food?"

"You don't want to listen to Savida's tales of adventure?"

He rolled his eyes. "I'm listening to my belly, and it says if I don't eat soon, I'm going to be the one firing arrows."

"That's a lot for one organ to say," I said but agreed and

stood up since I didn't want to be surrounded by the strangers looming over our table any longer. I informed Daithi we'd be back with food, and he nodded. Charlie led me through the crowd, who all gaped at the sight of me, back to the dining room. A shiver ran down my spine.

Charlie scoffed as we approached the queue for the food. "It's like they've never seen a titan before."

"They haven't." I took the plates he passed me and continued shuffling along the queue.

"There's no need for staring." He glared at a male who stood open-mouthed behind us.

I smiled at his protectiveness and teased, "Need I remind you of your reaction when you first saw us?"

He grumbled as he began picking up a spoon and loading his two plates. "I still think they are weird."

"Are you making a plate for Clawdia?" I assumed he passed me the extra plate for me to make something for Daithi and Savida to pick at.

"Yes," he replied, and I began filling my plates. "Where is she anyway? Surely it doesn't take this long to get ready."

I shrugged. "I'm sure she'll be along soon. I'm glad she is getting time to talk to females."

"I don't think she's ever had girl time before. It might be a bit much for her."

"She'll be fine."

Just as we collected cutlery and headed back outside, we spotted her walking through the crowd. She saw us as we dropped our plates on the table and strode toward us, three other females in tow. But I couldn't see them. They were background, as was everyone else, because my little cat looked completely different.

"Little Cat," I gasped as she came within earshot of us. "You look—"

I couldn't put it into words. Her hair was darker, shorter,

128

and styled in a way I'd never seen before. Her lips and eyes looked bigger and brighter, her cheeks were sculpted, and her skin was clear of any blemish left from a traumatic few weeks. And her dress hugged her like a bandage, showing the curves and soft skin I was intimately familiar with. It made me feel both proud and possessive. I wanted to cover the eyes of all the males who glanced her way. She was not for them. She was mine.

Charlie turned at my exclamation and found his words faster than I. "Stunning."

"Beautiful," I agreed quickly and preened as she shyly bowed her head and blushed.

"Do you really like it?" she asked quietly.

"Get over here," Charlie demanded and held out his hand. She took it ,and he raised it above her head, saying, "Spin," and offering us both a full look at the outfit. He pulled her close and then muttered, "Gorgeous," as he pressed his lips against hers.

A cough interrupted us, and suddenly the rest of the world swarmed into sight again. But it was quiet, hushed. I cast my eyes around, confused at what would cause the party to die down, and then it became clear as I followed the gaze of staring party members back to Clawdia and Charlie. Some faces were puzzled, others sneered, but no one seemed to share in the joy of two people in love.

Why is that? I reminded myself to monitor the situation. *The last thing we need is to be trapped on an island with people who hate us.*

I returned my attention to Clawdia as she introduced her new friends. "This is Karin and Naomi and Natasha."

Ingrid's daughter had the same intense and uncomfortable gaze as her mother, but the other two girls smiled warmly.

"It's nice to meet you all," I said.

"You're fairy godmothers," Charlie exclaimed and twirled Clawdia again. "You've turned our feral cat into a princess."

"Feral?" She glared and looked at me. "I wasn't feral, was I?"

"Never, Little Cat." She smiled shyly, moving from Charlie's embrace into my arms, and I pressed a kiss to her silky soft hair.

I must learn how to replicate this style. It's my responsibility to keep her hair beautiful.

"Suck up," Charlie coughed.

"You're cute together," one of the twins said, although I couldn't say which. All that differentiated them was a colored bracelet.

"Can you feel Clawdia like a normal familiar?" Karin asked, and the joyous atmosphere was suddenly doused.

The twin with the blue bracelet sighed. "Karin. Honestly. Take a break."

"Karin is a witch genius," Clawida told us, "She's going to help us figure out how to stop the knife Mary gave to Fafnir."

"Do we think he still has it?" Charlie asked.

"What do you mean?" Clawdia frowned.

"Didn't it get lost under the rubble of the factory?"

"Maybe," she drawled, a puzzled expression on her face as she thought back to our escape. "But it's better to be safe than sorry. Karin has also offered to help you learn witch things."

Both Charlie and I eyed Karin suspiciously, but she innocently smiled and said, "It would be my pleasure to help."

"Oh, yay, another tutor." Charlie rolled his eyes. "I've not had this much academic attention since I hacked into the school reporting system to change my grades." He leaned in to whisper into her ear. "I made the mistake of shooting too high. As soon as they saw the As, they knew I'd done something. Couldn't prove it, of course."

Clawdia laughed and playfully slapped at his arm. "Oh, Charlie. You're so naughty."

"Not as naughty as I could be," he growled and pressed her between us.

"Behave," she said in a voice that belied her words. She squirmed out from between us, stumbling a little as she went. "I'll get us something to drink."

I caught her and asked, "How much have you had already?"

"Not a lot."

"On an empty stomach." I frowned and picked up something from the plate behind me. "Eat this." My fingers grazed her lips as I pushed a sausage roll between her lips. Her gaze never faltered as she chewed, and something primal within me relished the action of feeding my soul pair. Especially when her violet eyes burned so intensely as I did so.

"Sickeningly sweet," the pink-braceleted twin said as she tucked her arm into Clawdia's and pulled her away. "Come and get something to drink, Clawdia."

"I'll bring you something back," she called as she merged into the crowd, the blue-braceleted twin following them.

And so we were left with Karin. She stared at us but made no attempt to start a conversation.

"So, you're big into the witch thing." Charlie broke the silence, rubbing the back of his neck. I picked up my plate of food and started eating as I watched them.

"You're not?" she asked.

"Well, I only just learned about it."

"So you don't care to learn." She crossed her arms, and her eyes narrowed.

"I want to learn. I just haven't had a lot of time yet. Dragons, evil witches." He chuckled awkwardly and shot me a wide-eyed look.

"Do you think having a familiar helps your magic? Do

131

you feel stronger?" she asked, returning to the topic of familiars.

"I didn't know I was a witch before, so any magical thing I was doing wasn't intentional. Getting Clawdia as a familiar and learning I was a witch happened at the same time, so yeah, I feel stronger, but it probably helps knowing more about my history and also that my familiar is half titan," he explained with a frown.

She turned to me. "I don't know anything about titans. What does it mean to be a titan soul pair?"

I gave her a brief history of the fall, and she stared at me with eyes burning with interest. But there was something unsettling in them.

Karin muttered to herself as she tapped her lip. "I knew she could heal, but I didn't know how or why it was so powerful."

"You didn't ask her earlier?" Charlie asked.

She rolled her eyes and waved her hand. "The twins were distracting her by asking questions about your relationship."

Charlie's eyes lit up with interest. "Oh? And what was she saying?"

"She didn't give any details," she mumbled. She pursed her lips, slumped her shoulders, and slunk off to talk to someone else.

Charlie smirked at me. "Clawdia, ever the lady."

I waited until I was certain Karin couldn't hear me before I said, "She is very odd."

"Like mother like daughter," was all Charlie replied since he turned his attention to his abandoned plate.

Clawdia returned, her smile bright, brighter than I'd ever seen, although her eyes seemed a little unfocused. *My Little Cat is drunk.*

She flung herself at me since Charlie's hands were full

and nuzzled into my chest, her hands wrapped tightly around a little plastic cup.

"Where's our drink?" Charlie asked with a laugh.

Her eyes widened. "Oh! I knew I forgot something."

"I'll forgive you," he said, taking the cup from her hands with a smirk and stealing a sip.

"I love you both so much," she sighed wistfully, leaning against me, and I wrapped my arms around her.

Charlie laughed and moved a strand of hair out of her face. "I love you too, but you are a soppy drunk."

"You don't like me soppy?"

"I like you always," he whispered.

"Charlie!" Savida called, and we all jumped. "This male would like to talk to you, if you can spare a moment from your love."

Charlie sighed and put the cup down before circling the table to shake a man's hand.

Clawdia's head rolled on my chest to look up at me. I didn't want to let her out of my arms yet. "Why don't we dance, Little Cat?"

The music had changed to a slow song many were singing. The lyrics about being perfect made it the ideal moment to share with her.

"A first dance," she breathed as I pulled her into the dance square. We swayed together, pressed tightly against each other. Her hands roamed my back in soothing caresses. As the sunset cast a dim glow, she whispered, "I love you."

"And I love you," I told her and chuckled as the song ended. I chucked her under the chin. "But Charlie is right, you can't hold your alcohol."

"You don't hold it, silly." She rolled her eyes. "You drink it."

I held my laughter behind tight lips. "Yes, you're right. Forgive me."

133

"I've never been drunk before. I didn't know it would feel like this. I feel like a bubble," she told me and hiccupped a giggle.

"You will not be saying such in the morning, Little Cat." I stroked her hair. "But I'll be there to make you feel better."

"You're always there." She smiled at me with such love in her eyes my heart lurched in my chest.

"Always."

To my shame, it was a lie. Another lie I told my soul pair to stop her from worrying.

I knew my fate.

CHAPTER 12

ZAIDE

"*D*o you think it's bad we are having fun when Baelen is hurt?" Clawdia asked in a small voice.

While I hadn't forgotten our soul mate lay asleep and injured, I was focused on us relaxing and having a nice time. At the mention of his name, guilt seemed to slip under my skin. *Could I have done something to help prevent him from getting hurt? Was I being a bad soul mate by having fun without him?*

I swallowed my guilt and pushed it away. She didn't need to feel all the anguish within my heart. Shaking my head slowly, I held her gaze. "I don't think Baelen would begrudge us our happiness, especially since we've had so little of it these days."

She hugged me, and as the song changed to something more upbeat, something I couldn't dance to without dishonoring my gods, I pulled her off the dance floor and back to the table. Charlie stood chatting with the twins, one of which was holding a tabby cat with a big black fluffy brush of a tail.

"Look, Clawdicat. A real cat," Charlie called as the cat was set down and began winding around Charlie's legs.

Clawdia pouted. "I don't know what you are trying to say by that, but I don't like it."

"This is Hex," the twins said simultaneously. "He's our fake familiar."

I stroked Hex under his chin, and his responding purr echoed loudly. "Little Cat, I think he likes me."

"No, he doesn't." She stepped between me and the cat, blocking me and crossing her arms. "I'm your little cat, and no other cats exist for you. Don't even look at him."

I couldn't help but tease her. "But he's so cute."

"I am cuter," she argued.

She is. In both forms.

But I was having fun seeing her face turn pink with frustration, so I reached around her and pet Hex again. His purr ramped up, and he rolled over, showing his belly, begging for more.

"You never purred like that," Charlie joined in the teasing, his lips twitching.

Clawdia gasped. "I did."

Charlie's laughter was loud and boisterous, drawing stares from people all over the party. He didn't seem to notice as he slapped his thighs and tears appeared in the corner of his eyes. I broke my serious facade and had to laugh too, which made the twins snicker behind their hands.

"Why are you getting so defensive?" Charlie asked between chuckles.

"I was … am … a great cat." Her gaze rapidly switched between Charlie and I. "Better than all the other cats. Right?"

"I'd argue you were the worst." Charlie scoffed. "Do you remember my thirtieth birthday?"

"No."

"Well, I got you cat wine, and you decided to push my cupcake off the table." He glared and slowly said, "You were a bad cat."

Her head tilted to the side. "That was your thirtieth? You celebrated with a cat?"

"You were the cat!" he exclaimed.

"You didn't know that." She raised her eyebrow and looked him up and down, regarding him with the same disdain she often showed him in her feline form. I covered my laugh with a cough.

One of the twins suddenly interrupted as the music changed, grasping Clawdia's arm. "Oh, I love this song. Clawdia come dance."

Her hands were taken, and she disappeared into a mass of females who descended on the dance floor in a similar squealing manner and began screaming the lyrics, which spoke of girls ruling the world.

Joseph approached us with a glass in his hand. He nodded regally in greeting. "Charlie, Zaide, I'm glad to see you having a nice time."

"Something tells me you're not here to make it better," Charlie mumbled.

He grimaced. "Forgive me for talking shop when we are here for pleasure, but I want to warn you. We are having a meeting tomorrow. We hope to have identified new Fafnir suspects, so we'll require you all to look through those images and let us know if we are on the right track."

Charlie shrugged. "Sounds good."

"We are going to try something in the morning to see if we can speed up the process, but we can let you know in the morning," I said.

"Excellent." He smiled and then tilted his head as he said, "I also had one other thing I wanted to let you know about. We had an interesting phone call earlier from a woman called Elizabeth. She offered information about Fafnir. Apparently, her family is descended from him and gave me

137

all the names of those that might be involved with him now he's back."

Charlie and I exchanged a quick glance before he smiled widely at Joseph and said, "That's great news."

He paused, assessing our faces, but nodded slowly when we didn't say anything else. "We've already got teams looking for them."

"I can help there if you need any hackers on the team," Charlie offered.

Joseph nodded. "Any help is always welcome."

"What are we planning to do against the hunters?" I asked. If I knew their plan, then I could rest assured I wouldn't be left to my fate alone, that others would be fighting for me.

But my heart sank as Joseph shook his head and sighed. "The hunters have always been a problem. They are like cockroaches. We are best off ignoring them."

"How can we ignore them if they are preventing us from protecting ourselves from Fafnir?" I asked.

"We won't solve that issue overnight." He waved his hand dismissively.

Charlie backed me. "They had a device that told them we are more powerful than Fafnir, which is why they followed us. If they are tracking supernaturals with this device by following the dragon, then soon they'll find members of your team."

"I understand hunters might seem a new threat to you, but we have been dealing with them for centuries. We can't completely get rid of them. When you chop off the head of one branch, another quickly rises. Avoidance is safer. And if they have a device to track the supernatural, let us hope they find and execute Fafnir before we do." He smiled and waved his hand with a drink around in a salute and walked away.

"We are to do nothing about the hunters, then? We'll

know nothing about them before they take me?" I asked, almost trembling with the rage that overwhelmed me.

They will do nothing? They will watch as the hunters find supernaturals and kill them? As they take me? While they hide here and govern their teams who risk everything?

I tried to calm the anger bubbling under my skin with deep breaths and a long drink of a cup I found full on the table behind me.

Do not act in anger. Control yourself.

Charlie's phone dinged, and he pulled it out of his pocket to scan the screen. "Fuck yes. Now I've got you, bastards." He looked up at me with a smirk. "That's such good timing."

"Who do you have?" I asked in my calmest voice.

"The hunters. They've broken into our old apartment and searched it. I got them on camera. There's no hiding from me now."

"And what happens when you find them? The council—" I ground my teeth to stop the growl from escaping.

"Are the council. We are us, " Charlie finished firmly, staring at me.

"And what will we do?" I asked.

"We make their lives a living hell," he said simply with a wide smile.

He scrolled on his phone for a moment before pressing something on the screen and holding it up to his ear. I took another drink and watched Clawdia dancing while Charlie spoke to someone.

"Hi, Adam." He chuckled. "I could update you, but you wouldn't believe me. Yeah, don't worry about it. No bodies to transport. Just your average seek and destroy. Money's no issue, Adam. You know that. So, can you help? I'd do it myself, but I've got a thing and want this info urgently." He laughed again. "I'd invite you, but I know you hate tiny food. Thanks, Adam. You're the best." He tucked his phone back into his pocket. "There. Sorted. Now I can get shit-faced and still be productive."

What am I doing to be productive? What is my role? How can I help? Or do I just wait for my fate quietly?

"You okay?" Charlie asked, noticing my silence. I hesitated, not wanting to voice my insecurities but he insisted, "Better out than in. What's wrong?"

"I am to be taken captive by hunters, and yet there is nothing I can do to guarantee my safe return. I feel trapped and helpless awaiting my fate with no productive outlet."

"Like a mouse in a trap." He nodded understandingly. "But I don't think you're looking at it the right way."

"What do you mean?"

"You aren't trapped. Fuck what the council are doing. The Fafnir thing for us is personal. The hunters are a serious threat to you. We aren't going to lie down and think of England. We are fucking powerful bastards. Weapons. We're a catapult. We're waiting for the moment the string is cut and we are thrown over the gates to cause serious destruction. We are the bad thing about to happen to them. So, you'll train —we'll all train—so that when the time comes, we know what we are capable of. Knowing your strength is half the battle."

Train? Train what? How to heal? How to dreamwalk? My power is neither defensive nor attacking. The only way I would get an attack power is if Baelen and I consummated our bond and I could use his power over blood threads.

But I couldn't lay all my thoughts at Charlie's feet. Instead, I asked, "How much of that have you drunk?"

"Why? Was I slurring?" He frowned. "I thought that was a great pep talk."

I laughed. "It was. Thank you, Charlie. I'll try not to remember our strength."

"Our strength."

I paused before saying, "This conversation doesn't get back to Clawdia. I don't want her to worry about me."

Charlie's brows pulled together. "Are you sure? You're already in the doghouse for not mentioning that Baelen might be in trouble."

"It's another thing she can't do anything to fix. Worrying is useless, and she's already had such a terrible time the past few weeks."

He shrugged. "It's your funeral."

"This has been the best night ever!" Clawdia exclaimed as she stumbled toward us and threw her arms around my neck.

I brushed her hair back from her face, and she nuzzled into my hand. Her eyes were unfocused, and her makeup, faded, but her smile was so big and bright it made my heart lurch. "I think it's time we get you back to the cabin," I told her.

Charlie stared at her, assessing her state too. "Water. Lots of water."

She pouted. "I don't want to leave yet."

"The party is over, Clawdia," Charlie lied.

But Clawdia was so drunk she didn't notice. "No. Come on. Please. I want to stay. It's still a party if we stay."

"I didn't want to do this, but you leave us no choice." Charlie sighed. "Zaide, get her."

I rolled my eyes. "I'm not your servant to be bossed around." But I picked her up and cradled her anyway as Charlie pushed through the crowd, making way for us as we walked back to our cabin. Clawdia's eyes closed the moment her head rested on my shoulder, and I chuckled. *She is going to have such a sore head in the morning.*

"Like you're not loving the excuse to have her all over you," Charlie chuckled.

"Jealous?" I smirked as I walked past Charlie, who held the door open to our cabin.

Clawdia groaned and tried to roll out of my hands. "I don't … feel well."

"Oh, God," Charlie said, and I hurried to the bathroom.

I placed her on the edge of the bath, and she swayed. "What's wrong with me? Why is everything spinning so much?"

"Who let her drink this much?" I mumbled.

She bolted, her eyes suddenly wide as she pushed me out of the way and lunged for the toilet. The room was quickly filled with the sound of retching and the vile smell of vomit.

Charlie cringed as her body heaved. "She was having a good time."

I shook my head. Pulling her hair back with one hand and rubbing soothing circles on her back with the other, I said, "It's all fun and games until the sausage rolls are regurgitated." Her heaves turned to sobs. "There, there, Little Cat. You'll feel better once it's all up."

"I'm so sorry—"

"No need to apologize, Little Cat. Let's get your teeth brushed and tuck you into bed."

* * *

FOR SOMEONE who had spent the evening with her head in the toilet, my Little Cat sat cross-legged on the bed early in the morning looking surprisingly fresh.

"Wakey wakey, I bought bacon," she sang.

"Are you still drunk?" Charlie asked in a sleep-thick voice as he rolled over.

"I don't think so."

"How are you awake and not hungover?"

"Advantages of youth." She stuck her tongue out.

He glared. "You've gotten lippy, and I'm not sure I like it."

"Zaide does." She smirked and crawled over to curl into my arms. I squeezed her tight and pressed kisses over her face, and she reached across to the side table to pick up bacon.

"He's a suck-up." Charlie pouted.

"He gets bacon first now." I opened my mouth as she fed me a rasher.

"I don't think you should play us off one another. That's how jealousy issues start," Charlie grumbled and snatched the next rasher she offered to me from her hands.

"You've been to check on Baelen?" I asked before they could begin to argue.

She looked back at me and nodded. "He's still not awake, but his threads are still green. I just hope it means he needs time to wake up like the protector."

"Let's focus on what we can control."

Her lips twisted, and her eyes narrowed in concentration. "Getting the council an image of Fafnir. How can I help?"

* * *

AN HOUR LATER, Clawdia and I knocked on Savida and Daithi's cabin and were greeted by a freshly showered demon. "Friends! Come in. Come in."

Savida chattered about the troubles of washing wings in a compact shower stall as he clicked the kettle and set out some teacups. Daithi joined us only a few moments later. He looked much improved since yesterday but eyed me suspiciously. "You are here early."

"We assumed from the sound of retching that your visit would be … later." Savida explained with a cheeky grin.

Pink colored my soul pair's cheeks, but she waved a hand. "That's all forgotten now. We'd much rather be productive."

"You are going to dreamwalk?" Daithi asked.

I shook my head. "No, we are going to induce a vision."

There was a long silence as he took a sip of his tea, refusing to look at me. Eventually, he said, "I'm uncertain this will yield results."

"Daithi hasn't been feeling—" Savida started.

But I interrupted. "This is the safest option for us all. It will work."

Daithi hesitated, clearly not believing me, but said, "If you say so."

"I do."

We made ourselves comfortable, Daithi lying on the small sofa and Clawdia kneeling at his side on the floor while I sat in the armchair. "Clawdia is going to hold your hand and focus on images of Fafnir. All you need to do is follow my instructions and allow any visions to come into view."

He nodded his agreement, and Clawdia took his hand.

"We start with our breathing—" I began. I talked him through relaxing of all his muscles one by one, and when I saw his breathing deepen, I knew it was time. "Open your mind's eye and be thankful for the visions you are given. Ask for the Fates to guide you. Ask them for sight of our enemy. Of Fafnir."

Clawdia peered anxiously at Daithi. *"Is it working?"* she asked me silently.

"We can only wait and see."

"Should I keep hold of him?"

"If it worked, I think you can let him go."

We waited in silence for half an hour. Clawdia let Daithi's hand go and joined me on the armchair, snuggling into me and enjoying the quiet. Savida fluttered around, trying to keep himself busy so he didn't focus on the unnatural still-ness in his soul mate. A loud gasp startled us, and Daithi jumped up, blinking rapidly.

"I saw him ... I saw what I wanted to see."

I stood as elation raced through me and spread a huge smile across my face. *It worked.* "I knew you could do it."

Daithi looked disbelieving and confused but not unwell. "How?"

"Because you do it all the time but in a much slower way. You wanted to find me my soul pair, and eventually, you saw a vision. So many times, you've asked for a vision but gave the vision no time to arrive, so it forces you. Makes you ill," I explained. "How do you feel?"

Daithi blinked. "Unchanged."

"What does this mean? You feel unwell?" Savida asked frowning and fluttering around Daithi anxiously.

"No, I feel as though I did before the vision. I feel as though I had a nap." Daithi shook his head, utterly bewildered.

A knock sounded at the front door, drawing our attention away, and Charlie pushed into the cabin. "Council has called us. It's time to plan a dragon roasting."

CHAPTER 13

CHARLIE

"$\mathcal{W}$hat are you doing here?" I stopped abruptly as I entered the dining room of the main house. Clawdia bumped into my back, but I didn't move. I stood frozen at the sight of my birth mother sitting at the table with the council members, sipping on a cup of fucking tea like it was just an average Tuesday.

She just arched a perfectly plucked brow and smiled. "You asked me to come, did you not?"

The room turned silent as everyone watched our exchange.

My eye twitched as my blood pressure spiked. "How did you even get here?" I asked.

"By plane." She sighed and set her cup down like I was an exasperating child. "Really, Charlie, it's as though you've never seen someone travel before."

I scoffed and stepped back in disbelief. *The nerve of this fucking woman.*

"I've never seen my birth mother in person before, so forgive me for being a little stunned that you're suddenly here."

She shrugged. "I'm the same as I am in a dream."

"Okay, yeah, it's totally not a big deal at all. I'm actually bored of you already," I said sarcastically and looked at Zaide with eyes that said "Can you believe this bitch?"

"Charlie …" she sighed.

Marianne coughed, drawing all eyes to her. "As much as I love watching a family drama, can we get on with our meeting? Time is of the essence."

Clawdia took my hand and squeezed, looking up at me with questioning eyes. I squeezed it back and pulled her to sit at the table, trying not to feel the piercing gaze of my birth mother watching us.

"Clawdia, Charlie, Zaide, would you mind taking a look at our new suspect pictures? We'd like to update the team as soon as possible."

"We can do one better actually," I said as I swung an arm around the back of Clawdia's chair.

I needed her close. *We joked last night about her being an emotional support animal, but maybe that's not untrue.* I was stressed but playing it cool in front of my birth mother, yet Clawdia placed a hand on my thigh, and I suddenly felt like I could breathe again. *Is this a love thing, or a familiar thing?* I had no real way of knowing, but fuck if I wasn't going to take advantage of it. I covered her hand with mine and squeezed her shoulder.

"I have seen him in a vision. I can show you him," Daithi said. He was also playing it cool. No one would have guessed that only a few moments ago, he'd stared in utter confusion as he was able to control something that had been like a curse to him all his life. *And all he needed to do was to stop being a know-it-all prick and listen to Zaide.*

"Please. Go on." Joseph waved a hand.

Daithi took a deep breath, and suddenly, in the middle of the table was a large hologram of Fafnir. The human version, which suddenly shifted into the dragon and back. The collective gasp that came from the council and my mother made me smile smugly. I wasn't shocked by Daithi's illusions anymore.

When you've seen him accidentally turn a cat into a human, everything else is a bit boring.

Marianne looked through her phone and quickly checked her photos against the image. "None of the new suspects are him."

Joseph took a picture. "I've just sent the image to the teams. If they are in the right place, they should get sight of him soon."

"He doesn't look like he could eat you when he's this small." Samuel waved his hand through the illusion.

"And Clawdia doesn't look like she'd piss in a litter box," I said with a shrug, "but she has."

Clawdia gasped and poked me in the stomach. Hard. "Do you mind?"

"Not at all." I grinned, unrepentant, even as I rubbed the spot her boney finger stabbed me.

"You can go off some people you know." She turned her nose up at me, which only made me want to piss her off more.

"You can't go off me, Clawdicat." I whispered, my lips brushing her ear, making her shudder. "You're literally attached to my soul forever."

It was still a weird thought, that she'd be with me until we died. We'd gotten magically married without ever discussing it, but a part of me was glad. You didn't get to keep a lot as a foster kid. At least I knew I'd never lose Clawdia. And, in turn, never lose Zaide or Baelen.

Elizabeth's gaze moved between Clawdia and me before she turned to Joseph and asked, "Have your team found anything on what Fafnir might be doing? Has anyone reported missing people?"

Joseph shook his head. "They haven't found anything yet. No reports have come in about missing members of our community, so we can only assume he's regaining his strength another way."

"Or your communication is being sabotaged," I muttered under my breath. Alex shot me a sharp look, and I shrugged. "There's no way he's just biding his time. He'll be building. So either he has a way of stopping you guys hearing about people going missing, or he's got a collection of people who have been 'missing' for a while now that he can snack on."

"People have been going missing for months now. You think not all of them have been taken as slaves?" Clawdia asked.

"It's easier to prey on people in panic." Zaide said in a voice so low and deep that it sent shivers down my spine and silenced the entire table. His jaw was tight, and Clawdia pulled his hand onto her lap, offering him the same comfort she offered me.

"Enough with the conspiracy theories please, Charlie. We deal with facts of matters here. We don't have evidence of anything you are saying." Joseph sighed and rubbed his forehead. "We are looking for Fafnir. That is all we can do for now."

You aren't utilizing your resources properly or thinking like the enemy. You're doing the bare minimum. My teeth ground together as frustration burned through me.

"What about finding my family?" Elizabeth asked.

"They are searching," Joseph said with an edge of irritation.

I leaned forward, taking my arm back from behind Clawdia to put it on the table as I stared Joseph down. "How are they searching? Physically? Magically? Digitally?"

"Charlie, you need to trust that our teams know what they are doing." Marianne added, her mouth pursed in a frown.

Through gritted teeth, I said, "I just want to know so I can tell you if I can do it faster."

"Be our guest." Samuel grinned mockingly and waved his hand, which really fucking irked me.

"The council is really starting to piss me off." I told Clawdia.

"Don't rise to it," she replied quickly and squeezed my thigh.

With a forced smile and fake cheer, I said, "Great. Forward me the email Elizabeth sent with the information on the family."

"Now?" Joseph asked.

"Now." I pulled my phone out of my back pocket and opened up my desktop on it. "I guarantee I'll have at least one local location for your team to check out by the end of this meeting instead of them just looking up at the sky for a dragon."

"Watch the attitude." Alex growled at me, but I wasn't paying him any attention. The email came through, and I got to work.

"We are all on the same team. Let's try to remember that," Elizabeth commented pointlessly.

"Exactly, Elizabeth." Marianne's voice brightened. "Thank you for your information. I'm sure it wasn't an easy decision to give up your family. But you have decided to join us here, and we'd like to know why."

I listened to the conversation with one ear as I did what I did best. Tapped and typed and found things.

"I heard you are currently missing your head of witches." Elizabeth began her pitch. "While Deborah Delaney is a strong witch, her power and, of course, her knowledge comes in second place in comparison to me and my family.

I'm offering to support you in your efforts as the head of witches, with the knowledge I have, in order to defeat Fafnir."

When I lectured her in our last meeting, I hadn't imagined she'd actually take any of what I said to heart. I definitely didn't think come here to try to lead the witches.

Joseph cleared his throat before he began, "You are welcome at this table to help us if you have knowledge and power to share. However, the issue of the head of witches is one we won't be dealing with until Deborah can have a trial and face punishment."

"Respectfully, I disagree," Elizabeth replied. My eyebrows rose at the balls of the woman, but my eyes didn't move from my screen. "Without a leader, witches will be more likely to be swayed and taken to support the wrong side. They need a leader who can forgive them for being misled and encourage them to rejoin the right side and write the wrongs they've committed."

Marianne replied, "We have a substitute leader here in the form of Ingrid Holm. Her family is also very knowledgeable, and their ward currently keeps us safe. The witches are looking to her for guidance at the moment."

"Which is fantastic. However, no official appointment has come from the council. You are leaving them open to be purchased by extremists, offering them the community and safety you do not."

"They are safe," Alex growled.

"Not all of them. There are witches beyond these wards, fearful and looking for help. Someone needs to be on the podium, in the spotlight, guiding them back to us."

"Why d'you wanna be a council member anyway?" Samuel asked, nothing but curiosity in his voice. But he was the lie detector.

"My family has been in hiding for a very long time. In

hiding, we've allowed the witch community to be without our knowledge and therefore make mistakes that have cost us all." She sighed. "I don't particularly relish the thought of being a council member, but I know it must be done to ensure that the education, history, and rituals of our community aren't lost or twisted to suit the gain of others."

"How very cryptic," Joseph muttered.

"You'll be required to share a more detailed monthly update on issues within the communities so we can pool resources for resolutions," Marianne informed her.

"That won't be a problem. I intend to do a deep dive into the covens and families."

As the room fell silent and a page took forever to load on my phone, I looked up to see the council exchanging glances, having silent conversations as they deliberated Elizabeth's request. Finally, they turned back to my birth mother just as my page loaded and I continued my quest.

"Thank you for thinking of the good of the witches. We'll appoint you as the temporary new leader, but be prepared for pushback," Marianne told her.

"While Fafnir is out there, pushback from the witches is the least of my worries."

Isn't that the truth. I frowned.

Joseph asked, "Do you have any other information you could give us about him? His aim? His powers?"

In my peripheral vision I saw her shake her head. "Although, I have bought diaries from my great-grandmother. She may have written down something that could help us. I started the first one on the flight over."

"Excellent. Keep us updated. After this is over, stay while we draft your announcement."

The tension in the room seemed to deflate as I put my phone face down on the table and sat back in my chair. Victorious.

"Mission accomplished," I told Clawdia, the smugness only in my tone, not on my face.

She squeezed my leg and squealed in my mind. *"That's brilliant, Charlie. You showed them. You're so talented."*

"So much praise for little old me."

"Don't get used to it."

Joseph coughed and rubbed his chin. "Our next item of discussion is something I didn't want to bring up last night where people could overhear, but your friend … the one in the medical center—"

Alex interrupted with a sneer. "Your friend managed to portal, and not only that, but come through century-old wards. How?"

"Truth please. Remember, I hate to smell lies," Samuel said with a smile that suddenly looked more threatening than friendly.

Clawdia jerked back and shook her head as she stammered, "We—we don't know. We were just as shocked."

Zaide's large hand cupped the back of her neck, and his thumb stroked in reassuring caresses. His eyes met mine, and I could see he was as pissed off as I was that they were being so hostile to our girl.

"How did he find you here?" Marianne asked calmly, bringing the tension down a few notches.

"I couldn't tell you. We've never met in person, but he's our soul mate, so maybe through our bond?" She shook her head. "I'm still learning, so I'm not even sure if that's possible."

I looked at Daithi and Savida, who'd been sitting in silence this entire time. "Is it?"

Daithi nodded. "Not usually before the bond is consummated, but he's—you all are—very powerful. Who knows what you are capable of."

Marianne raised a brow and said quietly, "He's not a vampire of mine. Where has he come from?"

"He's half akari, half titan. He's the son of the titan gods," Clawdia said, "But we don't know how he got here. We thought the portals were closed because of the protector, and we thought the wards were stopping anyone from finding or coming to this island."

A silence descended amongst the council as they glanced at each other.

"The portaling is a concern since we also believe that the protector's life keeps the portals closed." Joseph rubbed his jaw.

Clawdia shook her head. "It didn't look like a normal portal, though. It was black and smokey. I'm not sure if he was able to find a way of portaling from another realm to avoid the protector's safeguards because all of us are still unable to portal to another realm. Right?" She looked at Daithi.

Daithi closed his eyes, concentrated for a moment, and opened them once more to nod. "Yes."

There was a collective sigh of relief. Joseph narrowed his eyes, but his mouth smiled as he said, "I suppose we will have to wait for him to wake to know for sure how he managed it."

"And the wards?" Alex asked.

Samuel pursed his lips. "He is certainly powerful, but more powerful than Fafnir?"

"Who's to say?" Marianne mumbled.

"It doesn't hurt to take precautions." Joseph nodded.

"What are you talking about? Take precautions with what?" I asked. I could feel Clawdia's anxiety rocketing. No doubt she thought they were going to do something to Baelen. *Like we'd let that happen.*

"Our safety on the island, of course. There are many

supernaturals here seeking refuge, and it would be a feeding ground for Fafnir if he found us. Not to mention, we have the protector, his oldest enemy. We must ensure the wards can keep him out," Joseph explained as he stood and walked around the table to open the door. "Ingrid, could you come in for a moment, please?" he called into the hallway.

"And you think that because Baelen came through that the wards can't keep Fafnir out? That they'd fail?" Clawdia asked.

"The Holm family regularly add power to their wards to ensure they are up to scratch," Joseph said as Ingrid gleefully came skipping into the room at the call of the council. "That's correct, yes?"

She nodded. "Our wards are immensely powerful, and we ensure they are bolstered almost hourly. We wouldn't promise what we couldn't deliver."

Why would they regularly add power, especially hourly, to the wards if they worked as they should? I frowned.

"Then we will all add power to the wards as well. We have some very powerful guests, and this will help settle some of our more nervous guests," Joseph stated and looked at us all intently. Subtle, he was not.

"Yes," Ingrid said quickly, and her eyes had that weird intensity to them again. "That is an excellent idea. And much appreciated. I bet the wards would be thrilled to have more variety of power."

A shudder ran through me. The way she spoke about the wards was like they were power-sucking leeches like Fafnir. *And what the fuck do I know. Maybe they are.*

"Ingrid, would you mind asking a few people to help you power them while we finish this meeting?" Marianne asked.

"Of course." I think she would have curtsied if her trousers had enough give in them. She skipped back out of the room and closed the door behind her.

Marianne smiled as she turned back to us. "I think that's all we need for the moment. You're free to enjoy the rest of your day."

My eyebrows shot up at the dismissal. *They certainly aren't pretending anymore.*

"I see you were unable to succeed in your challenge, Charlie." Joseph smiled plastically as he sat at the table again. "But rest assured that our trained teams will soon have locations for all involved in this problem."

I copied the same fake smile the council had pasted on their stupid faces and inclined my head. "June Olsson is currently staying at the Motel L Älvsjö in Stockholm. There seem to be a few warehouses in the area, so they might be worth checking out since we know he likes to hide in warehouses." I pushed out of my chair so I could stand over them. "I actually finished before you began interrogating my familiar about her soul mate, but I thought it would be rude to interrupt."

"Only one? And you had time to spare?" Samuel asked mockingly.

I laughed. "You only need the one name and location because they are all together." I shook my head and crossed my arms, avoiding the sharp gaze of my birth mother. "I get that you guys have teams and people you trust. But you don't know me. Don't know what I'm capable of. Don't know what *we* are capable of. So don't make the mistake of underestimating us, because it doesn't end well. You want our help? Happy to. But give us details so we can better support the people putting their lives on the line to get information for us."

"You've made your point, Charlie," Joseph said drolly.

"Good." I looked at the other council members, who stared back at me blankly, and pinned the fake smile back on. "Have a great rest of your day."

I pulled out Clawdia's chair, took her hand, and pulled her toward the door. The others quickly followed suit, and just as I moved to close the door behind us, Elizabeth called, "Charlie, we'll talk later."

"Sure." I waved a hand and slammed the door closed.

I glanced at my misfit friends, and all our shoulders dropped in one collective sigh. I nodded to the door, and we filed out of the house and headed down the hill.

"The council seems ... stressed," Savida remarked as he stroked the leaves of bushes we passed.

"That's putting it kindly, Savida." Clawdia offered him a small smile.

"I'm glad that is over. Now we can all go and play the game we found in our cabin."

"A game?" I asked.

"Yes." His wings flapped with excitement. "It is a board with black and white squares and black and white pieces. Although it seems some are missing."

Clawdia nodded. "It's probably chess or draughts. I can come round and teach you later."

"Why not now? Where are we going?" I asked.

"We're going to check on Baelen," Clawdia said.

"You checked on him this morning."

"I'm going to check him again. He isn't a plant, Charlie. I'm not going to just water him once a day." She scowled at me, and Zaide coughed to cover a laugh.

We waved goodbye to Savida and Daithi as they broke away to their cabin, and we turned down toward the medical center.

"They've worried you by asking questions about him," Zaide remarked. He took her hand and pulled it to his lips for a kiss. *Suck up.*

"I don't want anyone to think he is too dangerous or too

big a risk to have around and try to hurt him while we are busy. I'd never forgive myself."

"The council probably won't hurt him. I think they do trust us a bit," I agreed grimly. "But there's no accounting for the witches. They were easily misled before. They'll be in sheep mode again if someone pipes up about Baelen overpowering the wards."

And as if to prove my point, a scream broke the quiet of the surrounding area, scattering birds from the treetops with the shrill sound. Without thinking, we all ran toward it. Toward the medical center.

CHAPTER 14

CLAWDIA

"*B*aelen?" I cried out as we pushed through the wooden door to the medical center. But the screams weren't coming from Baelen's room. They were coming from the protector's.

"Where's that doctor?" Charlie asked furiously as I rushed to the room.

The sound of pain and fear drawing me like a moth to the flame, I cracked the door open to see complete darkness.

"Sigurd?" I whispered. The screams were now whimpers. "Are you all right? What hurts?"

The afternoon sunlight flooded the room as I creeped in, illuminating the empty bed. Sigurd was on the floor, panting, his long blond hair splayed around his head like a halo and his body curled in on itself.

At the sound of my voice, his head snapped toward me, and he choked out, "Margaret?"

It wasn't the first time he'd called me by my first name, my old name, but I'd brushed it off as coincidence. But now it was clear as day. Even though his bloodshot eyes were hazy with pain, there was a familiarity there. He knew me. Somehow. But I couldn't dwell on that. I schooled my face and locked my feelings behind a cage in my mind. He didn't need my confusion or questions right now. He needed help.

"I was," I agreed quietly and approached him like I would a cornered animal. "Are you all right? Why are you screaming? Let me help you."

His threads were orange, but I couldn't see anything that would cause him to scream in such a pained manner. *Perhaps it was a nightmare?*

"How are you here?" He slowly rolled to sit up, clutching his stomach. "I thought—"

"I'll explain everything, but I'd really like to check that you are all right first. Is that okay?"

He nodded mutely. I dropped to my knees at his side and touched his shoulder, funneling power into him and turning his threads from orange to green. His breathing slowed, and his muscles relaxed. He closed his eyes and leaned his head back on the side table beside him.

"You healed me? Raised me?"

"No. God, no," I automatically said. I wasn't the witches who wanted to bring him back, who took the lives of demons to do so. But it was my power that brought him back. I had healed him. "Well, maybe a little by accident."

He opened his eyes to assess me and then nodded. "Your magic feels familiar."

I felt the need to explain. "Zaide and I tried to heal you before. And Zaide helped Alcor and Savida heal you completely. They are demons. We aren't sure why you kept getting so drained after we healed you, but that doesn't seem to be a problem now."

I finished healing him and sat back on my heels and stared openly. The last time I saw him, he was a crippled old man, unable to move or speak. Zaide had explained the effect the demons had on healing him, but it was still so surprising. It was like I was talking to a completely different person.

But I wasn't.

He was risen from the dead. Constantly drained and unable to heal. Aware but in constant pain. Probably confused about where he was and unable to ask questions. Or to fight against his ill treatment. And I thought I'd had a rough few weeks.

How he's suffered because of the wills of others. He's probably so frightened.

We were shadowed as Charlie and Zaide stood in the doorway, blocking the sunlight behind them, and stared at us with concern in their eyes.

"Margaret ..." Sigurd began drawing my attention back to him.

"I go by Clawdia," I told him quietly.

"Why am I here?" His piercing blue eyes were serious yet hypnotic.

Charlie coughed. "Why don't I get some food in, and then we can explain everything?"

Sigurd nodded. "I'd like to wash up too."

"That can be arranged." I smiled and stood up. "Charlie, don't tell anyone he's awake. The council ..."

"Yes. I know," was his reply as he strode away with a wave.

* * *

AFTER SIGURD HAD CLEANED up and Charlie returned with food, we ate on the sofas in a strange silence, all staring at each other, unsure how to begin with the questions.

Finally, as Sigurd placed his empty teacup on the coffee table, he said, "Margaret Claudia Jenkins."

I shuddered. His words felt like ice water washing over

me, sweeping me away to the dark places of my memories. Zaide squeezed my hand encouragingly, reminding me of the safe place I had in him.

My voice wobbled as I said, "I don't consider myself a Jenkins since my marriage lasted only a few hours. But somehow, you knew that."

"Yes." He bowed his head.

"Can you tell us how?" Charlie asked, leaning forward. "What happened to you last time you were revived?"

Sigurd tipped his head back, and his eyes glazed with memories. "The witches didn't know that raising me would also raise him, and they died because of it. He killed them and took their magic. Their power gave him the recovery he needed to escape. I was still too weak to follow him. With the war happening, I thought he'd be in the midst of it, reveling in the chaos. But it was years later, in England, that I found him. I had a dream. I met an akari woman who told me she could see the future and knew where he was, what he was doing. In exchange for the information, she asked me to do something. Before I confronted Fafnir, I was to sneak into his home and place a vial of poison and a note in a box in the floorboards."

An akari woman ...

I gasped. "Nisha?" Although I didn't move my gaze from Sigurd, I could feel the puzzled gaze of my men.

"Little Cat?" Zaide whispered in my mind.

"It can't be a coincidence," Charlie mumbled in an accidental projection.

Sigurd raised a brow. "Do you know of her?"

"I met her in a dream, as you did." I shook my head. "She told you to place the vial? She wanted me to die?" I don't know why I felt so betrayed, but my heart stung even as I reasoned that she saved me from a fate worse than death.

Charlie narrowed his eyes on me. "This is why we don't trust women that steal us from dreams."

"Did you know she'd come back as a familiar?" Zaide asked, staring blankly at the protector.

Sigurd shook his head.

"Did she? Nisha?" Charlie asked.

Sigurd's gaze darted between us all. He shrugged and sighed. "If she did, she didn't tell me. I was very surprised to see you alive."

I nodded but needed to clarify, so I asked, "Nisha told you to make sure I drank it and died? Or just to place it where I could find it?"

His blue eyes softened with sympathy. "She told me to place it there, but after learning of the horrors he had inflicted on his other wives from the diary, I knew she meant for you to use the bottle to save yourself. I confess I didn't think about why she might have had interest in you. She was an akari seer but saw visions about a human bride and her feared husband? It didn't make sense but who am I to question the work of the Fates."

"You knew what he was going to do to Clawdia and were just going to let it happen?" Charlie hissed, his hands shaking with his anger. "Did you hope that she found the poison before he beat and raped her? You weren't going to confront him? You know, the fucking thing you were meant to do?"

Sigurd's eyes bulged as he exclaimed, "No! No. I couldn't leave. I waited outside, and he came home with a malnourished, dazed, and frightened bride."

My stomach dropped as I made the realization. "You knocked on the door." Flashes of the past slapped me like the belt that gouged my back that evening. But I was saved by the knock on the door. Saved by Sigurd.

"I did." He gave me a small smile, and his eyes brightened.

He chuckled and rubbed his chin. "It wasn't well planned but I could hear screams. I wanted to give you time."

If he hadn't knocked when he did ...

I frowned and blinked through the memories. "He came back and got his coat," I whispered.

Sigurd nodded and explained, "I left a pin on the doorstep. A pin that belonged to his father. He died with it, and I took it from the grave. He knew I was out there."

"That made him grab his coat and leave?" Charlie asked, his brows drawn together.

"There's nothing Fafnir loves more than attempting to kill me." He smiled ruefully. "Our rivalry runs deep. He can't miss an opportunity to attack me when I'm so close."

"So, he left to find you?" I asked.

"I led him as far away as I could. When he caught up to me, I attempted to cage him, but he broke free." His expression faltered and became somber. "We nearly killed each other again, just like the first time. But we crawled away, and he disappeared."

The silence was long and fraught with tension. Sigurd seemed lost to his memories. Charlie's mouth opened and closed like he was about to ask something but stopped himself.

"Thank you. You saved me when you knocked on the door and gave me the opportunity to take my life back," I said around a lump in my throat and the gloss of tears in my eyes.

He closed his eyes and grimaced as though my thanks hurt him. "You aren't the first victim of Fafnir. You won't be the last. But I was glad to have done something to save you. To enable you a chance at a new life." He opened his eyes and smiled. "It seems fate had a lot in store for you. You have reconnected with your titan soul pair."

Zaide's large hand still clasped mine, and I looked up at him, my lips curving upward as I stared at his beautiful face. "Yes."

"I haven't seen a titan in many centuries. Are soul pairs more common now?" he asked, the curiosity clear on his face as he looked between us.

Zaide shook his head. "No. The gods seem to think we are the only ones, if not one of the only ones."

"Nisha must have known you'd be important," Sigurd said.

Charlie crossed his arms and huffed as he leaned back into the cushions. "I don't like that this woman has been meddling in your life for over a hundred years. Why the fuck does she care so much? What's it to her if you lived or died?"

"I'll have to ask her if I see her again," I replied simply and rolled my eyes at his dramatics.

Charlie turned back to Sigurd. "And that was it? You never saw Fafnir again?"

"A young witch found me. Healed me. I built a life with her. Had children." He looked down, his jaw and hands clenched. We stayed quiet as he composed himself.

He had a family. I couldn't imagine how hard it must be to be alive again, knowing all your loved ones are dead. My rebirth was a second chance. His rebirth was torture. I swallowed hard, wishing there was something we could do for him. Wishing there was a way for him to go back to his peaceful afterlife. To finally defeat Fafnir and never be used as a protector again.

No one deserved to be enslaved for all eternity, no matter how important their power.

Sigurd cleared his throat and looked up, his eyes clear and angry. "I never stopped looking for him. I visited every coven in the UK and asked if anyone was missing. I gave them a description of Fafnir. Warned them of the danger. But if he was attacking witches, then it was the ones who didn't know they were witches, the hidden ones, the supernaturals with the smallest amount of magic inside them. And there was no possible way I could track that."

"There wasn't a magical way of tracking him?" Charlie asked.

"Of course. I tried that too." He sighed and rubbed his chin. "But the pin was gone, and I had nothing else to use to find him."

"But he must have died before you. My mother said—" Charlie stopped abruptly.

Sigurd raised his brow but didn't comment. "I became ill in my old age and traveled back to Sweden—"

I interrupted. "Why did you have to go back there? If you had stayed in England, you wouldn't have been revived again."

"It's part of the spell we are both bound to. We must return to our original graves in case I am ever needed again."

"That's not right." I frowned. *The witches were so cruel to do that to him.*

"How did Fafnir get caught in that spell, though? Surely they would have cast that on you alone when you were given your powers?" Charlie rubbed his as he thought. "Or is that another myth retold incorrectly?"

Sigurd blinked and hesitated. "Yes. Now that you mention it, he shouldn't have been affected by my need to be buried in the same grave. He was not spelled."

"But when you went to Sweden—" Charlie prompted.

"As my children dug up the grave, they told me there was already a body there. I knew it was him. I didn't know when he died, but I was relieved it was before me." He shook his head and frowned so deep grooves appeared on his brow.

"But in retrospect, he had no reason to be there unless he planned to be reborn."

Charlie nodded. "That fits with what we know."

"But for what purpose does he wish to live again? What is he planning?" Sigurd asked, half to himself.

"We were hoping you might be able to tell us that," I replied softly.

CHAPTER 15

CLAWDIA

Sigurd stood up and started pacing the floor as he considered. "I know he has always wished to venture into the interlinked dimensions. Which, of course, he couldn't do because the natural portals are protected, and when he began attacking witches and I was spelled, I prevented others from opening portals to other realms."

"Okay, there's a lot to unpack there," Charlie said, rubbing his head. "You know about natural portals?"

"What are natural portals?" I asked, frowning because Charlie hadn't shared his knowledge of natural portals with us, and I didn't like that.

Sigurd replied thoughtlessly as he eyed Charlie with suspicion. "A portal that exists, and has always existed, to link the realm together. But they are the best kept secret in the realms. Which begs the question, how do you know?"

"I'll explain later, but I did ask you first, so … age before beauty," Charlie quipped with a cheeky grin.

Sigurd's eyes narrowed even further. "You are very insolent for a male witch."

I coughed to cover my laugh, but I must not have been

very convincing, because Charlie glared at me. *"Keep laughing. See if I don't spank your arse."*

"You can't threaten me with a good time," I replied, mostly because I'd seen something similar said in a film and wanted to pretend like I hadn't just shivered at the thought of his hands on my behind.

Sigurd sighed and sat back down on the sofa. "The portals have been guarded by my family since the fall of the titans. We had the most knowledge of the otherworlds and their people and spent so much time around the natural portals that we were used to such power. It wouldn't overwhelm us. That's how I was chosen to be the protector."

My eyes widened and snapped in Charlie's direction. He was just as gobsmacked. *"Are you okay?"*

"For a kid who grew up with no family, they seem to be sprouting up all over the place now."

"Family is good," I replied.

He met my gaze with somber eyes. *"Unless it isn't."*

Charlie swallowed. "So, you're like my uncle from a thousand years ago?"

"Sorry?" Sigurd spluttered.

"My uncle," he repeated and then explained, "My birth mother's family guard the natural portals. They also happen to be descendants of Fafnir. I think he found one of your sister's descendants and married her after Clawdia died."

"He ... married into my family?" Sigurd's skin turned mildly green, and he leaned to hide his head in his hands.

Zaide mumbled, "It would make sense if the portals were what he was after."

After taking a few deep breaths, Sigurd shook his head. "Perhaps he did find my family. After all, he knew there was a reason I was chosen. But the natural portals are a secret we guard with our lives. We take an oath—" He slapped his hand over his mouth and spun to look at Charlie. He pointed, confusion and anger in his eyes. "An oath we have just broken. How?"

"I haven't made an oath. And maybe the oath you made has faded because you died? Or maybe because you aren't in the family anymore?"

"Charlie!" I gasped.

"It's all right. He's correct." His lips were pursed as he said, "With my deaths and my marriage, I could hardly claim my name."

"Bloody matriarch," Charlie grumbled.

"We are going to be stuck for last names, then, because I don't like either of mine. Zaide doesn't have one. And I'm not sure about Baelen." The words were out of my mouth before I could stop them, and the resulting silence made a blush creep up my neck to my cheeks, making me really warm all of a sudden.

"Cute that you're thinking of getting married already, Clawdicat," Charlie chuckled as Zaide squeezed my hand and smiled, "but I think we'll just pick a team name. Like Avengers or Famous Five."

I narrowed my eyes. "There's four of us."

"Fantastic Four, then." He threw his hands up. "What do you want from me? There are more important things going on."

With Charlie's reminder, our joyous interlude turned sour, and I turned back to Sigurd to see his head buried in his hands.

In the silence, he whispered, "I cannot believe I so freely betrayed my family."

He kept that secret for so long, only to blurt it out now to strangers. Even if one of them is a descendent ...

"You weren't betraying them," I said as realization hit me. "You were just talking to a really watered-down version of your family."

"Yes! That is it." The relief on his face looked almost painful. "You are kin." He told Charlie. "Your family is mine."

"We won't say a word," I said.

Zaide nodded his agreement. "Of course not."

"You'll have them swear?" Sigurd asked Charlie, his eyes darting between us all.

"Sure." He shrugged and said, "I don't know how, but I'll get Elizabeth to do it."

Nervous energy stuck to my skin, and I felt the need to shake it off as I walked to the kitchenette and filled a glass of water.

Charlie asked, "So, you were chosen from the family to close the portals made by other races. How does that work?"

Sigurd explained, "Since males don't carry the line, I was chosen for the task. It was experimental magic, and no one knew if it would work. I was imbedded with portal magic from races who can portal. I was also given more magic so the ability wasn't based on conscious thought or action. I only needed to be alive for it to work. It took many years."

I imagine it wasn't nearly as simple or as painless as he makes it sound.

Charlie shook his head in disbelief. "You gathered species who could portal in one place when you were trying to stop someone from portaling?"

"Thankfully, Fafnir was too busy working on his own theory to bother with us. He was attacking witches and trying to use their magic to gain the power to portal himself."

"You didn't stop him from attacking the witches?" I could see Charlie attempt to control his face and voice so the disapproval and judgment didn't come across so obviously.

I didn't work, because Sigurd sighed and stared at the ground. "We had some people trying to distract him, but our most urgent work was to ensure that I could stop him from escaping." He clenched his jaw and said, "We let too many die."

"How do you know he wanted to portal himself away?" I asked. "Why do you think he was trying to use the magic instead of just consuming it?"

"Ah." Sigurd nodded. "You don't know the truth, only our myth. Allow me to give you all the knowledge I have on our enemy. Clawdia, would you mind?" He looked at the glass of water I held.

"Oh, of course." I hurriedly turned around and filled three glasses of water before carrying it over.

He's parched from talking so much after being dead for years, and you're standing around only looking after yourself.

It was my mother's voice. With everything going on, the dark thoughts had no time to shake me. But they did now. I swallowed as I handed the glasses to the men, my smile tight.

Talking about Fafnir was bringing Margaret Claudia back to the surface. But I was a different person, and her fears and behaviors weren't welcome.

As I calmed myself, Sigurd took a long drink of his water and began. "Fafnir is part Drakorian—"

"That's an old name for somewhere in Sweden?" Charlie asked.

"It's a realm. My brother is in Drakor," Zaide said, sitting up straight.

"And Drakorian's do what?" Charlie asked.

"They are people who share their soul with a dragon."

Zaide thumped his head. "Of course they are. Witches cannot turn into dragons from stealing magic."

"So, the magic-stealing thing is a Drakorian trait?" Charlie asked.

"Dragons have hoards. Things they collect and treasure. Hoards are usually made of physical things. There are hoards

of gold, glass, plants, food … but Fafnir hoards magic."
Sigurd's words were punctuated by a shocked silence.

Hoards magic? "Doesn't a hoard imply something that is
kept and not used?" My head tilted as I considered this.

"Exactly." Sigurd nodded and took another drink.

"But he's taking magic from beings. How is he doing it?" I
asked.

"People of Drakor have an unbelievable sense of direction
for items they want to hoard and an uncanny way of taking
what they want if it doesn't belong to them."

"He has other powers that allow him to collect magic?" I
recalled Nisha telling me how he'd been able to draw on the
darkness in the hearts of my parents to ensure I was truly
broken before he married me. *But is that his dragon, or just
manipulation?*

"As I said, it's uncanny."

I shook my head free of the memories and concentrated.
"Fafnir's hoard is magic. So, he's taking it and putting it
somewhere? But you said you believed he was trying to use it
to portal."

Sigurd nodded and leaned back into the sofa, settling in
to tell a long tale. "Fafnir's father, Hreithmar, was cast out of
Drakor. My parents often told us of the day it happened
because they were guarding the portal he was pushed
through. The portals hadn't been used since the fall. They
hadn't ever witnessed someone coming through before, but
when a beaten male collapsed in front of them, pleading for
mercy, they spared him."

*"I'm forever learning things about my ancestors that make me
stabby."* Charlie's sigh echoed in my mind, and I gave him a
sympathetic smile.

Sigurd must have read the thoughts on our faces, because
he said, "I agree. Had my parents known the problems his

son would create, I know they would have chosen differently."

But if he'd never been born, I wouldn't be here. I wouldn't have taken my life, I wouldn't have been reborn a familiar, and I wouldn't have ever met Charlie or Zaide or Baelen. And it hurt my heart just thinking that I could have missed out on them.

"Hreithmar …" Charlie repeated hesitantly, wrapping his lips around the old name. "He knew about the natural portal because he came through one. Maybe he told Fafnir about them, and that's why he targeted your family?"

Sigurd shook his head. "They swore him to secrecy in exchange for his life."

"And he said he'd been cast out of Drakor?" Charlie continued, rubbing his head. "It's not a great way to convince someone you aren't dangerous."

"He told them his magic was different to others of his race and he was therefore beaten and rejected. He leaned on their sympathy, and they helped him," Sigurd explained.

"He had the same power as Fafnir? To steal magic?" Charlie narrowed his eyes, and his fingers tapped anxiously against his leg.

I knew what he was thinking just from looking at him. His birth mother was concerned that because the males in the family turned into magic-stealing dragons, the same would happen to him. *"You haven't turned into a dragon. You don't steal magic. You have your own magic,"* I told him. His eyes flicked to me but returned quickly to Sigurd.

The protector shrugged. "I believe he also hoarded something intangible, but he didn't attack anyone or take magic, so I'm unsure what, exactly, his dragon desired."

"So, your parents helped him and had you, and at some point, he must have had Fafnir?" Charlie asked.

"Correct. He stayed in the same village, and Fafnir and I grew up together."

"You grew up together?" I asked, my distaste clear in my wrinkled nose.

"We were not friends," he assured me. "His mother was a witch from a nearby coven but quickly died after his birth. Hreithmar's mind deteriorated, and Fafnir dealt with a man who often forgot his existence, punished him lawlessly, and could often be found lying in the main square, talking to the earth."

Everything seemed to stop. The small, unnoticeable noises were gone. There was no movement. I existed in a frozen space with my thoughts. And I could see it. I could see a little boy wandering around a farm, gently stroking the animals while his father screamed inside a small home. I saw the fear in his eyes. His little legs were shaking. The scene changed, and suddenly, I was watching the boy, even younger, surrounded by other children, observing them all. There seemed to be a bubble around him all the children moved around. No one approached him. Spoke to him. Or even looked in his eye. He was completely alone. Different.

As the images cleared, leaving me back in the room, my heart squeezed, and my eyes welled. I could barely concentrate on the story Sigurd continued with.

"My parents tried to intervene, but to no avail." Sigurd's jaw tensed. "On Fafnir's twelfth birthday, he changed. His eyes flashed yellow, his body shimmered with scales, and he transformed into a dragon. We were not afraid, since we knew this was possible, but in his next breath, he picked up another child and crushed them in his jaw. As we all rushed to contain him, he flew off, and we realized a more sinister fate. The child he'd crushed had also been drained of his magic."

"Evil—" Charlie started.

But I interrupted, "He was only a child himself."

"Nah. No. Stop." Charlie raised a hand and shook his head. "I don't care if he was five and told to take magic to save his dying sibling. Fafnir's evil."

"No child is evil," I told him sincerely, seriously, staring into his eyes.

Charlie clenched his teeth and whispered, "Clawdia, the man tried to rape you and take your magic."

I swallowed and nodded. "The man. Not the child. He had no mother. No guidance from his father or village, and he was so young when his power emerged, a power that wasn't understood by his own people. It must have been quite traumatic for him."

Zaide's eyes darted between us, but he remained silent.

Charlie made a noise between a gag and a growl before standing up and waving his hand in my direction as he yelled at Sigurd, "Do you see what you've done? You've made him a sympathetic character, and now she's going to hesitate when we need to defeat him."

Zaide squeezed my hand and drew my attention to him. His purple eyes glowed as he said in a low voice, "He had many obstacles against him, Clawdia, I agree. But he has not risen against them. Instead, he followed the path laid out for him to a dark future. The boy may have been innocent and worthy of sympathy, but he has not been that boy for many centuries, and his path has only gotten darker."

"Your titan is correct," Sigurd said. "Do not waste your sympathy on Fafnir. And while he might be a child to you, he was an adult in my society. He knew his actions were criminal."

Charlie asked, "What happened after he killed the child? Did he turn back? Go home?"

Sigurd continued, "He didn't come back. We don't know where he went, but we began hearing of coven's missing members and knew he was flying to other covens around the country, killing and moving on. Which is when we collectively began planning. We asked Hreithmar how he was draining magic and why, and he was able to explain more about the nature of Drakorians. We also found out from a witch Fafnir had gotten close with that he was hoping to go to Drakor through a portal. He was looking into ways in which that could be made possible, including finding other supernatural beings who could portal, demanding witches to summon demons to create a portal for him and using the magic he stole to create his own portal."

"Wait." Charlie held up a hand. "He demanded that a witch summon a demon and make it create a portal? And that didn't work?"

"He couldn't resist adding more magic to his hoard and drained the demon of its fire before he had a chance to fulfill its role. Apparently, it happened on more than one occasion. Which is why we were so fearful of him getting near stronger supernaturals, in the human realm or in another realm. It was clear he couldn't control his impulses."

"He's trying to get to Drakor to find people like him? Are there no other Drakorian descendants here?" Charlie asked.

"None." Sigurd shook his head regretfully. "They were made extinct a long time ago when dragon slaying was a popular sport."

Charlie asked, "So back to the original question. If he's just taking magic for his hoard, where is he putting it? And why does he think he can use it?"

"His mother is a witch. He believes if he has magic, he can use it. And because his hoard is intangible, he has to keep it close to him. We don't think it ever leaves him."

"How can that be?" I asked with a frown. "Is it inside him?"

Sigurd shook his head, but his eyes sparkled with interest.

177

"From what we learned from Hreithmar, we believe he keeps it attached to him somehow."

"He has magic attached to him?" Zaide asked, his face a picture of puzzlement. I was just as confused.

"We weren't sure exactly how, but we imagined it sewed together like a patchwork cape," he explained.

"Like Frankenstein's monster," Charlie muttered.

I shook my head free of the strange image they presented. *This doesn't sound right.* "He isn't consuming the magic? It's not a part of him?"

"He doesn't get stronger in the manner one would if the magic had truly become part of his being."

I thought back to the warehouse. Fafnir said "meal" and "taste." He wanted a witch for power and because he was hungry. While it's true he wasn't getting obviously stronger, if he was using magic to feed himself, it wouldn't make him stronger. Only satisfied.

"Can dragons feed on their hoard?" I asked.

Sigurd shook his head. "Drakorian's are protective of their hoard. They organize it, stare at it, pick up items and sit with them. It's rejuvenating. And this is important for the relationship between the dragon and the Drakorian. So, when a dragon's desire is to hoard something intangible, it has detrimental effects. It puts him at the bottom of the social scale in Drakor since they take great pride in showing off their hoard and forces the dragon to seek more because it cannot see what it has. Fafnir cannot see his hoard and revel in its glory. Nor can anyone else. He is being driven mad with instincts he cannot satisfy."

He certainly doesn't seem mad. His every action seemed purposeful, carefully planned, and manipulative. He was a puppet master not a puppet. But Sigurd knew his history …

Confused, I shook my head. "None of this makes sense. He isn't mad. He's just as clever as ever. And if he was wearing the magic like a cape, then surely the hunters would have been able to sense the magic on Fafnir, magic he's been gathering for centuries, as opposed to us being made out to be stronger."

"We don't really know how the device the hunters used worked, Clawdicat. I don't think we can assume it would even pick up magic that wasn't inherently part of a person. We don't even know what they are measuring."

"Perhaps his death took away his magic and he needs to gather more," Zaide suggested.

"And that might be true, but why would he consent to dying early if he was going to lose his hoard? There is logic to his actions. Madness implies a sense of chaos and unexpected behaviors. So far, all we have learned about Fafnir is that he has been planning for a long time." I turned back to Sigurd, my confusion spilling over. "And you keep saying magic is intangible, and while you might not touch it like you hold a spoon, you can put your hand in it. Like moonlight, it is there. You can see it. We've all seen it."

"Perhaps it is spelled to stay invisible. Everything we believed hasn't been confirmed, Clawdia. I'm sharing the theories, but your knowledge is welcome. It's multiple minds that will solve this issue."

But you are stating it like a fact. And now I'm doubting everything you've said.

"So, you think he has the magic somewhere else? In jars? Like the witches did with the fires?" Charlie asked me.

"I don't know. He was talking about it like it was food. He certainly seems to think it feeds him, but if it feeds him then it can't be his hoard," I replied, my head hurting with all the conflicting information.

"We aren't going to figure it all out right now. But we have a lot more knowledge of our enemy than we started with." Zaide patted my leg reassuringly.

179

"Yes." I nodded and smiled reluctantly at Sigurd. "Thank you for answering all our questions."

"This world needs to be rid of Fafnir for the good of all the realms. I am happy to help however you deem appropriate."

Deem appropriate? He isn't keen to fight his enemy and lead us? The longer the conversation went on, the more suspicious and confused I became. I asked Charlie, *"Are you as confused as I, or am I being unreasonable?"*

"Something smells fishy for sure."

I smiled at Sigurd before standing. "You've been speaking for an awfully long time now, so I think it's time we leave you in peace."

Charlie joined me. "We'll inform the council that you're awake and let them know everything you've told us. You shouldn't be subjected to their questioning."

"And dinner will be served in a few hours," Zaide said in his gorgeous low voice.

"Thank you for your help in healing me," Sigurd replied.

As I turned to leave, my eyes brushed past the door which housed my soul mate. While I wasn't sure I could entirely trust Sigurd, asking him about Baelen might help me heal him.

"Oh, before I go, I do have one more question for you." He smiled kindly and waved me on. "Have there ever been instances of portals opening while you were alive?"

He raised an eyebrow. "None that I am aware of."

I bit my lip. "If there was such an incident, what would be the effect on the person who crossed?"

"The spell that gave my essence control over portals is tied to blood. I was imbedded with blood from all the realms' creatures to prevent the use of portals outside. If I had to guess the effect of someone who has circumvented that spell, I would assume their magic would be warring with their blood. I couldn't imagine how that might affect them, but I don't imagine it's pleasant."

"Could I heal that?" I said more to myself than to him, but he tilted his head and replied.

"I don't know the extent of your magic, but a war isn't something that is healed."

I huffed out a breath. "So we'd just have to wait to see what wins the war?"

"There are no winners in war."

Flooded with a sense of dread and helplessness, I closed my eyes.

Baelen ... what have you done?

CHAPTER 16

BAELEN

I didn't know how much time had passed when I became aware of voices.

"He is still not awake?" a male's voice asked. It accompanied the snick of a door closing and footsteps approaching me. I didn't recognize the voice, but my mind hadn't yet caught up with itself, and I was only able to listen.

I felt the soft blow of air over my face, and a female voice replied, "I don't know why he hasn't woken up. His thread is green. He should be fine."

Her hand stroked my brow in gentle repetitive movements. It was soothing. *But why do I need to be soothed?*

"The protector couldn't say what might help him?"

"Nothing helpful."

"Perhaps I can help."

She coughed out a laugh. "I assumed that's why you were dragged in here."

"The dragging was unnecessary," he replied, a smile in his voice. "I'm in need of gossip since yesterday was quite eventful. How did the council take the news?"

"They were angry we didn't immediately go and get them,

but we explained that I had a history with Sigurd which needed to be explained privately." She paused. "Once we told them everything, they seemed as confused as I was. They are questioning him today."

"The poor male."

She made a noise of agreement. "I don't have any other gossip."

"Where are Alcor and Arabella?" he asked.

"Apparently, I do have gossip." She chuckled. "Alcor and Arabella have been moved to a cabin … with Isaac."

He gasped. "And Isaac is glad about that? Arabella must be very stressed."

"I'm sure they are all very confused and annoyed. Arabella and Isaac want to get back to their team and help look for Fafnir, but with Alcor's memory, they are worried about him joining them."

"He wants to join them?"

"Won't let them leave without him. He's being very stubborn about it. But if he remembers what happened while they are in hiding, it could be disastrous and not just to them."

"Arabella hasn't explained why she took his fire in the first place?" he asked, and I felt hands on my chest. Large hands. My heart rate picked up as I felt power shift over me.

"I'm not sure she did. But it's their business," the female said, but I could not concentrate on her words anymore. The magic the male searched my body with awakened me. Not literally. My eyes didn't open, but I suddenly remembered everything. The shadows attacking me. Kaatu … taking over my body … portaling.

"Yes?" the male asked.

"You're being very serious and quiet. It's unnerving," the female said. It was a familiar voice.

Clawdia? I struggled to move, to open my eyes, to do

183

something. But my body wasn't cooperating. *What's wrong with me?*

"I can't heal anything." The male sighed and removed his hands from my person. "But these dark spots on his skin … I don't suppose they were there before?"

"They weren't."

Dark spots? What dark spots?

The male spoke again in response to my soul mate's obvious concern. "We will try again tomorrow. We will try every day until he can awaken and tell us what ails him."

"Thank you. I appreciate you trying."

"I am in your debt. You tried to stop them. As a small animal, you tried. Then you gathered my friends and led them to me. Thank you, Clawdia."

It is her. Who is the male? He doesn't sound like Zaide or Charlie.

"No debt. We are friends."

"Friends. I like that. Does that mean I can comment on how you have three males attending to your every whim? Because Daithi said I couldn't bring it up."

Three … He is aware she is mine, then.

"You can bring it up. I know how lucky I am."

"I probably shouldn't mention that you smell like Charlie and Zaide and have a glow to your skin like you were well pleasured?"

Jealousy burned in my chest at the knowledge that she'd been intimate with them and not me. She had a soul connection with both of them, but I was so far behind in my relationships with my soul mates. *And what can you offer them? Even your fathers can't stand you.*

"I—well—no, you probably shouldn't bring that up."

"It's good to know where the line is." The male's voice was serious, but I heard the edge of laughter in it.

I coughed my amusement, and suddenly, small hands pressed against my chest.

"Baelen?" Clawdia asked. "Are you awake?"

"Sunlight?" I grunted as I tried to open my eyes.

My mind became aware of the throbbing pain throughout my entire body. My head felt so full and fuzzy.

Why do I feel like this? What happened to me?

"I did." a voice in my mind whispered darkly with a laugh.

Then suddenly I was shoved out of my own mind. I lost control of my entire body, and my consciousness was pushed to the back of my mind. Forced to watch passively as my eyes blinked but I didn't feel, I felt the shadow of another person overtake everything. Through the panic and helplessness, I realized who I was now sharing my body with.

"Kaatu."

"Hello, Baelen. Hope you don't mind, but I'll be taking over your body until we can get our portal fixed and my realm can heal."

"Get out of my body." I started to struggle against the dark strands of shadow holding my consciousness hostage. I pushed and pushed against them, and my body jerked with the internal struggle.

"Stop struggling."

"Never."

"I'm here. Are you okay?" Clawdia's voice called like a siren's song. I felt pulled closer to her. Sinking into my body, I felt the effects of being pulled into another realm via a shadow. My entire body hurt, but I was now in control, and Kaatu struggled in my mind against me.

"What did you do to me?"

"What I needed to. Now you can spend time with your soul mate. You should thank me."

"Mates. And I'd rather destroy my relationship with them than use them."

"But you aren't going to be the one in control."

"I am for now." But I knew it was only a matter of time before he managed to take control again. He was too strong. And he knew it too.

"Baelen," Clawdia whispered. "Please answer me."

"Hurt," I huffed, glad I could reply to her but not without fighting for the control of my mouth and with pain draining my energy with every small movement.

"Where are you hurt?" Her voice hitched, and her hands roamed over my chest again, searching for injury. Her long hair brushed my arm and chest. Her face was the picture of concern.

"Everywhere," I grunted.

She was just as beautiful as she was in our dreams. But I could feel her properly. Touch her. See the blemishes on her skin, see the pale blue veins pulsing temptingly under her skin.

I wanted to ask what happened to her when she left the dreamscape and what I've missed, but the smell of her heady, delicious blood distracted me to the point my fangs dropped. I salivated.

Her hand cupped my cheek and searched my eyes. "Baelen, your eyes. Was there always a dark ring around them?"

I couldn't respond as Kaatu took advantage of my distraction and took over again, pushing me back into the empty, feelingless place in the back of my mind. *If he takes over entirely, I'll go mad in this place.* Watching but not feeling. Screaming but not being heard. I felt as though I was in a nightmare. A horrible nightmare.

"No," I screamed. *"You can't do this to me. I don't want to lie to her."*

"We lie to everyone we love, Baelen," he replied solemnly.

"Yes," my voice growled.

She frowned and pulled away. "I don't remember that.

Maybe it's different in the dreamscape?" she asked, looking at me for confirmation, but I was too busy pushing Kaatu out of my mind. She shook her head. "Never mind. That doesn't matter. I can't see anything on you, and your thread is green. Savida tried to heal you too, but nothing happened. Will blood help?"

"Savida?" Kaatu asked.

"Present," the male voice cheerfully announced, drawing our attention.

"A demon," Kaatu acknowledged as we took in his dark skin, leathery wings, and flame-red hair.

"You know about him. He's the demon who had his fire stolen by my witch, the reason this whole thing started for us. Remember?" Clawdia stared at us in a way that made it clear she was concerned for my mental health as well.

With him distracted by Savida, I managed to push him hard enough that I fully embodied myself again.

"Ah, yes. Nice. To. Meet. You," I stammered out as Kaatu battled against me.

"You're making me look bad. I know who Savida is. Let me answer these kinds of questions," I told him, trying to convince him that he needed to stop fighting me, that we could work together.

He sneered. *"I don't care about the silly opinions of strangers. Once you have consummated your soul bond and have their gift, you can heal the portal, and I'll leave you. Just let me work quickly."*

He continued pushing for control, regardless of whether he knew enough about my life to act convincingly, because he knew I'd get tired, beaten down, and go mad living help-lessly in an empty space in my mind. And that person would do anything to be rid of him. Even sacrifice his soul mates.

He was strong, but I was the son of gods. I wouldn't give in so easily.

187

"I'm not consummating anything while you reside in my head," I growled.

Soul bonds were sacred, and I wouldn't allow him to poison such an important moment for us all by being there. Especially if it was him in control. My soul mates would be unaware of who was engaging with them. A shudder ripped through me at the thought. Everything felt so hopeless.

And he reminded me as such. *"You will not always be in control. And if you do not consummate, then as soon as I am stronger, I will take them to the portal myself and force them to do my bidding. I do not need you if I have them."*

I couldn't risk him hurting them. Draining their gifts to heal something that died eons ago was certain to do that. Consummated bond or not, I couldn't allow it, and he knew it. He wanted me to follow his plan because it saved him energy, humiliated me, and got him the use of someone with the power to heal anything.

"They will know something is wrong with me," I warned him. Because they would. Surely.

He leaned on my insecurities and made me even more uncertain and helpless. *"They don't know you well enough to know you are behaving strangely."*

"They are going to see ..." But I said it with less confidence.

He pounced again. *"Me. They are going to see me. You'll go where I want you to go. Do what I want you to do. You have no choice."*

"You sound like you're in pain, Baelen. What can I do? Do you need blood?" Clawdia's voice sounded distant as I felt myself being dragged back.

With all my strength, I pushed him back down, pulling myself back up and gasping like I'd been underwater. *"No. I'm not going to let you take over so easily."*

"Get out!" I suddenly screamed, and it was me. It was my voice. What I wanted to say.

But I said it out loud. To my soul mate. When she was offering me blood. I felt sick, but hunger roared inside me again, and I salivated at the thought of her sunshine flavored blood.

She jolted to her feet, tears pricked her eyes, and my heart sank. "I'm sorry. I'm just trying to help."

Kaatu didn't fight me as I pushed myself up from my prone position in the bed, grunting with the pain, and took her hand before she could back away from me further.

"I think he means me, Clawdia. Feeding is a private matter for akari, and he'll not want me around," Savida said, but he stared at me like he didn't believe what he was saying. Clawdia said nothing, but her hands were shaking as she flicked her gaze from me then back to Savida.

"I'll leave, Baelen, but don't hurt her." He pointed at me, and I wanted to be offended that he thought I would hurt her.

Ordinarily, I wouldn't. But with a shadow interloper inside my mind, I didn't trust myself.

He turned, and Clawdia gave him a soft smile as he closed the door on us.

"You didn't have to shout like that," she whispered, and her hunched shoulders and saddened eyes hurt to look at. "He was here to help. I've been worried."

"I'm sorry," I panted.

She stared at me. Her violet eyes were penetrating and unfocused, telling me she was checking on my thread.

"Do you need blood?" she asked once her eyes refocused on me.

"I don't want to taste blood. I'm not akari." Kaatu sounded almost petulant.

I scoffed. *"I don't care what you want. Get out of my body."*

"I'm not leaving. You know my terms. I think you'll bend to them sooner or later."

"Then you'll deal with the consequences of inhabiting an akari body."

"Don't touch her wrist, or I'll make you sorry," he snarled.

"My body needs to recover from whatever shadow magic you used to get us here. You want my body to be able to move to consummate my bonds, yes? Or should I ask her to sit astride me right now and do all the work," I sneered.

He ignored my tone, speaking calmly, which only angered me further. *"Admittedly, I didn't think it would make you feel so terrible. Akari are cousins to shadows. You should have traveled more easily."*

Fury made my heart race and my jaw ache from clenching it, but I turned my attention from the tormentor in my mind and hissed, "Yes," in answer to my soul mate's question.

Kaatu tried to stop me, tried to push me out, but he wasn't prepared for how strong a hungry akari can be for blood or how powerful the promise of his soul mate's blood could be. But he was clever, and he'd know for next time.

I need to make sure I get enough to last me however long this shadow intends to hold me hostage inside my body, I told myself pragmatically. *He is sure to make this my first and last time feeding.*

"All right." She sat on the bed and offered me her arm. I sucked in a breath of her fragrant skin and watched the blood pulse in the blue of her veins. My tongue swept across my lip as I salivated. Dying for a taste of sunlight.

Control yourself. Don't hurt her. Don't drain her. She's offering salvation, I reminded myself.

She must have sensed my nerves, which gave me hope that she could read me and know I'm not entirely myself, because she assured me. "It's okay. We've done this before."

"Nothing is going to compare to the reality of you." I stroked her arm and peered into her eyes.

A blush rushed up her neck. "That's sweet. But you're hurting. Please let me help." She raised her wrist to my lips and smiled gently.

Unable to stop myself, I plunged my fangs into her and groaned as the taste of rich sunshine spilled over my tongue. Flicking my eyes up to look at my soul mate, I saw her close her eyes, her lips parted and her arms relaxed as my bite pleasured her.

I pulled her toward me so she could be in the crook of my arm, holding her wrist to my mouth as she lay limply, her face tucked into my neck, and I enjoyed the feel of her. Her weight and warm body against me for the first time … I relished it. As I sucked another gulp of the ambrosia seeping from her wrist, she groaned, twisting her legs and nuzzling into my chest, her lips grazing my chest and making my cock stiffen painfully.

"Baelen," she whispered.

My high was rudely interrupted. *"I didn't know taking blood had this effect on the victim."*

"She is no victim. Go away. You're ruining this for me."

"I feel violated tasting this."

"I feel violated by you being in my head, so we are all losers."

I took my last draw of blood and licked across the puncture wounds. Pressing a kiss to her wrist, I said, "Thank you, my sunlight."

"You're welcome," she whispered, suddenly shy. The blood rushing into her cheeks assured me I hadn't taken too much and colored her cheeks prettily. "Are you feeling better?"

I nodded. "Much."

"What happened? How did you get here? Who did this to you?" She stroked her hand across my chest. "You look like you've been bruised all over, but I can't heal it. Is that something to do with the shadows?" She stroked her hand across my chest, and I focused on the skin of my chest. Blotches of black seemed to move like ink and water under my dark skin.

"What the fuck? What have you done?"

"An unfortunate side effect. You'll be fine."

Anger bubbled under my skin, my jaw locked, and my hands shook as I stared at my skin. *Not only has he taken my body; he's made it something I don't even recognize.* I opened my mouth to tell her exactly what happened, exactly what was happening to me as we were speaking, that she shouldn't trust me and that Kaatu was going to use me, and them, to further his own agenda. But he knew my intention.

"I think I've let you have enough time to get what this body needs," he said smugly and easily pushed past me in a cloud of black, and suddenly, I was pushed out. I couldn't feel my body anymore, and even what I could see and hear felt distant.

"Everyone was gone. Shadows surrounded me," Kaatu replied to Clawdia.

"Stop!" I shouted.

Panic ripped into me. Like fighting invisible ropes, I struggled to take control of my own body. But I knew he meant to keep me here for good, and if I gave up now, he'd do the unthinkable.

The rage that boiled inside me focused my attention, cleared my panic, and started my ability to plan.

I was not going to let this shadow commandeer my body as though he had the right. I wouldn't let him poison the budding relationships I had with my soul mates. Or endanger them on a mission to save his land.

I understood the need to save his people. I'd been rescuing titans for so long to save Tartarus from desolation, but I hadn't done anything so morally gray as to steal someone's body and intend to form a soul bond with his mates.

But if he intended to have control of my body, I would ensure he had no access to my mind. If he wanted to pretend to be me, he would have to do so without my help. I imagined locking away my mind, forming an impenetrable barrier of blood and threads around it. I couldn't be certain whether it would hold, and while he was able to find out that my soul bonds had not been consummated, it was all the information I would allow.

I hope possessing me drains him of enough power that he can't possibly search my mind too.

"But how did you get here?" Clawdia asked, her eyes bright with concern. "Your portal … it looked strange. "

"You don't need to concern yourself with that." My hand waved dismissively, and I hated the pain it caused her.

"Of course I do," she cried out, looking utterly confused and hurt. "I was worried about you. You've been out of it for days. I thought the council were going to try and hurt you because it's impossible that you are here."

"Yes, the protector. He is the one who has closed the portals, correct?" my voice asked.

"Yes … but you already know that."

"This protector. How has he closed the portals? Can it be undone?"

"Why would we want it to be undone?"

"There is a dragon who is stealing magic, yes? I'm trying to think of the next steps the dragon might take."

She eyed us suspiciously. "I think the simplest way to get the portals open again is to kill the protector. I don't know any other way. But maybe we can ask him. I think he's awake now."

My head nodded. "He is being protected, I assume."

"We are on an island that has wards hiding us from anyone looking for him magically. And everyone here wants to ensure his safety, so yes, he's protected."

"And his power affects the natural portals too?"

"How do you know about natural portals?"

"I am the son of gods."

"Oh. Of course. I'm not sure. I'm told they haven't been used since the fall. But it's another question for Sigurd."

"Where is the titan?"

I almost laughed at how easy he was making it for her to figure out that I was not myself. *"I would know the name of my soul mate."*

"Be silent."

Clawdia's face crumbled in concern and all I wanted was to console her. "Titan? You mean Zaide?"

My mouth opened again. "Yes. Where is he?"

"He's just outside. Do you want me to get him?" Clawdia leaned back and moved her feet back to the floor.

My hand struck out to prevent her moving further away. "No," Kaatu said.

She frowned and sighed. "You avoided the question earlier. How did you get here despite the protector's magic and the wards?"

"I cannot tell you." My eye twitched.

Does it do that a lot? Do I have a twitchy eye? I questioned myself, but while I was stuck in the back of my mind, I made a note to watch for that.

"Why not?" Kaatu didn't respond, so she tilted her head and guessed, "Were you spelled?"

"In a manner of speaking," he replied vaguely, but it was enough to reassure her.

Her shoulders relaxed, and she nodded understandingly. "But the way you portaled, it's not something that can be replicated by another? It's only something you can do?"

"Yes." My head nodded, and I got a little dizzy from the strange view.

"Oh, good." She sighed and chuckled in relief. "I can

194

assure the council that we won't be expecting any more surprise guests. No matter how welcome." She smiled, lighting up the entire room with her beauty. "I'm glad you managed to get here, despite the obvious pain it caused you. Waiting until Fafnir was defeated for us all to be together would have been torture."

She squeezed my hand, and more than anything, I wanted to grasp it and pull her closer, to kiss her, in the flesh, finally, and tell her I was also glad to be with them. But I couldn't.

Kaatu was also stunned by her, because he told me, *"She's a beauty. You're lucky to have her as your soul mate."*

While I didn't think he was being disingenuous with his statement, I also believe he wanted to frustrate me. He was seeing the side of her that should have only been reserved for me and her other soul bonds. He was an interloper on a moment that should have been special to us. The start of our relationship. But she wasn't speaking to me. She was talking to him.

"I have two soul mates," I replied, trying to lean into the envy I sensed in his statement.

"I'm not interested in men," he scoffed.

Panic surged as I realized he didn't intend to consummate my bond with Zaide. Only Clawdia. He would try to seduce Clawdia and be cruel to Zaide. My titan soul mate already feared akari and thought the worst of them. It wouldn't be difficult for Kaatu to shut him out, but it would destroy us before we ever started.

And so I vowed to do the opposite. When I fought back control, I would push Clawdia away and keep Zaide close. Even though it would kill a part of my soul to do it.

"Do you feel better now?" Clawdia asked, bringing our attention back to her.

"Yes, of course."

She pursed her lips. "Are you sure? You're acting so strange."

"We've met only a handful of times in a dreamscape. Do you think you know all about me?" Kaatu tried to make us smile, to lessen the biting words, but Clawdia's face dropped, and she stood up.

"Perhaps not." She straightened her shoulders. "And if this is the way you aren't going to act, maybe I don't want to."

Kaatu clenched my fists and jaw as he watched her slam the door behind her. I said nothing but couldn't help feeling smug. *He's not the female-charming seductive shadow he believed himself to be.* My soul mate was no fool, and Kaatu's plan would fail. If I couldn't ensure that myself, I could rely on Clawdia to see through this farce.

I hope.

CHAPTER 17

ZAIDE

J was dishing up afternoon meal items onto plates when Clawdia slammed the door closed behind her and stormed straight toward me, wrapped her arms around me, and buried her head in my chest. I automatically returned her embrace but remained tense at her odd behavior.

"Well, what's the diagnosis, Nurse Clawdia?" Charlie asked lightly but raised his brows at me over her head.

"He's awake," she mumbled.

"Savida told us. Is this not good news?" I asked hesitantly as I stroked her hair.

I wanted to go in and talk to him, assure myself he was well, but Savida told us he was feeding. Although I hoped to get past my aversion to blood and feeding, I knew I couldn't see fangs in my little cat and not feel disgust, anger, and fear. It was still too soon.

"I'm not sure." She sighed and withdrew from my arms to sag onto the sofa. "He still has the black spots, and he's acting strange."

"Strange?" Charlie asked, walking around the sofa to sit

with her. He offered her a biscuit from the packet he held, but she shook her head.

"What's so strange about him?" I asked.

She began counting on her fingers. "He shouted for Savida to leave. He hasn't healed. He has a dark ring around his eyes." She looked at me with a kind of wild desperation in her eyes. "Did he have that before? I can't remember. We can look different in the dreamscape …"

If there was one thing I remembered clearly about my soul mate, it was his eyes. His eyes that I fought so hard against and then to care for. I knew them. And there was no dark ring. "No. Just blood red."

She nodded solemnly and continued her list, "He asked for the 'titan,' as if he'd never met you before. Do you think he's brain damaged?"

"He can't be that brain damaged if he's speaking," Charlie added around a biscuit.

"Something is wrong." She stood up again and twisted her hands with panicked energy. Her voice got higher, and her words came faster as she ranted. "He didn't tell me what happened with the shadows and couldn't tell me how he got here. A spell of some sort prevents him, but I think they've done something to him. He's so strange, and I know we don't know him that well, but my stomach is in knots, and my brain is screaming that something is …"

I took her hands and squeezed them. Her eyes met mine, and I said, "Little Cat, please, calm down. Your worry is probably making Charlie feel sick."

"True story," he garbled around yet another biscuit.

She turned to glare at him. "It could be that he's just eaten half a packet of biscuits."

"Nope, definitely your emotions." He shook his head and smiled, his teeth full of crumbs.

His dramatics did not entertain Clawdia. She snatched

her hands from mine and crossed her arms. "Well, I'm sorry for feeling."

"No one is telling you not to feel," I told her calmly.

"Something is wrong, Zaide," she hissed.

"Perhaps it is," I agreed and pulled her back into my arms. Pressing a kiss to her forehead she sighed and relaxed her arms. "But we can't do anything about it yet. Let us be calm. Let us watch. Wait. And when we can do something, we will."

"I'm sorry," she whispered. "It's all very …" She swallowed before continuing. "I don't feel great. My stomach hurts, and I've got a headache."

Her whimper hurt my heart, and I hugged her tighter. She was so good at looking after others, but she needed someone to look after her.

"Don't be sorry. You are stressed, Little Cat. I was just setting out lunch. Let's feed you and give you something to drink. That should help your headache."

I didn't move immediately, as she seemed content in my embrace. Just as her body started to relax and lean into me, the bedroom door opened, and Baelen wandered out holding a towel. Clawdia pulled away and turned to face him.

"I'd like to shower. Where is the bathroom?" he asked blandly, as though this were an ordinary day and not the first time we had seen each other since shadows attacked us in the dreamscape.

I expected more—something—from him. Relief, maybe, that I was all right and not lost in the dreamscape. Or a smile to reassure me he was all right, but he didn't even meet my eyes. He only looked at Clawdia.

We pointed at the door, and he nodded without saying another word.

"See," she muttered as he closed the door behind him, and she caressed my chest where my heart throbbed with pain. "He didn't even say hello to you, Zaide."

I kept my eyes on the bathroom door. "I noticed."

"He wouldn't do that." She shook her head fiercely. "He wouldn't hurt you like that."

"You don't think he's in his right mind?" I asked as I walked back to the counters.

"I don't know what's happened, but he isn't himself."

"We will have to wait and see, Little Cat. Try not to worry." I handed her a plate while Charlie loaded a video about midwives on his phone for us to watch while we ate.

Clawdia hugged him and pressed a kiss to his stubbled cheek. "How did you know I used to watch this?"

"Because it's so you." He winked and frowned playfully. "We're starting from the beginning, though, so no spoilers please."

We finished an episode and our lunch, and my gaze turned to the bathroom. "Should I make sure he's all right?"

"He's probably struggling to have a shit. He's been asleep for days." Charlie said as he put another biscuit in his mouth. "Poor guy."

"Don't be vulgar, Charlie." Clawdia snatched the biscuits from him. "And stop eating those before you really are sick."

As the kettle clicked and I made tea for my humans, the bathroom swung open. Baelen strode straight back to the bedroom, not glancing our way. His towel around his waist, I could see the dark spots on his skin, but his thread still showed as green. I could see why Clawdia was worried, but I didn't want to upset her further by agreeing.

"What are we going to do?" Clawdia asked in a worried whisper.

"What can we do? We don't know enough yet." I handed her and Charlie the mugs.

"I think you're overreacting slightly," Charlie said as he blew on his tea.

Clawdia's cold silence made his eyes shift to meet hers.

The violet of her iris burned with violent intent. She asked slowly, "I'm overreacting?"

His eyes widened, and he straightened but ignored me as I shook my head. He shrugged and told her, "I just mean he's up and walking. Shouldn't we be celebrating? He was comatose for days, and now he's not."

"Celebrating? Celebrating potential brain damage of our soul mate?" Her voice rose to a shrill shriek.

"I'm just saying—"

"I heard what you said, Charlie." Her voice shook with her fury, and she stood up to hiss down at him. "You think I'm being hysterical."

I'd never seen her so angry, and I don't think Charlie had either, because he tried to back track. "I never said—"

I tried to help. "I don't think Charlie meant—"

But she turned on me, pointing her finger. "Don't you back him up. I know what you are doing, both trying to placate the crazy woman. Keeping things from me. Whispering about your bro code. Well, I'm sick of it. I feel like an outsider in my relationships with you. I'm worried about Zaide getting taken from us and Baelen having spots, and everyone else is acting like it's all fine."

We froze. I didn't realize the effect we were having on her. In trying to comfort her, we were invalidating her feelings and making her feel ignored.

I almost laughed at how similar we were, how our anxieties mirrored each other. I felt left out of the human culture conversations Charlie and Clawdia had and the shared memories they had with each other. But now was not the time to bring that up. My soul pair was hurting.

"Little Cat—"

"No." She held out her hand, her chest heaving and her jaw clenched. "I'm done with this."

"Done with—"

Before Charlie could finish his sentence, Clawdia dissolved until there was only a pile of clothes on the floor where my soul pair had stood and underneath it was a squirming bundle of fur escaping the fabric. In her feline form, she wasted no time in jumping onto the kitchen counter before hoping even higher onto the fridge.

"Little Cat, what are you doing?" I asked.

"Get down from there," Charlie called. "Why are you a cat?"

Clawdia stared balefully down at Charlie before turning her back and licking her paw. I had to smile at her easy frustration of him, even if I didn't like that she felt so annoyed that she'd rather be a cat again.

It reminded me of the first time she turned back. When I thought I'd never have my soul pair because she was so heartbroken. When I thought I'd never talk to her again. It might have only been a few hours, but I the food had tasted even blander and my heart felt empty.

When we realized she could be both human and cat, I promised I'd ensure she was so happy she wouldn't need the comfort of being a cat.

But I'm failing. As I'm failing at everything else.

Charlie continued to rant. "Did you just ignore me? Are you really just going to pretend I'm not here? I'm sorry, okay? I don't think you're crazy, and I'm sorry."

"That doesn't seem very genuine, Charlie," I whispered.

He growled back, "I'd like to see you do better when you're faced with this infuriating demon-cat."

Taking a step toward the fridge, I called softly, "Little Cat, please come down, change back, and talk to us. We didn't know how we were making you feel. We understand you are concerned, and you have every right to be." She huffed but stopped licking her paw, turned, and lay down to stare down at me with those familiar violet eyes. "We are all new to being in a relationship, and it is more complicated when there are more than two of us. We are going to make mistakes, but we all want to support each other. We are here for you, Clawdia. Come down."

"You do the apologies from now on," Charlie whispered.

"Please?" I didn't take my eyes from her, hoping she could see the honest intentions in my eyes.

She glared but sat up. I thought it was a positive sign until her paw *tap, tap, tapped* a small bowl next to her and pushed it straight off the top of the fridge. It shattered with a loud crash across the wooden flooring, pieces of pottery scattered in all shapes and shards. She watched the destruction expressionlessly, huffed again, and turned back around.

"You're going to break shit now? Is that the kind of woman you are? You're telling us you aren't crazy, but you're smashing bowls?" Charlie yelled, outraged.

"Really, Little Cat, this bowl was innocent in our disagreement." I bent to begin picking up the pieces.

Charlie made an exasperated growl and then also bent to help me. "Unbelievable," he muttered. "I feel like I've gone back in time."

"Why do you feel you have traveled back in time?" I asked.

"This is what I put up with every day before you guys arrived. The fucking sass, cheek, and temperamental behavior of a feline." He glared up at the fridge again. "I swear to God, Clawdia, I know you've got a human brain now, so I'm not going to put up with this shit. Change back and explain yourself like a grown-up."

"I think she is a little past the demands now, Charlie."

"She's being so …" He growled again. "How are you so calm right now?"

"If she's ignoring us, and especially ignoring us in her cat form, it's because she needs time. I'm just disappointed she sought to destroy this bowl instead of talking to us." I poured the shards into the bin and saw her sink low, flattening herself along the top of the fridge and curling her tail around herself.

"Ah, the old, 'I'm not angry, just disappointed' adage. That might make her wise up." Charlie chuckled, but I glared at him. He raised his hands. "All right, I'll shut up."

Voice's from outside the medical center alerted us to the presence of others, and I quickly picked up the clothes from the floor and folded the items into small bundles as the door opened.

"Ah," Joseph said as he stepped into the room and spotted us. He was followed by Sigurd and Elizabeth. "We hoped to find you all here. How is your friend?"

"Awake," I informed them.

"And yet Clawdia is in her feline form and ignoring us. Is something wrong?" Elizabeth asked.

"Just an argument. You know how temperamental cats are. Loving the belly rubs one minute, and biting your hand off the next," Charlie told her loudly, and Clawdia quickly turned around to hiss at him. He waved his hand in her direction. "See what I mean?"

"I suggest you stop attempting to irritate her before she really does bite your hand," I mumbled.

Joseph coughed. "Your friend. Has he mentioned how he got here?"

Baelen opened the bedroom door at that exact moment, dressed in the clothes we managed to gather for him. He joined us in the center of the room, the picture of confidence and self-assuredness.

"Unfortunately, I'm unable to say exactly how I got here, but I can assure you there is no way to replicate the process. I'm special." He winked, and I frowned. That very uncharacteristic.

"How fortunate," Joseph replied slowly with narrowed eyes.

Sigurd raised his brow. "I understand you cannot speak of it, but I am so curious to know how you did it. After all, my purpose is to prevent portals."

Baelen shrugged like the entire matter was inconsequential. "You must not have had the blood of the titan gods. As I am their son, I portaled."

Sigurd rubbed his chin. "I did have titan blood."

"A broken titan with half a soul and no power is not the same as a titan of old." Baelen scoffed. "They were gods."

This alarmed me more than any of the other strange behavior I had seen of him, because he hadn't ever referred to me as a broken titan. But his fathers had. *Have they done something to him?* I knew his relationship with them was tempestuous, to say the least, but would they hurt Baelen in this way? But why would they make him behave like this if they wanted him to be with us? *Perhaps they don't.*

But where do the shadows come in?

Regardless, Clawdia was right. This was not our Baelen. Whether brain damaged or under some mystical influence, I needed to observe and work out this problem. This, at least, I could do. My frown deepened, and I sat on the sofa to watch.

Everyone was silent for a period after Baelen's announcement. Sigurd finally said, "I suppose that must be it."

"I'm glad to satisfy your curiosity. I wonder if you might assuage mine." He paused, looking around the room but still not meeting my eyes. "Privately."

What could he possibly want to ask privately of a male he has only just met?

"Of course."

Charlie's eyebrows shot up, and his eyes flicked over to my Little Cat, who still had her back to us but was clearly listening and speaking to Charlie. "I'll come with you."

A dark look crossed Baelen's face like a shadow before it cleared. "Private means—"

Sigurd tilted his head as he interrupted. "Charlie is my distant relative. Anything you have to say can surely be said with family present."

The silence as Baelen considered this echoed. When he eventually muttered, "Of course," and gave a false smile, everyone seemed confused.

Charlie followed them into the bedroom, and voices reverberated through the walls of the cabin.

"Strange," Joseph remarked. "Is he always like that?"

"We are assessing the effect the portal might have had on him," I replied diplomatically. "Did you get all the information you needed from Sigurd?"

"Yes, he confirmed all you told us. It's helpful to know he is a creature of the realms. We hope to find living relatives of other Drakorians who might have information about their hoards."

"Sigurd told us the descendants are dead."

"Nothing truly goes extinct here. We are so accessible by the other realms that we'll never just be a realm of humans."

"And have your teams had any news on Fafnir?"

"Not yet. But with Arabella and Isaac back with their teams, we should have better coordination and better results."

"They've gone already? Where is Alcor?"

"He's gone with them but as a civilian. He is not to be involved in any missions." But the turn of Joseph's lip seemed to suggest he didn't agree with the decision.

I worried for our demon friend. Being so close to the danger and having no recent memories of the woman who betrayed him was a recipe for disaster. I wished I had had the opportunity to speak to him before he left. To assure him he always had a home with us if worse came to worst. I sighed and reminded myself to ask Charlie about getting contact details for them, just in case.

The bedroom door opened, and Charlie, Sigurd, and Baelen stomped out.

"All done?" Joseph asked, not disguising his curiosity.

Sigurd and Baelen remained silent and rigid. Charlie grimaced and replied with an awkward, "Yep."

Sensing the odd energy, Joseph clapped his hands. "Well, I suggest we all leave Sigurd to rest. He certainly needs it." Sigurd gave him a smile and a grateful nod. Joseph looked at Charlie, Baelen, and me with a false smile, which set my teeth on edge. "I wanted to remind you of our meeting yesterday, in which we all agreed to support and fill the wards. With your very rare gifts, I'm sure you will be very helpful in ensuring we are kept safe here. We don't want anyone finding an excuse to throw you off the island." He chuckled, but the threat was made very clear.

Clawdia dropped down from the fridge and walked out of the door, her tale swatting from side to side as she wandered into the green landscape.

Joseph chuckled again. "That's the spirit, Clawdia." He turned back to us and waggled his brows. "You are certainly in the doghouse with that one." He walked slowly after her, still chuckling.

I sighed. "I'll leave your clothes in the cabin, then," I called after her, but she'd already disappeared.

I have much making up to do with her. But I was also a man of action. I wanted to be able to tell her she was right to be concerned, inform her of my suspicions with examples of his behavior, and offer a solution. And that would only happen if I spoke to Baelen myself.

"Charlie, I wondered if you have time for some training today?" Elizabeth asked. "Ingrid has a library here that we have been offered to use."

Charlie glanced at me but nodded. "I don't have any other plans, and my familiar is pissed at me, so I might as well get out from underfoot."

"We can also discuss that." She raised one brow in the way a disapproving mother does. I huffed out a laugh. Charlie might not have had a mother growing up, but Elizabeth was displaying all the same behaviors my own mother had. It sent a pang of longing through my chest.

He widened his eyes and replied sarcastically, "Ah, just what I've always wanted. Advice about women from my birth mother. Another tick off that life goal list."

She left, ignoring him, and he nodded at me as he shut the door behind them.

I was left with my soul mate.

But was it really him?

CHAPTER 18

ZAIDE

*S*igurd looked between us with interest as a cold tension swirled like a frosted window. There were no smiles from my soul mate. He had more interest staring at the protector as though he had the secrets of the realms written on his forehead.

"I'm sure you have much to discuss since you have been apart for so long." Sigurd coughed and bowed his head. "I will leave you to your conversation."

Baelen watched him go with assessing eyes before turning in my direction, still not looking me in the eyes. He smiled widely. A smile I'd never seen before. A smile that seemed sinister somehow. "Am I to join you in your cabin now that I'm well?"

"Are you well?" I raised my brow and crossed my arms.

"Of course I am." He walked to the window and looked out.

"Why won't you look me in the eyes?" I asked as I crowded him.

He scoffed and said, "You are afraid of them." In the

209

reflection of the window, I saw his sneer. "I don't want to make you afraid of me."

"I'm not afraid of you."

If he truly was concerned about my fear of him, as I had been when we first met, then I wanted to assure him. But I also said it to warn whatever was influencing him. Whether that be his fathers or something else, it was clear this person was not the modest, genteel male I knew.

He turned around, and his red eyes met mine. The dark ring around them was like a smudge and shifted the blood red of his iris to a thin line around the pupil. Like the ink splodges on his skin, it seemed to move, retract.

He smiled, and it wasn't the sinister one from before. It was small and soft. "Am I to join you? I understand if I am not welcome. You are all much better acquainted with each other than I am with you."

"You are always welcome, Baelen." The vulnerability in his words made my heart lurch, but I couldn't trust this switch. It was more like Baelen, but he was still a proud male. He wouldn't pout. I continued, "However, there is only one bed. Charlie, Clawdia, and I have been sharing but you may not feel … and there isn't a lot of room."

He shrugged and pushed past me to the sofa. "Is there a comfortable lounge chair like this one? I can stay there. I don't want to be away from my soul mate."

"Soul mates," I corrected with a frown as I followed him.

"Yes." He held up a finger as he picked off lint from the sofa and inspected it. "I want to talk to you about that."

"About what?"

"I don't intend to consummate my bond with you."

My mouth dropped open with surprise, and I flinched back. "What? Of course not. We are still getting to know one another."

"I mean ever."

I sucked in a sharp breath and staggered as though a knife had been plunged right into my heart. My eyes stung but I clenched my jaw as I tried not to show more emotion.

Baelen's head tilted as he watched my expression avidly, a cruel smile playing at his lips. He was enjoying my pain. But I had to believe it wasn't really him who spoke those words. Who wanted to cause me pain. Something strange was afoot, and no matter how hurt I was, I needed to discover what it was.

This can't be Baelen.

It took a few seconds for me to find words. "Is that right?" Although my voice was calm and unaffected, my shallow, shaky breath betrayed my hurt.

"I only want Clawdia," he clarified.

"May I ask why?"

He shrugged as though it was unimportant and he was only humoring me. "She is female. Beautiful. A soul mate to be proud of."

My eye twitched. *Do not react. Do not show your hurt. This is a lie.*

"You did not say any such thing in the dreamscape."

"Why would I? Clawdia cares for you. Hurting you would ruin my chances with her, and since she is the only one I want, I pretended I wanted you."

I bit my tongue and paused before nodding. "Why do you think I wouldn't tell her now?"

"You?" He laughed, the sound loud and obnoxious. "Who keeps secrets from her? Whispers with Charlie? You coddle her and are a masochist. You'll allow her happiness even if you never find yours. The self-sacrificing nature of a healing soul."

"And if I do tell her?"

He narrowed his eyes and hesitated for a moment before

shrugging. "It's not going to stop us from coming together. We are meant to be."

"And we are not?"

"No one can love someone's entire soul. There is always a dark, unlovable part, which is where all the bad and the trauma and the unkind words have been kept. You are that side of the soul, Zaide. Were you female, I'd still not want you. But at least I'd be able to fuck you."

Although I thought I had steeled myself against the effects of his cruelty, doubt and hurt crept in.

Maybe he really doesn't want me. Maybe he was acting before in the dreamscape. Maybe this is the real him. Who am I to assume that the son of the gods would love me? Why would an akari ever treat me with kindness? Perhaps the dreamscape is just that ... a dream.

I closed my eyes and clenched my fists as I tried to shake off the negative thoughts. *Ignore the pain. Don't doubt yourself or Clawdia. Seek out the truth.*

Baelen picked up a cup and swirled the contents, inhaling the smell of the leftover tea inside, and as I watched him, I reflected on what he said.

Is it a message for me? Is he talking about himself? Is this person the dark part of his soul instead of something causing his behavior?

Finally, I said, "You are not a cruel person, Baelen. What has happened to you? I want to help you."

"Help me?" He raised an eyebrow and smiled.

"You're my soul mate whether you want it or not. I will always help you."

His eyes narrowed, and he put the cup down to consider me. "If I asked you to do something for me, something dangerous, would you do it?"

Something dangerous? I frowned as worry crept through me like a vine. It was confusing that he would ask, especially considering he was being cruel and pushing me away. If I told him no, would he try to use Clawdia in his dangerous task instead? And yet, he was my soul mate, if he needed my help, I would never reject him.

"I would. As long as Clawdia wasn't involved."

The smile that crept across his face was slow and wide. "That's very good to know."

I tensed to prevent a shudder but asked, "Will you let me help? Can you tell me what happened?"

He waved me off. "You can help when I want you to help. At the moment, you aren't needed."

"But am I needed by the real Baelen?" I asked, praying that pushing him would force some kind of telling reaction.

But he scoffed. "Are you really so desperate for me that you'll believe I am a different person instead of the truth I am giving you?" He approached me slowly, disgust clear on his face and giving me flashes of my akari master with the same expression. His voice was low but firm as he said, "I do not want you. The Fates had no choice in making us soul mates, but you are the side dish I can pick up or leave, not the main meal."

My heart couldn't take much more. Just talking to him was like volunteering to be flayed alive. But it was an interesting analogy, and it made me ask, "Do you eat, Baelen?"

"Of cour–No, only blood."

"You can't enjoy meals even though you are half titan?" I asked, clarifying again.

"Apparently not," he mumbled.

I wasn't sure what to make of that. I didn't know the correct answer, but his replies were strange enough to make me believe more firmly that this wasn't my soul mate. And if it was, then he was under someone else's influence. I just needed to prove it.

"Take me to the cabin," Baelen demanded. "I'm tired and I'd like to rest."

* * *

AFTER TAKING Baelen back to the cabin, where he made himself comfortable on my side of the bed and waved me away as if I were a servant, I left the cabin at a jog. Away from everyone, I had time to process my feelings. And soon, the hurt and pain turned into anger that burned brightly inside me. I needed to find a way to release it or risk doing something I'd later regret.

How dare someone turn him against me? As though things aren't complicated enough, the Fates want to take away the joy I might find with my soul mate too?

I cursed under my breath as I found myself running deep in the wooded forest of the island, twigs slapping me as I passed. My speed increased as my legs pumped in time with my heart. I needed to get lost. To be away from everyone. To break down where no one could see. To punch and kick and cry at the turbulent emotions twisting inside me.

My mind was a mess. Daithi's vision, the slow progression of finding Fafnir, and my own helplessness in it all already occupied a huge part of my mind. And now Baelen's cruel words filled the empty spaces in my thoughts until they were all I could think about. Until they consumed me.

Perhaps that is why I get captured. I throw myself at the hunters in a desperate attempt to end this torture.

Panting, I came to a small clearing where a large tree stood in the center. Its roots were as big as the trunks of other surrounding trees and rose in waves and dipped under the ground. I approached it slowly and swallowed.

Then, clenching my fist, I pulled back my arm and punched it. Hard. I cried out as my fist smashed into the wood and splintered the bark. The branches shook above me, and leaves dropped in a shower. But it was cathartic. All my built-up rage had an outlet, and I battered at the trunk of this old tree. Repetitively. Rhythmically. One punch after the other. Bellowing. Roaring. Until all the poisonous thoughts had been pushed back and blocked out and all I could focus on was my movement.

Breathing hard and tired enough to feel my aching body, I hugged the tree, leaned my head against the trunk, and closed my eyes. It had been a long time since I had exerted myself in such a way. Sweat dripped down my back, and my fists were broken and bleeding. But I felt numb. And that was better than hurt and angry and confused and scared.

Eventually, I moved to sit at the trunk of the tree, one leg bent up while the other stretched out over the grass as I watched the birds high in the branches and glimpsed the fluffy white clouds passing by between the gaps in the canopy.

Timid steps approached, and I knew who it was without even looking.

"Go away, Clawdia."

"Oh. Am I interrupting? I'm sorry." My gaze moved from the sky with a sigh and focused on my soul pair. She hugged her middle nervously but stared at my hands with a concerned frown before quickly kneeling next to me and picking my hand off my thigh. "Zaide? What have you been doing? Why does your hand look like this?"

"I'm fine." I snatched my hands away, and she flinched.

I shouldn't have been angry with her, and I'd later regret how I made her afraid for even a second, but I'd reached my limit. Despite relieving some of my anger, I hadn't calmed enough to cover my true emotions. Everything I'd ever repressed came to wait just under the surface of my skin. It made me itchy and irritable.

"You don't look fine," she whispered, her violet eyes big and sad.

I looked away. "Why are you here?"

"I came to explain. I ran into Natasha. She listened to me rant about the two of you and then offered me some good advice. She made me realize that I am not angry with you at all. I'm frustrated with everything, and Baelen not behaving like himself just tipped me over the edge. But that is no excuse. I'm sorry for being rude and smashing the bowl."

I listened but didn't react. She needed to talk, but I didn't have the emotional capacity to absorb or respond to her apology.

She licked her lips and knotted her hands. "I know pushing the bowl wasn't acceptable, and it's the last time I'll ever do that. I don't want to be destructive when I'm angry. I know how terrifying that can be, and while I'm sure you and Charlie would be the last people to be scared of me, I don't want you walking on eggshells and hiding the nice plates when I'm in a mood.

The truth is that I'm still getting used to being human again. It's been a baptism of fire, and I think this island, where it's safe, has just allowed me to process it." She sighed. "I'm still making excuses. I'm sorry. Truly. I'm sorry you and Charlie were the ones who were mistreated, and I'm going to do my best to recognize when I'm misdirecting my anger and stop before I hurt you. I don't want to hurt you. Although, I think Charlie enjoys when I'm sassy Clawdicat. It reminds him of the good old days." She laughed a little, but it couldn't bring a smile to my face.

All the hurt and anger flared back up from one small phrase. I sneered, "The good old days before I came to the human realm?"

Her mouth dropped open, and panic flared in her eyes. "What? No! Zaide, I'm trying to apologize—"

216

"For what? You can do no wrong, Clawdia." I stood up to get away from her as small resentments came bubbling to the surface and flooded out before I could stop them. "I'll love you even if you throw a bowl at my head and wish for my death. I'd lie on the floor bleeding, loving you, and hope my end gave you what you needed."

"I would never—" She shook her head and blinked rapidly. "I can't believe what I'm hearing. Do you believe I do not love you with the same amount of devotion?"

I crossed my arms. "You have other males to consider."

"So this is about jealousy?" Her voice rose as she matched my anger.

Why am I saying any of this? I'm not jealous.

"No." I sighed, covered my face, and took a deep breath, attempting to calm myself.

"Then what is this? I know you were disappointed with me—" Her voice broke, and she swallowed. "—but I didn't think you were so angry that you'd believe I don't love you."

I shook my head but still couldn't look at her as I began pacing. "I'm so angry. I'm so angry about everything. Not you. I-I am becoming a worse version of myself. I'm losing control, and you will see."

"I will see what?"

"I try every day to be calm and collected. Someone you can rely on. I let you down when we were in the cave. I fell into my memories and dreams as our bond was formed. But I try."

"Of course you do. I never—"

"I want to be someone who gives you peace. The kind of peace you gave me the moment I saw you, the moment I recognized the missing part of my soul."

"You do. Zaide, I'm sorry if what I said made you feel—"

"If I cannot give you peace, if I cannot keep you happy as a human, if I cannot get along with your other soul bonds, I am useless to you. Isn't that true?" I stopped dead and stared at her, panting.

"No." She grasped my hands and repeated firmly, "No."

"I cannot offer you my concerns or worries because I am holding yours," I told her, and her frown deepened. "I temper Charlie's behavior, and he helps support me so we can support you."

She dropped my hands and sighed. "Then you have a partnership with Charlie and not one with me."

"You are not to worry, not to fear. You have had enough of that already." I sat back down at the base of the tree.

"And you don't?" She paused, watching me as I picked at the grass. "You told me you wanted a family. You want people who will never leave you. Who love you unconditionally. You want back what you lost."

"Yes."

"Families protect one another, yes, but families support each other. You are letting Charlie support you but not me? How am I supposed to feel about that? Do you not trust me?"

My head snapped up, and I glared. "Do you trust me? You left and didn't wake me. Didn't trust me to keep you safe as you stood against him."

"That wasn't about trust. That was about an akari seer making me believe that if anyone came with me, they would be killed."

Logically, I knew that already. But evidently, I couldn't stop myself from spewing all my repressed emotions.

She kneeled in front of me and placed a hand on my knee. "I don't understand where this has come from. We are going around in circles. Please. I want to help us both. Can you explain what's going on in your head?"

"I'm ... angry."

"I see that. Is this about Daithi's vision?" she asked.

"In part," I admitted. "I feel ... useless. I'm awaiting this fate with no plan or hope. I lie awake all night thinking about how the council does not plan to do anything about the hunters and how they have still not found Fafnir. How Sigurd seems uninterested in taking up his role and ending him. All of which I cannot do anything to assist with. So when you explained your fears about Baelen and I saw his behavior, I thought I should try to work out the reason why."

"You believe me about Baelen?" She smiled, and hope filled her eyes.

I nodded. "He was cruel."

"Cruel?" Her face fell. "How? What did he do?"

"He told me he didn't want me." My lip trembled, and my voice cracked. I coughed. "He only wants you and lied in the dreamscape so you would like him. He said I wouldn't tell you because I coddle you."

"That's not true!" she exclaimed. "Well, you do coddle me, but Baelen wants you."

"I know. I hope I know," I whispered, "But he almost made me believe he didn't. He said some things …"

"What things?"

"They don't bear repeating."

"Zaide, my love, I'm so sorry." She pulled me into her arms, her hands and chest cradling my head. "I can't imagine hearing all that. No wonder you are so upset."

"I don't think he meant it. I think there is something at force here, magic or an influence or something, but it still cuts me to the core to hear his voice and see his lips say those things," I mumbled into her shoulder.

"We will work it out, my love. This is not yours to bear alone. We do this together." She stroked my hair, and for a moment, I let her, enjoying the sensations.

But I soon pushed away with a sigh. If she truly wanted to know what was in my head, I needed to be honest and allow her to support me.

"We are together, but we are not. You are making friends. Charlie is busy with his mother. Savida and Daithi are trying to make things up to me, but their betrayal still weighs heavily on my mind. I have chosen to forgive them, but I cannot forget. I feel as though there is a noose tightening around my neck and I'm alone."

She must have read something in my eyes because she didn't try to invalidate my feelings by saying I wasn't alone. She simply nodded, took my hand, and stroked her thumb gently over mine in slow caresses while she thought of her response.

"I don't think this is your main reason for helping, because I know you care for Baelen, but are you trying to decipher what's happened to him because you think you are useless to us if you do not?"

I nodded once, a small jerk of my head, and explained, "I need something to keep my mind off the impending doom I face, something to stop me from collapsing and pouring my fear into you. And I've failed. I'm failing you." I closed my eyes and leaned my head back, trying to keep tears at bay.

A gentle hand brushed my face, and I peeked through my lashes to meet somber violet eyes.

"Perhaps I've not made it clear or have been too weak for you to feel like you can lean on me, but I want your fears and worries. As much as I adore you for the peace you give me, it's not sustainable. Your actions and thoughts, especially the negative ones, shouldn't be repressed." She ran a finger down my face again and smoothed the scar under my eye. "This mask of perfection is not required for me to love you. It's not required for anyone to love you. When Charlie is grumbling and huffing, does that make me love him any less? Of course not. And despite all his misgivings, Daithi is still loved dearly by Savida. And while you might be disappointed in Daithi, it's because you love him. Love doesn't fade with bad behavior. If you want to scream and cry and shout and rage, I want you to." She gave me a wan smile. "We are two sides of the same coin. Here you are destroying your knuckles on a tree to get rid of the same angry and scared energy which made me push that bowl. Do you still love me?"

"Always."

She pressed a soft kiss to my lips and continued quietly, "I know how you feel. I was so frightened that there was something inside me that made me unlovable. I tried so hard to be good for my parents, and yet they failed me. It took becoming a cat to help change the beliefs they gave me. And if I could turn you into a cat so you could learn that too, I would."

"I don't think being a cat would help any more than you already have, Little Cat."

"You are not and should never strive to be perfect. But you are perfect for me, to me, in all your multifaceted parts. You are loved. So loved. And I don't want you holding yourself back because you fear rejection. As Charlie said, there is no divorce for us. Whatever happens, we are a team for life. So, share everything with me, as I share with you."

My jaw clenched as memories of the past flashed in my mind, and I explained, "When I was a slave, being loud or expressive made me a target for the Akari master. He would take blood and give it to his friends. If I made too much noise, I'd be made to fight in the rings for days without rest. Quiet was safest. I was silent for a year after Daithi and Savida saved me. I didn't want to say anything that would make them regret bringing me with them. I was not interested in roaming the realms, but I wanted Savida to be happy."

"You do not need to be quiet with me, love. And you are not useless. I understand if you want to be busy so you are not concentrating on the vision. But you don't need to do anything to be of value. You are already essential to me. My heart and soul," she whispered against my lips. Her lip twitched upward, and she said, "However, I do think we both need to work out better ways of expressing our fear and anger."

I nodded firmly, furious with myself for my behavior. "I do not wish to frighten you with my anger."

"That isn't what I meant." She looked down shyly with her lips pouted. "We should find better ways of releasing our anger … together."

I was still confused as she stood up in front of me. But as she reached for the edge of her shirt and pulled it up over her head, my mouth dropped open as understanding hit.

"Little Cat?" I whispered, "Here?"

CHAPTER 19

CLAWDIA

I don't know what came over me. Seduction wasn't something that came naturally to me, and even though my body burned for him, my pussy aching for the stretch and pleasure he could give me, I still felt scared and embarrassed.

As I tossed my borrowed shirt onto an upended root, I bit my lip, watching Zaide's face carefully for a sign. He remained frozen.

If he doesn't move soon, I'll have to put my shirt back on and bury my head in the sand for all eternity.

Goosebumps pebbled my bare chest, and my arms tensed to stop the instinct to cover up. Just as I was about to chalk it all up to a bad experience, he moved. His eyes darkened. He slowly rose to his feet and then pulled me into his arms so fast our chests collided. My hardening nipples brushed the cotton of his t-shirt, and I shivered as I wrapped my arms around his neck. I pressed a kiss to his chin and nipped along his jaw.

"Are you sure?" he asked. Lifting my chin, he assessed my eyes.

"Yes."

His eyes were bloodshot and puffy from holding back tears. His knuckles were still bleeding and swollen. He was sweaty, and his muscles bulged, veins popping with the recent exertion. I shouldn't have found any of it attractive. But I did.

The demonstration of strength was probably to blame for my desire. Females were designed to look for strength and not just in how he'd made visible dents in the tree trunk. He wanted to protect me, even from himself. He held himself back despite all the emotion he carried. But when I told him he could trust me, could rely on me to love him through it all, he let me in. And that required a different kind of strength. One I could appreciate even more.

"You want us to make love angry?" His brow furrowed as he stroked my jaw.

I took his hand and kissed his knuckles as I whispered, "I want you. Angry. Sad. Hurt. Afraid. I want you."

"You do not need to prove that to me. I believe you," he replied. But his voice was low with desire, his eyes fixated on my lips as his other hand moved up my ribs so his thumb rested under my breast.

I shook my head. "I want to. We should let go. We should do everything we want, even if it scares us." The longing in his eyes gave me the courage to lower his hand from my lips to my breast. A whimper escaped me as his fingers flexed, squeezing slightly. "We should be everything to each other."

"Little Cat," was all he managed before his lips crashed into mine.

His hands moved from my chest to my behind as I reached for the bottom of his shirt and began pulling it up over his defined abs and pectorals, which I lovingly stroked. He took over, quickly throwing his shirt into the surrounding grass. He reached for my leggings as I reached for his trousers. We managed to get them halfway down before our lips collided together again. We were ravenous for each other, kissing hard as our hands roamed, caressing, scratching, and pinching at bare skin.

His erection was huge and jumped against my stomach as I bit into his lip. He groaned, and the sound set me alight. Liquid desire coated the inside of my thighs, and I clenched them to feel something. Anything. I whimpered.

He broke away, as breathless as I was, his lips shiny and swollen and his eyes burning. He gripped my hips and turned us, and then spun me, so I was pressed into the tree trunk, the bark harsh and unforgiving against my sensitive skin and nipples. But it was exactly the sensation I wanted. Needed. I craved the pleasure and pain, the reward and punishment.

His lips caressed the shell of my ear and I shivered. "Are you ready for me, Little Cat?"

I felt like I was. I wanted him so much. But he was so big. *What can it hurt if we just forgo the foreplay?*

"Yes. Please. Zaide, I want you."

I wiggled against him, and he stopped me, squeezing my hips and pressing me more firmly against the tree. His large body surrounded me, protected me from the chill in the wind, but being so confined made me even more needy.

He pressed my hands flat against the bark and said, "Do not move your hands." His voice was a low growl, and the command made me shudder.

His fingers spread my arousal up to coat my clit. I arched my back and tightened my thighs, whimpering as I felt his large finger surging through my folds.

When his finger pressed at my entrance, he demanded, "Open for me, Little Cat."

"I am." I wriggled again, bearing down on his finger.

"You aren't." He spread my lips, and I spread my legs a much as I could while my leggings circled my ankles like manacles. His long, thick digit finally sank deep inside me, and I moaned, my forehead pressed into the bark as I desperately rode his hand. "You're so small, and I don't want to hurt you."

I shook my head and whined, "Hurt me. I want to feel you stretch me. I want to feel it burn. I want you to hold me against this tree and fuck me so hard you hit my cervix with every thrust. Please, Zaide. I need you."

He stopped moving, and I felt the hiccup in his breath. "You are going to kill me."

I smiled, unable to stop my pride at being able to affect him so much, and sassed, "Not before we cum, I hope."

"If you want hard, Little Cat ..." He caressed my back before he pulled his finger out and spanked me. Not my backside. My pussy. I gasped, and sparks flashed behind my eyes. "I can give it to you hard."

His voice was calm and controlled, and it didn't feel fair that he was still composed while I felt so completely wild. So, I started talking in an attempt to make him as impassioned as I.

"I want you to mark me. I want you to see me, see the bruises and the bite marks you put on my body, and know I'm yours. That you did that to me. I want to feel you tomorrow. I want my pussy so open to you that you could slip inside me at any time, for the rest of the day, as though I was made just for you and your pleasure."

"Gods, Clawdia. Your mouth." His teeth bit onto my neck just hard enough to make a mark and hurt for a second, until he peppered the imprint with kisses.

He lined his cock up at my entrance and pressed into me. Our groans were loud and synchronized as he filled me. As much as I wanted him, it was a struggle taking his cock in this position and without much foreplay. But I loved the burn. It was perfect. When his pelvis pushed against my backside, I gagged, swearing I could feel him in my throat, he was so deep. His hand pressed against my pelvis, tilting me in just the right way for him to thrust again, hard and fast, while my clit nudged against his palm.

"Is this what you wanted, Little Cat? My big cock forcing your small pussy open."

I was mindless with pleasure and whimpering. It was exactly what I wanted. Despite desperately wanting to chase the orgasm coming my way, my movement was restricted by the leggings around my ankles, the male at my back, and my hands, which had been ordered to stay on the tree. I was unable to move, and for some reason, that only made me more desperate.

"Zaide, Zaide, Zaide!" I called on repeat. Every thrust made my breasts swing, and my nipples grazed the bark in a tantalizing brush of pain.

"Give me your pleasure, Little Cat, so I can spill inside you and mark your insides."

It was enough that I immediately cried out, screaming, my whole body tightening as pleasure wracked and ruined me. Stars burst behind my eyes in violent explosions, and the whole world fell silent. All I could hear was my heart. My legs were shaking as I came back to earth and moaned when Zaide's release flooded me, filling me as he also cried out.

He soon pulled his softening cock out of me, and I gasped as his come poured out of me. I shook a leg free of my leggings so I didn't ruin them, and he turned me and lifted me into his arms, hugging me tightly to his chest. I sighed, relaxing into him, nuzzling into his neck, and wrapping my legs around his waist.

"I don't have the words," he said quietly as he continued to catch his breath.

I licked my lips and shook my head. "Neither do I. That was incredible."

He chuckled and nodded his agreement. He combed my hair out of my face and wiped my forehead. "We look wild."

"Your braid is a complete mess," I told him as I pulled it through my hand, trying to smooth and clean it.

"We were wild, Little Cat. And it was unbelievable. I love you." He kissed my forehead, and despite all we had done, despite the fact that I was naked, wide open, and in his arms, it felt like the most intimate touch. Love lightened my heart.

"And I love you." I held his face in my hands and kissed his nose. "I think this is a much better way of releasing anger."

"I agree." He smirked. His eyes trailed to my neck, and his expression faltered. "Although Charlie might be concerned about those bruises. I'm sorry."

"Don't apologize. They are war wounds, and I'm proud of them." I raised my brow and smiled smugly. I also took the time to sneakily push power into his threads to heal his knuckles.

"You should be. You worked hard for them."

"I'm glad you think so."

We chuckled together, and after a slow, lingering kiss, Zaide put me down, retrieved my shirt, and helped me put it back on.

"I need a shower," I remarked. "I also said I'd go to see Karin about adding power to the wards. Do you want to come with me?"

He shook his head as he dressed. "No, I need to find Charlie and get some help on what could have happened to Baelen."

"Without a shower?" I asked.

"I'm not ready to wipe away the evidence just yet. Let me have this." He kissed my forehead as I carefully pulled my underwear and leggings up.

"You can have whatever you want. Always," I told him.

And some primal part of me was glad he would be walking around with my mark on him, just as I had his marks on me.

Considering Daithi's vision, it might be all I had of him soon.

* * *

"I WONDERED where you had gotten to," Natasha called as I approached. She was sitting outside of the medical center on the wooden step and stood to greet me. "You look … Is that dirt on your cheek?" She gasped and waggled her brows.

I rolled my eyes. I didn't have to see myself to know I was covered in dirt. And probably walking strangely.

"Yes. I'm just going to have a shower, and then you can take me to the wards. I haven't forgotten." I walked past her, heading to my cabin, but she grasped my wrist and tugged me toward the hill instead.

"No need to shower on our account. It won't take long," she said cheerfully.

Easy for her to say when she isn't the one with cum running down her leg.

"Oh, but—" I tried to pull out of her grip. "I really need to —" She wouldn't let me go, and I was already too tired from the day to fight anymore. I sagged and let her drag me along.

"You went to apologize?" Natasha asked with a knowing smile.

"Yes," I replied.

"And?"

"We had a really good heart-to-heart," I hedged as we neared the top of the hill and the large house.

"Looks like you had a really good penis-to-vagina too." She raised a brow and smirked.

"Ah Satan!" I exclaimed dramatically. Natasha laughed

boisterously at my use of her naughty name, and I smiled despite the embarrassed blush covering my cheeks.

"You should just tell me exactly what happened since I am living vicariously through you," she suggested and guided me past the house, toward a shed further on.

"I can't tell you. But it was very good." I gave her a coy smile, and her eyes widened.

"That is so cruel, Clawdia." She pouted. "No one likes a tease."

I opened my mouth to respond, but behind us, a door slammed, and Karin stormed out of the house. We stopped as we waited for her to catch up with us, but her mind must have been somewhere else, because she furiously muttered at the ground and stomped until she saw us and changed her demeanor. Her foot missed a step, but her shoulders relaxed, and she managed a smile.

Natasha called, "Karin, we have a sacrifice for your wards."

"Her wards?" I asked. *Why are they hers?*

"Karin covets them," Natasha pretended to whisper but spoke loud enough for Karin to hear.

Karin narrowed her eyes at her cousin but smiled at me. Her voice was light and breezy when she said, "I just like to make sure they will never falter."

Natasha explained with a roll of her eyes, "She manages the schedule of who is supposed to top up the wards and when. She takes her job very seriously."

Manages the schedule? Does she not top them up herself?

I thought it impolite to clarify, so instead, I asked, "Are you all right? You seemed angry when you left the house."

"I'm fine." She smiled, but something I couldn't decipher flashed in her eyes. "I can't wait to see your magic and how the wards respond to it."

Karin opened the door to the shed, and I stepped in to see

a salt pentagram surrounded by lit candles on the wooden floor.

I swallowed nervously. "So, how do I help?"

While I wanted to help and be of use to the wards keeping us hidden, I wanted a shower more, so this needed to be over and done with fast.

Karin shut the door behind us and waved her hand over the salt. "This pentagram links directly to the wards. If you step inside, you should be able to push power into them and all their places across the island."

"That's it?" I asked with surprise.

"Told you it doesn't take long." Natasha smiled. "I do it in about two minutes."

I stepped into the center square, settled on the ground, then crossed my legs. "I just ... push ... power?"

"That's right." Karin said, watching me avidly. I hesitated, and the confusion must have been written on my face because Karin sighed. "You're a familiar. Have you forgotten that you can give power? It's in your nature."

I didn't like her tone but decided against snapping because I wanted to get it over and done with before I checked on Baelen and had a nap. The day felt never-ending.

Getting comfortable, I took a deep breath, closed my eyes, and focused on the well of magic that lived in my center before gently pushing it out from my hands and into the salt.

A flash of white light burst from the pentagram as my magic was absorbed, and I gasped, my eyes flying open. My observers were standing open-mouthed. *Was that not normal?* The pentagram had formed a thin, clear barrier around it, which reminded me of the way Winnie had trapped and drained Savida of his fire. As I mentally made that connection, my eyes widened, and something from underneath me seemed to hook onto my hands and pull more magic from me than I offered.

231

The sickening sensation reminded me so much of Fafnir's touch that I flinched away. Or I tried to. My hands were stuck on the ground.

"What's happening?" I called to Karin and Natasha, a little bit hysterical as the flashes of my past surged to the surface of my mind. "I can't move my hands. It's just taking more magic. What should I do?"

"What?" Natasha's eyes widened, and she looked to Karin for help.

"It's all right," Karin replied calmly. "It just means the wards like you. They should release you soon."

But my panic was overwhelming, and I began feeling dizzy and nauseous. I didn't know if that was because of the draining or the memories, but I quickly reminded myself never to offer to do this again. I groaned, closed my eyes, and said, "I feel sick."

"It's never done that before, and she feels sick," I heard Natasha whisper furiously. "How do we get her out?"

"Don't touch it, Natasha!" Karin shouted. "We'll lose the magic."

"She doesn't look well. You need to get her out. Now."

Like a light turned out, suddenly the pressure holding my hands and drawing magic was gone. The barrier had vanished, and the room was as it was before. Except I was confused, drained, panting, and unable to walk.

Natasha rushed toward me and gripped my forearms as I sagged. "Are you okay?"

I blinked. "I'm all right. Just shaken. I won't be doing that again in a hurry."

"Sorry. It's never done that before," she said as she helped me up.

Karin beamed at me as I hobbled out of the pentagram. "Well done, Clawdia. That was such a huge amount of magic and power. I can't believe you hold so much in your body. You're the perfect familiar."

It was similar to how Winnie would praise me for helping her with her spells and giving her magic, but it made me uncomfortable. And it bothered me that Karin seemed to only value me for what I, as a familiar, could give a witch. While I used to feel tired after helping Winnie, I'd never felt sick before. Something about all this felt wrong.

I nodded at Karin and asked Natasha in a small voice, "Can you help me back to the cabin?"

I BARELY LOOKED AT BAELEN, Daithi, or Savida as I walked into the cabin. I didn't question why they were there. I headed straight into the bathroom before stripping off my clothes and hoping into the shower. I turned the temperature up to scorching and let the water wash over my neck. After the short walk back in the fresh air, I no longer felt sick, and the extreme fatigue had faded, but throbbing over my eyes told me there was a headache imminent. I used the extreme temperature of the shower to head it off.

I tried not to think about the strange sensation of the wards or how upset Zaide had been or how Baelen wasn't acting like himself. I only wanted to calm down under the hot spray, wash, and go for a nap. The fatigue, both mental and physical, started to hit the moment I got warm.

Stepping out of the shower, I wrapped myself in a large, fluffy towel and wiped the condensation from the mirror. I filled a cup of water from the tap and greedily drank the ice-cold water. It was one of the sensations I loved when since becoming human again, so I did it as often as I could. Cold water after being in warm water was so refreshing.

My stomach cramped suddenly, and I tensed with the

pain of it. *What now? Haven't I been through enough emotions today? I can't be a cat again, Zaide will have another breakdown.*

As I pressed a hand to my stomach, I frowned in confusion as it cramped again. Almost like I'd eaten something that disagreed with me, my stomach rumbled, but then I felt a swoosh like I'd just wet myself and knew exactly what was happening.

But how? I'm a familiar?

I sat on the toilet and wiped myself and saw, as I expected, blood.

I'm menstruating again? How? Why?

Unable to do anything else, I tided myself up and washed my hand, staring at myself in the mirror as I tried to work out how I felt about this development. It meant I was functioning like a normal woman and not a familiar. It meant I was a healthy woman. It meant I could have children one day.

I had a flash of an image, three little boys, one with yellow eyes and scales, one with golden skin and blue eyes, and one dark skin and red eyes. And a baby, a girl, a bow in her golden hair but nothing else indicating who her father was. I blinked, and just as suddenly as they came, they were gone.

What was that? A vision?

Despite the confusion, I was bereft. My stomach rolled as emotions hit me like a train, and I sat on the lip of the bath as tears welled in my eyes. I took a deep, shaky breath as I closed my eyes to focus, to bring them back, to work out what that was and how I'd seen it, but nothing happened.

The one little boy had scales. I didn't know what that meant, but it made me sick with anxiety.

If this is how Daithi feels every time he has a vision, it's no wonder he's miserable. I felt awful.

Despite all the questions and fears around the sudden vision and my period, one thing was certain. Those children were mine, and even though I only glimpsed them for a moment, I loved them so much. I wanted to see them again. My heart was full at the thought of meeting them and watching them grow up.

Thoughts about their fathers and how they would also love their children made me stare off into space, dreaming and smiling to myself.

If that was the future, then it is a bright one. No matter what we have to face, I should remember their faces.

Blinking out of my daydreams and thoughts, I realized I was bleeding rather heavily into the bath. I cleaned myself up again and wiped the bath down before my stomach reminded me I needed painkillers. I picked some out of the bathroom cupboard, popped open the tabs, and threw them in my mouth, following it up with water from the tap.

The pain and suffering women had to deal with for a week of every month was barbaric. But why would I allow myself to suffer when I could just be a cat?

Closing my eyes, I attempted to change forms, but nothing happened.

I can't turn into my familiar form?

Trying to stop the sudden anxiousness from over-whelming me, I took a deep breath and tried again. But still, nothing happened.

I can't be a cat again? Ever? Or just during my cycle?

My connection to Charlie hummed between us, our familiar bond, alive and well. *But is it temporary? Am I going to stop being a familiar? Am I turning more human? Can a human have a familiar bond?*

All I cared about was whether I'd lose Charlie. While never being a cat again would be sad, I prepared myself for that eventuality when I first became human again. But not having my bond with Charlie…It would kill me. If whatever was happening to me didn't kill me first.

But I'd been given hope that we'd survive whatever was happening through the vision of the children. I can't have children if I'm dead. *And perhaps I do lose our familiar bond, but I don't lose Charlie. He loves me. He wouldn't leave me.*

Taking deep calming breaths, I mentally planned how I was going to tell the others.

I screamed when the door suddenly banged open, and the lock, which I had drawn across it, pinged into the shower curtain. Baelen's chest heaved as he stared at me, red eyes swirling and fangs protruding.

CHAPTER 20

BAELEN

*M*y hands wrapped around a cup I couldn't feel. Kaatu examined it, my fingers following the pattern. He'd been touching everything like that as he walked around the cabin and picked up items. Although he didn't say so to me, from what I saw of his realm, I assumed it had been a long time since he'd seen anything like the things in the human realm.

My head almost always remained facing the window, my eyes looking longingly at the greenery. I could sense the urge he had to explore and touch things outside, but for some reason, he decided to stay indoors, where Zaide had left us.

I would feel sorry for Kaatu, but the longer I remained hidden in the back of my mind, the harder it was to fight him for control of my body. I felt weak and beaten down, which was only made worse when I saw the devastation on Zaide's face when Kaatu spoke those vile words to him. Denied him. I'd screamed and screamed for him to stop, to just leave things be so there was something in our relationship to be salvaged when this nightmare was over, but I don't think even Kaatu could hear me, I'd been so pushed out.

My vow to prevent Kaatu from having any knowledge of me had also been broken when Zaide asked about food. Kaatu panicked when I wouldn't respond to him and so pushed himself into my mind in the blink of an eye. If I had control of my body, I imagined I would have shaken with anger and nausea. Instead, I was a ghost of myself, trapped in my mind.

It's hard not to feel hopeless when things look so bleak.

"Stop your complaining back there. This is going to end soon, and we'll all get what we want." Kaatu rolled my eyes as he paced the room.

He could hear me, so perhaps he was weakening. Or bored. Or simply ignored me as I tried to save my soul bond.

"What makes you believe this is about to end?"

"You are a handsome male with teeth that give a female pleasure. It's only a matter of time before she falls into your arms."

Despair filled me. If she fell into my arms when it wasn't me at the helm … I couldn't imagine a worse betrayal for either of us.

Kaatu continued, oblivious, *"And the protector assured us that the natural portals aren't affected by him. I'm moments away from saving my realm."*

"I'd be happy for you, but you've taken my body, destroyed my relationship with my soul mate, and intend to rape the other."

"Rape? I won't rape her. She'll want it." He stopped moving, and his voice was shocked.

"She isn't consenting to sex with you. She believes you are me. It's violating enough that you are in my mind without you also taking an innocent female too. One who is my soul mate. Perhaps you have been so isolated you've forgotten what a blessing a soul bond is and how it should be cherished."

"You are upset about the titan." He sighed as though I were a child having a tantrum over something silly, and it enraged me.

"Upset isn't even close to describing how I feel," I hissed and hoped he could feel it. The fury. The indignation. The despair. I hoped he knew that although saving his realm cost him nothing but power, it cost me everything. I was being sacrificed. The worst of it was I would have helped willingly if he'd only allowed me and my soul mates more time.

"We'd all do terrible things to save the ones we love, Baelen. It doesn't make me a villain."

"It does in this story."

We were silent as he walked back to the window in the kitchen area and looked out, his—no, my eyes, following the roll of leaves being swept away by the wind.

"It's an interesting place, this human realm. So green. I'd forgotten what that looked like. I look forward to seeing my homeland flourishing again once more." I did the bodiless equivalent of crossing my arms and turning around. I didn't want to listen to him anymore. It only gave him more power. *"Ignoring me won't work. I am in your mind and body. You are stuck with me."*

I had to wonder why his plan wasn't to portal them and force them to heal the portal instead of using me. Asking the question could have given him ideas, though, so I refrained but thought maybe he didn't have the strength to use my power to portal all of us.

I also could have told him that he didn't need to consummate the bond to use their powers. It would spare Clawdia, but it would mean he could simply steal her away the next time she was alone with him. The portal was so broken that I worried attempting to heal it would kill whoever attempted it. Kaatu wouldn't allow for failure. He'd push until either it worked, or we were dead.

"Your soul mate offered anything to save his pair from pain. It was interesting."

Kaatu's words seemed innocuous, but I heard the deeper

meaning and had I a spine, shivers would have been sent down it. It was clear he could hear some of my inner thoughts; the way he replied to me earlier proved that. But other thoughts, I believed I'd guarded.

Yet Kaatu responded with a parallel line of thought. Zaide offering anything to save Clawdia told me he knew something was wrong with me and told Kaatu he would be a good secondary plan if Clawdia didn't fall into his arms.

A knock of the door jolted us both out of our minds, and Kaatu turned us to see Savida's flame-red hair poke through the crack. "Baelen?"

"Demon," Kaatu replied.

"You aren't even trying to disguise it," I thought with disgust.

Savida walked into the cabin, his wings jostling past the door frame. He was followed by a faei with green hair and eyes I wasn't familiar with.

"Savida." The grinning demon tilted his head to examine us and then waved his hand at the other male. "And this is my soul mate, Daithi."

"Soul mate," Kaatu repeated.

"Yes." Savida nodded happily and settled on the edge of the sofa so his wings weren't squashed.

Kaatu's chuckle sounds strange from my mouth. "Forgive me. I've never met soul mates."

"Are your parents not such?" Daithi asked with suspicious eyes. I wanted to laugh.

"Oh. Yes, of course. I meant outside of the family," Kaatu tried to explain. It wasn't clear whether Savida and Daithi fell for the excuse, because their expressions didn't change, but Kaatu blundered on, "I confess I don't know much about soul mate lore. I didn't expect to find a soul mate, and my parents did not provide details. Could I ask you questions?"

Daithi raised a brow but said, "Of course."

"Using each other's powers. How could one achieve that unbonded?"

"So you do have a conscience," I said but cursed internally. He would find out what I'd been hiding from him, and then it would be anyone's guess what he would do. I just prayed they found out he was possessing me before he could do anything.

"You need only touch each other. Although it would take a very strong and compatible pair to do that. Savida and I have been bonded for many years and do not use each other's power." Daithi's words made me want to sigh. I saw how still my body went as Kaatu absorbed that information. I couldn't tell what he was thinking but knew it was bad.

Savida frowned at his soul mate. "You don't know how to use your visions, and you've never taught me how I might use your illusions. And until Alcor helped me learn my name, I haven't been able to use my gift. So, we have never tried. But maybe we will now. More power can't hurt when we are in such dangerous situations."

"The dragon?" Kaatu asked, boredom in his tone now.

"The dragon." Savida nodded, but he looked at us with more suspicion than previously.

Clawdia interrupted any further questioning as she opened the door and came in looking drawn and tired. Just the sight of her drew me closer. She smelled like Zaide, sweat, magic, and plants. But there was something else. A tinge to her scent that made me want to be near her. The effect of which was Kaatu shoving me back. I hadn't even realized he'd allowed me to regain some of my senses until they were gone again and the scent of her was a memory.

Surely this meant he was weakening. Hope bloomed within me even as I lost all feeling and returned to the ghost-like state and watched.

She didn't acknowledge anyone as she headed straight into the bathroom, and we all watched her quietly until we heard the sound of the lock being drawn across the door behind her.

"It seems your soul mate has had long day." Savida said with a sympathetic smile. He exchanged a glance with Daithi. "We'll leave you in peace. Please tell her we hope she feels better soon."

They filed out, and Kaatu watched them with narrowed eyes until they reached their cabin. I couldn't tell what he was thinking as he stood outside of the bathroom and listened to the sound of the water falling from the shower.

"What are you doing?" I asked.

He didn't respond, which only fueled my panic. The shower stopped, and there were sounds of cupboards opening and closing. Listening closely seemed to pull me closer to my body until I could vaguely feel myself breathing and smell the floral scent of the soaps she used.

She gasped, and before I could question why, the most delicious smell seeped out from the cracks of the door. I couldn't resist. It was a siren call even Kaatu couldn't defend from, and he was pushed out of control completely as my akari nature took over with full force.

Despite knowing Kaatu wanted me to form a mate bond with Clawdia and gain her powers, at the first opportunity I was given to talk to her as me, to push her away to protect her, I failed. The second I could smell her blood, I cracked.

Not only her blood. But menstrual blood.

It smelled like sunshine lathered with honey, and I was drooling at the thought of licking her clean. My fangs descended, and without a second thought, I charged the door, broke the lock, and flew into the bathroom.

She gaped at me. "Baelen, what's wrong?"

Dressed only in a towel and soaking wet, she was the most beautiful thing I had ever seen. Her cheeks were rosy, her skin plump and dewy. A rose after spring rain couldn't compare. I wanted to tell her. But moreover, I wanted to pull her into my arms, run my nose down her neck, and kiss my way down her body to her sweet center. My cock was painfully hard at the thought of her. There was nothing more akari loved than a bloody sword, and I tingled at the chance.

"Do it. Take her. She's yours," Kaatu urged, and the sound of his voice made me hesitant.

I should stop. I shouldn't touch her. This is what he wants.

But I wanted her so much.

"Baelen, you're worrying me. Are you okay?" She came over to take my hands.

"You're bleeding," I explained, lisping around my teeth.

"Oh." A blush bloomed on her cheeks, and she locked her thighs together. "You can smell that? It's not—I'm not in any pain. Well, I am, but I'm not hurt. No one's hurt me," she stuttered, and for the first time since this nightmare began, I smiled. She was so sweet.

"Sunlight, I know exactly what that scent is," I whispered. I pulled her close so her wet skin dampened my clothes and, with my lips at the shell of her ear, continued, "And I'm dying to taste it. Please give me that honor."

"Honor? Taste?" She pulled away and stepped back, her face the picture of horror. "But I'm bleeding."

"And I adore your blood." I smiled, but she remained unmoved. "Akari only menstruate once a year, and their partners take the day to help ease them."

"Ease them?" she asked, her curiosity getting the best of her.

"Eat them, Sunlight," I replied with a wicked smile. She tried to hide her shiver of desire, but her eyes darkened, and her fists clenched.

"I'm not sure." She pursed her lips as her brow furrowed. "You've not exactly been yourself, and I'm really tired. Today has been a lot."

All valid points, and had I been able to think past the incredible smell of her, I would have agreed and let it go.

But as it were, I replied, "I've never felt more myself, Sunlight." I stepped closer again, backing her against the bathtub so she had nowhere to escape, and caressed her face. She leaned into my touch. "But if you are truly too tired and too pained, I will settle you into bed and fetch food. Would you like that?"

It would be a struggle to be near her and not crave her taste, but I would do it and pray she felt better the next day.

She watched me intently. "You do seem more yourself …"

With my other hand, I pulled her tightly against me and let her feel my desire press into her stomach. She gasped and licked her lips.

I brushed my nose with hers and whispered, "You're in pain. Let me help."

"How will that help with pain?" she asked, a quiver in her voice.

"Orgasms are a natural painkiller, and stimulation helps with cramps," I told her as I pressed kisses across her jaw and down her neck.

She relaxed into my kisses with a breathy sigh and rubbed my chest. "And it's an honor where you are from?"

"The greatest." I wasn't lying about that. There was nothing more an akari male dreamed of than this moment.

My hands roamed her towel, clenching and unclenching, testing at the corner folded into itself across her chest. She shivered, and her hands crept to my waistband, pushing my shirt up so she could feel the skin of my abs. I barely restrained a moan as her nails gently scored over my chest.

"I don't want to hurt your feelings," she whispered. But the heat in her eyes suggested that she was teasing more than honestly feeling pressured.

I assured her, nonetheless. "It's not about me, Sunlight, it's about you and your needs and your desires. If you are uncomfortable, I will not pry."

"I'm not uncomfortable ..." she said quietly and bit her lip.

Her hands rested on my back and pulled me closer, but I pushed away for a second to tear my shirt off and throw it to the floor. Now she could touch me as much as she wanted. I lifted her chin to meet my eyes and watched her pupils dilate as she returned my stare.

"I will lick you until you scream your release. You'll sit on my face like a queen on a throne as your juices fall down my throat. I want to keep you in raptures so much so that you never feel any discomfort from your cycle." She swallowed, and her chest heaved. "May I?" I whispered.

"Yes," she gasped. "Please."

Victorious, I swiftly tugged her towel off and lifted her into my arms. Her legs came around my waist, and I moved from the bathroom to the sofa. My lips touched hers in a frenzied kiss that built and built. The smell of her arousal amplified the scent of her blood. My cock was impossibly hard. So hard I ached. My fangs throbbed, and with every graze of her lips against them, I longed to sink my teeth into her lip.

But that wasn't the blood I craved more than life itself.

I nipped my way down her jaw to her earlobe, lightly biting on the soft tissue and pulling a delicious shudder and sigh from my mate. Her nipples pebbled against my chest, and I directed my mouth in their direction. She pushed my hair back and gripped my head tightly to her chest as I sucked and pulled on the berry-red protrusion. She groaned and squirmed. "Baelen. That's so good. But I need more."

I smiled, proud she felt comfortable enough to ask me for what she needed. "You are a beautiful woman, my sunlight. I could gaze upon you all day. And one day, I will. But your blood calls to me. I need to taste it." I pressed heated kisses to her stomach as I trailed down toward her mound.

She nodded desperately, her hips twitching, urging me to where she needed me most. "Please," she whined.

I pushed her legs up so I could get a better view of her. White skin, pink lips, and between them, the smallest sliver of red. Saliva pooled under my tongue as the scent of her intensified. But rather than diving in with my tongue, I ran my finger between her folds, gathering her juices and massaging her clit with them. Her legs trembled at my touch, and she whimpered. I held her violet gaze as I lifted my finger, sucked it into my mouth, and licked the blood off with a groan, my eyes rolling back in my head at the taste of her.

When I opened my eyes, her eyes were blown wide, her chest heaved, and her skin was pebbled with arousal. I couldn't hold back any longer. I had to bury my face into her weeping center. She whimpered as my tongue buried deep inside her, as deep as I could go. I curled my tongue, pulling her sweetness into my mouth and groaning at the rush her blood gave me. I'd never known anything like it. I dug my nails into my hands to stop myself from coming right there and then. I felt stronger, as though her blood had a special power I wasn't aware of.

I gorged on her, and she squirmed, needing more. She sobbed as my lips closed around her clit and sucked.

"Are you going to come, my sunlight?" I asked in a growl.

"God, yes."

"There is no god here, Sunlight. Just the son of ones. But if you'd like to make me one, you have to pray to me." I lightly blew on her clit, causing a shudder. "What's my name?"

"Baelen," she whined.

"Do you want to come?" I asked.

"Yes," she whimpered.

"Scream my name as you do. Pray to me."

My tongue licked at her rapidly and without mercy, and soon she was crying out. "Baelen. Baelen. Baelen."

I bit into her thigh, and she screamed. Wetness gushed over my face, and I turned wild. Gorging on the blood from her veins and the blood from her pussy, I was overcome with light and thirst.

But of course, such a moment couldn't last forever, and the door flew open, revealing the horrified faces of Charlie and Zaide.

CHAPTER 21

CHARLIE

"Quite the day," Elizabeth commented dryly as we walked toward the main house along the forest's path.

I laughed. "All of our days are like this at the moment. Just one massive rollercoaster after the next."

"It's an interesting time in your life."

"I don't think this is what they mean when they say your best years are behind you." I hesitated and added seriously, "Thank you, by the way."

"Thank you?" she repeated.

"For coming," I explained and shrugged. "A little warning would have been nice, but I appreciate that you're trying to help."

"You're welcome." Her smile was small and almost shy.

"Who's guarding your portal?" I asked.

"No one. I've trapped the house. If anyone I don't know enters, I'll know." I nodded, and there was a brief silence before she said, "You didn't tell me you were in love with your familiar."

I frowned and asked, "What difference does that make?"

She raised an eyebrow disapprovingly. "She's a familiar. She might look human, but she isn't."

"Ah, yes." I rolled my eyes. "I completely forgot all that instantaneous knowledge I gained when my ex accidentally let slip I was a witch."

Elizabeth stared pointedly. She didn't like the sarcasm, but I didn't like the disapproving mom look. I'd gone many years without it, and I definitely didn't need it now.

She huffed and continued, "She's bound to you for eternity. She can never leave you even if she wants to."

"You aren't telling me anything I don't know."

"A hostage can't love you."

I stopped dead. "What are you talking about? I'm not holding her hostage. I locked her in my house one time because she was tearing the shit out of my t-shirt and I wanted to catch her before she escaped without punishment."

"Her soul, Charlie."

"I'm holding her soul hostage?" I exclaimed, but after a bit of thought, I agreed, "Yeah, okay, maybe, but only because it was about to fuck off into the sunset and Zaide would have gone all Romeo on me if she'd died. No one would have preferred that."

"It's not my place to say anything." I rolled my eyes. *Not her place to say anything after she's already said something.* She continued, "But I'll be looking forward to getting to know her."

I laughed, remembering Clawdia's fury when I told her about meeting Elizabeth the first time. "I told her you almost dusted me, and she's a little miffed about it. So good luck with that. She can be a fierce little thing when she wants."

"Of course you did." She sighed, but the small curl of her lip told me she wasn't upset. "Why was she angry earlier?"

"The classic Clawdicat protest." I sighed. "I may have

suggested she was being irrational. And yes, I already know how bad an idea that is, but despite being able to read her mind and feel her emotions, I'm still a dumb man. I can't be prince charming all the time."

Elizabeth heaved a long-suffering sigh, as if she'd raised me and was sick of my shit after years of putting up with me. Or maybe I had that effect on everyone regardless of how long they'd known me. But before she could retort, the door to the main house swung open, and Ingrid stepped out onto the porch to greet us.

"Ingrid, you look fantastic," I cheered with a charming grin, which she returned. "We're really looking forward to having another look at your library, aren't we, Elizabeth?"

Drawing Ingrid's attention to my birth mother was a bad idea, because her face fell into a smooth mask. "Forgive me, I'm afraid we haven't been formally introduced yet, although I did see you at the meeting this morning."

Elizabeth had the same bland smile the other council members wore when they were about to be arseholes. "I'm Elizabeth Olsson, the temporary council representative for the witches. I see you've already met my son, Charlie."

Ingrid's face seemed to freeze and buffer before she blinked, resetting, with her bland smile, which now seemed a bit crazed. "I'm sorry, did you say temporary council representative?"

"Yes."

I could really do with some popcorn for this show.

Ingrid's mouth gaped open and closed like a fish. "I wasn't aware they had already made a decision about such an important matter."

"I offered to step into the role urgently since I know many witches will be feeling guilt and fear from their involvement in Deborah's plot. They need to be resolved of guilt and given a new mission to amend for their wrongdoings."

A great campaign slogan, Elizabeth, but it is a bit preachy.

Ingrid tried to prevent the scoff in her voice but failed. "And you are the witch for that?"

"Of course. You know the power of my family?" Elizabeth's shoulders straightened.

The old 'do you know who I am?' Classic.

"Your name does sound familiar," Ingrid admitted.

"Our family line is the same as the protector's. It is very old, so old we had been assumed dead. But we were hiding."

"The protector is your family line?" Ingrid's question was breathy, and she wilted, knowing the competition was lost.

"Yes. It is also of Fafnir's line."

Elizabeth is taking no prisoners. She might as well just say, 'Bitch, I've got portal magic and dragon blood. You're no match for me.'

"That is powerful blood," Ingrid managed to say. She turned to me with a bright smile. "No wonder your son has managed to hold such a powerful familiar."

Elizabeth nodded. "And he needs to learn the power of his heritage. Urgently."

Ingrid snapped into her gracious host persona and ushered us inside, saying, "Yes, of course. You are most welcome in our library."

As I stepped on the stairs up to the library, I realized no one was following me. Both Elizabeth and Ingrid stayed in the hallway, continuing their weird witch-off.

Elizabeth said, "Ingrid, I would like your help with my new role, if you would be so kind."

Like someone had plugged in a Christmas tree, Ingrid lit up and smiled brightly. "Of course. I'd be pleased to help you with your task, Ms. Olsson."

This lady needs to get her nose out of people's arses. It's just sad.

"I'd like to get to know the witches here, research their covens and family lines. As they are residing in your home, I'm sure you, as the intelligent witch you are, made sure to know them." Elizabeth nodded and glanced up at me. "I'll just set Charlie up with a few tasks, and then I'll be down, and we can get started."

Ingrid vibrated with excitement. Her need to help in this important task, as the underling of the temporary witch's council member, was written over her face. She waved me up the stairs and flitted away into the dining room. "Karin is in the library at the moment. Don't hesitate to ask for her help if you need it."

Elizabeth followed me up the stairs, and when we reached the landing, I muttered, "Well, that was awkward." I glared at her. "We are trying not to upset the locals, and you're here for all of ten seconds and being all ice queen."

She rolled her eyes but asked, "Why are you trying not to upset the locals?"

"Because they look at us like the villagers that hunted for witches."

"That may be because you are an interesting bunch."

"It's not curiosity on their faces," I muttered as I pushed the door open to the library.

"Truthfully, Charlie, you're sleeping with your familiar, who is in human form. If witches had a porn category, that would be the most taboo one," Elizabeth said dryly, and my mouth dropped open in horror. "I expect it's that."

"You watch porn?" I gagged.

* * *

I WAS LEFT ALONE with a book on defensive spells and placed at a small desk in a corner of the library. Training to be a witch should have been an epic montage scene of ropes, chants, and practicing spells where magic popped from our hands like a shower of glitter, followed by a scene where we put creepy crawlies into a boiling cauldron. But instead, I felt like I was back at school and in detention.

Sighing, I looked around the library as my mind wandered. What were Clawdia and Zaide were up to? Was she still being a sassy cat? Had Zaide figured out what was up with Baelen?

I got up from my desk and started circling the shelves. If the books were in any kind of order, it wasn't apparent to me, and I started flipping open ones that called to me. Which tended to me the ones that looked like they belonged in a castle. I was lazily flicking through the pages of one when a sheet of folded paper fell out. Picking it up, I unfolded it to see what was written inside.

The handwriting was awful and not in English, but there was the image of a pentagram with had arrows pointing downward at each point of the star. The number thirty-five was also written with a question mark, but I couldn't decipher anything else, and since the book also wasn't in English, I couldn't figure out what it might have correlated to.

I put the book back on the shelf and headed toward the section of books with modern covers. I found one which screamed "take me," and … of course, it was a why choose romance book featuring foursomes and guy-on-guy action.

They can't say that I don't do anything for them.

"Hej, Charlie."

I wasn't ashamed of the squeal I made as Karin creeped up behind me while I was reading spicy scenes. Nor was I ashamed that I hid the book behind my back like a child when I turned to greet her. "Hi, Karin. You okay?"

She chuckled. "I'm sorry. Did I scare you?"

"Just a bit. Although to be fair, my heart was just settling

down from the events of the past few weeks, so it was probably good you restarted it for me."

She quirked a brow. "I'm glad I could help. What are
you looking at today? Maybe I can help you get your
books?"

I scratched my neck. "Elizabeth has me looking at defensive spells in that corner."

"Great! I can show you some of the best ones!" She turned
around and walked toward the corner, and I followed, interested in a magic display instead of reading anymore of the
stupid textbook. But she disappointed me when she picked
up another book and started flicking through the pages. She
continued, "There's an invisibility spell in here that's
different to the other ones because it uses approximately ten
percent less magic. There are studies I can show you to back
it up."

While I really didn't want to read the study, I was interested in what she'd said. "How do you measure magic?" I
asked.

She turned to me, her eyes sparkling as she began
explaining. "Well, it was through experiments. They would
drain someone of their magic until they were almost
completely empty."

"Wouldn't that kill someone?" I asked, thinking about
Fafnir and his draining powers.

"Sometimes." She shrugged, which I thought was weird,
but continued, "Then they'd divide up all the magic they took
and add it back into them in sections to see how much was
needed for each spell. The development of science revolu-
tionized magical practices for the better."

"And what's a few deaths for science," I replied sarcastically.

She clearly didn't see it that way. "They were paid. How
else would they get witches to offer themselves as experi-

ments." She smiled and handed me the book. "You can read more about it here."

The way she shrugged off the morbid history like it was completely fine was strange, but I didn't say anything. I just walked back to my tiny desk to add the new book and the one I picked up for Clawdia and Zaide to my pile. *Ergh, more reading. I really am at school.*

"Let me know if you need anything else," Karin called. "Anything at all. I'll just be over there, researching."

I sighed and started reading again, but I could feel her eyes on me. I turned around to catch her, but she held my gaze.

Out of nowhere, she asked, "What's it like having a familiar?"

After the questions she asked at the party, I knew she'd been waiting for another opportunity to grill me, so I answered with a shrug, "It's pretty great. I didn't set out to get one like other witches, but it worked out well."

"And you can hear her thoughts?"

"Yes."

"All the time?"

"No. She has to want to talk to me for me to hear it. I think I'd go mad if I had to listen to her all the time." I chuckled.

"And you can feel her emotions in the same way? When she wants you to?"

I shook my head. "That one's more like if we don't want each other to feel stuff, then they don't."

"Handy when one of you is in danger and needs help." She pursed her lips as she thought.

"I guess." I turned back to my book and flicked a few pages. "You asked me questions about familiars at the party too. Why are you so curious about them?"

"I did but I wanted to know what it's like since I haven't

255

ever met one or anyone with one before."

"There's probably more to learn from your books than from me. I'm still learning myself."

I jumped back as Karin suddenly sat on my desk and pushed my book out of the way. "Books are great, but there's something to be said about experience."

I looked up, confused. "Is that why you're hanging out with Clawdia so much? Because she's a familiar?"

She shrugged and crossed her legs. "I think it's fascinating that she was able to turn human. But it helps that she's a nice girl too."

"She can be," I muttered, thinking about the broken bowl.

"But nice girls don't have as much fun as bad girls," Karin whispered, "We could be bad together."

I froze. "Are you coming on to me right now?"

I took a moment to actually look at her face and saw … desire? But it looked strange. *What the fuck is going on here?* She knew I was with Clawdia, so I didn't know why she thought it was a good idea to come on to me.

But I gasped as a sudden wave of lust hit me out of nowhere. *And why the fuck do I have a hard-on right now?* I looked down at the traitorous cock. *Why the fuck are you here? There's nothing good happening right now.*

"If it's not obvious, then maybe I should do something to make my intentions clearer." She leaned closer, and I scrambled out of my seat away from her.

"Er—no. Thanks."

"I'm not stupid, Charlie, I can see your cock is hard." She nodded at my dick like I wasn't aware.

I covered my crotch and explained in a rush, "That is not about you. It's not even about me. This is one of those mystery erections the universe likes to throw at guys for jokes."

But when my knees almost went from under me and I

had to grab on to a shelf for support, I realized what was actually happening.

Clawdia and Zaide were having make-up sex without me. *Fucking bastards. I'm here working, and they are prating around.*

"Charlie? Are you okay?" she asked, getting off the table to approach me.

I picked a book off the shelf and held it in front of me to warn her off. "Yep. Fine. Thanks."

"You look uncomfortable. Let me help you." She walked like a cat stalking their prey, swaying hips and narrowed eyes.

Jesus Christ, is this actually happening? "I'm totally fine, thanks." I stumbled behind another desk to shield me. I hadn't been pursued like this since primary school when the girls played kiss chase.

With a huff and a stomp of her foot, she stopped. "Are you really so besotted with her? She's your familiar. She has a soul pair and a soul mate. You don't need her."

I gaped at her. "I'm not sure why you thought I'd be into you. You know I'm with her. I love her. And this whole thing has come out of nowhere. The only person you've shown interest in is Clawdia, and that's because you want to know about familiar stuff. What the fuck, Karin?"

Her face changed, and she sneered, "I didn't want you anyway," before storming out of the library.

What the hell was that?

When Naomi—at least I thought it was Naomi, because I couldn't tell the difference between the twins—walked into the room, I was still standing there, processing the trauma of it all.

I'm going to fucking kill Clawdia and Zaide when I see them. I thought inopportune boners were a thing of the teenage past. Fucking horny bastards. And not even going trying to wait until I got back. Rude.

"Everything okay in here?" she asked, her eyes wide and full of mischief. "I just saw Karin storm out."

I blinked. "I'm not ready to tell you."

She raised a brow but looked down at the book Karin had been reading. "Researching enchanted blades. Very Karin," she muttered.

"Is it very Karin to come on to someone out of nowhere?" I had to ask.

"She did what?" Naomi gasped.

"Wanted to know if I wanted to be bad with her." I felt sick repeating it.

"Oh, goddess. She said that?" Her expression echoed the disgust I felt.

"Unfortunately."

"No wonder you're in a state of shock."

"One moment, we're talking about measuring magic, and the next ..."

Noami clicked her tongue and made a noise of under-standing. "She doesn't know a lot about flirting. But she can tell you a lot about magic. She plays to her strengths."

"She knows I'm with Clawdia, so even if I knew she was flirting with the magic talk, she shouldn't be trying to move in on me." I growled. Now that I was recovering from the shock, the anger settled in.

She shrugged. "I don't know what to tell you."

"Why the hell would she do that?" I threw my arms out in exasperation. *This day has been so fucking weird.*

"I don't know. But if I had to guess, I'd say it was about power." Naomi leaned against a shelf and crossed her arms.

"Power?

"You're powerful. You've got the blood of some of the most amazing witch families. You have a familiar, and your familiar is a titan soul pair. You have so much potential.

You're probably the most powerful witch ever. If you don't count half breeds."

"While I appreciate the ego stroke after the trauma I just suffered, I don't see what this has to do with Karin," I said as I returned to my seat.

"You don't seem to understand what you have. But Karin is painfully aware of what she doesn't have."

"What does that mean?" I sighed and rubbed my forehead.

"Our family stays here to keep safe, to guard the records and books we keep and ensure the wards stay up and help us."

"Right … and?"

"And she can't ensure the wards stay full with her amount of magic. She can barely put a candle out."

"If that's the requirement for a good witch, then I'm useless," I remarked.

"You just haven't learned anything yet. But it's made her feel inadequate. So, she's made up for it by learning everything she can about magic. It's the one thing that sets her apart and makes her feel valuable. Without power in the witching world, you aren't anything." She raised her brow. "Half the reason we follow lines through the matriarchal lines is because boys don't tend to be as powerful as girls. You're a real rare gem." She winked, and I laughed.

"That's what I always tell myself."

I refused to feel sorry for Karin after today's crazy but acknowledged that it would suck to be so passionate about something you couldn't take part in. I added, "And thanks for the insight."

"No problem. Now you need to answer something for me."

"Sure." I shrugged.

Her eyes laughed, and she pointed at the book on my desk. "Why are you reading my why choose romance book?"

CHAPTER 22

ZAIDE

I strode into the library in the main house and spotted Charlie sitting alone at a desk with a tortured look on his face. I coughed to announce myself, and his head snapped up from his book.

"God, you have good timing. Please get me out of here. I'm so bored I could die." I chuckled at his dramatics but then his eyes narrowed, he stood up and charged toward me. "But first," he began and punched me hard in the arm.

I didn't flinch since his fist felt like a rock bouncing off my muscles and raised a patient brow as I asked, "Why do I deserve to be assaulted on sight?"

"Because you and Clawdia decided to get your freak on and gave me a boner at literally the worst time," he hissed, despite no one being around.

I laughed loudly. *I hadn't considered that Charlie would feel our pleasure, and from the look on his face, he didn't enjoy the experience as much as I had.* My chuckles died down, but when I saw his snarling face, I started laughing again.

"Would you stop?" he exclaimed. "It was so traumatic. My dick may never recover."

"I'm sure that's not true. Your dick has always worked." I laughed again.

"Just because my first erection wasn't at the sight of my true love doesn't mean I'm hard all the time. And I don't want to be."

"You've had more erections than I've had hot meals," I retorted.

His mouth dropped open. "Oh, God, that's depressing. What a way to bring down the mood, titan."

I chuckled again and nudged his shoulder. "Why was your erection at the worst time, I thought you were in here learning." He glared at me, and my eyes widened as a thought crossed my mind. "In front of your mother?"

"Worse." He gagged. "In front of Karin."

I bit my lip to stop from laughing. "You should have blocked us out."

"I tried. What the fuck were you doing?"

"I think you know how it works, Charlie, you gave us a lesson." I gave him a sly smile. "We were embracing our wild side."

"You have a wild side?" he asked, crossing his arms and pouting.

"Are you upset?" I asked.

He sighed and leaned against a shelf. "I'm jealous as fuck. I've been tortured here, and you guys have been experimenting without me. And I was the one who got a bowl almost dropped on my head. A blow job would be the least she could do."

I smirked. "She'll apologize properly to you, I'm sure."

He waggled his brow. "Was that what you got? An apology?"

"We worked out a lot of things that had been bothering us," I told him blankly.

He narrowed his eyes. "You're being cryptic, and I just

want to ask more questions."

"I'm not going to tell you more."

"And I even got you a present." He picked a book up off the desk and slapped me across the chest with it. "Even got the gay sex you need to get started with Baelen." All my humor faded, but I held the book in place as Charlie asked, "Wait, was Baelen involved?"

"No." I stepped back and rubbed my head. "That won't be happening any time soon. And that's why I'm up here. I want to search for things that could cause Baelen's strangeness."

"She's convinced you?"

I shook my head and let my eyes tell Charlie how serious I was about this. "He convinced me. He only wants to consummate the bond with Clawdia. The way he spoke. The things he said. He was …"

"What?"

There was only one way to say it in a way he'd understand. "A complete arsehole."

A slow smile crept across his face. "Is it wrong to be proud that you just said that?"

I nodded, my lips twitching. "It's strange."

"You know, they say the first sign of a relationship is when you start sounding like each other."

"You are my boyfriend-in-law in this strange harem we have going on." It was the same thing he said to me when he pulled me from the car crash.

"Stop. You're making me blush." He batted his eyelashes at me, and I laughed. "Okay enough fun. You think Balen's under some weird spell or something?"

"Yes."

"Could he be dangerous?" His voice was low.

I hesitated. "Not to Clawdia, but I think you and I need to be wary of him. Something isn't right."

"Charlie?" Elizabeth's voice called as the door to the

library pushed open.

"Hide me," Charlie whispered as he darted behind me.

Elizabeth sighed as she walked in. "Charlie, why are you hiding behind your friend?"

"Because if I have to look at another book about spells, I'll run away." He peeked around me and glared. "You know there are other ways of learning, don't you? I'm more of a hands-on learner."

She rolled her eyes and said, "Yes, well, I'm sorry it took a while for Ingrid and me to plan our next steps."

"I'm so glad you've managed to become besties while I've been planning offing myself," he replied sarcastically.

"You're so dramatic," she sighed, and I had to agree.

He caught my side-eye and playfully pushed me as he stopped hiding and came to stand in front of his mother. "Anyway, now you're here, question for you: Is there a spell or potion that could change someone's personality?"

My gaze snapped to Elizabeth. I hadn't thought to ask her about our issue since I wanted to keep it between ourselves. *Charlie must trust her more than he lets on to involve her.*

"Asking for yourself?" Elizabeth asked with bored eyes.

Charlie gave her a fake smile. "Hilarious. No."

"Baelen isn't acting like himself," I explained.

"That could be caused by anything. Didn't you say he came through a strange portal?" she asked.

"You think it could be the portal affecting him?" I frowned. *Why would a portal have any effect on someone?*

"Portal travel can be a dangerous thing. If he'd managed to warp one to get here, then it's likely he's suffered some kind of damage."

"We thought that was the reason he wasn't waking up, but could it give him a personality transplant?" Charlie asked.

Elizabeth pursed her lips. "I would think it would look more like a concussion. Not a personality transplant."

"What could cause someone to completely change? For them to act indifferent to their soul mate?"

"He's indifferent to you?"

"And cruel."

"And he wasn't before?"

"No."

She tapped a finger against her lip as she thought. "There are dark spells that can influence behavior, but I've never come across nor heard of a witch who could wield them."

"And how many witches would be in the realms to put a spell on him?" Charlie asked, frowning at the ground. His gaze flicked to me. "Unless you think someone here did it while he was unconscious?"

"I think it's possible," I conceded.

"Who would do that? And why?" Charlie waved his hands in exasperation.

Elizabeth interrupted with a shake of her head. "Ingrid has just gone through pictures of each and every witch on this island and told me of their families and specialties. No one here has that kind of magic."

In the silence that followed, I deliberated on what we knew about Baelen's condition. Other than acting differently, the only other clues we had about what happened to him, were the strange portal and the shadows who might have attacked him in the dreamscape.

"What do you know about shadow people?" I asked.

She jolted with surprise and frowned. "You think shadows have done this?"

"They attacked him in the dreamscape. The portal was smokey."

She tilted her head. "Their natural portal was destroyed in the fall, but our family continued to guard it. They could move with the shadows, live in them. It's how they can access the dreamscape. In the shadow of their mind."

"Could they possess a person by being in the shadow of their mind?" I asked.

"I don't think it's possible, but if you're sure it was shadow people who attacked him …"

"We are used to the impossible happening to us by now." Charlie sighed and rubbed his eyes. "What can we do? How do we get the shadow out? And why would it only want Clawdia? What's the plan here?"

"Who knows what the shadow wants. But they must be very powerful to have possessed someone through a dream-scape and then use their power to portal here."

"Their power?" I asked as a shiver ran down my spine. "The shadow might be able to use Baelen's powers?"

"Shadows can't portal. They travel through shadows."

"How do you know this?" Charlie asked.

"We know a lot about the people of the realms. We have to."

"So we really think Baelen's possessed?" He asked.

"You'll need to watch him carefully."

"We need to watch everyone carefully. Why is nothing simple?" Charlie moaned and nudged my arm. "Let's head back. All this talk of possession is making me itchy."

"Charlie," Elizabeth called as we passed her. "Tomorrow, I expect a little more focus on your studies."

His shoulders slumped as soon as we left the library, and he mumbled, "I'm back at school again. This is a nightmare."

"Charlie, my soul mate may have been possessed by a shadow. That is a nightmare."

He patted my back. "We'll figure it out."

As we were walking back down the hill, two familiar figures were walking in the opposite direction.

"Zaide, Charlie!" Savida waved, his big grin bright. "We are just on our way to dinner."

"God, I'd kill to order a pizza now," Charlie muttered. "I

don't want to go back up there after I've just escaped. Even for food."

"I just want to check on Clawdia, and then I'll go and get some for us," I told him.

Savida looked between us. "Yes. She stormed into the cabin while we were talking to Baelen. She looked very pale."

"Your soul mate seems to be very uncertain about what it means to be soul mates. I thought he would have known more since his parents were such," Daithi added.

I frowned. "He does know about soul mates."

Savida shook his head. "He was asking us about using each other's magic."

My eyes widened. This was it. Actual proof that it wasn't him. "He knows how to do that. We did it in the dreamscape."

"He wants her magic?" Charlie asked.

"But not from me," I added.

We exchanged a panicked look.

"Shit," he said.

"Shit," I repeated.

And we raced back down the hill, leaving Daithi and Savida in the dust.

We were breathless as we threw the door open wide to see Clawdia with her legs spread on the sofa and Baelen lapping at her pussy like it was his last meal. The door smacked into the wall, and Clawdia screamed and yanked her legs up to cover herself.

Baelen's head snapped toward us, and the look in his eyes made me step back. *He looks feral.* Blood smeared around his mouth, his eyes red and bright.

"What the fuck is happening right now?" Charlie shouted.

"Why did you charge in like that?" Clawdia squeaked as she kneeled on the sofa, and her expression changed from shocked to concerned. "Is something wrong?"

266

"Clawdia, get away from him," I whispered, unable to tear my eyes away from Baelen.

He hissed, snarled, and showed off his bloody fangs, yet Clawdia patted his head like she was soothing an animal and asked, "What's happening?"

"Why is he like that?" Charlie's lip curled.

Baelen, despite his feral state, seemed to understand Charlie's derision and responded by standing up and growling at him.

Clawdia rose behind him and caressed his back, imploring us with her eyes as she tried to pacify him. "Baelen, calm down. It's okay."

I held Charlie back with an arm across his chest. "Stop. Don't move."

"What the fuck?" Charlie flinched away from my beastly soul mate as he stepped in front of Clawdia and bared his teeth. "Get away from her!" Charlie shouted.

"Why are you shouting? Just calm down and explain. You're scaring him." Clawdia tried to get around Baelen, but he held her behind him as though protecting her from us.

"*You* should be scared of *him*. Now get away." Charlie lunged around me and grasped her arm.

Baelen's eyes flared, and preempting his movement, I stood between them so Baelen charged into my chest, almost bouncing away. I swallowed, his red eyes giving me a flicker of fear before I forced him back.

Charlie shouted a phrase, and suddenly a cage flared around Baelen. His eyes widened, and he roared as he charged into the bars that now held him captive.

"What are you doing? Let him go!" Clawdia yelled and fought Charlie's hold on her arm.

Charlie let her go and sagged onto the sofa with his head in his hands. "Oh my fucking god. I'm so sick of this day."

"How did you do that?" My mouth was agape. Seeing

Charlie use magic somehow made it everything we knew, more real. He was a witch. He had magic. He was also part … Drakorian.

Charlie sighed but answered my question. "I fucking hate learning by reading, but after spending all day looking at pages, something must have gone in."

Clawdia stomped her foot, and we looked over to see her hand on the cage, her eyes flared dangerously. She whispered darkly, "Someone explain what is happening right now."

Baelen rested his forehead on a glowing bar, his shoulders heaving, his eyes closed.

"He's possessed," I told Clawdia before she began shouting.

She paused, her hand falling back for him. "Possessed?"

I nodded. "By a shadow, we think."

Her face fell. She looked from me to Baelen and back to me. "No."

Charlie's head snapped up. "What do you mean no? You were the one who was insisting he wasn't himself."

"He … he was himself just a moment ago. We—" Her breath caught, and she pressed her hand pressed against her chest as her eyes grew round.

"Yes, we saw how quickly you believed in him again when his head was between your thighs," Charlie grumbled quietly.

Clawdia composed herself and asked, "What do you mean possessed by a shadow? Did you find something?"

I took a hesitant step toward her as I quickly said, "He was last with shadows. The portal was all shadow-like, and Elizabeth explained they may have the power to possess people. They move in the shadows. Including shadows inside a mind."

She shook her head. "There are no shadows in our minds. Light doesn't touch the brain."

"Does science explain the shit I just did?" Charlie asked, waving his hand at the cage.

"I thought maybe a spell but—" She swallowed and bit her lip as she shook her head again. "He can't be possessed," she whispered at the ground, her shoulder trembling.

"Why not?" Charlie asked.

"Little Cat." I approached her carefully and tilted her head up to look at me. The gloss in her eyes and the quiver of her lip made my heart falter. I pulled her into my arms. "Do not get upset. It's all right."

She whispered, "If he is not Baelen, who is he? Why would he …?"

"Gods." I clenched my jaw and pulled her tighter to me as I realized her issue. The shadow was intimate with her. *She thought Baelen was who she was with, but if he is indeed possessed, who's to say who was with her?*

I pulled back to look at her. She wasn't crying, but her brow was furrowed, and she refused to meet my eyes. As I smoothed her shoulders, I noticed something run down the inside of her bare thigh. Blood.

I gasped and stepped back. "Little Cat, you are bleeding from your legs."

"What?" Charlie stared at her legs in horror. "Jesus Christ."

My voice rose. "Why are you bleeding between your legs? What has he done?" I turned to glare at Baelen, my hand twitching with the need to punch him. He stared blankly back at me.

"Nothing." Clawdia patted at my chest and regained my attention. "Nothing," she assured me.

But I remained confused. "Nothing? You are hurt." I snarled before a realization hit me and I gasped. "Was it me? Did I—?"

"No. No." She seized my hands. "Stop panicking."

"It's her period, Zaide," Charlie muttered. He looked at Clawdia and asked, "Why do you have a period?"

She looked down as she whispered, "I don't know."

"What is a period? Why are you bleeding?" I asked looking between them, my panic lessening.

My question seemed to confuse them. Clawdia looked at Charlie, whose mouth opened and closed before attempting to say, "It's … it's …"

Clawdia's mouth began to turn up into a smile. "Yes, Charlie, what is it?"

He glared. "You can explain it."

"You are joking. This is not a serious condition?" I asked.

Clawdia squeezed my hand and replied calmly, "Women bleed for a week every month. In short, it is the end of a fertile period."

"Fertile period?" I asked and blinked. My mind whirled, and I gasped. "Children?"

Charlie smothered his mouth with his hand. "Periods usually mean there aren't children."

"No children," I repeated.

"Yet," Clawdia added.

"Is anyone really fucking hot all of a sudden?" Charlie announced and stormed to the kitchenette to throw open a window.

"We may have children?" I asked. My heart fluttered with the thought. *Children … We could have children …*

"One day." She squeezed my hand, her eyes lit with joy. "I saw them."

"What?" Charlie choked and spun around. "Them? Saw them how?"

She shook her head, but the happy smile remained. "It was so strange. I looked at them and knew exactly who they were. I can't describe the feelings, but I love them so much."

"Children." Charlie braced himself on the cabinet.

"Yes, Charlie. Are you all right? You're green." Clawdia let go of my hands to reach for him. She stroked his hair while he took gulping breaths and attempted to compose himself.

"I just didn't think," he replied, and she patted him sympathetically as she smiled over at me. "How did you see them?"

"It was like a flash. A vision. I was thinking about what my courses mean, and then suddenly I saw them." Her smile was full of longing. "I wish I could see them again."

"What did they look like?" I asked, gravitating toward her.

"There were four," she began.

"Four?" Charlie squeaked. While he seemed terrified, I was giddy with excitement, listening for every small detail, eager for more of the future she painted for us.

She laughed but continued. "Three boys and a girl. A boy who looks like you but with blue eyes," she told me. "Another who looks like Baelen with dark hair and red eyes." I followed her eyes as she looked over at the cage and saw Baelen's eyes were wide and glassy, his mouth open. She swallowed and added with a stutter, "Another who had scales and yellow eyes."

"Scales?" Charlie yelled. She covered his mouth with a hand, and through it, he mumbled, "He'll be a dragon?"

"I don't know."

It did not matter to be if he was born with a tail. I would love them all the same.

"And the girl?" I asked as I came behind her to wrap my arms around her waist.

She leaned back against me and replied, "The girl was a baby with a little bow on her head. She didn't look like any of you, but she was still beautiful."

"If she is ours, there is no doubt about that," I whispered, and Clawdia smiled brightly.

Charlie asked, "You think it's the actual future? It's definitely going to happen?"

"I don't know. But I want it to happen." She squeezed his hand.

"You do?"

"Don't you?" She raised her brow. She didn't look concerned about his reaction but instead seemed amused.

He clenched his jaw. "The dragon kid means Elizabeth is right and boys turn into evil dragons."

"Unless another is to join us? And the girl is yours?" I suggested. Although I couldn't foresee another soul bond joining our family.

"Another man?" Charlie gasped.

She squeezed his hand again to stop his imminent panic. "I don't know what it all means, Charlie, but I can't pretend I'm not happy to see a possible future with so much love and potential," she said quietly but with so much passion it was hard not to feel excited. I pulled her closer and pressed a kiss to her shoulder.

Charlie hesitated. "Even the scaly one that might eat magic?"

Clawdia laughed. "Even him. He was so beautiful."

"I can't wait. When are your fertile times, Little Cat?" I kissed the shell of her ear, and she shivered.

Charlie pulled her out of my arms and glared. "Slow down, buddy."

"We aren't having children just yet." Clawdia told me and patted my chest.

"Of course. After we've defeated Fafnir," I conceded.

"And after we've found your siblings." She added.

I pouted. "We cannot have children and search for them?"

"You are too eager, my love."

But how could I not be? Now that I knew of another possibility, a bright and happy future, I couldn't wait. And the future Daithi saw for me would be bearable knowing that I had joy waiting for me.

CHAPTER 23

CLAWDIA

"*T*his is remarkable, Charlie. And you've been able to keep it up for all this time?" Elizabeth circled the magic cage that contained my soul mate.

As soon as we'd calmed down, I was able to tidy myself, and Charlie rushed off to grab dinner for us all and bring his birth mother to help us with both mine and Baelen's predicament.

I sat kneeling on the sofa as near as I could to Baelen. Despite what Charlie and Zaide said, I couldn't believe he wasn't himself while we were intimate. I couldn't believe it. He called me sunlight and had the same shocked awe about him as the moment he realized we were soul mates. The aggressiveness he'd had when he woke up and the way the words from his mouth sounded strange had gone. I was so sure he was mine again.

He leaned his head against the bars of his cage, watching us all but making no remark. Even after all the conversation about children, he didn't say a word. I'd never wanted to know the thoughts of a man, quite so much.

His eyes had not been wild, but nor had he had the arrogant sneer on his lips. He was my Baelen again, and although I didn't know what caused the change, I suspected it was my blood. So, I vowed to stay close.

Charlie rolled his eyes as he leaned against the kitchen counter. "As you can see."

Elizabeth straightened with overly wide eyes. "And here I thought you were learning nothing."

"How do we rid him of the shadow?" Zaide asked from beside Charlie as he made tea.

While I wasn't convinced it was a shadow causing his strange behavior, Zaide was, and Baelen didn't confirm or deny the accusation. But I'd witnessed the shadows in the dreamscape. If they were so powerful and had such ability, why didn't they possess him or me when they fought him then?

Elizabeth sighed, and her expression turned somber. "What can we do? I don't know how to ensure his shadow leaves him." She moved away from the cage and took the cup Zaide offered her.

"We just keep him in a cage?" I asked, outraged. *This is not a solution.* It was clearly uncomfortable for him to sit so cramped, and more to the point, I wanted him with us, with me. I didn't want him captive.

Baelen's lips quirked, and he said, "I am fine in here, Sunlight. I'd rather you be out of reach."

"What does that mean?" I asked, pressing my hand against the cage. He opened his mouth, a desperate want in his eyes, but no words came out. His face darkened as he choked and gasped, his mouth tight and his brow furrowed with pain.

My heart stuttered, and I tried to reach through the bars to touch him, but the barrier around him stopped me. "Okay. All right. Don't try to say anything more on the topic. We're going to help."

He coughed again, but the panic in his eyes dulled and he

whispered, "You cannot help me, Sunlight. But I appreciate you trying."

"Are you hungry?" I asked him, my voice low. Zaide didn't like seeing him feed, but if it kept the real Baelen with me, I'd try anything.

"No." He smiled, and amusement made the red of his irises swirl. "But you cannot delay the inevitable by speaking with me."

"Inevitable?" I asked quietly.

"You must speak with Charlie's mother." He raised a brow.

"How did you know?" I asked in a surprised whisper.

"You wear your feelings on your face." He smirked, and my heart leaped at the sight.

I pouted playfully. "I don't want to."

He gave me an affectionate smile that made me giddy, but when he waved his hand urging me away, I sighed. Standing, I turned to the kitchenette, where Zaide opened his arms for me to curl into. He was being very protective since I told him about my vision, which melted me. *He will make such a lovely father.*

"We haven't officially been introduced," Elizabeth said and held her hand out.

I took it and shook once, keeping my face blank so she didn't know how awful I thought she was for treating Charlie so poorly when they first met. "No. I'm Clawdia, Charlie's familiar."

"And I'm Elizabeth." She grimaced. "Despite being his birth mother, I tried to kill him."

Surprise made me blink. "At least you own up to it."

I eyed Charlie, who grinned at me and confirmed my suspicions. "I warned her about your bloodthirst, Clawdicat." He glanced at Baelen and mumbled, "Although maybe it's not the time to bring up blood thirst."

Laughing, I patted his hand and ushered Zaide out of the way of the sink so I could wash our plates.

He didn't move too far and picked up the dish cloth, ready to help dry as he said, "We are encouraging her temper."

"We are?" Charlie asked with a laugh.

"Perhaps not this week, though," I muttered as I handed Zaide a plate. He gave me a wicked grin that sent a shiver down my spine.

Elizabeth cleared her throat and set down her cup. "While I appreciate the invitation for tea, I assume it wasn't just for me to witness the cage you fashioned?"

I felt Charlie's gaze but kept my eyes in the sink as I replied, "No. Although we are very proud of Charlie for his first magic trick, I have a … question. About familiars."

"Magic trick?" Charlie's indignant voice echoed in my mind, and I lowered my face to hide my smile.

"Oh?" Elizabeth asked, "What's the question?"

I handed Zaide the last plate and used the end of his dish cloth to dry my hands. I licked my lips and said, "I am … bleeding."

"Bleeding?" I peered at her from under my lashes and saw the moment it dawned on her. "Oh." Her brows slowly rose. "Oh."

"Is that bad? What does it mean?" I asked.

Elizabeth coughed and sputtered, "It means you will need a potion for birth control."

I frowned, and my panic subsided. "But aside from that. Familiars are fertile?"

She pursed her lips and shook her head. "Generally not."

"So why am I? Or is that not what it means?" I gulped, and tears flooded my eyes as I thought about losing that vision of the future just as I realized it could be true. Zaide took my hand and squeezed it.

"Why don't we sit down?" Elizabeth said, and my hackles rose. Sitting down always meant bad news, but I followed her back to the sofa and sat next to Baelen's cage again, wishing I could touch him. Zaide and Charlie took seats at the table and waited for Elizabeth to continue. I braced myself, but she asked, "What do you know about familiars?"

I shook my head. "Just that they are souls that needed a second chance and are tied to witches to support them and share power."

Elizabeth closed her eyes and grimaced, "Familiar documentation is largely witch propaganda, but to know so little about yourself is criminal."

"What do you mean by that?" I asked.

"Let me explain the history, because it is clear it is yet another thing that has been lost to time. Familiars are the human realm's only naturally occurring magic other than the portals. They are animal gods. When humans worshiped an animal, the prayer and faith, which is a kind of magic in itself, awakened a consciousness inside them and gave them power."

I was still reeling from hearing a familiar was a kind of god but managed to ask, "What kind of power?"

"The power of any god, a way to help their worshipers. Cats in Egypt could sense when vermin were near the grain stores without being close by and were able to kill them before they could spoil the food. A bull in Greece was able to regrow its horns in a matter of hours and sharpen them in seconds to protect its people. I even read about how the jaguar gods in the Mayan civilization could call other animals and creatures into action at times of war."

"So what the fuck happened?" Charlie asked, clearly as interested in the story as I was.

"You said they developed a consciousness from worship? So, they weren't human souls?" I asked.

277

She shook her head. "No. Souls are souls. They don't have a specific race or creature allocation. All living things have souls."

"So, how did it become that familiars had past lives?" I asked.

"All souls have had other lives. A new soul is rare indeed. The real question is why do you remember that past life, and that lies in the witches' summoning spell."

"So, witches saw these animal gods and decided to keep one?" Zaide asked, his eyes dark with anger.

Elizabeth continued, "After the fall of the titans, the shadow portal crumbled, and their connection to the inter-linked dimensions was gone. Much of the shadow magic in the portal was absorbed into the earth, and the realm recy-cled it by placing it in animal gods who, with this magic, could then speak to humans telepathically and alter their forms."

Shadow magic? I have shadow magic?

I looked at Baelen, who stared back at me, his face frozen, but I couldn't read the emotion I saw there. Anger? Fear? It worried me because if he really had been possessed by a shadow, was it because of me? Did they know their magic resided in familiars? *Am I the cause of his suffering?*

"Does anyone else find it weird that all we are hearing about at the moment is shadow this and shadow that? For a realm with a dead portal, they are coming up an awful lot," Charlie said with his usual skepticism.

I didn't want to get distracted, though. I needed to know more. How I existed. "Alter forms?"

Elizabeth nodded. "To be as their worshipers are. Human."

"Human," I repeated, a little dazed. "Daithi didn't do this to me? I could always turn human?"

Elizabeth nodded. "It was always within your ability. Daithi probably forced the issue."

"Wow." I took a moment to process that and then frowned. "But I was summoned. I wasn't an animal god."

Elizabeth tilted her head in agreement. "Animals aren't worshiped anymore. There aren't many animal gods, if any, left in this realm. Witches saw animal gods become more powerful and wanted the power for themselves."

"Bloody typical," Charlie mumbled.

His hatred for witches would have been comical, especially considering he created a magical cage only hours ago, but I couldn't bring myself to laugh. I felt like I was on the verge of something, learning something that would change everything.

Elizabeth continued unperturbed. "They discovered the animal gods now had some shadow magic. Shadows have a bond, which they reserve for their mates, that ties their souls together. They become one. They can feel each other's emotions, hear each other's thoughts, and share power. They die together. As the shadow magic wrapped so tightly with the animal gods' own magic, they changed and became, in a small part, shadow."

My eyes widened. "The bond—"

Elizabeth nodded. "You recognize it. It is the bond you have with Charlie. "

Charlie's face was serious, but I felt lighter, relieved. "So, it's like my pair bond with Zaide and my mate bond with Baelen. It's for mates."

Elizabeth's pause chilled my blood. Her voice was low as she said, "Your bond is warped."

"What?"

She held up a hand to stop any more interruptions and hastened to finish. "Back when animal gods roamed, a few

279

witches were able to tether their souls together. It's unclear in the texts about whether it was a consensual bond or not, but the effects were the same. The witches had access to the shadow magic residing in them. But as animal gods dwindled and the shadow magic was homeless but unattainable to them, witches decided to find a way to make the animal gods."

"How did they do that?" I asked quietly.

"A spell. A very complicated spell that requires months of preparation to call a soul, gather shadow magic, and reap magic from faith and prayers."

"How—"

"Like I said. It's extremely complicated, which is why so few witches have familiars, thankfully." She huffed out a breath and continued, "No one truly knows for certain what happens when we die, but we do know that some souls stay around. When a soul that hasn't been reborn naturally is called, it remembers its past life, which works in the favor of the witches."

"Unless their past life was as a slug," Charlie mumbled.

"How do you call a soul?" I asked.

"In a similar fashion to calling a demon. By opening a portal through the veil to the afterlife and pulling the first soul that crosses." Her lips curled in disgust.

My stomach dropped, and I whispered, "I was placed into a cat?"

I felt sick at the thought. *My feline body isn't mine? I've taken the place of some other soul?*

"No. Your feline body is a part of you. Once the soul is called and the prayers and faith are applied, it forms the basis of the animal god. The shadow realm's magic creates the form based on the soul's previous life."

I let out a sigh of relief.

"This is making my head hurt." Charlie rubbed his head with a groan.

"Once the animal god has been created, witches must turn that creature from god to slave." Elizabeth's voice lowered, and her eyes narrowed.

"Slave?" Zaide asked, his voice equally dark, and his eyes met mine.

I didn't pause on the word. While Winnie had obviously used me for my power, she never once made me feel like a slave, and I was grateful for the love she gave me as the trauma of my past life lingered in my heart and mind.

I asked, "How do they bond a familiar with a shadow bond?"

"With a tether. Shadows use their own shadow-made tether to wrap around each other, but witches create a magic tether, like the cages we are so fond of, and tie it around the animal," Elizabeth explained.

Zaide asked with pain in his eyes. "Do you remember any of that, Little Cat?"

"No." I blinked and tried to recall my first days in this life. I shook my head. "My first weeks alive again are a blur. I was scared a lot."

Charlie shook his head, his voice serious. "I didn't tether her. I would have remembered doing something like that."

He thinks he enslaved me? I tried to reassure him. "It's all right, Charlie. Our bond is different."

"Describe to me what you did to save her," Elizabeth said calmly.

"Zaide told me to imagine a thread and to pull it toward me." He exchanged looks with Zaide, who nodded.

Elizabeth leaned back into the sofa with a small smile. "You let her tether you, Charlie."

"What do you mean?" he asked.

"The thread you saw. You tied it from Clawdia to you, did you not?"

"Yes."

281

"You are bonded but not in the same way as the shadows, or the witches. Witches tie from themselves and force the connection. Shadows tie each other. You allowed her to tie to you. Although that does mean you are still unbalanced. If you want an equal bond like that of the shadows, Charlie must also tie Clawdia."

"I don't feel like we are unbalanced," I commented.

"The person in control of the bond always feels less. You may not have had time to notice, but it may be duller, quieter than your last bond."

I thought about that and realized she was right. With Winnie, I was always heard and could always feel her. With Charlie, I had to want to be heard and felt only what I wanted to feel. But he'd felt my extreme emotions even when he didn't want to. We were unbalanced.

I gave him an apologetic glance. "I just thought it was because Charlie is calmer than Winnie."

Charlie laughed. "No one has ever accused me of that before."

"I agree, Clawdia, Charlie is never calm," Zaide added with a chuckle.

"We'll fix it," I told him.

"I'll add it to the to-do list."

We sat in silence, lost in our own thoughts for a moment as we processed all the new information.

Eventually, I realized my original question hadn't been answered. "So, even though I have shadow magic and can change forms, you didn't say if the fact I have my courses is normal or not?"

Elizabeth's eyes were soft as she lifted a shoulder in a half shrug. "In truth, Clawdia, I don't think familiars called by witches are fertile. But you and your men seem to be the exception to many of the rules. What people won't tell you about bonds is that you share more than just power. Perhaps when Zaide regained his fertility, so did you. And although it's not documented, I like to imagine that the animal gods of the past and the witches they were with had a romantic bond that allowed for blessings like children."

It was a nice thought and made me smile. *At least there is hope. I might not be normal, but I am blessed.* "I think that would be wonderful too," I agreed.

My dislike of her lessened as she smiled understandingly. Her gaze moved to the window, and I noted how dark it was outside now. She slapped her knees and stood up. "Anyway, I'll leave you to your evening. It's been a long day, and I'm sure you still have a lot to think about."

I rose to see her out. "Thank you, Elizabeth. I appreciate your knowledge and help."

"No thanks necessary." She waved, and I closed the door behind her.

With her gone, the remainder of my energy seemed to fall away, and I was suddenly exhausted. I yawned, and Zaide wrapped an arm around my waist as he guided me to the bedroom. "Come on, Little Cat. Off to bed."

I stopped and looked back at Baelen, feeling ridiculously guilty that we were going to bed and leaving him in a cage without so much as a pillow or cover. "Are you going to be all right in there? I hate that you can't come to bed with us."

He smiled patiently and waved me away. "I'll be fine, Sunlight. Have sweet dreams."

I fell asleep before my head touched the pillow, and morning came all too quickly.

My eyes fluttered open to the cracks of sunlight shining past the edges of the curtain, and I sat up to see that Zaide had already risen. The morning felt quiet and still. But it wasn't the peaceful kind. Instead, the air seemed to vibrate with the kind of electric tension that suggested something was coming. Be it a storm or something else. When I looked at Charlie, he was already awake and staring at me with the same puzzled expression I'm sure I wore. He felt it too.

But if our experience on this island was teaching us anything, it was that we couldn't control everything. We just had to put on a smile, see what happened, and hope everything worked out.

CHAPTER 24

BAELEN

"*M*orning," Zaide said as he opened the door to the bedroom, the squeak of which woke me up.

Blinking groggily, I became aware of my stiff muscles from being stuck in a cage with my legs bent and my neck hanging all night. It was better than the alternative. And I was glad to be the one that opened my own eyes.

When the three of them went to bed last night, I stayed awake for hours, staring at the clock on the wall, fearful that if I fell asleep, I would wake up to find myself stuffed in the back of my mind once more and watching as someone else controlled my movements.

As it was, the morning was peaceful. The sun rose in the sky from beyond the window in the kitchen, and I admired my soul mate's bare back and legs as he made tea in his shorts. I'd never been attracted to a male before, but with Zaide, our bond drew me to him. It was impossible to deny while I was in control of my body. My eyes trailed over him languishingly, caressing, observing, and admiring.

He finished making his drink and turned to face me,

leaning on the counter as he sipped from the cup and considered me.

I didn't avoid his eyes, but I dreaded to think what he thought of me.

"Stop with the love eyes. You're making me feel sick," Kaatu announced loudly.

He'd been suspiciously quiet since last night when we learned Clawdia's nature as a familiar was tied to shadow magic. It concerned me that he would think it even more perfect to use my soul mate to fix his portal since she housed some of the magic the portal had lost. *But what would that do to her?*

I flinched and looked away, clenching my jaw to reply. *"I'm in control right now, so I can do what I like."*

"Right now, you are in a cage and can't do anything. It's the only reason I haven't bothered to try and take control again, even though I know it would be easy."

"What is happening in your head right now?" Zaide asked quietly.

I opened my mouth to say something, anything, that would help them, tell them they were right, but Kaatu pushed for control again, and I was left gasping and choking as I desperately clung to the control of my body.

"Why won't you let me tell them? They already know."

"They know nothing."

"They believe a shadow has possessed me, and that's why we are in this cage."

"If you confirm anything, they will find a way to be rid of me before I am ready. And if the touch doesn't work, then I'll need Clawdia to still believe you are without influence to consummate the bond."

"You aren't consummating anything with her. Stop talking about it."

"But you are so adorable when you are angry."

Zaide sighed, placed his cup on the side, and kneeled in front of me. "You are feeling yourself today?"

I managed a quick nod.

"And yesterday evening was akari bloodlust?"

I nodded again.

He sighed, his shoulders sagging with relief, before standing and heading to the bathroom without another word.

Clawdia and Charlie left the bedroom only moments later. My sunlight took one look at me and came straight over, her face scrunched with concern.

"How did you sleep? I'm so sorry you had to stay there." She rested a hand on the cage.

"I've slept in worse places." It was true. In my hunt for titans, I'd often had to wait out the slavers in strange places until I could rescue the new recruits. But it was never pleasant.

She huffed out a breath, and her eyes looked sad as she said, "We should have asked Elizabeth to make a bigger cage so you could at least lie down."

I shook my head. "It was a long night, and no one was thinking clearly."

"You seem to be thinking clearly." She tilted her head as she examined much in the same way her soul pair had.

"I am," I confirmed. Her eyes were bruised with exhaustion, and as she crouched in front of me, I could see how she pressed her stomach into her bent knees and hugged them tightly to add pressure. "How are you feeling this morning, my sunlight?"

She sighed and whispered, "Bloated. Achy. I barely slept because I was worried I'd make a mess and scare them."

I frowned, wishing I could pull her into my arms. If I were myself, I'd be on my knees in front of her, easing her pain, divulging in her delicious blood. "It disheartens me that it causes you pain and worry," I told her, then smiled. "But you smell delicious."

She chuckled. "I'm going to take that as a compliment."

"You should," I replied, feeling better now I'd made her smile.

"What are you two whispering about?" Charlie asked.

She winked at me and turned to face her witch. "Nothing for your ears."

Charlie seemed to guess just from looking at her and pointed. "You can't fault me for freaking out a bit. I know it's a natural thing, but I didn't grow up with girls, and the whole thing scares me. What kind of people bleed for a week and just carry on with their day."

"Women," she replied blandly, and I laughed.

He shuddered. "Scary."

"So dramatic." She shook her head but smiled at his antics.

Just as with last night, I watched their easy banter, and longed for nothing more than to be a part of it. I hadn't been part of a family for a long time and with Clawdia's vision, it made me hopeful for the future.

She turned back to me. "Are you hungry?"

I shook my head and chuckled. "No, Sunlight. I've never been so well-fed."

Her eyes softened, and she said quietly, "I don't know how often you need it. I don't want you to feel like you have to ask me."

"I'm well," I assured her.

Charlie watched us. "You're being normal today."

I nodded. "For now."

He narrowed his eyes at me. "You aren't getting out of the cage."

"I know." I couldn't help the smirk. His suspicion was entertaining and worked in my favor.

"And you can't tell us anything?" He raised a questioning brow.

"No."

He paused, still considering me intently, then shrugged. "We'll figure it out. And when you're back to normal, it'll be good to have you here helping us with Fafnir."

His easy acceptance of my place in his—their—lives, despite having only met me once, in which I also hadn't given a good first impression, warmed my heart.

"Of course," I choked out.

Zaide left the bathroom holding a brush. "Little Cat, can you help me for a moment?"

She rose, took the brush from him, and had him sit on the chair so she could begin combing through his long white hair. He closed his eyes, savoring her touch. *It's a kind of torture, being inside a cage watching, unable to touch or be touched.*

"You don't want me helping you with your hair?" Charlie asked playfully.

Zaide's eyes cut to his friend, and he replied, "Little Cat has to comb out the tangles she put there."

"And I still have no details." Charlie pouted.

"You'll have to live in suspense," Clawdia teased.

"Why?" he asked and flicked Clawdia's braid.

"Because it's between us and the birds," Zaide said, a wicked grin on his lips.

"Birds? You were outside?" Charlie's mouth dropped open. "You were literally wild, and I was reading a fucking book. So not fair."

"You can't be there all the time, Charlie." Clawdia laughed as she finished braiding Zaide's hair and put her hand out for him to hand her his tie. The tie had a little prayer stone similar to the one he gave me in the dreamscape.

"I know. I just want to be." Charlie sighed and began

putting his shoes on. "Anyway, I'm off. I need to talk to Elizabeth."

"I'll come with you, Charlie." Zaide looked up at Clawdia. "Little Cat?"

She shook her head and said, "I'm going to visit Karin and get some more pain killers and female products."

Charlie straightened with a frown. "Be careful with her."

His tone startled her, and she dropped Zaide's braid. "What do you mean?"

"She was being weird yesterday."

She narrowed her eyes. "Weird in what way?"

Charlie seemed to choke on his words as he said, "Just … okay, well, she, she came on to me."

"What?" She recoiled. "What did you do?"

"I told her I'm with you," he replied quickly, and her shoulders relaxed. Pulling her into his arms, he kissed her forehead and said, "I thought it was weird that she was flirting with me because she knew I was with you."

"Do you think it was because I'm with three men that she thought you were also open?" She asked, and her face fell even further as something occurred to her. Her mouth ran away as she jabbered, "Assuming you aren't. I mean, we've never talked about it. I suppose it's greedy of me to assume you'd never want anyone other than me, and I'm only your familiar—"

He covered her mouth. "I'm not. I know Baelen and Zaide have each other as well as you, but for me, it's only going to be you. I can promise you that right now."

"What if you find a soul mate?" she asked quietly.

"Witches don't have soul mates."

"Drakorians do."

"Well good for them, but that part of me is literally a drop in an ocean of Charlie. I'm not a dragon. And I don't want anyone else. I just wanted to tell you because I know you don't want secrets anymore and she might try to bring it up and make me look bad."

Her eyes narrowed again. "Why would she bring it up if nothing happened?"

"She's clearly got some agenda here because although she came on to me, it didn't feel genuine. It was like she was doing it to see if I'd fall for it. I'm not sure what she's up to, but just ... be careful." He cupped her face and examined her eyes. "Okay?"

She nodded. "All right. I'll be careful."

"Good." He let her go, picked up his phone from the table, pocketed it, and nudged Zaide. "Come on, then. The day's a-wasting."

"See you later, Little Cat," Zaide said as he stood. He leaned down to kiss Clawdia.

"Love you," she replied breathlessly as he pulled away.

"And I you."

Charlie glared. "You're making me look bad."

"Then kiss our beautiful little cat and tell her you love her too." Zaide shrugged and walked to the door.

"Love you, Clawdicat." Charlie kissed her with no less passion than Zaide did. "See you in a bit."

I sighed. "No kisses for me." They all paused to look at me. I didn't think they'd forgotten I was there, but they were surprised to hear me make a joke, because all three of them gave a startled laugh.

Charlie winked. "I'm sure you'll get plenty of kisses when we've fixed you. Bye, Baelen. Be a good little vampire for Clawdicat while we're away."

The door slammed behind them, and then it was just Clawdia and me. She went to the bathroom, and I picked at my nails as I waited for her to come back. When she did, she sat near me again, and I relished in the smell of her, the warmth radiating from her.

"Are you all right?" she asked eventually, hesitantly. I tilted my head. She knew I couldn't talk about my situation with Kaatu. "I mean, after what I said last night. About what I … saw."

"Ah."

She wrung her hands nervously and explained quickly, "You didn't say a word last night, and you're talking now, and I just wanted to know if it was because you couldn't talk last night or because you didn't want to."

"I couldn't." But not for the reason she thought.

Visions were something I had an uncomfortable relationship with since my mother had been cursed to see the future when the titans fell. And Clawdia's vision, whether it was such or not, was a frightening prospect for someone whose fathers disowned him.

"Can you talk now?" Clawdia asked, her expression earnest. "I know you don't have a great relationship with your fathers. Are you worried?"

I blinked, shocked at how easily she saw through me. "I suppose I am."

She nodded. "That's understandable. We're all still getting to know each other."

"Zaide is uncomfortable around my eyes. A child—"

She interrupted my thought before I could finish it. "Zaide couldn't be more excited for children. He'd love them all. I could give birth to kittens, and he'd raise them with pride." She laughed, and I had to smile.

"I just need time to process," I told her and changed the subject. "Have you ever had a vision before?"

"Never. I can't even be sure that it was a vision, but it was so clear and so sudden. Even if it's not a vision of the future, I know what I want it to look like. And I think that's really helped Zaide in particular."

I changed position, trying to get more comfortable, and

cast my mind back to when my mother was still around. "My mother's visions were always sudden. She'd be in the middle of something, then gaze off for a few minutes and eventually return to us, blinking away whatever she saw."

"Your mother had visions?" Her violet eyes were alight with interest. How I wanted to touch her. I didn't imagine when we shared our lives and spoke about the past that I'd be in a cage.

"She was cursed with them after the fall. It's not a typical akari gift." Clawdia blinked, opened her mouth, closed it, and tilted her head. I frowned. "What is it?"

"Is her name Nisha by any chance?"

It was my turn to be shocked. "Yes. How did you know?"

She gasped and sat up, enthused, and exclaimed, "I've met her! I know her. She …" She stopped and blinked, realizing something. "Wow. She's been seeing me since my past life. She told the protector to hide the potion in Fafnir's house so I could find it."

I didn't know what she was talking about, and she must have remembered that, because she explained everything the protector had told them and also added how Fafnir was, in fact, Mr. Jenkins, her ex-husband.

The Fates had us tied up in threads we couldn't escape even if we wanted to.

She was meant for me. Zaide was meant for us both. And my mother had been assisting my future from before I was born. It made me feel … loved, to know she'd been looking out for me for so long and continued to do so. I wondered if she'd had a vision of me, as Clawdia had a vision of our children. But it was just another question I wanted to ask her when we finally met again.

"She must have known you were meant for me and ensured you could have been reborn," I said, and Clawdia nodded her agreement.

"Were you born when I was living my past life?"

"No." I was not over one hundred years old. I was half that, even if I didn't look at it. But I didn't tell her that. Regardless of gender, no one wanted to admit their age, especially when the person asking was so much younger.

"I've met your mother, and she doesn't look old, but according to you, she was there for the fall of the titans, which was ancient Greek days, yes?"

"Yes."

"So, you're immortal?"

I shook my head. "Akari live very, very long lives. As did the titans when they had their souls. So do the faei. All our realms have magic to sustain us. Yours does not, and so humans are relatively short lived."

"Unfair." She pouted, and I laughed.

"You'll live as long as I do when we are bonded." She gave me a shy smile, which did nothing to stop my desire. Changing the subject again, I asked, "Did she look well? When you saw her? My mother?"

She frowned. "You haven't seen her?"

I shook my head slowly. "She left my fathers many years ago. It was part of the plan for her to hide somewhere even I wouldn't know about."

"What—"

"It's a very long story, my sunlight." I sighed. She looked a little disgruntled, and I assured her, "I will tell you one day. But not today."

She hesitated and then smiled as she said, "Her house looks like a fairytale cottage, and she's beautiful, like you, but she was worried, talking about the future and gazing off."

Her words lit me up from the inside. "You think I'm beautiful?"

She gave me a look. "You know you are."

"It's nice to hear." I restrained my smile, barely, and changed positions again.

When I looked back at her, she was staring at me again with a kind of melancholic gaze that made me want to embrace her. "You will be all right, won't you, Baelen?"

I placed my hand on the cage, barely touching it so it didn't hurt me. "Of course. No matter what happens, Clawdia. I'm going to be fine. I want us. I want our family. And I'll fight for it if I need to."

"Good. Because we need you. I need you," she whispered.

Of course, Kaatu ruined it by reminding me of how powerless I actually am. *"How touching."*

CHAPTER 25

CLAWDIA

"*T*hank you so much for this, Karin." I sat on her sofa, sipping on a tea that was easing the ache I'd had deep in my stomach all morning.

When I turned up that morning and explained I had my courses, was in pain, and had no products, she immediately ushered me in, cooing over me with sympathetic noises. Which was really nice when compared to the horrified look I'd received from Charlie and the confusion and panic from Zaide.

Karin handed me products, showed me how to use them, and let me pick which one I wanted to start with. Then she settled me on the sofa and handed me a freshly brewed tea she assured me would make the pain a distant memory.

"You're welcome," she replied easily as she joined me with her own cup.

I shook my head. "You don't understand. This is exactly what I needed. The guys weren't that helpful. But Winnie … she would have done this for me if she were still here."

"You loved her," Karin said, her eyes soft and wistful.

I nodded, remembering snuggling on the sofa, helping

her choose outfits, and having deep discussions about race, sexuality, history. "We were like sisters."

Karin stared at me with that intense gaze she had. "When she took Savida's fire, did your feelings for her change?"

I shook my head. Despite what she'd done, despite the betrayal and the disappointment, I'd always consider her family. "I was disappointed she couldn't see what she was doing was wrong. I wanted her to listen to me and stop. But she didn't. And she'd been using me to find information out on them all so she could make that plan. She drugged me to keep me out of the way. Betrayed me."

"But despite that, you loved her." She said it like a fact with a smug tilt to her lip I didn't quite understand.

With Charlie's warning ringing in the back of my mind, I eyed her as I said, "She was the first person to love me and treat me well in a while. I probably overlooked a lot because of that. But yes. I loved her. Even now, I miss her."

She set down her mug and leaned close. A manic look in her eyes had me leaning away, my body tightening with sudden tension. She asked quietly, "What if you could have that back?"

"What do you mean? Have Winnie back?"

"The easy life. The sister relationship with a witch who will love and appreciate you."

I frowned. "Charlie loves and appreciates me."

She scoffed and glared out of the window. "Charlie doesn't know how to use you."

My eyebrows flew into my hairline, and I repeated, "Use me?"

"You have so much power, almost an unlimited amount, and he could draw on that. He could do all kinds of spells. He could be great. But he doesn't care about being a witch, and he doesn't have the knowledge. It's such a waste."

After everything that I'd learned about familiars and their

history, it frustrated me that she believed having power automatically meant it should be used. The animal gods had power but were tethered to witches who wanted to use that power to boost their own. Greed was a common trait amongst humans but even more so in people with a touch of power already.

I swallowed my frustration and replied calmly, "Charlie's got plenty of time to learn all that yet. We aren't old. He can grow into a great witch who can utilize all the power we have. He does care about being a witch. He's just been busy."

Not that it is any of your business.

"Busy. Yes, you've all had quite the adventure. Isn't it time it stops?"

"That would be great," I replied with a snort. "As soon as Fafnir is defeated and Sigurd is put back to rest, we can dedicate ourselves to the things we really want and are destined to do."

"And they are?" she asked, curiosity overtaking the manic gleam in her eyes.

I relaxed slightly and managed a chuckle. "It's quite a list. There's going to be lots of traveling around the realms."

She sneered. "Charlie? Traveling around the realms? What a thought." Her laughter was cruel, and my stomach dropped. Talking with her was like playing Russian roulette. One moment, everything is fine, if not a little tense, and the next she says something so ... wrong. It made me wonder which was the real Karin.

"That's the second disparaging thing you've said about him. Why is your opinion so low?" My hands clenched around my cup tightly, and anger bubbled under the surface of my skin.

She shrugged. "He's just very immature. You should have seen him in the library yesterday. He was so bored he was flirting with me to get out of reading."

I huffed and slammed my cup on the side table. "You're wrong about him, and whether you think he was flirting or not, nothing else would have ever happened. He's with me."

She raised her brow at the mug. "Finish your tea."

The fact she completely ignored my statement told me she didn't believe it, which only made me angrier.

Gritting my teeth, I stood up and said, "I think I should go."

"Because you don't like my opinion of Charlie?" She blocked my path as I headed to the door. "You could do so much better than him. Have a witch that knows what they are doing. That can support you on your adventures. I've read so much about the other realms. Did you know there is an island in Álfheimr that is completely underwater? It's—"

I blinked in confusion and interrupted, "Karin. None of that matters. It's not what I want—"

"You don't?" Her eyes lightened, and I felt even more confused as she continued brightly, "Oh, well, that's even better, then. You could be a cat again—"

I held up a hand as I interrupted again. "What are you talking about? I can be a cat whenever I want." *At least, I could before. Who knows how my cycle has affected me.*

"If you don't want to travel the realms, then we could just have everything could go back to normal …" She was speaking fast, and my brain couldn't process the words. Nothing was making sense.

Why does it feel as though we are speaking different languages?

Words poured out of me, stopping her in the middle of whatever she'd been saying. "Karin, nothing can go back to normal. My normal was licking my fur and watching Call the Midwives on the television because it reminded me of my past. I'm human again now. I have men that love me and want to be with me. I get to talk to other people again and feel like I'm more than the magic I have. All of that isn't something I want to give up. Too much has happened to go back." I took a deep breath but pressed on before she could interrupt again. "And I was trying to say that I don't want a witch to support me on our adventures. I have a witch. I have Charlie, and whether he can offer magical support to us is irrelevant. I need him for more than magic. Just as he needs me for more. We love each other."

"You love each other." She repeated the words like I was her love interest in a film and I was trying to let her down.

She stumbled back, her face blank but her fists clenched.

"Yes. I thought you knew that. I told you about them, him." I don't know why I felt sorry for her. We barely knew each other, but it felt cruel to leave her when she was clearly upset. I approached her like I might approach a cornered animal. "Where has all this come from?" I asked carefully.

Her lips tightened before she announced, "I want you to be my familiar."

My silence was stunned. "Well, I'm flattered, but I can't be anyone else's familiar. I'm Charlie's. But that doesn't mean we can't still be friends."

"Friends?" She scoffed. "Friends can't share magic."

"So you only want me for the magic I could give you." I had to sit down, as my legs suddenly went weak. Disappointment and anger had that effect on a person. Or so I thought.

"We could do such amazing things together." She paced in front of me, seeming to blur with how fast she moved.

"Like what? Cure cancer? Take over the world? What do you need magic for? You've never left this island." I tried to wave my hand, but all my energy seemed to have been zapped from me. The previous day had been long and draining, so I wasn't surprised, but my lethargy couldn't have come at a worse time. I needed to leave.

"Charlie, come and get me. You were right. Karin is being really strange. She seems to think you and she can be my witches."

But Charlie didn't reply, and as I reflected on my words, I realized I was wrong. Karin didn't think she and Charlie could be my witches. She was smart. She no doubt knew how familiars were created. She also knew Winnie had died for Charlie to take over as my witch.

A sharp inhale drew her gaze to me. She asked, "Has it worked? The tea?"

The painkiller tea. My eyes shifted to the cup, and hurt reverberated through me. It was almost exactly the same situation I had with Winnie, and for the second time in this life, I'd trusted a witch, only for them to drug me and attempt to hurt someone I cared for.

No more taking food or drink from witches.

"Is that why I can't move?" I asked weakly.

She didn't respond but began gathering things, and I knew she was about to start the second part of her plan. Kill Charlie. *Distract her. Stop her.*

Despite my lips and tongue feeling heavy, I fought the effects of the tea to say, "Karin, Karin, I don't understand. Why would you do this? Why couldn't you just summon a familiar?"

She glared at me. "Because I have no power. Because it wouldn't be as strong as you. But don't worry. I've thought this through. If you do start to die before I can transfer your bond to me, I'll drain your power and use that to summon a familiar."

Charming.

"You haven't thought this through. I'm connected to more than just Charlie. If you try to hurt him, Zaide and Baelen will stop you to protect me."

"Taken care of." She waved a hand and continued to pack her bag.

I blinked and tried not to let the panic surging inside me

take over. I asked her, "What do you mean?" while I called, *"Zaide. Zaide, can you hear me?"* in my mind.

She sighed as she stood over me. "You ask a lot of questions. We'll work on that."

Anger suddenly overtook the fear, and I growled, "How did you imagine this would go? That I'd be glad you killed someone I love? That I'd just let you take my power without question or thought? I'm done with that. I'm not going to make this easy for you."

She shrugged. "Nothing worthwhile is easy. I expect you to fight back, Clawdia, but I've been planning this for days now, and it's faultless. I'm going to get everything I want."

"Power. But no friends. No love," I choked out as my eyes began to strain.

"That might seem like a tragedy to you, Clawdia, but my parents do love me, and they'd want me to choose power. They know what this means to me."

"You think this is all going to go your way, but if you hurt him, even if you become my witch, I'll never forgive you. And I'll take my life to stop you from using me. From making me your slave!" I shouted and desperately struggled against the haze coming over me.

Please, please. I can't lose him.

She scoffed. "No, you won't. You've a soul mate and a soul pair. You'll be attached to me, doing all I want you to, because if you don't, I'll hurt them."

I would do anything for Zaide and Baelen if it saved them pain, and I couldn't imagine them being so easily controlled by this powerless witch, but I'd already underestimated her so much.

"You have no real power of your own, so you're going to take ours and use it against us? Why? What do you hope to accomplish?"

She picked up her bag and threw it over her shoulder.

"Nothing. I have no plans for world domination. I don't want to hurt anyone. I just want to be able to use the power I have learned so much about. I want to spend my days researching and experimenting with my own power and limits. I want what everyone else has taken for granted. I want to be respected and needed."

"All of which are admirable," I coughed, "but doing this doesn't help that. You're going to hurt him. And me. Please, please reconsider."

She shook her head slowly and walked toward the door. "I'm not going to let this opportunity slip through my hands."

No.

And as I heard the door slam shut, the world went dark.

CHAPTER 26

CHARLIE

*E*lizabeth was wide-eyed and bushy-tailed in the library, sipping on what smelled like coffee and scouring a book.

I called, "Good morning, woman that birthed me."

She looked up as we walked in. "Good morning, Charlie. Zaide. How is everyone today?"

I shrugged as I sat next to her at the table. "Clawdia is in pain, and Baelen is himself again, but we don't know how long that will last."

"Has he told you anything?" she asked.

Zaide joined us, the chair creaking as he sat down. "Nothing. I think the shadow prevents him. He was able to more or less confirm that he's currently in control and is happy to stay in the cage."

"That's a good start. Perhaps the shadow's influence is weakening," Elizabeth suggested.

I nodded at the book she was reading. "Have you found anything that could help?"

"I've been reading up on demons and how they are

recalled from possession." She pursed her lips and set her coffee down as she flicked back a few pages.

"It's not a priest throwing holy water at them?" I asked jokingly.

"No." She gave me an unamused look and turned back to her book, her fingers following the words on the page as she searched for something.

"Holy water?" Zaide frowned.

"It's a religious thing. I'll explain another time," I said. Knowing him, he would love the idea of blessed water.

"Demons are recalled from possessing their host by calling another person, or themselves, using their name to go back to their body," Elizabeth read.

"But shadows don't have a true name, do they?" Zaide asked.

"No. And shadows are themselves shadows. Their body morphs with them, so we can't recall him to a body," Elizabeth added.

"None of this sounds positive," I remarked, hoping she actually had something useful to say soon.

"It isn't what is written, but what is not," she said, her eyes sparkling with interest. "How does the shadow keep himself a shadow for so long? Their nature is to morph and change like the mist and clouds."

Zaide caught on faster than I did. "You believe he is leaving Baelen at certain times?"

"I think if he hasn't already, he will. And then we only need to capture him and find out his intentions with you all."

I huffed out a frustrated breath. All that lead up for nothing. "So, we have no solution. Only a wait and see. Again."

"All good things come to those that wait." Elizabeth said to lighten the mood, but it didn't work.

"Sure." I folded my arms, and my stomach rumbled which only made me grumpier.

Elizabeth continued, "In the meantime, you can continue with your studies while Zaide helps me search for more information about shadows."

My studies. God, I hate having to read all this magic shit. Although I should read up on making a magical tether so I can even the bond with Clawdia ...

But just like I had in school, I distracted the teacher with questions. "What have the council said about Fafnir? Have they found him yet?"

Elizabeth sighed as she pushed a book in Zaide's direction. "Not yet. I'm inclined to believe there is something strange happening in their teams because they are struggling to find anything."

Something strange happening in the teams? I couldn't stop myself. The need to find the information and solve the mystery curled inside me. I made a mental note to hack into their phones to see what was going on later.

Zaide flipped open a book and got to work, ignoring both of us. As much as he pretended to be cool and calm this morning in front of Baelen, I know he was still freaking out about the situation and desperate to change it.

"Can you do anything about the teams?" I asked.

"I'm still new to the council. They aren't going to share any secrets with me just yet." Elizabeth shrugged. *Fucking politics.*

"What about finding your relatives? Have they managed that at least?" I asked.

She shook her head. "Nothing."

"I fucking told them where they were!" I exclaimed. "What more do they need? That should have been an easy win."

What the fuck? I ran my hand through my hair and tried to shake the anger creeping over me. *But how the fuck could they fuck that up?*

"Apparently, no one was there when they turned up," Elizabeth said calmly.

"And they couldn't find anything telling them where to go next? They didn't ask me to have another look?" I stood up, breathing hard. "These people are supposed to be the supernatural council's best. The most trained. Specialized. And they can't catch people when they are given an exact location?"

"Why are you so distraught about this? There will be other opportunities." Elizabeth frowned as I began pacing.

"It gets harder to track people when they know they are being tracked. That was our best shot, and a good team should have been able to get our family members and find out what the fuck Fafnir's plan is and where he is."

I blamed whatever weird tension was in the air for my sudden flare of temper, but in all fairness, I'd been as good as gold for our little vacation away from the action. Everyone else had had a breakdown. Surely it was my turn to have a wobble.

"Charlie, are you well?" Zaide asked.

"No. I'm not fucking well."

He stood and put a hand on my shoulder, stopping me mid-pace. "You are a catapult, Charlie. Take a deep breath and make a new plan."

Despite being angry and frustrated, I smiled. *He's the best boyfriend-in-law a guy could ask for.* "New plan," I repeated. He nodded and sat back down.

My leg began vibrating, and I pulled my phone out to see Adam's name. *He has great timing.* I needed a win. I pulled my phone out and waved it at them. "I need to take this. But I'll be back with food."

They nodded, and I headed out of the room. "Adam?" I answered.

But Adam's voice wasn't the cheerful, triumphant call I

expected. He whispered quickly, "Charlie, listen, I don't know how much time you have."

My stomach dropped, and I rushed down the stairs of the main house and out the front door. "What's happened?"

"Your seek-and-destroy turned the tables on us," he breathed. "They hacked me, found the location of your call, and they are on their way."

"No." I froze. "How the fuck?"

He groaned as he explained, "I've no clue. I managed to get the bare minimum on them and went to bed. I woke up to this shit storm. I don't know how long you've got before they come calling."

"Jesus, fuck." I crouched and buried my head in my hand.

Do the wards stop technical tracking as well as magical? Is the island invisible if they manage to turn up here? God, I should have asked more questions about them.

"I'm sorry, Charlie. I don't know what kind of organization these people work for, but they've got mad resources to beat my security in such little time." Adam's voice was like a quiet buzz in my ear now as my mind raced.

"Thanks for the warning, Adam." I wanted to hang up, but I knew how people like this worked. "Are you going to be okay?"

"I've got things in place for this kind of thing. Don't worry about me. Just get yourself out of there and lie low. Text me when you're safe so I know you're still alive."

I swallowed thickly. "I will. Thanks again."

"Good luck."

I hung up and almost threw my phone. "Fuck!" I yelled.

"Trouble?" a voice asked curiously.

"Karin. Shit. Yes. Maybe." I ran my hand through my hair and tried to calm down enough to think clearly. "We need to get everyone together. Strengthen the wards."

"It's okay, Charlie." She smiled sweetly, and I was so in my own head it didn't even occur to me that it was weird. "Whatever it is, we'll sort it."

"Yeah." I nodded. "Where are the council?"

"Come with me. I'll take you to the council, and they'll help you." She started walking, and I automatically fell into step next to her.

Panic battered at me. My head was spinning, my heart racing. I felt sick to my stomach that I'd lead the hunters right to us. I was so cocksure. *And now look at what you've caused.* The witches here didn't need this panic. Sigurd certainly didn't need to be hunted when he was the very thing stopping Fafnir from terrorizing the other realms.

I wasn't concentrating on anything, too involved in my own head, the panic and guilt overwhelming me, to see where I was going. But it was when the door behind a small cabin closed that I realized I was standing inside a large salt pentacle that I knew I'd fucked up. Suddenly, a transparent wall flew up around me, and I was trapped.

"What the fuck is this, Karin?" I tried to stay calm. I really did. But the last thing I needed was to deal with whatever Karin's agenda was as well as hunters.

She giggled and almost danced on the spot with glee. "You're so silly, Charlie. You just let me walk you right in here."

"Listen, whatever fucked-up shit you're going to try to do, can you leave it for now? We are about to be attacked!"

"Charlie, you've already been attacked."

She looked so pleased with herself it confused me, and I had to ask, "What?"

She waved her hands at the cage I found myself in. "Don't bother struggling. It's too late for that."

A shocked laugh startled both of us. I was hysterical, laughing until tears streamed down my face. When I was calm enough, I said, "Your seduction tactics need work, but seriously, you need to let me out now. I need to talk to the council about hunters."

"Who said anything about seduction?" She set her bag down and started pulling stuff out of it.

I had no clue what she was doing, but the more pressing issue of the hunters made me call out to Clawdia. *"Hey, Karin's trapped me in a circle, and I can't get out, but can you go to the council and tell them the hunters are on their way. They need to lock this place down right now. Then come get me."*

Usually when I spoke to her, I could hear her response or feel her presence. But it was like she'd disappeared. *Why the fuck can't I hear her? Feel her? Why isn't she replying?*

I looked at the witch in front of me, the witch I knew Clawdia was going to see today and currently had me trapped. Suddenly, this didn't seem like a game or a prank anymore.

"What have you done to Clawdia?" I asked darkly. *If she's harmed a hair on her head …*

"Oh, that?" She didn't even look up as she replied, and I froze. "Nothing. I just didn't want her to be able to contact anyone or you'll be able to stop me."

"Stop you doing what?" I asked, the knot in my stomach turning to ice as I realized the seriousness of this.

"Getting a familiar, of course."

"What do you mean? How is trapping me here going to get you a familiar?"

"I'm not trapping you. I'm killing you."

I coughed, choking on my own saliva. "You're crazy. You literally tried to seduce me yesterday, and now you're going to try to kill me?"

She stood up and shrugged, her eyes serious and … bored. "Just testing how I could get you alone. Thankfully, you provided me with just the right opportunity at the right time."

I shook my head and stepped back until the cage zapped me to stop me going any further. "You don't have any power. You can't kill me."

Her bored expression fell away to reveal an evil sneer. "Not with my power, no."

"What does that even mean?" I asked, my eyes getting bigger as I took in my surroundings, looking for bottles of fire or other magic that she might have hoarded.

"You didn't come here to donate magic to strengthen the wards. Clawdia did, though. Yesterday. We managed to get a good bit of power from her. Enough that I could create the tea she so willingly took from me this morning. Ironic, really."

"You've been draining the wards to use the magic?"

She gave a slow round of applause. "Very clever, Charlie."

"You can't drain the wards, Karin." I stepped closer, panting as panic clawed up my throat. "Please listen to me. The hunters know about this island and are on their way. We need the wards—"

She interrupted me. "But if I do, I'll be able to kill you, drain your magic, bind the most powerful familiar in the world to me, and then I'll be able to stop the hunters before they step foot on land."

"You're so dumb," I choked, actually shocked at how pigheaded she was being when we were about to be attacked.

"You can't stop this from happening, I'm afraid."

"Will you just warn the council then? So they are prepared in case you can't stop the hunters." In a last-ditch attempt, I started begging, "Please. Fuck, if you're going to kill me, I need to know the others are going to be okay."

Is this the moment Zaide gets caught? Because of me? And I'm fucking dead, so I can't even find him?

I'd never felt more helpless in my life, and I prayed for some miracle. For someone to find me. For Clawdia to hear me. For the council to get wind of the attack and protect everyone. But miracles were for believers, and I knew I was well and truly fucked.

"That's not your concern anymore," Karin said, and I saw it in her eyes. The dismissal. The end.

This is it.

With a few mumbled words from her, the place lit up like a rave. But this wasn't a party I wanted to attend. I screamed as pain, the most I'd ever experienced, caused my knees to buckle and my mind to shatter.

It was like being back in that clearing, being drained by the witches but only ten times faster. In seconds, I was falling to the ground. Magic tore from me like I was bleeding out from every pore, and I genuinely thought it was the end. Images of my life flashed before my eyes. Smiling faces of people who knew me, liked me, cared about me. Friends, co-workers, foster parents. My birth mother and the pictures of the sisters I'd never met.

And then there was this cat. A fluffy cat with violet eyes that seemed to smile with mischief. The same eyes that looked at me so adoringly from a beautiful human face. Zaide. Savida. Even Daithi.

I don't want to say goodbye to them. I don't want this to be the end.

Tears leaked from my eyes as I held on to the image of them until the gold thread, the magical tether I'd tied to myself, snapped, and I took my last breath.

CHAPTER 27

ZAIDE

I glanced at the door for the third time in the last few minutes. "Charlie has been gone for a while."

"He's probably run away so he doesn't have to look at the book again," Elizabeth remarked without looking up from her book.

"I don't think it's that. He promised to bring back food." I tapped my fingers against the desk and continued to stare at the door.

Something felt off. The day had been going well, but upon waking there, had been something in the air that was making me nervous. I thought it was something to do with Baelen, but considering Charlie's reaction to the news that the task teams were unsuccessful and how long he'd been gone, I was starting to worry.

"What do you think it is?" Elizabeth asked, drawing my attention back to her. She was looking at me, and concern darkened her eyes.

"He made a call at the party before you arrived to tell an old friend about finding the hunters that broke into our apartment to find us. I think the phone call is his friend calling him back with news." I closed my book.

"What makes you think that? It could have been anyone."

"Charlie doesn't have anyone other than us," I said, and her face shuttered. It hurt her to know that her son had been alone for many years, but she'd made her choice, and I wouldn't withhold information on account of her feelings.

"Why would that news make him stay away so long?" she asked, trying to understand why I was agitated.

"Maybe he's planning something we wouldn't approve of." Charlie was the type to rush in without a second thought if something was urgent. *Maybe the information he gained about the hunters is prompting him to act quickly.* I stood up. "Something doesn't feel right."

Elizabeth stood with me. "Let's go find him if you are so concerned. It's about lunch time anyway. He'll probably be eating."

It frustrated me that she would make such a remark, and I snapped, "You might think he is silly and immature, but Charlie is hardworking, loyal, and very insightful when he wants to be. He often pretends he is not so no one expects too much of him and he can't let anyone down." I raised a pointed brow. "Something I think he learned with families that weren't his own."

"Yes." She coughed and looked away. "Well."

We were walking down the stairs as lightbulbs suddenly burst above us and the earth shook, causing the paintings on the walls to crash to the ground. Glass shattered everywhere. And the underlying feeling of magic that the island had from his ancient protective wards suddenly vanished.

"What was that?" I gasped as I grabbed the railing to steady myself.

Elizabeth crouched against the wall and held on to the

stairs as tremors shook the house, her face pale. "I think it was the wards."

"They've failed?" I asked, horrified.

As soon as the shaking stopped, she stood up and ran down the remaining steps and out of the house with me following closely behind. Screams sounded from down the hill, but from our vantage, I could see the edge of the lake. And there were large boats heading toward us. Three large boats carrying cars and figures in uniformed clothing decorated with an embroidered red arrow.

Hunters.

"We've been found," I whispered.

Elizabeth licked her lips but straightened her shoulders. "I must get to the council and see what the plan is."

"The council won't have a plan. They ignore the hunters." I was angry because I knew this was it for me. I knew this was Daithi's vision coming to fruition. And the council ignored our request for something to be done about the hunters. But in the same breath, I hoped they did have a contingency plan for this situation. No one deserved to be captured and killed for their power.

Making a quick decision, I started running down the hill and called over my shoulder, "You must hide. I will find Charlie and my soul mates."

I headed straight toward the cabin, believing Charlie would have headed to Clawdia if he saw what was happening, but a shout from the trees on the other side of the path stopped me in my tracks. "Zaide!"

Turning, I saw Lawrence, his face white and serious as he waved me over. I went to him and whispered, "Lawrence. What is happening?"

"I don't know. All I know for certain is that the wards have gone and it looks like we are about to have company. I don't know if they are friendly." He spoke quickly and suddenly nodded his head for me to follow and started jogging away. "I need your help."

"What is it?" I asked as I followed him. We were heading to the medical center.

"The protector. He needs to be taken away from here right now."

As much as I wanted to go back and see Clawdia, Baelen, and Charlie and make sure they are okay, I knew our priority had to be to ensure that Sigurd lived to protect the realm another day. "I'll help."

We stormed through the door, and as I recognized the green hair and the black leathery wings of the people in the sitting area, I let out a relieved breath.

"Daithi, Savida. Thank the gods you are all right. What are you doing here?"

"We were just chatting with the protector," Savida explained.

"We heard the screams. What is happening?" Daithi asked, but the somber, more so than usual, expression on his face, told me he already knew. He'd seen it. He knew.

"Sigurd?" Lawrence asked.

"Yes?" The blond man in question directed his attention to us instead of the book he had in his hands.

"Come with us. We need to get you out of here," Lawrence told him sternly. Without asking another question, Sigurd stood up and followed him out.

"Zaide?" Daithi asked again quietly, his voice a plea.

I sighed and offered him a small smile. "I think you already know the answer to that, Daithi."

"No," Savida breathed, and his eyes welled with tears.

"Yes, my friend. It's time," I told him quietly so he wouldn't hear the quiver of fear in my voice. He pulled me into his arms, wrapping his wings around me so I was cocooned in his embrace, and I closed my eyes to savor the touch before reluctantly pulling away. "Come," I said and pulled them both out of the cabin.

Lawrence was waiting for me. "Can you watch out as we go? I need to concentrate on where we are going."

"Where are you going?" I asked.

He pointed toward the thicker part of the forest. "There's a tunnel not far from here that leads to the other side of the island. There's a boat we can use to row to the next island. Finding the tunnel is a bit tricky, though, and I might have forgotten the instructions."

"I can help you get to the tunnel, but I can't escape with you. But I think these two should. Daithi can form an illusion around the boat so you escape without being spotted, and Savida will be able to heal the protector should anything go wrong."

And it would make me feel better knowing they were safe.

He stared at me before nodding. "Good idea. Let's go."

We took off at a slow jog through thin trees that were packed tightly together. Lawrence occasionally stopped to feel the bark of one tree in a particular spot or search the ground for a sign that he was going in the right direction. I remained at the back of the group, watching our surroundings for signs the hunters were nearby or that someone was following us.

"Here it is!" Lawrence whisper-shouted as we approached a large stone. He pushed at it, and after it refused to move for the third time, I urged him out of the way and rolled the stone to reveal dirt stairs descending into the ground.

"Thank you," Lawrence said as he waved Sigurd to go on in front of him. The protector nodded his thanks as he moved without fear into the darkness. Lawrence held his hand out, and I shook it as I knew humans liked to do. "I hope to see you again soon." And then he, too, was gone.

A flare of light inside the tunnel made Savida loudly sigh his relief that he wouldn't be underground in the dark again. I knew how difficult that would be for him, if not completely immobilizing.

"Goodbye, my friend. Please stay strong." Daithi put his hand on my shoulder.

"I will." I smiled through the fear and focused on the image Clawdia painted of our lives. "I have a bright future to look forward to."

Savdia took my hand and squeezed it. "We will find you."

"I know."

Daithi added, "I won't abandon you again."

"Thank you." I took a deep breath and tried not to let my emotions get the better of me. I shooed them on. "Now go and stay safe. I have to find the others."

I gave Savida's hand a squeeze as he looked fearfully toward the hole before handing him over to his soul mate, who gently tugged him forward. With my family waiting for me and in danger, I didn't stay to watch them go. I headed back the way we came, faster now that I was alone and not looking for guiding landmarks. I passed the medical center and slowed as I approached the path.

There, dressed in all black and holding large guns with both hands, were three male hunters, the same symbol on their chests as the others that had chased us, but I didn't recognize them. They weren't saying anything. They were behind a cabin, just watching the main path for something. Or someone.

I hunkered down behind a large trunk and deep into the long grass and examined my new dilemma. I had to cross the path to get to my cabin but could think of no way to distract them long enough to make a run for it.

Luckily, or not so luckily, another hunter, a young male, came strolling down the path as though he owned the island.

He smiled at the group and waved a hand to bring them out of hiding. "No one seems to be around. We'll need to do a thorough search of all the cabins and make sure that anyone hiding gets taken into custody."

Custody? They aren't killing anyone? Why? I frowned as I listened harder. *I suppose I'll find out soon. But not before finding the others and getting them safe. Then fate can do what it will with me.*

"Why don't you come with me, and we can start at the big house on the hill while everyone else searches here?" the young male suggested as he spoke to a smaller male.

"If you're going to use this as an excuse to prat around ..." That hunter's voice was older, tired.

The young male spoke again, "I'm serious about this. It's big. I get it. We want to do well, and we will." His grin was wide. "But there's no harm in having fun when we find it, right?"

The sentiment that capturing people different from yourself for nefarious purposes was fun made my hair stand on end and my stomach flip. And I would have to survive being captured by them. The shame of it made nausea rise into my throat.

The group headed out, and I turned slowly to look toward the lake. I could see that only one of the boats had been able to pull into the tiny harbor and sent a prayer of thanks to Riseir. They couldn't get everyone on the island, but they had enough reinforcements that I couldn't attack them. I would have to sneak as many as I could into the tunnel and hope they eventually gave up looking for people when they believed the island was abandoned.

Double-checking no one was around, I dashed toward the cabin, but instead of going inside, I ran around the outside to look in through the windows. No one was there, not even Baelen. *How did he get out of the cage?*

Crouching down again, I called, *"Clawdia, where are you? Is Charlie with you? We are under attack, and we need to leave."*

But I received no reply. And I couldn't feel her awareness as I usually did. *Has something happened to her?*

Panic churned inside me, and just as I started planning my next steps, I saw a dark figure in the tree line in front of me. I froze. Red eyes flashed, and I sighed, relief pouring from me. Until I saw another figure behind him. A gun pointed at him. Without thinking, I charged. The gun fired but too late for it to hit Baelen. I'd already gotten between him and the hunter, gripping his arms and turning him so he faced me, but my back faced the shot.

I jolted forward as the force of the shot pushed me into him, and then we seemed to blur, smoke surrounding us. Suddenly, we were somewhere else, lying in the long grass but no longer looking at the cabin.

"Titan?"

Not my Baelen, then. I sighed as a strange sensation, like the spread of ice-cold liquid across my skin, began from where I was shot. "I'm fine," I replied. "But I don't have much time. I am going to be taken. I need you to find Clawdia and Charlie and get them to safety. Portal them away somewhere."

He looked at me as though studying a foreign language. "You won't ask me to portal you away?"

"I can't avoid my fate, and creating a portal would draw attention that could be dangerous to Clawdia and Charlie."

"You are interesting, even if I am not interested in you," he concluded and sat up.

I ignored that because I knew it wasn't Baelen talking and didn't need a shadow's interest. "You have to move quietly. In the shadows. Find them," I told him, my eyes pleading with him. "Shadow, and Baelen, if you can hear me, please look after them. I don't know what your plan is, but please don't hurt them. Keep them safe for me."

Something shuttered in his eyes, and his body shuddered. But he nodded. "I won't harm them."

"I suppose that will have to be good enough." I sighed and lay my head back as the numb sensation took my legs, chest, and arms. "Go. Quickly," I urged. I could feel my eyes and body getting heavier, and when his form blurred in a smokey plume, I lost the battle with my eyes and closed them.

I tried to call out to Clawdia, to tell her I loved her and that I would fight to get back to her. But it was clear I was shouting into a void. Our bond was silent, but I prayed she was well. That she was with Charlie.

The mutter of male voices was distant in my confused state, but I could vaguely feel hands lifting my legs and pulling my limp body across the ground.

And then the earth shook, and gasps erupted from my captors as a loud roar echoed across the island.

Was that a dragon?

CHAPTER 28

BAELEN

*A*fter I'd been left alone in the cabin, I fell asleep again, safe in the knowledge that Kaatu wouldn't attempt to overtake me again until I was set free from the cage.

Yet, when I woke up suddenly, there was a tension in the air that made me alert. Sitting up, I listened for something but heard nothing but the odd movement of creatures in the woods outside. Then tremors rocked the cabin, screams echoed loudly from nearby, and magic felt as though it had been sapped from the earth.

"What's happening?" Kaatu asked, his voice quiet as he also listened for the cause of the screams.

"I don't know." I braced myself, my nails scoring the floor-boards as the room continued to shake and a glass fell from the counter. *"We are both in this cage."*

I hoped the others were safe from whatever caused this shaking, but Kaatu was more concerned about us. *"How do we get out of here?"*

"I don't know. The spells of human witches weren't something I was taught. Were you?"

"Obviously not."

"Then we have to wait."

The screams from outside subsided as the tremors stopped. Yet the magical cage around me began to vibrate and flicker.

"What does that mean?" Kaatu asked again, his impatience becoming more grating.

"I don't know." The cage flickered again, and I put my hand out to touch it. It zapped me when it materialized, but it wasn't nearly as painfully as it had been in the past. *"Maybe Charlie's spell is failing."*

"Freedom at last." I heard the smile in his thoughts. *"Nothing is going to stop me from saving my realm and my people."*

I'd admire him if I wasn't the collateral damage in his campaign. *"You know, even if Charlie and Zaide did find a way to eject you from me, I wouldn't forget your plight. I would ask them to help. They are good people and wouldn't leave you and your people to die any more than I would."*

After spending days in my body, observing them as I did, I was sure he already knew that. But there was no harm in telling him the truth. *"But when you have defeated a dragon, which, by the way everyone has spoken, is not going to be soon. They may be good people, but they are going to choose themselves. As they should. But I am choosing my people. My realm. Myself. And I have the power to make the decision for you all."*

"I understand." My lips twisted, and I sighed as I leaned my head on the flickering cage again. *"I hate that it's come to this, but I do understand."*

"Don't lie, youngling. It's me you hate." He chuckled.

I could only shake my head. *"I can hate you and also understand you. I hate that you made me speak so terribly to my soul mate and spoke about forcing our soul bond with the other like it wouldn't be a complete betrayal for us both."*

"I'm sorry."

His apology was so jarring and uncharacteristic that it put me on guard. *"For what?"* I asked slowly.

"This."

The next thing I knew, I was thrown back into the corner of my mind and locked away in my own shadowy version of the cage Charlie locked us in. I was dizzy with the suddenness of it and tried to fight back, to push against the shadow bars, but they were like stone and seemed to close in the more I struggled. I forced myself to still, and the bar retracted slightly. Enough for me to concentrate and see what Kaatu was now doing since he'd commandeered my body.

The cage around us was gone, and Kaatu moved my legs to stand. The flickering cage must have vanished entirely, and Kaatu took advantage at the just the correct moment for him to force us into action.

Then he was running, throwing the door open, and storming from the cabin.

"Where are you going?" I asked, but I sounded quiet even to my spirit ears. Kaatu ignored me as he ran around to the back of the cabin and into the forest behind. From the safety of the trees, he turned us to face the harbor, where a large boat was docking and two other identical boats waited further out on the water. *"What is going on? Who is that?"*

It was my understanding that the island had wards. *Did they fail? Or are these people friendly?*

As we watched, people dressed in all black and armed with weapons exited the boat and began walking onto the island. They didn't speak. They held their weapons close to their chest and watched their surroundings with the kind of careful awareness that only trained soldiers had. *Not friendly.*

"But the perfect distraction," Kaatu whispered, excitement in his voice.

"Distraction from what?" I asked, but he ignored me again

as he headed up the hill, through the trees, and toward the main house.

Charging into the house from the backdoor, we found people cowering in the dining room. I didn't recognize any of them. Kaatu announced, "People with weapons are here. I think you should hide."

They let out startled gasps and whimpers before scrambling to find somewhere to hide.

"That was kind of you, but you aren't here for them."

"No. I need Clawdia." I didn't need to question why. He was going to attempt his plan, but for once, I wouldn't try to stop him. I'd rather her be with us away from the humans with weapons, even if Kaatu could hurt her in his attempt to revive his portal.

"She went to visit a witch friend," I told him as he began throwing doors open in the house and calling, "Clawdia!"

"Which is why I came here."

"It doesn't look like she is here," I murmured. He turned around in the last unaccounted-for room and huffed a frustrated breath when he saw she wasn't in there.

"I'll try the cabins." Heading back down the hill through the trees, we seemed to blur with speed until we stood back where we started. Except now, the armed humans were nowhere in sight, which made me even more nervous.

What if they've already found Clawdia, Charlie, and Zaide? What if they've already been killed, and I didn't know?

Just as panic started to set in, I saw a glint of gold and let out a mental sigh as Zaide dashed around the back of the cabin and crouched in the grass.

"Go to him. Help him," I urged Kaatu, not sure why we weren't already moving.

"He's not the one we are looking for."

I tried to stop the automatic surge of anger at his cruel

words because I knew better than to argue right now. *"He might know where Clawdia is. He's probably guarding her."*

If he knew he was being manipulated, he didn't show it, but before we had a chance to approach him, Zaide's eyes met ours and then widened. But it wasn't with shock. Fear.

Too distracted both, Kaatu and I had missed any indication that someone was approaching. Before either of us could react, Zaide had cleared the distance between us and spun me away, blocking the shot of something, which pushed him into our arms.

If I could have felt my heart, I'm sure it would have stuttered as he collapsed and Kaatu blurred us away from our attacker. Disorientated, we fell into the grass, and his stillness made me freeze. *Darkness, I wished it was me holding him. If he's been killed and this is goodbye, I want it to be me holding him.*

"Titan?" Kaatu asked.

Zaide stirred, and I could have cried with relief. Whatever they shot him with hadn't hurt him, but when he didn't move, I suspected the weapon had a different purpose.

"I'm fine," he replied. "But I don't have much time. I am going to be taken. I need you to find Clawdia and Charlie and get them to safety. Portal them away somewhere." Kaatu seemed thrilled to have permission after a little back and forth. Zaide finished by saying, "Shadow, and Baelen, if you can hear me, please look after them. I don't know what your plan is, but please don't hurt them. Keep them safe for me."

Without complaint, Kaatu allowed me to take control, and I made the only promise I could. "I won't harm them," I said. Even if I meant so much more with those words.

I didn't know why Zaide believed he was going to be taken, that it was his fate, but for his only thoughts and desires to be for Charlie and Clawdia's safety made me fall a bit more in love with him. He was the kind of soul that would love fiercely. I'd never questioned my reasons for being alone before, but it was clear now that I was waiting for them. After having so little love, I would only accept something that couldn't fail me.

I just needed to not fail them in return.

"I suppose that will have to be good enough." Zaide lay his head back and whispered, "Go. Quickly."

Kaatu stole control of my body back again and didn't pause for me to say goodbye before taking off at a sprint toward a cabin, blurring us into the shadows so we remained unseen by the armed humans strolling up the main path and pushing into cabins.

Although Kaatu wasn't focusing on it, I saw the bodies of fallen witches being pulled along the ground toward vans at the edge of the forest. *Why are they kidnapping them? Who are these people? Is this what Zaide meant by saying they were going to take him?*

But no matter the questions and the panic, I could do nothing but watch and pray that Kaatu rescued my soul mate and her witch from such a fate.

We threw open a few doors to different cabins and found nothing. But in the fifth house, our eyes zeroed in on a prone female lying passed out on the sofa. "Clawdia?" Kaatu shook her, but she remained unconscious. Her body was limp as we picked her up and settled her over our shoulder.

What happened to her? Why won't she wake up? I wanted to run my hands over her head and check there weren't any injuries which could have caused her unresponsiveness.

Kaatu held my hands out in front of us, and a portal began forming in the middle of the room.

"What are you doing? We can't leave Charlie. If her witch dies, so does she."

"I don't need him to heal the portal, and I don't have time."

I wanted to roar in anger. I'd promised Zaide I wouldn't

harm them. If something happened to Charlie, if it killed him, it would kill her too, and I wouldn't be able to live with the knowledge I'd destroyed my family before it began.

But I was helpless to stop him.

He charged through the portal, and it disappeared behind us as we fell into a cave. But it wasn't the one in Ombra. The ground wasn't black, dusty, and drained of all magic. We must have been at the human realm side of the portal.

It was then that I realized how powerful Kaatu was. The only way he could have been able to portal here was if he'd been here before or seen it in some way. Which meant he'd been here when the portal was functioning. Before the fall. He was as old as my fathers and mother.

Kaatu crouched and pulled Clawdia down from his shoulder and into his arms. She was still unconscious and limp, but that didn't stop him from closing his eyes and reaching for the tentative bond between us and drawing on her power.

I almost hoped it wouldn't work, that our bond was too frail to hold the enormous amount of power she held. But that wasn't the case. As easily as he took from me, he took from her, pulling the power through us.

When he opened his eyes again, threads of red, threads that were so thin and brittle that they looked as though they would snap, appeared across the large boulders of rock cast about the back of the cave. Without a thought to the consequences, he suddenly poured magic into the threads.

Kaatu was not a titan. He probably knew the threads were a very small part of the fabric of the universe. But he didn't know titans were cursed. Manipulating the threads too much caused drastic imbalances across the realms. And pouring raw power into threads, enough to heal a long-dead portal, as he was doing, would no doubt get the attention of the Fates.

And no one wanted their eyes on them.

Yet I had to question whether this wasn't exactly what the Fates wanted. To realign the balance in the realms and save Ombra from certain doom. Righting the wrongs caused by my fathers' mistakes.

He groaned as power poured from us, desperately trying to plump and change the color of those shriveled portal threads.

Even if it killed us all.

CHAPTER 29

CHARLIE

"*F*afnir," a voice whimpered.

Fafnir? What's a Fafnir? I swung my head around, which felt heavier than usual, and squinted my eyes.

Why does my head hurt so much? And why are the colors so fucking weird looking? I had to close my eyes to keep from getting dizzy.

I couldn't understand what happened. All I knew was that there was a gaping wound somewhere on my person, and I was bleeding out. I could feel it draining my energy, causing me pain I'd never experienced before and utter misery. Whatever was causing the pain had to be bad. I just couldn't pinpoint exactly where on my body it was. My body felt bigger, stranger ... winged? I tried to turn around to investigate, but my feet weren't cooperating.

"Please don't hurt me. I'm sorry. I didn't know," a voice said again. It sounded familiar but made me irrationally angry, so I must not like the person.

I squinted again as I opened my eyes to look around, disoriented but clearer headed. Everything looked smaller. A blond woman with blue eyes wide with fear and glossy with tears stared up at me.

"What the fuck is your problem?" I tried to ask but made a noise like a roar. She whimpered, and the smell of piss reached my nose.

That's odd. I usually couldn't smell for shit. I'd drunk milk that's been days out of date and only realized when my cereal had lumps in it. I'd never been able to tell anything from smell alone.

My nose couldn't have picked a worse time to smell things, and I recoiled. I stared at her trembling and scared and couldn't help but feel a little proud of myself. I've never made someone piss themselves with fear before. I'm a badass.

But why is she so afraid? What did she do to me? What have I done?

The door to the fence I stood in opened, and another extremely small blond woman peeped in. She also looked up at me with fear and moved very slowly into the … pen? *Am I in a pen?* But when her gaze flicked to the other woman, the anger was undisguised.

"Karin. What have you done?" she hissed.

Oooo, interesting. The one that pissed herself has clearly done something wrong. Something to do with me?

"I didn't mean to. I didn't know," the one on the floor whimpered.

What didn't she know?

Another voice sighed. *"She didn't know about me."*

"You? Who are you? Where are you?" I tried to turn to see where the voice was coming from, but it felt like my head was on a stalk and I couldn't get my neck to bend the way I needed. It was a whole thing. I'm sure the two tiny ladies were enjoying the circus show.

The voice continued calmly, *"I am you. You are me. We are two souls sharing the same bodies. One Drakorian. One dragon."*

331

That didn't make any fucking sense. I might be confused, but I knew I wasn't a dragon. Or a Drakorian. I was Charlie. Very human. Very boring. Very good at tracking. Charlie.

But I went along with it. What else was supposed to do? *"Dragon. Do you have a name, dragon?"*

"No. I share your name."

Maybe I don't want to share my name. You're already sharing my head, I thought, pouting only because this voice was being far too reasonable when everything was very confusing. *"But you are you,"* I tried to reason.

"Yes," he replied simply, and it made my head hurt.

"So can I call you Dralie? Like Dragon Charlie?"

He hesitated, and I took the time to look down at the tiny women. They were whispering, but I wasn't interested in what they were saying. There was a greater mystery occurring in my mind. Finally, Dralie said, *"I've never had a name before."*

"You share bodies with a lot of people?" I asked. *Maybe this is a normal thing, and I didn't know. I do seem to have forgotten a lot of things.*

"Not many. But Drakorian's have always preferred to think themselves in control."

"What's control? Can't control much in life. Seems wrong you don't get a name. So, what's going on, Dralie? How come you're here?"

"I've awoken. Usually, I awake during the pubescent stage of life, but I can see here that you are much older."

I could hear page flipping. *Is he looking through notes on my life? This is crazy weird.* I hoped it had the last few chapters in there, because I didn't have a clue what happened or what I'd missed. It would be good to know.

"So, you're awake. Great to meet you," I said, actually a bit excited. I didn't know what it all meant, but company was always nice.

He returned my happy sentiments. *"I look forward to gathering our hoard together. We have many years to make up for if we are to attract a mate."*

"A mate?" Something tickled at the edges of my mind. A thought or a memory or something, but I lost it before I could see exactly what it was.

"Yes. But we can do that later. We are in my form, so we must be in danger. Don't worry, Charlie. I will guide us out of this."

"Charlie?" The sound of the small woman's voice drew my attention back to her. She did look very familiar, but as I reached for the thought or memory, it slipped through my reach.

"Yes?" I replied, trying to be polite so she didn't continue to look so frightened. There was only so much fun to be had when someone was terrified of you for an unknown reason. I didn't want to realize that I was actually just Spongebob with bad breath when I believed I was a petrifying bad ass.

But when I opened my mouth and said the word, I made the same strange, gargled noise as before. And the same reaction happened, white faces and the overwhelming smell of sweat.

"You are in your Drakorian form, Charlie. You must stop roaring," Dralie told me, and I paused. It was the second time he mentioned this Drakorian thing. And roaring? People can't roar. *Wait. Am I a dragon?*

The woman spoke again and took a hesitant, shaky step toward me. "Charlie. Please. If you can hear me, I need you to listen. We don't want to hurt you, and you don't want to hurt us. Calm down."

It felt like a lie, even if I didn't have my memory to prove it. I knew the one woman had already hurt me because I was still bleeding out somewhere and dying. Just reminding myself of the pain made me furious, and I said, "I am fucking calm." But there was no denying it this time. I roared.

And clearly, she didn't believe me, because she muttered a spell and tried to trap me in a cage. But it fizzled when it touched me, and I choked on a laugh as her face fell from determination to fear.

"Oh, goddess," she whispered, and the other woman whimpered again, scooting back to the wooden fence. Which, now that my head and neck were pointed in the correct position, looked less like a fence and more like a small wooden wall. *Is this a home? Where is the roof?*

"Dralie, did you see that? The woman tried to attack us with magic! When I wasn't doing anything wrong!"

"I did see, Charlie. Allow me to deal with this. We should leave before anyone else tries to hurt us."

I knew Dralie had my back. *"Do the honors. I can't believe she'd try to hurt me when I'm already clearly wounded."*

That gave him pause, and he asked, *"Wounded? Where?"*

I mentally shrugged. *"I don't know for certain. But it feels like something inside me has died."*

But just as Dralie was going to impart some amazing dragon wisdom, the woman tried to attack us again, mumbling something and changing her stance.

Suddenly we seemed to merge. I was Dralie, and he was Charlie. We were one big-ass fucking dragon. And we knew how to work this dragon body.

We simply flicked the woman away before her magic could even form. She hit the wall, bashing her head hard, then fell to the floor. I winced as the wall collapsed on top of her, and the other pathetic woman who whimpered and cried the entire time also got knocked unconscious by a falling structure. *Nasty. But efficient.*

We didn't know if they were breathing, and we didn't care. Anyone who hurt us would pay.

We took off, large wings loosening from behind us as we walked through the remaining standing walls of the cabin and stretched our wings wide. It was then I got a good look at my new body. My yellow and orange scales glinted in the afternoon sun. It was a happy color, but I got the impression it didn't exactly suit me. Or maybe it was ironic.

We flapped, testing the strength of my new appendages and finding them to be the perfect vehicle for our getaway. With a lot of effort and a helpful gust, we soared up into the air, and suddenly, I could feel the wind over my scales and under my wings, and it was incredible.

As we sailed through clouds over the island, a small projectile fired into the air in front of us, causing us to come to a stop.

What was that? We dove down, angry and full of vindication, and roared, and small people dressed all in black pointed their sticks in the air and began shooting more small projectiles at us.

That isn't very nice.

We dodged and weaved and flew as though we'd been doing it our entire lives. Like we should have been doing it our entire lives. It was exhilarating and freeing and amazing. Flying couldn't get any better.

As we flew away, a glint of gold on the ground made us hesitate. Gold wasn't our choice for a hoard, but it was always pretty to look at, and since we had so much gathering to catch up on, we swooped in that direction. But we found another of the shooting men with his hands around the gold, tugging it away.

My shiny!

We were suddenly furious and roared to scare off the male and take our prize, but they only dropped the gold thing and reached for their weapons. More of them appeared and raced toward us. Inhaling, we gathered all the anger we had and let out a huge breath. A fiery blast knocked most of the males away.

Yes! We reached for the gold with our hind legs and pulled it up to admire. But the gold was not gold. It was a person. A being with golden skin and long white hair. *Not a treasure for a hoard.*

Huffing with frustration, we dropped the being and flew off, leaving the island behind.

As we glided toward another small island, suddenly very tired and in pain, we wondered when we would get our memories back. We needed to know what the woman had done to us so we could find a way to heal the wound. A dragon couldn't collect his hoard when he was in pain. A dragon couldn't impress a mate when he was in pain.

From Dralie's past experiences, we knew being damaged could take away our ability to bond and transform as we were supposed to. We certainly hadn't had a typical introduction to each other too, so who knew what effect that would have on us.

How long would we be a dragon? Where were we going? Will we get our memories back?

As we landed in long grass, and waddled into a wooded area, we tried to think about our past but it only made our head hurt. We didn't need any more pain so we immediately stopped trying to remember.

But the empty hole inside me still ached, and we didn't know why.

CHAPTER 30

CLAWDIA

*B*ellowing pulled me from sleep. Although I couldn't open my eyes long enough to look for the culprit, I fought the complete exhaustion I felt with a small dose of adrenaline which I got from hearing the loud noise.

Something about it made me scared.

Squinting, I peered into the darkness. But the sound had vanished, and I was distracted by the dreadful feeling throughout my body.

Why do I feel like a stone? Gravity had never been so hard on me. My bones felt like steel, and I could barely move. Yet it also felt as though I was being emptied, drained, and I was shriveling up as more of something important was pulled from me. *Magic?*

A flash of something moving from the corner of my eye startled me, and I jolted. With another burst of energy, I could see that I was in someone's arms as they panted and heaved, touching a large rock.

"Almost there," a voice said. I recognized the voice. Baelen.

Suddenly I was awake, my eyes wide and my mouth agape as I remembered everything. *Karin drugged me and wanted to kill Charlie to take me as her familiar, but how did I get here? How did Baelen get out of his cage? And where is Zaide?*

My head lolled as I attempted to get a better look at my surroundings. We were in a cave. I couldn't see anyone else. But the rocks were floating. I wanted to rub my eyes to clear my mind of the obvious delusion, but my hands continued to lie limply at my side, grazing the hard stone beneath me. *Why are the rocks floating? How are they floating? Is Baelen doing that?*

It didn't matter how long I stared, the rocks rolled and moved and floated, rearranging themselves so the largest ones were at the bottom as a base and the others piled precariously on top of each other until they met in the middle, creating a large archway.

"What's happening?" I slurred but couldn't be sure how much sense I made since my tongue felt alien in my mouth.

Baelen groaned again, and I felt our bond straining through our touch, our magics being forced out. *He is using my power, but how? I can't move things.*

Crack.

It wasn't a physical noise. The stone arch remained upright. But something snapped inside me, and a piercing scream echoed around the walls of the cave. My scream. My back bowed as pain threatened to rip me in two. I could barely catch my breath as agony overcame me.

Baelen's voice was a welcome distraction from the trauma. "Hold on for one more second, Clawdia. I need this. We are so close."

But I had nothing to hold on to. My bond, the golden thread I'd tied to Charlie, had been obliterated. I had no witch. And Charlie … was he dead? I choked on a sob as tears rolled down my cheeks in rapid succession.

No. No. No. It can't be true. Karin can't have succeeded. Baelen and Zaide should have saved him. He can't be dead. He can't. I won't believe it.

But the proof was when I choked, coughed, and spluttered on a thick liquid that began bubbling up my throat to my lips and poured out of my mouth. I was dying. My body echoed the death of my witch, being drained, and losing an essential bond. Baelen's eyes widened as he looked down at me, but he didn't take his hand from the rock. He didn't stop pushing magic from us.

Baelen, my Baelen, would have stopped the moment he realized this was causing me pain. But without my witch, I was as good as dead. I couldn't stop him. Couldn't speak. Or move. The last vestiges of my power poured from me to him and into this cave.

Blue light suddenly flooded around us as the archway lit up, and Baelen's breath caught. *A portal? He was creating a portal?*

He dropped me, and as I hit the ground, something happened. Something clicked. And my body changed into the smaller, fluffier form I loved so much.

I panted, lying on my side, unsure what just happened. Or why. Although I felt dreadful, I no longer felt like I was at death's door. Blood didn't seem to be pouring from my mouth, and if I were going to die, why would my body waste energy transforming me into a cat? Nothing made sense.

But this whole situation was like a fever dream. I just hoped my survival somehow meant Charlie was still alive. I couldn't feel the bond between us anymore, but I didn't let that stop me from hoping.

"It worked. It worked." Baelen shuffled on his knees toward the portal.

And then collapsed.

I jumped up and ran over to him without thinking, and with my cat eyes, I could see more clearly as the darker spots on Baelen's skin began to move, merge into a pool of ink on his chest, and then seep out onto the stone. I skittered back as the spot moved toward me, but then it grew. It grew until it looked like … a shadow. A shadow of a male figure against the cave wall.

And then it became solid, and I got a glimpse of the person who'd invaded my soul mate. Pale gray eyes stood out against his black skin, and thin braids of gray hair fell to the nape of his neck. A thin, flowing skirt didn't conceal much beneath, and I averted my gaze.

He smiled at me, and I trembled, shaking with fear. This person had possessed Baelen, made him say cruel things to Zaide, and tried to be intimate with me. I felt dirty and uncomfortable and … wrong. But he stood there smiling.

Rage boiled up inside me, and I did what every cat did when they were mad. I fluffed up and hissed.

His smile turned to laughter, and I hissed again and took a swipe with my sharpened claws, which he easily dodged. "It's been a pleasure, Clawdia. If you ever come to Ombra, pay a visit to the king. It would be an honor to see you again." He stepped over Baelen and headed toward the portal. "You'll understand why I don't wait for Baelen to wake up. I'm sure he'll explain the entire saga and paint me in a very poor light. But I want you to know there is very little I wouldn't have done to save my people, and I will not apologize for those I have to sacrifice to get what I wanted."

I couldn't say anything in response. I just remained staring at him, hunkered down, attempting to cover Baelen. Although his words did give me pause to worry. *The sacrifices were us? Did he have something to do with what happened to Charlie? Or Zaide? And why aren't they with us?*

Without another glance, he turned away, and the portal swallowed him in a cloud of blue.

It was a terrible thing to hope for, but I wished the portal didn't lead him back to Ombra. I hoped he walked for years in the blue smoke and realized he'd failed.

Turning away and relaxing, I blinked, and the anger, and my claws, disappeared. Baelen lay still, which frightened me, and I clambered onto his chest so I could feel the rise and fall of his breaths. Despite being pained, confused, and exhausted, I couldn't sleep. My mind remained buzzing with the remainder of my adrenaline and thoughts battered my fragile state of mind.

How did we get here? Did Baelen have any control when the shadow possessed him? Did the shadow know his thoughts and was able to act like him? Was it the shadow who gorged on my blood? Did Karin do something to Charlie? How am I alive and a cat when my bond with Charlie is gone? What happened?

I sat there, thinking, worrying, and processing, for a long time until Baelen finally stirred. "Clawdia?" he called, his hands coming up to tentatively touch me. His eyes were still closed, so he must have been confused about the strange weight on his chest.

I meowed, and his eyes flicked open, wide and confused as he took me in.

He tried to sit up, keeping me in his arms and dragging himself toward the cave wall to rest against. "Why are you a cat?" he asked, his hands roaming me, checking for injury or harm. "Are you all right?"

I meowed again and hoped he could see I was fine. Or as fine as I could be, considering the circumstances.

He frowned, and his eyes, thankfully back to the pure red they'd been before, darkened as he stared at me. "What happened? Why can't you change back?"

I hadn't tried to change back. My body, mind, and soul were so battered and bruised that I knew I wouldn't be able to. Baelen must have seen something because he sighed but didn't press. Instead, he asked, "Is he here?"

I knew to whom he was referring since he'd said hello before disappearing through the portal. I shook my head in a very un-cat-like movement, which was actually very difficult to achieve.

His jaw clenched, and he lowered his gaze. "I'm sorry, Clawdia."

It wasn't your fault, I wanted to say. *You didn't want to be possessed.* But I had to settle for bumping my head into his chest and meowing softly.

"I will tell you everything. But not right now. I'm so tired." He stroked lightly over my head, and I nuzzled into him, purring to soothe and heal us both. He was tired and no doubt traumatized from the ordeal. Everything else could wait. We could stay here, rest, gather our thoughts, and breathe for a moment before we attempted anything else.

Sometimes, all you can do is breathe and hope the next day is better.

The blue swirl from the portal cast interesting, hypnotic shadows and patterns along the cave walls, and before long, Baelen was snoring. I wanted to drift off too, but fear burned brightly inside me. Fear that remaking the portal had noticeable effects across the realms that could lead people here, where we lay alone, exhausted, and powerless.

I won't let anyone hurt him again.

So, I catnapped. I awoke with every squawk and rustle from outside the cave and jumped when the hum of the portal changed as a fridge did sometimes. More than any noise, my thoughts kept me awake.

Charlie might be dead. Zaide could be anywhere, and we are still under threat by Fafnir.

What a catastrophe.

To be continued

EXCITED for the next installment in the Tales of a Witch's Familiar series? CATASTROPHE is up next!

THANK YOU!

Another cliffhanger. Shocker.

I'd be sorry but I love a cliffhanger, it brings out the psycho in me.

As always I want to thank you for continuing to follow Clawdia and the gang on their journey, it means so much that you've fallen in love with them as much as I have and I can't wait to tell the next part of their Tales.

This was definitely my favorite book so far, although writing it nearly killed me, and I hoped you enjoyed it too! Whether you loved or hated Catapult, please take a moment to leave a review and hopefully other wonderful readers will be able to find, read and love/hate with you.

Thank you to my family and friends, your support means the most to me. Even if I leave you on read in the group chat most of the time because I'm in the writing dungeon, I am so grateful for your patience and so lucky to have you. Love you all to the moon and back.

To my proofreader Victoria, and my cover designer Christian, this book wouldn't look half as good as it does now without you. You continue to make my dreams a reality and I can't thank you enough.

Until next time!

FOLLOW FOR MORE FUN!

Need to share your frustration at the cliffhanger?
We're here for you!

Confused by Charlie's English slang?
Explanations await!

Want to share pictures of your familiar?
Give me those cute pics!

Come and join the reader group The Familiar Forest Facebook page to talk about The Tales of a Witch's Familiar series.

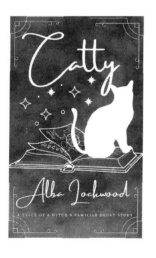

You can also sign up to my newsletter and receive a short story called Catty which reveals more of Clawdia and Charlie's hilarious relationship before the start of Catalyst!

ABOUT THE AUTHOR

Alba Lockwood is a debut author who writes reverse harem, paranormal romance and fantasy. When she isn't writing about cats, witches, Gods and other realms, you can find her losing sleep reading books from other amazing authors such as Katie May, Raven Kennedy, Tate James and Jaymin Eve.

Alba is from and currently resides in Birmingham, England with her parents, her brothers, and her precious black and white cat, Daisy who inspired this series.

Printed in Great Britain
by Amazon

31051776R00202